Kylie is a long-time fan of erotic love stories and B-grade horror films. She demands a happy ending, and if blood and carnage occur along the way, so much the better. Based in Queensland, Australia with her two children and one wonderful husband, she reads, writes and never dithers around on the internet.

D1036311

Also by Kylie Scott

Hot Down Under Short
Room With a View

Flesh

Kylie Scott

First published by Momentum in 2012
Pan Macmillan Australia Pty Ltd
1 Market Street, Sydney 2000

A CIP record for this book is available at the National Library of Australia

Flesh

EPUB format: 9781743340806
Mobi format: 9781743340813

Cover design by Carol Kabak
Edited by Tina Louise
Proofread by Red Dot Scribble

Macmillan Digital Australia: www.macmillandigital.com.au

To report a typographical error, please email errors@momentumbooks.com.au

Visit www.momentumbooks.com.au to read more about all our books and to buy books online. You will also find features, author interviews and news of any author events.

For Hugh. With thanks to Babette and Louise.

CHAPTER ONE

53 days post-apocalypse

Daniel looked down the barrel of the shotgun all set to blow his brains out and grinned. These days, even a gun-toting, trigger-happy female was a delight to behold, and she was perfect.

Sunlight streamed in through the kitchen window. She all but shone with it, like an angel or a princess or something. Something a little overdue for a bath and a lot on edge, but something very good just the same. The feeling of sweet relief rushing through him nearly buckled his knees.

Tall and curvy, around thirty at a guess, and uninfected, she was by far the best thing he had ever seen in jeans and a t-shirt. Not even the dried blood splattered on the wall behind her could diminish the picture she made.

Sadly, his girl did not appear to share his joy.

Wary gray eyes devoid of even a hint of elation watched him down the barrel of the gun. He refused to be discouraged; his smile did not waver. "Hey."

"Gun on the floor. Slow." Her voice sounded dusty with disuse. "Eject the clip."

"Okay." Daniel did as told, keeping his happy face on her the whole time, hunching a little when he stood back up. He gave the old rucksack at his feet a nudge with the toe of his sneaker. It currently contained the sum total of his worldly goods, but she was welcome to it. "There are just a few cans of soup, and Irish stew. Help yourself."

Plush pink lips parted as though she might speak but then she paused, as if she thought better of it. The grimy finger squeezing the trigger shook some. It was good to know she wasn't completely okay with blowing his brains out right here and now. That

1

was nice. Of course if her nerves got any worse, they might be in trouble just the same.

He softly cleared his throat, trying not to startle her. "You've, ahh, got the safety on. You see there?"

Daniel nodded to the dangerous firearm pointed his way and waited for the confusion to cross her pretty face, for the golden moment of distraction to appear. It didn't happen. Her lips puckered, but not for kissing. The withering glare confirmed it.

God bless her. She wasn't falling for any of his bullshit. Which made it time for Plan C. Plan A would have had her falling into his arms, demanding immediate sexual gratification. He wished. And B was for the Bullshit, which had not gone down, thus leaving only C, for Clusterfuck.

Then, everything happened at once.

He grabbed the barrel of the gun with both hands and shoved it skyward. Her reflexes kicked in, and her finger jerked hard on the trigger. The resulting boom was beyond deafening. Heat seared the palms of his hands. His ears rang as if a brass band had set up shop in his head. A shower of plaster dust rained down on the two of them like confetti at a wedding, which had to be a good omen.

While she coughed, sneezed and shook off the dust, he grabbed her. He pulled her in against him with one hand while keeping a good grip on her gun with the other. She and the gun definitely needed to part company, pronto. His arm wrapped around her belly and her ass tucked in against his hips. Testosterone and pheromones ran riot, and his blood surged hot – the bulk of it heading due south. His brain was on its own. Fragrant or not, she felt beyond good spooned against him.

So. Very. Good.

Unfortunately, there was still the matter of the gun. She clung to the thing like a lifeline.

"Let it go," he ordered. She ignored him, not a surprise.

Daniel held the weapon high above her head, waiting for gravity to take its eventual toll. The woman stretched and strained, stubborn as hell, but her stranglehold slowly slipped away until she was clawing at thin air, sliding down his body till the heels of her boots reconnected with the kitchen floor.

"Easy," he soothed, and flicked the safety on the gun. He slid it across the kitchen counter, far from temptation.

Her body trembled and her hands latched onto the arm around her waist. Shit, he didn't want to scare her. That wasn't the objective. But her fingernails were digging deep, drawing blood and stinging as she tried to push him off. Small sounds of distress came from her throat like a wounded animal. She had probably been on her own since civilization came to an end two months back. What must she have been through? While one wrist wasn't hard to catch, two was tricky when his girl was so determined. "Calm down. Please, I'm not going to hurt you. You're the first uninfected I've come across in weeks. Talk to me."

"Let. Me. Go," she gritted out between clenched teeth. Music had nothing on the sound of her voice.

"I'm Daniel Cross. What's your name?"

In reply she growled and squirmed and carried on. Her soft warmth was heaven, causing his body to respond for the first time in a long time. Having her rub up against him was worth almost getting shot any day of the week.

Her t-shirt rode up a little and her jeans eased down some. His fingers made contact with silken, smooth skin and the curve of a hipbone. He had to remind himself to breathe. The urge to wrap himself around her and hold on tight was huge. She must have felt his hard-on nestled against her ass because the wrestling kicked up a notch. But she wasn't going anywhere. No chance. His girl disagreed.

She slammed her head back, catching him on the jaw and coming close to dissecting his tongue with his own damn teeth. It couldn't have done her precious skull much good either. "Shit! Damn it. I am not going to hurt you. Stop it."

She, of course, chose not to, going wild in his arms for all the wrong reasons. In the end he let her wear herself out, waited till she hung limp in his hold, damp with sweat and sucking in oxygen as if she'd run a minute mile.

"Are you finished? Going to be a good girl for me?"

With a sullen little huff, she nodded her agreement. The dark blonde ponytail, littered with plaster dust, bobbed up and down beneath his nose.

"Okay," he said.

Nice and slow he took a step back, reluctantly drawing his arms away from the warmth and softness of her. His eyes, however, didn't stray from her for a second.

It didn't take his girl long to react. An elbow flew at his face, and she spun around. Her own momentum delivered her back to him. Their chests collided in a wonderful manner. He locked his arms around her, giving himself over to the thrill of it. The press of her gorgeous, generous tits against him nearly stopped his heart. For a brief moment she wasn't fighting him. For a treasured millisecond she stopped to regroup and his soul swelled. She was his very own personal nirvana.

"You promised to behave," he scolded. "Bad girl."

"Fuck you."

"Good idea, I love where you're going with that. But let's say we talk first? Get to know each other?" He gave her the biggest shit-eating grin of his life, the one that had been dying to burst out of him since she'd burst in.

What the hell. He couldn't remember having this much fun in years, and definitely not in the last two months. The sound of his own voice was a novelty; having someone to hear him an absolute joy.

"You were going to tell me your name," he said, but his girl still wasn't done.

For her next move, she attempted to feed him his balls via her knee. He managed to block it by jamming his legs together to catch hers. Before she could start scratching or slapping, he pulled her wrists behind her back, securing them in one hand. This worked against him, however, because of the way her breasts strained against the front of her t-shirt. The lace cups of her bra bore a mesmerizing pattern.

It drove him crazy, as though the flowers and curlicues bore the code to all of her deep dark secrets. Damned if he wasn't going to pop a blood vessel trying to decipher it.

While he was distracted, the ingenious woman lunged at him with sharp little teeth. He fast risked losing a nipple to her fury.

"Now that hurts." A sound smack to her rear produced a startled yelp. The jaws of death unlocked. Thank God. Daniel wrapped her ponytail tightly around his fist to prevent a repeat performance and got down in her face, nose to nose, grinding his teeth and feeling more than a little annoyed. "That was not nice. Stop and think. I have done everything possible not to hurt you. I only want to talk to you. You've shot at me, scratched me, kicked me, and now you start biting. Apologize."

The woman jerked back, her eyes as round as the wheels on his trail bike.

"Well?" He waited with ill patience while she said nothing for a good, long time. More than long enough for him to notice she had a smattering of freckles across her nose and cheeks, like a scattering of sugar. He had never been into freckles but there was a first time for everything.

"What do you want?" she hissed.

"Let's start with being friends, that's probably going to challenge you enough for one day." He let out part of a breath. It wouldn't do to let his guard down fully when the girl was this tricky. "Why attack me? We're both on the same side, aren't we?"

She snorted. Her eyes skittered away from him, her body twisting, continuing to test his grip.

"Behave for a while and I'll try the letting-you-go thing again. In the meantime, why don't you try using your words? Talk to me." He hadn't thought her face could harden any further but she managed it just fine. Her mouth tightened, and stony, pretty gray eyes stared up at him, as if she was imagining the size of the hole she could blow in him with her big gun.

"I'm really happy to see you," he ventured. "You know we could go someplace safe, and share a can of stew. Or soup... Whatever. Your choice. I don't mind. Totally your call."

For a first date, it sounded shit even to his ears. She seemed less than impressed. The woman glared at him like he had grown a second head, and it wasn't any better than the first.

"Right," he said, straightening his spine. "Then we're just going to have to do this the hard way."

CHAPTER TWO

Ali glared at the stranger with all the animosity she could muster. Having spent eight weeks hiding in her neighbor's attic, living like a rodent while the world fell apart outside, there was a hoard of hostility at her disposal. An ample amount of petrified too, but hostility came in handier.

Do it the hard way? The fucker. She wanted to go medieval on his ass, but oh man, he was big. She wasn't tiny by any standard, but her neck ached from looking up at him. On a good day she would barely reach the notch in his chin.

Today was not a good day, which did nothing for her terror levels. Her heart tripped about in her chest like she was having a coronary.

She should have stayed at Mary's house, safe and sound and starving. How could she have missed him, even crouched down, rifling through the cupboard? All of the effort to be hypervigilant on her few trips out into the world, and yet here she was, caught. She had to escape. Civilization was gone. Law and order a distant memory. Who knew what people would do now that the rules did not apply.

Apart from his size, the stranger seemed normal enough, if appearances counted. A head of dark hair with traces of gray, broad shoulders, and a mind jam-packed full of plans, apparently. The way he stared disturbed her. And his long, lean face inched lower and lower, as if he planned to kiss her.

Had he forgotten she had teeth? She hadn't. He risked losing more than a nipple if he tried to kiss her.

Ali heard the moaning the same time the stranger did. His head snapped around as his big body tensed. The oversized paws dropped from her hair and hip, enabling her to make a dive for the shotgun.

All kinds of confidence rushed back into her once she had the weapon tight in her hands.

God, who to turn the gun on first, zombies or him? Her heart sped.

Ali had watched the world unravel through Mary's front window, her own neighbors murdering and looting. Once law and order were gone, no one could be trusted. She'd crawled up into the attic and pulled the ladder up after her, then stayed there a month after everything was silent, too scared to move.

A common enemy didn't mean a thing. This man had done little to engender her trust. He might not have hurt her so far, but he showed no signs of letting her go, either. Asshole.

Meanwhile, the asshole was all business. One hand retrieved his pistol while the other reached for his pack and delved within. He emerged with a box of ammunition, which he proceeded to load, every move calm and efficient. The loony smile was long gone, just like she should be. It was better to be safe than sorry.

The shotgun felt good and heavy in her hands. Survival was everything. She could only trust herself for that. She had to be alone.

"Sounds like we've got a group of them," the man reported, his big hands still on the go, seemingly unconcerned about her gun. How could it not occur to him that she might be just as much of a threat as the infected? "They're coming from the street out front. Go out the back door, I'll be right behind you. Go."

But she didn't move a muscle, just stood there, overwhelmed, trying not to empty the slight contents of her stomach onto the kitchen floor. This house wasn't secure. Escape meant going outside, where the infected were. The thought terrified her. Her mind became a mess of white noise. No choice, she had to go out there.

"What are you doing?" the man bellowed. "Run!"

Escape back to Mary's house. Back through the rabbit hole and up into her safe place in the attic. All on her own.

He could follow but, being built akin to the proverbial brick shithouse, no way would he fit through the hole in the fence. His surviving this long told her he could obviously handle himself and deal with the infected on his own. He would be fine.

Ali ran like a rabbit, straight out the kitchen door and into the midday sun, her gun held before her in a grip that could choke.

It was safer alone. Alone was best. If her own neighbors had gone nuts then strangers certainly couldn't be trusted. And this guy was the quintessential definition of strange. No need to feel guilt over leaving him. She didn't even know him. So why were her feet faltering? Why look back?

They were there, the infected, spilling around the sides of the house and into the suburban backyard, lurching forward in their fucked-up fashion. Far too close for comfort and far too many to fight. She broke out in a cold sweat. The tattered, bloody remains of clothing hung from their putrid flesh, rank in the summer air. No humanity left, walking nightmares. Hungry, yawning mouths stretched wide.

The acid burn of bile hit the back of her throat.

Ali turned away, clutched her gun tighter, pushed her legs harder, feeling the fire in her calves. Through the long, green, over-grown grass, past the bright, plastic children's swing set, and on toward the back fence she ran.

The stranger's heavy footfalls were close behind her when the toe of her boot caught in the cracked concrete path. Her balance deserted her. She threw a hand out, ready for the fall, but he was there. Fingers hooked into the back of her jeans, righting her before she could greet the ground. He kept her upright and on her feet. He saved her life.

"Keep going." Sweat had beaded on his brow, but the gun in his hand was steady.

Ali pushed herself forward.

So close.

Nearly there.

Shots rang out behind her, the noise startling against the chorus of moans and groans. She braved a quick glance over her shoulder and watched more and more infected stumble around the sides of the house, like a lunch bell had been rung. Or a shotgun discharged. Which she had done, back in the kitchen. Shit. Damn.

They might not enjoy sunlight but it wouldn't stop them if a meal was at hand.

Ali dived for the break in the shoulder-high fence and scrambled through on hands and knees, pushing the shotgun ahead of her.

She ran into something that stabbed through her denim, slicing into her skin. A sharp stab of pain shot up her leg and made her gasp. She ignored the pain and tugged herself free.

The escape hatch was three wooden palings with their bottom halves missing. She had to wriggle and wrench to get her hips and butt through, but it beat the exposure of the open streets. Eight weeks worth of dwindling rations and sitting up in the attic, sweating it out, had whittled her away, but it was still a tight fit.

Behind her the big guy swore as her rear cleared the rabbit hole and sweet liberty beckoned. His pack flew through after her, knocking into her heel. She stumbled back up onto her feet, ready to be gone.

The fence groaned and shifted behind her, protesting the weight as his hands gripped the top, boots scrabbling for purchase as he heaved himself up and over.

Shit.

Before his feet could hit the ground, she was off and running. On through Mary's prized rose garden, straight over the top of the spot where she had buried the old lady. Her stomach tumbled and turned.

The key was on its piece of string around her neck and she tugged it up and over, wincing when she nearly took off an ear in her haste.

He had to be close behind her, but there was nothing he could do once she was inside. Mary's house was Fort fucking Knox, bars on every window, deadlocks on every door. Not that it had helped. Back before anyone knew what was happening, Mary had taken a bite to the wrist. Apparently, the plague had been cooked up in a lab somewhere in Asia. No one would admit to exactly where. How it escaped had become another mystery, but it went global in days.

Nothing to be done. Not for Mary or anyone else. It couldn't be murder if the person was already dead. And infected was dead. Everyone knew it. Everyone who was left.

Luck was with her and the key slid in, the door clicked open. Everything unfolded as it should. She sobbed with relief. Get inside, and get safe.

The stale, oven-like air of the house greeted her with all the promise of home. She slid the gun onto the kitchen bench, gave both hands over to clenching the door handle and throwing herself against the solid old wood in a whole body effort to slam it shut. Lock the whole fucking mess out. Get back up into the attic. Pull up the ladder. Screw the light of day. She would stay up there till hunger or thirst drove her out, and that was a promise. You could go a long time on a box of cereal and a couple of bottles of water.

This was her home now. Her haven.

"NO!" the big guy roared on the other side. Then his hands were there, fingers jammed in, prying the door open and forcing his way inside. Too strong. She couldn't stop him. But she wasn't done yet.

Ali bolted for the ladder, panic pushing at her heels and sweat stinging her eyes. The door slammed shut behind her. The deadbolt was thrown.

A fresh cramp bit into her side, but no way would it stop her. Not a chance.

One hand hit the cool rough surface of a metal rung. Safety was so close she could taste it, sitting on the tip of her tongue like a tease. Her feet couldn't work fast enough. Her damp hands slipped, but above, the comforting dark of the manhole beckoned. The superheated air from the midday sun wafted down, furnace-hot and so welcome.

"No you don't."

Strong arms wrapped around her waist and pulled, prying her free of the ladder with disgusting ease. She shrieked every insult known to woman and man, fighting him off with all she had. "You fucker! You motherfucking cock-sucking asshole. Get your fucking hands off me! Get off me!"

She kicked, punched and flailed. His hard chest stopped her fist short, jarring her wrist. Pain shot up her blood-smeared leg as she kicked. She wasn't getting anywhere but she wasn't giving up, either. Whatever the fuck he wanted, he couldn't have it. She'd fight till her last breath. The big bastard took her down with ease, pinning her to the floor. Not crushing her, but giving no leeway.

Hot tears of frustration scalded her cheeks as she screamed words of abuse at her captor. They were a torrent, jumbled and nonsensical. She screamed till she choked. Then her cries morphed into gulping pleas for him to listen, to let her up and let her go. To leave her alone. Why the hell wouldn't he listen to her anyway? What the fuck was wrong with him?

This man was every bit as good at the silent treatment as she was. In truth, he was better.

Eventually, she stopped. The tears, the words, all of it.

They lay on the pastel linoleum floor in a mess of sweaty limbs. She could barely move with the big bastard on top of her, holding her down. Her arms were pinned by his hands and her legs trapped beneath his. Effortlessly, he contained her. Ali shut her eyes tight, blocking out his determined gaze. Now he'd take what he wanted and all she could do was survive. A cry caught in her throat. She'd seen a woman dragged out of her car and raped on the Neilsens' front lawn not long after the infection hit, when the police first abandoned the streets and chaos took over. But the man on top of her made no move. Apart from his breathing, he remained immobile. Waiting was the worst part. She'd suffocate on the scent of him before long. The house was oppressive, humid, with every door and window locked tight. Claustrophobia dug into her, its razor sharp fingers sinking through her neck, clawing at her throat.

Everything was locked out. She was locked in – with this stranger – with no escape. She was cornered.

The man said something, chanting it over and over. His breath was hot on her ear, and his body hovered above her, caging her in even though he carried his weight on his arms. She couldn't quite hear him over the pounding of her heart and the shit running riot in her head.

There was no air. No hope. No nothing. Sweat poured off her face as she gulped for breath. Her body was giving up, signing off, as all good little ensigns eventually did.

"Breathe, damn it. Breathe." The man was in her face, staring down at her, blue eyes shot with concern. "You're having a panic attack. Do you hear me? It's a panic attack. You're safe. Everything's okay. Now breathe. That's all you need to do. Just breathe for me."

His words unlocked something, flicked a switch in her head. Her airways opened and stale, fetid air rushed in.

The sudden rush of oxygen was magic. She couldn't get it down fast enough. Her head swam.

"Easy. Easy now, that's it." He stroked her arm, murmuring on and on.

Eventually he stopped too, rolled onto his side.

They lay in silence, him with a leg and an arm thrown over her, holding her down. He needn't have bothered. Exhaustion had already won the war. She wasn't going anywhere.

Both of them stared up at the hole in the ceiling as their heartbeats slowed.

CHAPTER THREE

"You weigh a ton," she said.

Daniel lifted his head off his little ray of sunshine's chest, ridiculously gratified by the calm, even thumping of her heart, and the steady, measured lift and fall of her ribs. She was alright. Never mind the griping.

His girl was okay, and on some subconscious, unchartable level, that equated to trust. It had to be trust. Or maybe she was just worn out. Oh well. He'd settle for what he could get, for now.

"Hey." He held both of her wrists in one hand, and used the other to wipe at the dirty tear tracks on her face, to tuck a strand of oily hair behind an ear more adorable than any ear had a right to be. He was grinning again, and he didn't bother to fight it. She was every Christmas all at once, tinsel and trees and the whole shebang. Sure, last Christmas had been spent fighting for survival, but this more than made up for it. What a wonderful present. He'd even gotten used to her smell. "How are you feeling?"

"Squished."

"Right. Sorry." In deference to her future goodwill, he shifted more of his weight off her and onto his side, leaving a leg thrown over her and her hands trapped, for safety's sake. Thankfully he had gotten his cock under control a while back. "Better?" he asked.

By way of a response, she snorted and stretched her fingers as if she was working out the kinks.

"Did you know it's Valentine's Day? And you still haven't told me your name," he said.

"It's Valentine's?"

"Mm hmm. February fifteen. I've been keeping track."

"Valentine's is the fourteenth."

"What's a day between friends? Anyway, we were talking about your name. Which you were going to tell me," he prompted.

She didn't even blink.

"Whenever you're ready. No rush at all."

Her focus remained fixed on a point above his head. He didn't need to look. He knew what she was staring at so wistfully – the gruesome hole in the ceiling. Her own perceived gateway to freedom. That bubble needed bursting. Obviously she'd been holed up in the attic since the shit hit the fan, given the state of her.

He waited while she deliberated.

Daniel sucked in some much-needed oxygen. Why had he held his breath? That was dumb.

Eventually, she blew a strand of hair out of her face, her throat moved, and she gave a bare inch. "Ali."

"Hi, Ali. I'm Daniel." He smiled, and like the turning of the tide, about an ocean's worth of tension eased out of him. "Well, I have a feeling this is the beginning of a beautiful friendship."

She gave a brief bark of laughter, or perhaps a cough. The house was dusty. It made it hard to tell. "Friends don't hold friends hostage. Generally speaking."

"Hmm," he nodded. "Friends also don't let friends live out their days in a stinking, dark, dusty hole. Or so I've heard."

She pinned her lips tight and turned her head away, making him feel ten types of asshole. Too bad.

There was a message to be delivered here, and he could not afford to fail. He couldn't face going back to being alone. Could not do it. Boy didn't that mess with his whole "man as an island" theory of a lifetime's making. "Ali, I know things are scary, but barricading yourself in here alone isn't the answer."

"Really?" She glared at him. It was a queenly glare. His girl pulled it off with aplomb, no matter the grime. "Living in a dark, stinking hole got me this far."

"Granted, but the worst is over. I'm not saying things are a party out there, but they have calmed down."

"Are you serious?" she asked, her voice highly skeptical.

"Hear me out." Her brow flinched for a moment, but at least he had her attention. Until she craned her neck and frowned at what his finger was up to mid-torso – the torso in question being hers. His digit was drawing circles around the dip of her bellybutton. Endless circles. They both watched his finger go round and round, dawdling over soft skin in a lingering caress.

He could have sworn the thing had a mind of its own.

"Get. Your. Hand. Off. Me."

Which, he had to admit, was fair enough. Maybe enough boundaries had been messed with on their first day together.

"Sure, sorry. Didn't even realize I was ... Yeah, never mind." He moved the hand back to his leg and let his fingers fidget on safer ground. They wouldn't stop moving, a sure sign of nerves.

"So. Life outside," he began. A sore subject, to be sure, but he had to sell it. "You realize situated on the edge of the city is a bad place to be? Inner city is thick with infected, but further out here in the 'burbs you're going to cross paths with other survivors."

"Oh, you think?"

"Be nice," he said. "Now, I'm guessing the people left over are going to be a mix of the lucky, like you and me, and the odd bastard handy with a weapon and happy to do what they need to get by. I'm guessing by now food and water are getting scarce for you. You can't stay hidden, can you? Not if you don't want to starve. You also know it's too dangerous to go out on your own."

"I've done okay."

"You need someone to watch your back. Can't do that on your own."

She tucked in her chin and said nothing.

"I'm not saying you didn't do good getting in here and staying put through the whole meltdown, but it's time to move on, Ali. I was thinking of heading south-west, find a nice rural area and set myself up, be self-sufficient." He would be self-sufficient alright, him and his hand, if she shot him down. More important things were at play here, though, because eventually, she would mess up and be dinner for the hungry horde. The thought made his heart kick over painfully. The infected were growing restless as pickings grew slim, branching out from the thick of the cities.

Soon enough, her little corner of suburbia would be overrun, if her own lack of food and water hadn't since made her flee.

"I'll grow my own fruit and vegetables, use solar panels for power. I was a mechanic, so I've got a good basic knowledge of all sorts of things. Sky's the limit." Daniel nodded, pleased with the sound of it. Plausible, warm and friendly.

Please God, he had to have won her over.

Instead she sighed. And it was long, drawn out and mighty fucking irritated. When women sighed like that it never boded well for anyone involved. "We discussed this."

"Huh?" He propped himself up on an elbow, bewildered. "No, we didn't."

"Fingers." Ali jerked her chin at the hand currently stroking her thigh, toying with the inner seam of her jeans, generally making itself right at home.

"Sorry ... my bad." He jerked his hand up, then paused. Amongst the dirt and dry stains on her jeans, something caught his attention. Dread slammed through him. The damage sat directly above her knee, and it was fresh. "You're bleeding."

"I'm fine."

"No. You're not." Daniel clenched his teeth and ignored the sick feeling building in his belly. "How did you get it?" When she hesitated a second too long he lost his cool completely, something rumbled in his throat and his voice rose to all new heights. "Now, Ali. Tell me now. How did you get it?"

"I didn't get it from one of them, okay? It was a nail or something going under the fence. I'm not infected. Stop yelling at me," she growled straight back at him, her gaze fierce. "Asshole. Get off me."

"You're sure?"

"Yes."

"Oh, thank fuck for that. I'm sorry, but I had to know." The minute he lifted his leg up off her, she tried to scurry away, scrambling backward on hands, butt and feet, crab style. The grip he had on her pants didn't let her get far. "Take them off. That needs seeing to."

"It's just a scratch."

"Don't give me that. You want me to lecture you on how easily infection sets in? How fast?" He scowled, clinging to the raggedy hem of her jeans as if she was his safety blanket. Her gaze flicked to her feet and his followed. One solid kick from those boots of hers and he would be in a world of pain. Important, given how clearly unhappy she appeared to be. "Please ... I mean."

The melting-glass glare and the jut of her chin relented, somewhat. Good enough.

"Anyway, you need a bath."

Her neck and face flushed, as the muscles around her mouth moved. The play of colors beneath her dirty skin fascinated him.

"Can you get out of my face for one minute?"

"Sorry, sorry. Though wouldn't you feel better cleaned up? Then we can see to that scratch." Daniel gave her his most trustworthy face, hooking a finger in a hole above the hem of her pants leg in case of failure. "Maybe some new clothes, too? What do you say?"

She sniffed disdainfully. "I wasn't sure if they hunted by scent, or … it was a safety precaution. Messing around with hair and make-up didn't seem wise, given the circumstances."

"I don't think they track by scent. Mostly they seem to rely on sight and sound. And, sorry again, but as emergencies rate, you having a bath is definitely one."

Her brows reached for the sky. "You are such an ass."

"But an honest one. Doesn't that count for something?"

"No. Not really." Gray eyes inspected the worn flooring with great care. Far more than it deserved. "Alright, but I'll deal with my own hygiene issues."

"I appreciate your willingness to cooperate. In that same spirit, you need to know that I'm sticking to you like glue. Where you go, I go." She opened her mouth to refute, but he got there first. "Nothing dubious, I promise. I'll turn my back, won't even peek. You can trust me."

"The house is locked up. I don't you need you watching my every move."

He shoved his free hand into the space between them, palm up and empty. "Ali, nothing is certain these days. Nothing. Consider it a necessary safety precaution because this can't work any other way. We need to stick together. I'm sorry, but shyness isn't a good enough reason for your premature death."

His girl frowned, stopped, frowned some more. Finally, she delivered one short nod of assent. "Okay."

"Seriously?"

Her chin moved in the desired direction, but she didn't meet his eyes. Not even a little.

She was nervous. The panic attack, running away, all of it. If he had stopped to think with his big head as opposed to the little one, he might have moderated his behavior some time back, but no. He had been gung-ho the whole way.

He was an ass.

But, he was the ass committed to keeping her in one piece.

"Good. Great." He released the death hold he had on her pants, something surprisingly hard to do; his fingers stiffly refused to uncurl. "Why don't I turn my back and let you get out of those jeans so you can get your knee cleaned up? I've even got a couple of extra t-shirts if you need, so you can cover up. I'm not going to see a thing. How does that sound?"

Her shoulders dropped. "Fine."

Turning his back was harder than letting go of her jeans had been. All sorts of conflict rose up inside him. The girl had no voodoo powers, she wasn't going to disappear into thin air because his eyes weren't on her. Christ, he was a case. A bead of sweat slid down the side of his face. His hands shook.

The tiny hallway led to a poky lounge with a couple of bedrooms situated off it. Not much chance she would run off on him. Surely.

He strained his ears but heard no sounds of a swift retreat taking place behind him. With the shotgun still in the kitchen, care of their mad dash, she had no weapon at hand. Behind him, the sound of shuffling told him she'd climbed to her feet and ditched the dirty, bloody jeans.

Still. You never knew. So he snuck a peek over his shoulder.

"Hey!"

He spun to face her at the tone of outrage, a hand held out to halt her not even happening escape. Ah, fuck.

The poor girl struggled to pull her pants back up. Going by the pained expression on her damp and pale face, doing so didn't come remotely close to being fun for her poor sore knee.

"Shit. I'm sorry. I'm really sorry. Okay, let's try again." Daniel shoved a hand through his hair, grabbed a handful and tugged. Holy cow did she look upset. Her eyes were once more skittish, searching for an out. His fault. "Ali, in case you haven't noticed, I'm excited to see you. No excuse, I know. I also seem to be a tad bit terrified that you're going to disappear on me. So I'm sorry. I shouldn't have cheated."

She showed him her teeth.

"I know. I deserve that, but still ..." She hesitated, and he smothered his own snarl of frustration. Buried it down deep in his belly where she couldn't possibly hear it and use it against him. "Ali, play fair. Give me a chance here."

"Why should I?" Ali sank back down onto the floor. She set her hands on the linoleum behind her, leant back, sort of Playboy Bunny-style, minus the thrusting out of her breasts. That was just his dirty mind filling in the gaps. Mostly, she appeared tired, cranky, run down. But it didn't matter. He stared at her, stunned. Poleaxed all over again by the pale, dirty woman who had shoved a gun in his face.

Aah, man. Forty-one was far too fucking old for love at first sight. He might as well throw himself at her feet and be done with it. Except he'd pretty much already done that. It hadn't gotten him anywhere.

She definitely looked twitchy again, like she would be making for the nearest exit at the first opportunity, sans him.

"Ali, if I break your trust again, I'll go fetch the shotgun for you myself. What do you say?"

"I say you're full of it." It took some time, but eventually she met his gaze. There was a lot going on behind those gray eyes. Too much. He stood in the proverbial cold, coming close to having the door to her heart and mind slammed shut in his face.

"Talk to me," he said. "Please."

Her body sagged, and her head hung low. "And say what? I was fine on my own."

"I know, I know. But for how long? Hmm?"

Nothing.

"All I want," he dropped to his knees before her. She hustled back on her butt till she hit the wall. Those wide eyes, so full of fear, made his heart hurt. Without her trust he had nothing. "All I want ... is to keep you safe."

"For what?"

"A long time. A very, very long time."

"Right." She partly turned her head, putting him in the corner of her vision. "You want a lot more than that."

Daniel held up a hand, stopping the notion right then and there. "But! But. Listen to me here because this is important. Not without your permission, Ali. That's the crux of it."

She watched him like he was a barely chained beast for several long moments, probably weighing his intrinsic value, or who the fuck knew what. He sat silent, out of tricks for now, worn down to his last argument. He held his peace.

"Okay, I promise I won't run. For now. Not that I'm committing to anything." The last she tacked on hastily to the end.

"Absolutely." His heart turned giddy cartwheels inside his chest. Clapping would probably be going too far. "God forbid."

"Up to and including agreeing to play Adam and Eve with you."

"Uh-huh. Got it." He nodded eagerly but kept his face bland. "But you know you just put the visual of you wearing nothing but fig leaves in my head."

She blinked.

"Sorry."

Ali carefully pushed herself up the wall, got to her feet. He followed. Not licking his lips.

"Where's the bathroom?" he enquired.

Gray eyes darted to a door down the hallway, but her hand pointed to another.

"There?" He gave the door indicated a nod, but kept the other in mind for later. It and whatever lay behind it. "Okay, let's have a bath." He paused. "I meant that in the singular, by the way."

CHAPTER FOUR

"How are you doing?"

"Hmm?" Ali rushed the razor over the back of her calf, swallowing past the lump in her throat, feeling stupid and self-conscious.

Gussying herself up because of the idiot, because his jibes had hit home. She had actually let him get to her. Stupid.

And her hands were shaking again. The combined effect of the oversized male lounging against the doorframe with his back turned and the infected banging around outside set her nerves to highly strung.

Both made her jumpy.

Eventually, the infected would lose interest and seek out other prey. Eventually, so too would the oversized male.

"I could give you a hand," he said, not for the first time.

She didn't bother to reply.

"You're killing me."

"I don't have my shotgun. If I was killing you I'd probably want that," she pointed out, in a voice so tight it wavered. Being without her shotgun sucked even more of the courage from her. "Where is it?"

His head turned far enough for her to sight his chin, but he stopped short of looking at her. Lucky for him. She had wrapped a towel around herself just in case his curiosity got the better of him.

Ali rolled her shoulders back, gave her armpit a quick sniff. Soap, not sweat. She smelt fresh. It did feel good being clean after so long. He'd been right. Not that he needed to know. The delicate power balance needed to stay in her favor. Trusting him was a tenuous thing.

The bathing had taken up a lot of her water supplies. But being clean was, apparently, a required luxury.

Jerk.

The infected outside bashed at the back door. She forced her shoulders back down from her ears, made herself ignore the sound. Slow, deep breaths.

"The gun's on the kitchen counter," he said, facing mostly forward. "Right where you left it."

"I saw that, mate. Watch it."

"Please. Did I turn once while you washed your hair? No. Some of those noises ... you should be ashamed of yourself," he ranted. Because he was crazy. Crazy with an offbeat charm she struggled to stay immune to. Beware the man that made you smile. "But wait, how about while you frolicked with the soap, did I turn then? No. No, I did not. I kept my word no matter how you baited me. That's because I'm pussy-whipped and proud."

"Pussy-whipped. Very nice." Something stung her knee. Wincing, she lifted the razor from her skin. Great. She'd nicked herself due to focusing on the view instead of shaving.

God, but he filled out blue jeans. His ass was paired with the strong line of his back, framed by a set of broad shoulders encased in a t-shirt that fit right. She tried to ignore him, but her girl bits lacked the moral fortitude, apparently.

And lacked priorities.

It had been a very long time between dates.

And he did have a stellar ass.

Her nipples pebbled from more than the damp. It was surreal to feel feminine. To feel human ... A drink would have worked, right about then. "You sure have a way with words."

"I can't hold back. You're such a receptive audience. You love me."

She snorted and hated herself for it.

"And it's great to have someone to talk to. Even if I can't face you while we're talking, which is plain rude. My mother would have been appalled." Daniel reached up and leant an arm against the top of the doorframe. His fingers tapped a beat against the old hardwood. Mary's house wasn't sized for him. He was going to knock himself out on a doorway if he wasn't careful.

"Give it up," she said.

"No chance. Not so long as my pathetic state of affairs amuses you."

It did. He wasn't even particularly funny. Probably stress.

Then the thing at the back door went thump. Ali jumped, slicing the side of her ankle. Proving the stress theory right. "Shit."

"What?" Daniel spun and his face screwed up tight in disbelief, brows drawing together. "You were wearing a towel? For how long?"

He snatched a facecloth from the counter and dropped to his knees, dabbing at the small cut oozing blood. "And you call me untrustworthy."

"You were fine where you were." Her hands clutched the top of her towel. "Going from being alone to having you around is an adjustment."

Daniel grunted. "Question. Have you even fired that gun before today? Not that I'm worried you'll kill me in my sleep or something."

"No. Today was the first time." She held still and watched him tending to the cut. In truth, she had survived more by cowardice, hiding in her attic hole, than cunning. "I probably couldn't hit a house."

"You did hit a house. You would have hit me just fine." Daniel smiled up at her.

There were creases at the edges of his baby blues, faint, paler lines against the tan of his skin. He was maybe forty. He wore it well. Lovely, faded, denim-blue eyes that held her rapt for a time. If in days gone by he had smiled at her from across a crowded room, she would have smiled back. That much was true.

"I nearly did shoot you," she said. "Why would you smile at that?"

"Because you didn't shoot me. Also because you're willing to defend yourself. Taken in the right context, both of these things make me happy." He grabbed a tube of antiseptic cream from the first-aid kit spread out on the bathroom counter and squeezed some onto his fingers. "Might as well deal with your knee while I'm here. Stay still."

He frowned and clucked his tongue, thick fingers stroking over the jagged cut on her knee. His touch was extraordinarily gentle.

With his face at her crotch level, she started to sweat. The old towel offered little protection. He was a stranger, although an attractive one. She had stopped sleeping with strangers years ago. Had stopped sleeping with anyone almost a year ago. A woman could be content with her own hand. Shower jet. Toys. It had seemed the simplest solution after the great breakup.

The jumble of emotions tumbling through her was all too much for one day.

"Probably just a nail going under the fence. I can do that." Ali made a grab for the antiseptic, but Daniel stayed ahead of her, tucking it behind his back. "Personal space?" she asked.

"Hush. This is not good." He continued administering to her, shuffling closer on his knees. She could feel his warm, damp breath on her leg where the towel skirted her skin. It tickled. "When was your last tetanus shot?"

"I don't know," she admitted. Another thing to worry over. "There might be some antibiotics in the cupboard. I'll have a look. I think we're done here."

"How does it feel?" The corners of his mouth lifted, slowly, and she stared for a moment, bedazzled.

Past time to pull herself together.

Nice face by no means changed the facts. He had barged his way into her safe place. Denied her liberty, yaddah, yaddah.

And oh yeah, she had lost it, big time. Hugely. Right up close and personal.

Shit.

Enough of her normal self remained beside the chunk of space the cowardly rabbit inhabited to wonder if she should be embarrassed or angry or what. He made her feel exposed in a way that had nothing to do with her missing pants.

The thing at the back door started up a dull, constant hammering. Maybe more than one of them, by the sound of it. They were out there, waiting.

What the fuck was she going to do?

"Hey. It's okay." His eyes were full of warmth and affection. It was the sort of gaze you got jealous over when another woman was on the receiving end.

How bizarre, he didn't even know her.

"No need to panic. We're safe," he said. "Everything's locked tight."

"Yeah." Her chin bobbed like a cork on the water. She was safe. In her head she knew it. But in the depths of her rabbity heart, she didn't believe it. "I should get dressed."

"Which makes it my turn to clean up." The big man rose to his feet, taking up all available air space in the tiny bathroom. She tried to withdraw, but the back of her heel connected with the bottom of the cabinet door with a thump. That smarted.

Luckily, Daniel didn't seem to notice her lack of grace. "Another question. Why were you heading for the roof when this place is locked up tighter than a vault?"

"The last news reports said they didn't climb well, so it's safer up there. They said to get onto rooftops, knock out staircases if you could ..." Ali shrugged and twisted her lips.

Why had she remained in the dirt and dark when there was a whole house at her disposal? It wasn't something she cared to review. "I felt safer up there. Can you move, please? You're in my way."

"Yeah, but ..."

"Move. Please."

Daniel said nothing and didn't move, he stood and stared back down at her from on high, his mouth open slightly. The look he gave said she was a hair's breadth off being loony bin material, but he was too kind to say so. Screw him. Ali bit her cheeks and fought the fear. Being cornered set her off in the worst way and the pushy bastard just kept doing it. He didn't understand shit. Why she cared what he thought was beyond her. But she did.

"Look, they could still get in. You don't know what could happen. If enough of them beat against the door, they could break it down. Last time I checked, no one had put out a survival guide for this particular scenario so you can keep your fucking opinions to yourself, okay?" The words poured out in a hot rush. Damn. Not good. Maybe she had lost it. "I want to get dressed now."

"O-kay." And if that wasn't said using a "don't spook the crazy lady" tone of voice, she would eat her big toe.

Ali shoved her wet hair back from her face, then took a breath and tried to calm down. "Can you move ..."

"We can find a safer place out west, you know." With no warning Daniel whipped his t-shirt off over his head, dropped it to the ground and started in on his belt buckle.

Like it was no big deal.

Holy hell he was fit. And standing way too close. His upper body was perfectly defined. What the hell had he been doing since civilization fell apart?

The oxygen had long since left the room, for her at least. She needed a paper bag to breathe into. Now would be good. "Wh-what?"

"Yeah, yeah. Something with a decent fence we can build up so we can be safe out and about during the day. Be able to see anything coming at us from a distance." Busy hands made short work of belt and button and zipper. Her face went nuclear. She held up her hands to cover her cheeks while his jeans dropped and his plans grew.

It was difficult to know which alarmed her more.

"I've been using a trail bike, but we could switch to a small four-wheel drive. We can just switch cars when we hit a roadblock we can't get around. What do you think?"

Think? Yes, she needed to think. To do that he had to stop. All of it. He had to stop pushing. "Wait."

"I say we head out tomorrow. You can get packed up by then, yeah?" He propped his hands on lean hips, thumbs tucked beneath the waistband of his black cotton boxers like a threat, or a promise. She wasn't sure which. His big hands framed the ridges and planes of muscle from abdomen up to his chest, fancy tattoos sitting atop each big buff shoulder, done in shades of green and gray and blue. He was a work of art.

Her knees wobbled.

With a particularly pained expression, he asked, "What's wrong now?"

"You. You need to back off." The flats of her palms connected with the heat of his chest as she did her best to shove him. "Give me some space. Now."

The big guy gifted her one small step backward and hung his head. Lips compressed and jaw stern, he looked up at her from beneath dark brows. "Ali ..."

"No. You need to back off. This isn't going to work."

The big man swore. Repeatedly. "You've been living up in the roof for what? Six, seven weeks? Coming down to scavenge when you have no other choice? That's not living, and we both know it. The world may have gone to shit but we're still alive, don't you think it's time to start acting like it?"

Her face must have conveyed her doubt over the pep talk because he groaned and ran a hand over the choppy, badly cut, short dark head of hair. He seemed beyond irate with his eyes narrowed. It wasn't her damn fault he barged in and took over without a thought. Various muscles around his mouth tightened, as if he wanted to yell at her but held it in. She could relate. It was going around.

Finally, he rolled his shoulders, like a fighter getting ready to head back into the ring. He gave her a long hard stare and she did her best not to blink. Her frightened inner rabbit wanted to scamper as escape scenarios raced through her mind. Daniel noticed her reaction and the growl amped up a notch as he took yet another step back. This one was sizably bigger than the last; he was almost back to standing in the doorway. "Better?"

She nodded.

"Fuck's sake." His mouth opened then shut, as if he too had just noticed the lack of oxygen in the room. "Fine, maybe you don't need me. Truth is ... I need you."

She stopped.

Daniel crossed thick arms over his chest and glared back at her. A purely defensive stance, she knew it well. Her own arms were crossed and bolted down over her breasts, which might have been his point. She was the one locked down. He simply mirrored her tight-ass ways.

And he looked downright stupid in Mary's flowery feminine house. He was so big and intimidating. No wonder she had run like a rabbit. She winced at the angry red lines crisscrossing his tanned skin. Her work. But struggling had gotten her nowhere. He stood there barefoot, waiting on her in his underwear.

She focused on his toes because they were easier to fix on than his face or the rest of his stupendous body.

What the hell was she going to do with him?

Suddenly, he stuck his hand out. "Shake. We're starting over. Clean slate. Pretend we just met, like it's our first date or something."

"Our first date?"

He gave a one-shoulder shrug, face carefully bland, but the lines around his eyes remained tight, sharply embedded. "You get the drift."

His big hand hung there in the space between them. In many ways, she would be trusting her life to that handshake. Not a "throw caution to the wind", idle sort of undertaking. All of this felt weighty, and she had no crystal ball to tell if he was good or bad, right or wrong. She had no way of knowing since the world had gone so spectacularly to shit.

Moments passed and the hand did not so much as waver. He waited her out with absolute patience. As signs went, it wasn't bad.

"Alright." She held her hand out, and he covered it with both of his.

"Daniel Cross, forty-one, single." He paused and gave her a wary glance, turned his face aside. "Divorced actually, a long time ago. Let's not discuss it. I'm a mechanic, or, I was. I've been travelling down the coast for the last six weeks, looking for survivors. Your turn."

"Ah, okay. Ali Jameson, thirty-two, was a secretary. I lived in one of the townhouses next door." Done. She shut her mouth and shuffled her feet. Ignored the tingling going up her arm entirely.

"Single?"

She gave another nod.

"Keep going," he encouraged.

"Well ..." What to say? Thinking back on it, her accomplishments were few. Best stick to the fresh stuff, what little of it was air-able. "Mary, the old lady that lived here, she got sick and asked if I would stay with her. She didn't have much family. Mine were all down south." Her voice wound down to a whisper, and he nodded in understanding. "There was no way out. Things went bad fast. People just ..."

"Yeah, I know. There wasn't as much military up north and what there was, was spread thin. But still, the streets were insane. You did the right thing keeping your head down."

She said nothing.

His smile widened, all enthused once more. It made her stomach flip with nerves. "Okay, this is good. We're getting somewhere. Tell me, Ali, did you have time to turn and run when you first saw me? You know the neighborhood well, don't you? You're one cunning babe. With a decent head start you could have lost me easily, I think. So why am I here?"

Ali's breath stopped, stuck somewhere in her throat. She hadn't seen it coming. She tugged on her captured hand, and his fingers tightened infinitesimally. "I did try to get away. It didn't work. You're very determined," she muttered hoarsely.

Daniel skewed his lips, took his time. "I know you tried. You were scared. Here's the thing though … I don't think you want to be alone any more than I do. Some part of you chose to face me, to take a chance that I would be a good guy, that I wouldn't hurt you."

"Are you a good guy?"

"Mostly. Define 'good'." The side of his mouth curled up and his gaze slid over her, making all of her tingle this time. Not good. First dates always made her feel awkward, stupid. This one blew them all to smithereens.

"For instance, do you mean am I good at certain things, or am I a good person? Because both are valid in their own way," he said. "And as for being a good person, just because my thoughts are impure doesn't mean my actions would be. Mostly, I manage to keep myself in check. But, with you, I'm a little overexcited. You might have noticed. You have, haven't you? I think I'd given up on finding anyone alive and you … well, you exceed my wildest dreams." He paused, stared at her for a moment, eyes intent.

Such blue eyes.

"But back to the question, I've been told I'm quite good at some things. I can give a demonstration if you like. You know, of things I might be good at. You could judge for yourself if you like. Do you like?" he asked.

She blinked.

"I'm babbling, aren't I?"

"Somewhat."

"You're very kind."

They smiled at each other. He had a nice smile.

It occurred to her then that, for a brief time, she had been okay. Fear had not ruled her mind. Panic had not owned her body. She was not cowering up in the sweltering heat of the attic, surrounded by dust and cobwebs, more frightened of the world outside than she was of the poisonous spiders sharing her space. For a few brief minutes she had been herself, holding a conversation even, albeit a rather odd one.

How perfectly, weirdly, normal.

"You okay? What are you thinking?" Daniel eased the grip on her hand, and she managed to draw it free. Stupidly, once back in her own possession, her fingers missed the firm, steady grip. "Not going to flip out on me again, are you?"

That was the question. She thought hard before answering.

"No. I don't think so." Ali rubbed her palm against her leg, wishing she could rub off the whole liking the hand-holding business.

It was the human comfort factor, no biggie. Without a doubt, she'd certainly been short on comfort. She might crave it, but she could live without it, as she had amply demonstrated over the past few months. The underdressed, oversized man standing in her bathroom eating her up with his eyes was entirely unnecessary for adequate levels of comfort. If only her fingers would stop quivering. If only she wore more than a towel.

"It's okay if you need to flip a little. I can deal with it," he said. Gentle fingers tucked a strand of wet hair behind her ear and then lingered for a moment before returning to his side. He had a way of moving into her personal space in the blink of an eye, before she even knew what was going on. Or, maybe he had never left and she had ceased to notice.

She'd acclimatized to his presence.

"You know, I kind of enjoyed you against me, not biting or anything. It was nice. I could get used to it. Shit, I really am babbling. I haven't talked to anyone in weeks." Daniel scrubbed a hand over his face then let it wander up to do the same to his choppy hair. "Funny thing is, before all this, my favorite thing in the whole wide world was to be left alone to get things done. I hated conversation for no damn purpose, for politeness's sake. Know what I mean?"

"Yeah," she said, understanding perfectly. More often than not, opening her mouth meant saying the wrong thing and being frowned at or ridiculed. Alone was a thousand times simpler.

He stepped closer. She stepped back, her butt hitting the sink.

"So ... Communal bathing? Too much, too soon?"

"Mmm." She tucked her lips in and gripped her towel, afraid it might slip to reveal more than he needed to know of her state of mind. The man had a way of seeing everything.

"Gotcha." His hands settled on his hips and he gave her a lop-sided grin. "I didn't mean to scare you with all my grand plans."

"I'm not afraid of you, or your plans." Mostly.

"Well, I didn't mean to push you either."

"Yes, you did," she laughed. "You're the epitome of pushy."

He sighed. "Busted. Out of curiosity, if you weren't scared, then what were you? When you were staring at me just now, I mean."

"Maybe a little scared."

"Ah. Okay. If I'm not allowed to get away with telling fibs, even the little ones that don't hurt anyone, same goes for you, babe." Blue eyes bored into her. "If it makes you feel any better, you scare me too."

CHAPTER FIVE

Daniel hated the moaning. It might drive him crazy.

One of them still bumped around outside, knocking over potted plants and banging into wind chimes. Daniel watched Ali by the light of the candle but she didn't stir, thank god. His girl needed her sleep.

She might have begun curled up in a tight ball but she was a bed hog at heart and after weeks of sleeping up in an attic, he didn't much blame her. He hadn't been able to sleep. Every time he lay down, his nightmares started.

Besides, her presence excited the hell out of him.

To have company was great, amazing. But to have her as company thrilled him right down to his toes and all the way back up again.

So instead of sleeping, he enjoyed the view, sitting at the end of the wonky double bed, which in all likelihood predated him. His girl defied the laws of gravity splayed out the way she was, with the sizeable dip in the mattress toward the center. She was lying on her back with her limbs spread-eagle, nothing more than white panties and a tank top covering her on account of the hotbox humidity.

Daniel couldn't help but appreciate the nice thin cotton.

Not only sensible for summer but perfect for spying what lay beneath, like the valley between her breasts and the shadow between her thighs. That he could make out the lips of her pussy was probably pure imagination.

Dark blonde hair was spread out across the pillow, her pretty face turned away. The slow, even rise and fall of her breasts mesmerized him. Hypnotized.

He could watch her sleep for hours.

He likely would.

He had considered taking himself in hand, getting some relief, but no. For some dumb reason it felt like cheating. As if it would take something away from finding her, from waiting for her and winning her.

And he would. His commitment was total.

Apart from the moaning, things were good – body washed, belly full, and his girl laid out for his viewing pleasure. Tortured, but good.

The window was boarded and a chest of drawers sat in front of the door, his girl's shotgun in pride of place on top. She had actually gone to sleep with it beside her. He'd moved it to higher ground at the first opportunity.

Besides the hundred and one locks and the bars on every window, no less than guns and barricades would have convinced her to sleep in the house as opposed to up in the attic.

He moved the drawers aside carefully, quietly, and stepped out into the dark hallway.

Ali had refused to use the main bedroom, wouldn't even go near the closed door. It was as if she hit an invisible wall a body's length from it and – bam! – got no further.

People had done some horrible things to survive. He knew he had, the worst of it keeping him awake at night, scared of what might come out of the dark. The virus had made monsters of everyone.

Deep down, he knew what he would find.

He didn't go in, just stood in the hallway and opened the door. The hinges creaked ominously as it swung open. No need for the warning, the smell was sufficient. The small flashlight he used gave him small, tight circles of light. Sensible, since the infected seemed to find their meals by sight and sound alone.

There was a lot of blood on the floor. The human body held liters of the liquid. It had seeped into the carpet and dried, making a stain of darkness among the pale pink. An old-fashioned marble lamp lay discarded close by, its heavy base covered in more blood.

This was Ali's secret then. She had bashed her infected, elderly neighbor's skull in with a lamp base.

His stomach clenched. Shit, his poor girl.

A gun was much simpler and cleaner by comparison. Faster, even if the eventual toll remained no easier to pay.

He pulled the door closed and continued on with his tour, up the aluminum ladder till he reached the manhole. He doubted she could have done more than move around the tiny attic on her knees. As lodgings went, it was hot as an oven and thick with dust, way claustrophobic.

Never the fuck again would she go up there if he had anything to do with it.

Daniel descended the ladder and padded back to the guest room, rearranged the drawers against the door and tugged off his t-shirt. Night had failed to appreciably cool off the house. It remained sweltering with the windows closed and no electricity to turn on the fans.

She had moved in his absence, rolled over onto her side so those pale plush limbs fell into alignment. She'd even tucked a hand beneath her cheek.

He might have offered to sleep on the floor as part of the giving her space and time negotiations, but he couldn't do it.

The mattress springs made a racket as he climbed on next to her, easing an arm over her waist and settling in to spoon her warm body. They fit together just right.

She murmured something but didn't wake.

The memories of the scene next door kept his cock under control, which was good. His poor girl. He wanted to comfort, pamper and protect her.

She needed that right now.

Being this close to her, his skin slicked with sweat in no time. He felt like he had a fever. No way was he moving.

Because, despite being this close to her, the in and out of her breathing soothed him. How she riled him up and calmed him down all at once, conscious or not, defied logic.

Weeks of exposure had taught him to block out the moaning coming from the street, to shove it to the back of his mind and not let it consume him. He could lie there and stroke her arm, breathe in the scent of whatever shampoo she had used up a bottle of and bide his time. It was all good.

For the first time in ages, he had hope.

CHAPTER SIX

Ali woke with a gasp, taking a moment to get her bearings.

The morning sun hadn't woken her, Daniel's wandering hand had. His hand and the whole body ache his touch generated. Her skin felt prickly, disturbingly alive and alert.

The hand cupping her breast would have been cause for castration, except for the fact that her hand was shoved down the front of his boxers. Her fingers curled around a hip like she owned it, with her wrist resting beside a sizeable appendage greeting the day in the usual way. Whoa boy. The head of his cock came close to peeking out from beneath the waistband of his boxer-briefs. His member matched the rest of him in size.

Wicked thoughts drove her silly. She needed to calm down. Do the deep breathing. Which was a mistake because he smelt good, warm skin and clean male sweat.

She inhaled him, just to double-check. He smelt amazing. A girl could get high on him. She wanted him. She did. Wanted to feel him inside her, wanted this ache to end. Desire owned her, and it was leaving her a big, wet mess. What a terrible power to hold over someone. He didn't even have to do anything to turn her to shivers, her own mind and body could run riot just fine.

But it was a natural urge, nothing to worry about. It had been a while, and a stressful situation and curiosity being what they were, blah, blah, blah. All the old clichés.

Curiosity. What a lame ass excuse. She could do better.

Thank god he wasn't watching her now. Her cheek rested on one sun-burnished pec and God help her if she had drooled on him in her sleep or something. How special would that be?

Someone so hard-bodied shouldn't have made such a comfortable mattress. She needed to get the hell off him.

Ali averted her gaze, pulled her mind out of his pants, then extricated her hand from his boxers one cautious millimeter at a time.

"You awake?" he murmured.

She whipped her hand from his underwear like her fingers were singed.

He chuckled, chest shuddering beneath her cheek. "I'll take that as a yes."

"I'll have my breast back now."

"Mmm." His fingers uncurled ever so slowly, but his other hand, the one resting on her lower back, moved not at all. "Heard a motorbike close-by earlier."

"What?" She scrambled up into a sitting position, startled wide awake, as if he had doused her in coffee. Her heart pounded, and every hair on her body stood erect. "When?"

"Hour or so back. Nothing since." He stretched both hands up, tucked them behind his head. How the hell could he be so relaxed? "Be calm," he said.

She shook her head in wonder. "Be calm? I haven't seen any uninfected around here in over a month. Bit of a coincidence them turning up the day after I fire the shotgun. They were searching for us."

"Maybe. Maybe not. Might be you're just feeling a bit paranoid, babe. Which, I would add before you rip my head off, is fair enough. Either way, unless you've put out a welcome mat they're not going to find us. Have you?" he asked, mouth twitching. "Is there some sign out there that you're in residence? No spray-painted announcement on the door? Another pair of these cute cotton panties left hanging from the mailbox, perhaps?"

Her face heated. The asshole. "No. Of course not."

He yawned and scratched at the short spiky dark hair pointing every which way. He was all over the morning appeal. In comparison, she probably looked like she had been tumble-dried. But he had a whole charmingly disheveled thing going on with his bed hair. If she hadn't been balancing scared shitless and embarrassed there might have been time to stop and appreciate it.

"Then, be calm," he said. "We're okay."

Ali bit at the inside of her cheeks, gave the small bedroom a detailed once over. The old chest of drawers still barricaded the door. The windows were still boarded and the shades still drawn. Everything was where it should be. The filtered light gave no clue as to the time of day or how long she had slept with him beside her. Beneath her. Bloody hell.

Things were heating up. Her skin was sticky, no matter the water wasted last night. Sticky and sweaty and she had been spread all over Daniel like honey on toast. Her fingers knotted themselves up in the top sheet. Over and over.

Alex had hated her clinging. Clinging being his term for any touching taking place outside of sexual congress. Oh, no, Alex had preferred to be adored from afar. Made it much simpler for her sister to slip on in and have him.

What a beautiful moment their wedding was. It had truly brought new lows to family awkwardness.

Ouch, a year on and still she felt the sting.

And why that old wound had chosen to pop up and nip her on the ass here and now she couldn't say. It fit with her flurried, messy state of mind. Hell, she didn't even know if any of her family were alive. Being betrayed dwindled in importance in the face of cold, hard death. Her insides felt strangely empty, as they always did when she thought of her family. She'd well and truly been left alone. Alone, except for the giant in her bed.

Daniel yawned again, cracked his neck and watched her. The other people out there wanting who knew what didn't seem to concern him. That made her want to thump him. Hard.

Right on his big, fat, pretty, patient head.

"Talk to me, babe," he said gently. When she didn't reply, he raised an arm, pointed a lazy finger toward the chest of drawers. "Your gun's up there. I didn't want you accidentally blowing my head off during the night. Because that would be sad, right?"

She smiled and rubbed the sleep from her eyes. "Right. Sad."

"I get the need to be cautious, Ali. I do. But you're assuming everyone's out to do harm before you have proof. Shoot first and ask questions later."

Tension drew her tight, across her shoulders, down her spine. She was a puppet at its mercy. "You've been on the road for six weeks and you think otherwise?"

"Yes. Though frankly, on the roads I used, I didn't see anyone," he said with the same cool, calm expression.

"We have a decision to make. We can stay here, holed up for a while, or we can sneak out. Avoid whoever the hell is out there and the infected, hopefully." Daniel rolled onto his side and put his head in his hand. The bed wasn't big enough for him, his feet dangled off the edge. "You know what I want, this decision is yours. I'm not going to push you into anything."

Which was a nice change from his high-handed pushy bullshit of yesterday. She kept her mouth shut, but her whole body leant forward, toward him. It was more than the dip in the mattress. Something about him drew her in, slowly but surely. A weakness in her armor needing remedy. Caring for someone else, given the state of the world, was crazy. She might as well just press the self-destruct button now and be done with it.

"We can give it some time, wait till you're ready. We do however need to make a move sometime, babe. You see that, don't you? Staying here ... it's not good."

The thought of leaving her hidey-hole had those rabbity instincts rising to the fore. Hide. Hunker down. And hurry up about it.

But where? Back up to the roof? For once, it wasn't the answer. Not after cleaning up, sleeping in a real bed, talking and interacting with someone as if she were a normal person.

Whatever normal was now.

Moving on would involve trusting this man.

Sprung so tight, she barely trusted herself.

"You think I'm going to get cornered staying here?"

"Yes," he said.

The rabbit kicked hard in protest. She rubbed her breastbone with the side of her hand. "Supplies are ... they're getting hard to find."

He nodded.

"Yeah." Her stomach dropped away, and she shut her lips tight to hold in the words for a moment longer. When she forced her mouth open, her jaw clicked in protest. "You're right. We should go."

He blinked, stunned. "Really?"

"Yes."

The big man whooped like a kid let loose in a toyshop. She sat in his lap, his arms wrapped around her, kisses peppering the top of her head before she even registered he had moved. "You won't regret it. It'll be great. Promise."

"Okay. Put me back." She swatted at his arms, a half-hearted protest at best. All the warm male skin surrounding her, the heat and scent of him, created a heady combination. The impulse to grab him back and hold on tight startled the crap out of her. "Enough."

"Never. Or not yet. We'll pack up what you want to take, and make for the highway. First, though ..." He rubbed his cheek against the top of her head and made a happy humming sound. "Quality time together is very important for new couples."

Sitting on his lap, the prod of the hard-on beneath her butt could not be mistaken.

"Since you're in such an agreeable mood we could have sex to celebrate. That would be nice. A real bonding experience," he mumbled against the top of her head, voice all low and rumbly. Highly sexed and self-assured, the arrogant ass. "What do you say, babe?"

She could hear the grin in his words, the amusement at her reaction. Her elbow caught his unprotected ribs.

He laughed outright at her then. "Ouch. Beat me, I don't care, this is worth it. Tell me I'm right again. Slowly this time. Really draw out the words, play it up for me. Feel free to pant in between if it feels natural."

"You're being an idiot. Let me go."

"I might be, but you're smiling and laughing. Why the hell would I care? I didn't get a response back on the sex issue either ..."

"Dan. Let go."

He stilled, his big arms wrapped around her. "You know, that's the first time you've said my name."

"Really?"

"Mm."

She shrugged it off, but deep down, it did feel kind of good. Warming, almost. Maybe she wasn't alone. "Let me go"

He sighed and the octopus grip on her eased. "Right. Sex later maybe."

CHAPTER SEVEN

Un-fucking-believable. They were arguing again.

Finn lay flat atop a cargo truck and watched through the scope of his rifle, rapt, as half a kilometer ahead the pair had it out in the middle of a four-lane highway.

These people defied logic.

They were an hour out of the city, with nothing but deserted cars scattered about and bushland on either side. No movement as far as the eye could see, and Finn was making sure he could see far and well. Those two made quite the target, hashing out their issues beneath the glaringly white, hot summer sky.

The woman had a shotgun nursed in her arms and the big guy had a pistol at his side. Neither kept watch. How they had survived this long, he did not know. The whole scene made the back of his neck itch.

He'd heard gunshots yesterday around noon, but arrived too late to find anything but a mass of infected loitering around a sub-urban street. Otherwise, everything still. No telling whether the shooter had gone to ground or been killed, though he hoped not the latter. Enough had died in the past two months.

He had climbed up onto the roof of a two-story place nearby, reluctant to give up on the possibility of real, live, uninfected company. He was numb to hope, but what else could he do? The only other people he had sighted had been criminal, trouble.

But maybe this time, maybe these people.

Watching and waiting was his lot these days. He had watched innocent civilians gunned down outside of hospitals, watched the bombing of Sydney. All those necessary measures decided and taken and the orders passed down. It all kept turning over inside his head. The eventual death toll was a figure that kept changing, never static.

He had been unable to help so many. Maybe he could save her. His scope wandered over the woman. She was more girl next door than beautiful, curvy with a few years on his twenty-six. Her loose-fingered grip on the shotgun told him all he needed to know.

Finn had been willing to give the big guy the benefit of the doubt, but test time was over. This scene more than convinced him the man wasn't taking care of her. He wasn't protecting her.

Not like Finn could.

It hadn't been easy, following them. He had hung back far enough that the purr of his motorbike remained undetected, close enough not to lose them. A time or two he had been forced to stop and wait, listening, tracking.

Thank fuck he hadn't lost them.

The psychotically loud trail bike they had been using sat nearby while they quarreled. Probably needed refueling, a straightforward process with all the abandoned vehicles about. Some had been run dry, but not all. Resources weren't an issue if you knew where to look.

And exactly what were they arguing about all this time? He neither knew, nor cared. The shadows were growing. The sun had begun its gradual slide into the west. There would be a couple more hours of light at best.

Time was slipping.

Eventually the big guy fled the fight, started siphoning fuel out of a nearby sedan.

Thank fuck he hadn't lost them.

Nothing was harming her, not on his watch.

They finished up, got back on the bike. So noisy.

Finn crawled to the edge of the truck, shrugged the rifle onto his back and dropped back to the asphalt. He moved out a minute after they did, rolling with the whole stalker situation for now.

What else was he going to do? Where the hell else could he go? Nowhere, that's where. He followed.

CHAPTER EIGHT

His girl was going to do herself damage if she didn't calm down.

Ali paced the top floor of the two-story brick house they had found in the middle of nowhere. Inspecting, staking out her territory, pacing her prison cell. Daniel wasn't sure which. Her shoulders twitched, and she wrapped her arms around herself, hanging on tight.

Downstairs, people had died. They saw lots of dried gore, though no bodies. He had ushered her through and up the stairs to the dank lounge at double speed. Ali hadn't spoken a word since their arrival, didn't even comment on the carnage.

He was terrified she would change her mind, demand he take her back to the pastel cottage in the burbs with its bedroom done in blood.

"You okay?" he asked.

She nodded, shoved her hands back to her sides. Inside him the worry escalated. He rubbed his fingers together, wanting to grab her but holding himself back. Maybe he shouldn't have pushed to move on so fast. It wouldn't have cost him to give her more time.

She crept up on the sliding glass door that led out onto a balcony. A timid hand reached out and slid the door open a handsbreadth, but left the curtains drawn. The setting sun gave him glimpses of a golden halo above her head as she peeked out through the gap. They were safe for the night.

"Careful," he cautioned.

Another nod.

Outside, the climbing jasmine turned the balcony railing into a tangled tropical garden. It also blocked out the worst of the smell from downstairs. The garden didn't warrant this level of fascination. Though clearly, his girl thought otherwise.

The highway close by made this place just a pit stop. There was nothing more than a couple of houses and a petrol station attached to a mini-mart named Creek's Bend. The mini-mart had long since been wrung dry and set on fire, leaving the inside a charred, black wreck.

They would need to restock soon, tomorrow perhaps. But tonight they were fine and dandy, if only she would speak. Sometime soon would be good.

A whole day of nitpicking and now nothing, his girl loved extremes. And to reach a time and place in his life where he was desperate for a woman to talk to him about her day, mood, choice of shoe color, whatever she wanted to discuss – he would do his best by the topic.

"You hungry?"

She shook her head.

"Thirsty?"

Another negative turn of her head.

Ali sunk down onto the carpeting, sitting cross-legged before the split in the curtains.

Maybe it was the novelty factor. She had only been on the road for a day. For him, the great outdoors had boiled down to flies during the day, mosquitoes at night. There'd been summer storms that whipped up the dust and debris and turned the earth to mud, making the going slow. The glare of sunlight toasting him throughout the day, followed by the long, long nights on his lonesome.

At least he had his girl. Something was going on with her, however. Something he hated to be left out of, needy fuck that he was.

Daniel crouched down behind her, not touching uninvited, though hovering damn close. "Quiet, isn't it?"

Another nod. A desperate mind might see it as gaining ground.

"What are you doing?"

She glanced over her shoulder, swallowed, and licked her lips with the tip of her tongue. "There is nothing to fear but fear itself. Right?"

Ah. Right. Sort of. "You're afraid?"

One terse nod. "Terrified. Have been all day."

"Oh. That's what the snarky was about. Got it. Okay. Now I'm understanding." He shuffled closer, daring to storm the fortress. He lined up the back of her arm with the front of his, leaning in till his mouth was next to her ear. "Keep talking. I'm listening."

She turned back and her eyes flew open. Her brows shot up, startled at finding him right there. But she didn't move away. Score one for his team. "It wasn't all me being snarky. You were being unnecessarily stubborn and pushy at times."

"I humbly apologize. Keep going."

"I'm starting to think it's just your nature." His girl almost smiled, the corner of her mouth compressing. "Uh ... I don't know. It felt so exposed out there on the road but now, stuck in this place, I feel weird. This was someone's home. And they probably died here. It's ... it's all so messed up now, isn't it? The whole world. Or what's left of it."

He nodded and smiled.

The brows descended further than necessary. "Why are you smiling?"

"Because, for the first time in my adult life, I'm getting where an equally adult female is coming from without bursting a blood vessel or something. It feels like a breakthrough. You're talking to me. I love it." Daniel ignored the scrunched-up face his honey dealt him. He dropped his shoulders with a sigh and smiled some more, relaxing into the conversation. "Yes, it's all messed up. And no, my nature is delightful. More importantly, however, this place has a flat roof. Once the sun sets, we could climb up there, star watch. Get a different perspective. What do you say?"

"The roof?" Her throat worked and her eyes searched the floor. "Ah. Wow. I don't think I could do that. Be out in the open again. Shit."

"Okay."

An infected stumbled onto the street outside; a long, low groan echoed across the empty landscape. A shiver slid down her back. Her hand, fingers trembling, fished for the shotgun sitting by her side.

"Ali, it's okay," he said, earning another nod. Actually, it was closer to a jerk, and far from convinced.

He had searched the place thoroughly, barricaded the door downstairs and the stairwell both; he'd junked them up with furniture. Nothing was getting near.

"You really think we could go up on the roof?" Her plush mouth was set in a super straight line of disbelief. She stirred up all sorts of tender in him. It shouldn't have been a surprise.

It had been a long day, and apart from riding him on each and every decision made, she had been a trooper. She questioned, but she didn't whine. A delicate line to tread, but one he'd begun to appreciate.

Especially since she kept checking him out when she thought he wasn't looking. Talk about life affirming. Turning around to find her focusing on a lower level, say where his ass had been. It made everything much more than all right. He loved it. The hitch in her breath and the telltale spike of those nipples through her t-shirt made life superb.

On the bike she had settled against him more with each passing kilometer. She held on good and tight, leaning into his back as they wound through build-ups of once upon a time traffic. He doubted the cuddling was conscious on her part, but it meant she was relaxing.

"We can definitely go up on the roof," he said. "It would even be safer than staying down here, when you think about it."

She paused, cocked her head. "You're smiling again."

"You make me so happy."

She snorted a laugh, which was quite possibly the cutest thing he'd ever heard.

"You know, I think you ran out of words," he said, earning another small smile. "You certainly used up a lot on me today with all the constructive feedback. Which I appreciated very much."

"You think?"

"Mm hmm. Happens to guys all the time. We have less words per day than women. I know this for a fact, saw it on TV once."

Ali darted the tip of her tongue across her lips, eyes flitting between him and the world outside. Like anything was happening out there. "I don't have a penis. In case you hadn't noticed."

"I had. I'm very grateful, in case you hadn't noticed."

"Actually, I had."

He nodded, shuffled a little closer. Close enough so he could see the goose pimples on the side of her neck rise when she felt his breath there. And she still didn't move away. "Thought you might have."

Outside, the sun sank, slowly turning the world to gold, then gray, then black. A solid black these days, being minus electricity.

The kind of darkness you only used to get out in the middle of nowhere.

The first star twinkled hopefully through the slice of life the curtains afforded.

"Make a wish," he said.

"Okay."

Daniel dragged over his backpack and cracked a can of soup. She had to be hungry by now, no matter how taken she was by the scenery. He fished out a clean spoon and filled it up with the cold and gelatinous but nutritional goop. With all due ceremony, he held it in front of her pretty pink mouth.

"Time to eat. Open," he said and she did, making him feel all sorts of good. Purring in her ear and rubbing up against her wasn't out of the question. Though he doubted she'd appreciate it. He alternated spoonfuls, one for her, one for him. It satisfied some primal caveman thing in him to feed her.

He wanted to do all sorts of things for her but, for now, he was stuck with what she would allow. The whole quiet, meditative state seeped into him and everything was good and mellow. He could roll with this.

His girl sat, frowning out at the horizon. Little lines sat between her brows and her concentration was absolute. It seemed like she was daring herself not to blink or turn away. Forcing herself to face up to the world. During the day there had been distractions, but not so now. She struggled but didn't back down. The least he could do was to be there for her.

When her hand strayed back to rest on his knee he stayed perfectly still and just let her. He doubted she knew she had reached out to him. That she touched him. His dick more than realized, the hair-trigger her presence inspired kicking in.

He thought about cold water. Ice-cold water. It almost worked.

Soup gave way to bottled water. Then he cracked open a bottle of fifteen-year-old scotch he had been saving up for just such an occasion. A celebration of being alive, drawing breath, being together. A celebration of her hand on his knee. "Drink."

She put her lips to the bottle, and he tipped, sending the very fine amber liquor straight down her throat.

Big mistake.

Ali sputtered and grabbed at the bottle, shoving it away before covering her mouth with a hasty hand.

"Damn it, sorry. I didn't think." Daniel set the precious bottle aside and rose up on his knees, pried her hands from her face. Hard to see much in the darkness, but her eyes were glossy. She choked and laughed in equal amounts. At least he'd made her laugh. "I should have warned you it wasn't water."

"Holy shit, Dan. It sure wasn't."

"I'm sorry, I was trying not to ruin your Zen silence overcoming fear thing. I thought we could have a drink, you know?" He settled back on his haunches, carefully wiped away the shining trail of tears on her cheeks. Second day in a row he had made her cry. At least this time it was due to well-aged scotch firing up her throat and not a panic attack. Or he hoped it wasn't a panic attack. Fuck it, the thought made him panic. "You're okay right? You'd tell me if you weren't? I mean, I know you're spooked, but you're not too bad, are you?"

"I'm fine. Be calm." There was a smirk in her voice. He could taste it.

A low chuckle escaped her and her hands patted down her t-shirt, most likely an attempt to brush off the spilled scotch. He did his best not to get distracted by the lure of her jiggling tits.

He was so easy for her, so head over heels it was ridiculous.

"Be calm," he growled. "Don't quote me to me, missy."

"I'm fine, Dan." She smiled, the white of her teeth cueing him in to the fact in the dim light. "You don't have to worry about me. I can keep myself together, despite earlier demonstrations to the contrary."

"I know. You're strong. Self-sufficient. I get that," he murmured, and she looked back to him. She was close enough to kiss, and he wanted her mouth.

"Dan ..."

"Hmm?" His gaze lingered on her lips, waiting.

After an eon, he had to admit to himself, it wasn't happening here and now. Okay. Alright. Still, there had been ground gained today. He could feel it.

"Dark enough now we can climb up onto the roof if you're game," he challenged, pushing to his feet. "Nothing to fear, remember? I'll grab the bedroll."

CHAPTER NINE

Her hands finally stopped shaking.

Ali watched as Daniel strode through the house. He was all easy grace with his long legs eating up the hallway until the shadow of him disappeared into a room.

So dark, she couldn't see for shit, but wow, could she feel. What she felt was jumbled. Complicated. It trumped the fear hands down.

She was so tired of being afraid, tired of living the rabbit. But the rabbit had kept her alive.

There was no sight of him in the dark hallway.

Daniel was gone. She missed him. Missed the press of his arm against hers. Missed the warmth of him at her back, despite the stifling heat. Not a panic thing but more of an ache, a yearning. The man couldn't go down a hallway without her getting clingy.

She usually didn't glom, no matter what certain asshole exes might have inferred for their own nefarious purposes.

Something had to be done.

She had been working herself up to taking some constructive steps in his direction, yet here she sat. Stalled, frustrated, and thinking about sex. Dwelling on sex since the "holy shit" of being far away from her hidey-hole had eased within her. It had eased because of him.

A moment later Daniel hauled the rolled-up swag out from one of the bedrooms, hustled it down the hall toward her. When he spoke his voice was lowered. "Open the sliding door, please. All the way. Remember, we need to be nice and quiet."

She jumped to her feet, pulled the door open as ordered. Her dinner curdled. "Daniel, I don't know …"

"Shhh, it's okay. You can do this. I'm a true believer," he said, pushing as was his wont. "Besides, we'll be safer up there. Safe is good, right?"

"Yes, safe is good." Ali studied his face to see if there was some dig in it but he smiled back, serene. Maybe a touch arrogant, but hey, that was him. "Alright."

The roof didn't extend far over the balcony. Daniel positioned a chair below the roof edge, put a foot up on it and tested it with his weight. Once satisfied, he motioned to her with a finger. "Slow and careful, got it?"

"Got it."

His big hands settled on her hips, and she stepped up onto the chair, stretched her arms up, hands reaching, and – fuck-oh-my! She gasped and strangled a girly shriek as he lifted her high.

The roof was big and lined with a low rim of bricks. Ali scampered up and over, coming close to landing face-first. Her hands fumbled in the darkness before touching down on the gritty surface. Concrete, heated all day by the sun, warmed her palms.

The world was large up there, huge. Large and huge and open. On the other hand, she was very small and insecure. But he was right about being safe. No infected could manage a two-story climb any time soon. Knowledge that had sent her up into the safety of the attic from the start.

"Babe. You okay?"

"Yes." Ali righted herself, hurried back to the edge and peered down into his face. His presence pepped her up immediately, bolstered her failing reserves. His unwavering smile. Her hands could shake all they liked. "No. Shit. Pass me the bedroll," she said.

A quiet chuckle drifted up from below. "Repeat after me, there is nothing to fear but fear itself."

"Shut up and gimme the swag."

First he passed up the pack, then the bedroll. He eased it up with a hand to the bottom, taking most of the weight. "Move back."

She did as told.

Big hands gripped the brickwork as he hauled himself up, muscles flexing and the sleeves of his t-shirt stretching. What a shame she only had moonlight to see him by. He was a whole display of delicious, packed full of win.

Shows of strength and daring had never really gotten to her previously. Not like this. Daniel made her stomach drop and swoop. He made her feel like she defied gravity. Every carnival ride she'd ever taken rolled up into one. She kept expecting the ground to give way beneath her feet, for his attention to wander and waver. But it didn't happen.

At the end of the day, she couldn't hope to live up to the hype. The truth of it stung. No, it throbbed like an old wound in damp weather.

The man in question put his feet on firm ground and started dealing with the bedding, spreading out the swag in the center of the space. He kept quiet, smiled at her once and watched her discreetly, which she shouldn't have savored but did. Stupidly, his smile made her feel safe. Wanted. Those sidelong glances were potent things.

He didn't say a word, however, and she could have done with a word or two from him right then. Next to him, the rustle of the breeze through trees and the chorus from the insects deafened. There were a lot of bugs carrying on, summoning up sex partners. She wondered if Daniel was thinking about sex – if he expected a suitable demonstration of her gratitude for dragging her reluctant butt back out into the world.

Maybe he thought of stripping himself out of the jeans and t-shirt and curling himself around her, the same as the night before, pressing every inch of his hot skin against her while setting her on fire. She had woken up aching that morning, and the feeling had yet to abate.

Was he really thinking about sex? Doubtful.

She couldn't see a leer on his face. No knowing smile, either. She had, however, managed to rile herself up. Damn nipples. Time to think other thoughts.

A mass of stars twinkled above their heads. Looking up made space seem much, much greater. She didn't do it twice. There were no lights on the horizon. No signs of life. The vast and silent land stood empty before her.

She focused back on Daniel before the agoraphobia could grab her by the throat and squeeze.

Dan squatted down with his back to her and fussed at his pack a minute. When he turned, a toothbrush stuck out of the side of his mouth. He held out its mate to her. A neat line of paste sat atop the bristles, brilliantly white in the darkness. He took such good care of her.

They brushed in silence. The spit, rinse, spit was soon done and the brushes returned to the pack. She wondered what came next. Not talking, apparently. He was probably tired. She must have worn him out.

Daniel sat on the swag and yanked off his boots and socks. Then he leant back, putting his hands behind his head, stretching out his big body. He was beautiful, inside and out, picture perfect masculine beauty. His patience hadn't gone unnoticed while she had taken her sweet time coming to grips with things. Everything inside her was raw and exposed up on the roof. Lust had long since gone to war against logic.

They had known each other what? Thirty hours. At most. She didn't dare touch him, not even a toe or the cuff of his jeans. Ali kept her fingers curled tight, out of temptation's way. There was so much tension in the air, such electricity. She would get zapped. Maybe he was immune to it. How disheartening. It was not particularly surprising, but truly disheartening.

Not knowing how he felt drove her nuts. Normally so damn chatty, now he chose to shut up? She couldn't stand it. The tension inside her twisted and turned, making sitting still impossible. It wouldn't do.

"Say something," she blurted out.

"Huh? What's wrong?" Daniel bolted upright. "What do you want me to say?"

"Shit." Ali crouched down at the end of the bedding. What a spectacular mess. "Never mind. God, I'm such a head case."

The man made a noise somewhere between disbelief and grand impatience. "Light of my life, come here, talk to me. What the hell have you been telling yourself for the past two hours, huh?"

She waved off the beckoning hand, settled her butt back onto her heels. Her own stupidity knocked her on her ass. "I'm sorry. Really, it doesn't matter."

The hand fell and tucked back behind his head. "If it didn't matter we wouldn't be having this deeply confusing conversation. Now, tell me what I'm supposed to say."

She didn't answer but felt the words like a tangled, festering knot inside her. Hanging her insecurities out to air would not help.

"I like you cranky," he said. "I like you cuddly."

"Are you trying to be Dr. Seuss?"

"Only if you find his works sexually arousing."

She snorted. "No. Not really."

"Probably for the best." His hand beckoned once more. "Come on, babe. Come lie down. You're safe with me."

"I'm safe with you?" she scoffed. Ali climbed over to him and the mattress on hands and knees. Sick of not being able to see him properly, not being able to read him. He pushed all her buttons with ease and was pleased by the response, if his smile was anything to go by.

"Are you serious? You're the least safe person I've ever met," she accused. "The very least."

"How so?"

"Oh, come on! You're always pushing for more. You scare the crap out of me."

"Everything scares the crap out of you. You face it down anyway. Try to run away afterward, sometimes, but still ... You get what I mean." He peered up at her. "Besides, you don't look scared to me."

"It's dark. You can't see a thing."

"Babe," he whispered, so low and gentle it hurt something inside her. She hadn't done anything to deserve such care from him. She had been a prickly pain at each and every turn, walls up, guard on high alert. It made her feel like a fraud when he put himself out there. He was fearless. "Ali, I see you just fine."

His face was all shadows. But his voice was clear as day.

All the reassurances a girl could ask for. There had to be a catch. But what if there wasn't? What if everything he said was exactly how things could be and she was too rabbit-hearted to reach out and grab him?

"Relax. Come and lie down. You can fight with me again tomorrow. I promise." He closed his eyes, yawned, and made a show of settling in for the night. Sleep sounded really good. She wanted to lie down beside him, rest her head on his shoulder and cut the shit for a while. To relax. Be calm. Get her head on straight and shore up her reserves for tomorrow.

Maybe the plan would be easier to deal with in the morning.

"I'm tired of fighting," she admitted in a very little voice. It leant toward the pathetic.

"Me too."

"Dan?"

"Hmm?"

"I'm sorry I'm such a pain in the ass."

"Me too." His hand shot out to catch her wrist before she could connect. How he did it with his eyes closed, she didn't know. Perhaps it was time to face the humbling truth: she was that predictable. "Sorry. Thank you for the apology. Can we sleep now?"

She hesitated and he tugged at her wrist until she lay on the mattress beside him. He softly laughed at her. It did bad things to the parts she tried to shelve. If only she could will her pussy and hormones and the whole shebang out of existence. How simple would life be then?

"Sleep, babe."

She made quick work of her boots and socks. The cool night air on her bare feet felt shivery, wondrous, and she scrunched and stretched her toes in appreciation. The little things in life made it bearable. Daniel wasn't little. He took up a lot of room. Life, however, wouldn't be easier minus her girl parts, which couldn't get enough of him and his teasing. There would still be scary shit lurking around each and every corner.

Daniel shifted beside her. "Stop it. Go to sleep."

"I can't."

He groaned. "Can too."

"Not."

"Ali. Stop. Sleep." The sleeping bag shushed as he tossed and turned. Maybe she should ponder the stars without freaking out. It had to have been years since she had slept out of doors. On the bed of a boyfriend's pick-up after a bonfire out in the bush – early twenties. Wow. Good times. Great sex. Then he'd moved away for work and that was that.

He was probably dead now. She swallowed.

Daniel executed another toss, turn and roll. He finally settled on his side, facing her, an arm arranged over her chest and one humungous leg thrown across the both of hers. Like he was pinning her down against a possible escape attempt.

He looked half asleep, totally relaxed. His limbs had definite weight. She should have minded, but didn't. It felt sweet and honest and caught her off guard. His fingers twitched and he snuffled. It was endearing.

And she had to face it, liking him was unexpected, but real.

His breathing was slow and regular, and the stars kept twinkling overhead. She dared herself to keep watching them. Made herself. None were falling.

There was a moan off in the distance, low and grating, but she ignored it and concentrated on the rest of what the world had to offer. Stars were far and away prettier to contemplate than whatever roamed out there, rotting and festering.

She needed to find her happy place.

His leg really did weigh half a ton. At least. Maybe more. She didn't want to disturb him, but she was losing sensation in her toes. Pins and needles started up in her feet.

Ali pushed against his thigh with both hands, wiggling out from beneath it. A hand closed firmly around her shoulder, holding her in place.

"Huh? What ..." Daniel's eyes flew open and found her and then his face relaxed. "What's wrong?"

"Hey. It's okay." She changed tactics, pushing against his shoulder until he relented and rolled onto his back, letting her go, re-closing his eyes.

He was clearly exhausted. She wondered if he had gotten any sleep the night before. Still, he remained full of tricks. She had no sooner stretched out, unencumbered, than he rolled back onto his side and grabbed her with both arms before returning to his back, taking her with him this time.

"Hey!" she hissed.

"Ssh, sleeping." His iron bars for arms held her to him. No, tree roots, thick and stubborn. She braced her elbows on either side of his head, and set her knees to the mattress beside his hips for leverage.

"Aah, man. Stay put, babe. Pander to me a little, please? That was a hell of a long day."

"Daniel, open your eyes. Look at me."

Sighing, he did, a scowl on his face, expecting trouble, obviously.

The wise words set to appease died on her tongue. She had no intention of going anywhere. He didn't need to worry. That was all she had been going to tell him, and it wasn't good enough ... Not by half.

She wanted more for him. Wanted more for herself.

When she pushed against his hold, trying to sit up, his arms fell away from her, falling back onto the thin mattress. He made a noise of weary resignation. "Fine. Better?"

"Yes." Before she could wuss out or lose her nerve entirely she whipped her shirt off over her head, tossed it out of reach.

There. Done. No turning back. She could control this. He was putty in her hands. The ultimate power of whipping out your tits, it got them every time. As ancient as Adam and Eve with her dropping the fig leaf. Absolutely perfect. There would be no heartbreak. No losses. She felt powerful sitting astride him, safe. Shoulders back, breasts thrust forth.

Perfect.

And Daniel's eyes bugged out of his head in a most gratifying way.

You would have thought she was in French cut lace, as opposed to some nice sensible dark cotton that had been washed a hundred times.

His hands flew to her hips and held tight, not in an "I have to have my hands on you" fashion. It felt closer to a "don't you dare disappear on me" grip. The look he gave her was mostly lust, but desperation tinged the edges. Shit, she couldn't be anybody's world. Handing over her heart to him couldn't happen, certainly not yet. When he looked at her like that, though, how could she hold back? Emotions were slippery things. Her grip on them might be more tenuous than she had imagined.

Maybe this could have waited for a better time.

No.

"I'm sick of being afraid. Daniel ..." All of a sudden the world tumbled. It happened so fast her head went woozy. Her back was against the mattress and Daniel loomed over her, his big body shaking with tension. Those blue eyes of his blazed with some internal fire. Her heart stuttered in her chest.

Maybe, just maybe, she had well and truly bitten off more than she could chew.

CHAPTER TEN

Holy shit, he was blowing it.

Ali blinked rapidly, eyes vague and confused. Daniel held himself perfectly still, resisting the urge to grind himself against her. Almost.

"You okay?" he enquired, heart racing, sweat beading on his forehead, running down his spine. Fuck. He would shake himself apart at this rate.

And he had scared her when she was being so damn brave. It made his teeth hurt. Shove a gun in his face, no problem, but risk herself with him? There was real fear, directly beneath him, skin gleaming in the moonlight, pupils dilated. "Babe?"

She gave a tight nod and shifted beneath him. In his great and mighty quest to get close and closer he was probably squishing her.

Maybe she couldn't answer him because he wasn't letting her breathe.

He took more weight onto his elbows but remained plastered against her. He couldn't deny himself. The press of her breasts against his chest and the way her hips cradled him blew what remained of his mind. No one else got to him this way. Every smooth move in him had left the building.

The way her thighs were willingly spread to take his body sent a fresh surge of blood heading straight for his dick. He was a goner.

And again with the no grinding rule. No matter how tempting. God help him if she changed her mind now. "Tell me you're okay."

"I'm okay."

She did not convince him.

Shit, if he said the wrong thing, she might put her shirt back on. He didn't know if he could take it. He might cry, and have his very own panic attack. "I'm an idiot. I'm sorry. Didn't mean to flip you like that."

She swallowed, relaxed a bit beneath him. "You, ah ... kind of took me by surprise."

"Yeah. Yeah, I know. Sorry."

"I only took off my shirt, Daniel. The bra isn't even all that revealing," she replied, cool as can be, plush mouth set all prim and proper. "If all it takes for you to lose your cool is the hint of hard nipples then I'm concerned on your behalf."

"Shit. Say hard nipples again."

Her body vibrated beneath him with soft laughter. "No."

He groaned, lowered his face so they were nose to nose, staring at each other. Each, perhaps, a little freaked out. Her hair had escaped the ponytail and lay spread across his sleeping bag. He rubbed a strand between his fingers, soft and silken. "God, you are so beautiful."

Ali's eyes skittered off, nervous with his praise.

"Say, thank you," he prompted.

"Thank you."

"Say, kiss me."

A smile curved her perfect mouth. He saw stars, dots dancing through his field of vision. This woman made his knees weak. Thank God he wasn't standing.

"Kiss me," she said.

"Whatever you want."

Daniel angled his head, brushed his lips over hers, getting the feel for her. He eased her into it, taking it nice and slow, making up for his earlier bad behavior. Sweetly, lightly, he licked at her lower lip, a nibble here and there. He was a man determined. She would never hesitate to throw herself at him ever again. Throwing her clothes to the wind would be the norm. He was a man with a plan to woo.

Hallelujah.

And the plan went straight out the window when she gave a growl, shoved her fingers into his hair and her tongue into his mouth.

His dick kicked against his zipper and he gave up, ground himself against her. He moved his weight onto one arm, all the better to scoop up an ass cheek and grope to his heart's content. She had the nicest ass. Her long legs wrapped around him. He could spend hours with her doing just this. Days. Sucking on her tongue, drawing her in, giving her absolute access to him then taking the same and, oh, yes. She gave.

And then some.

Kissing her was something he could see himself doing for a good, long time.

Daniel licked at her, stroking her tongue with his own. He explored.

Her hands trailed down his back. Pulled at his t-shirt.

She broke off the hot and heavy kiss to drag it over his head.

"Daniel," she panted, palms smoothing over his ribs. Her nipples poked at his chest through the thin material of her bra. "Your body is beautiful."

"Glad you approve. Let's lose the bra." He rolled them onto their sides, then attacked the clasp on her back and peeled the straps down her shoulders. She shrugged it off, tossing it to the wild blue yonder.

Sweet heavens her breasts were gorgeous, generous. They filled his hands like a dream. Alabaster pale against the tan of his fingers, nipples beaded hard against his palms. She was a fucking feast.

"Pants," she said. "Hurry."

Daniel dragged his gaze back up to her face. It was a very determined face, mouth set and eyes serious. "What?"

"Get your pants off."

"Right." He reared back on his knees and made quick work of the button and fly, getting his pants and boxers off while his girl did likewise.

Holy shit, the wriggling and wrestling, he couldn't watch or he'd blow. His dick tapped his belly as it was. But he couldn't look away. Ready, willing, and peeling off her jeans, kicking them off. Hooking her thumbs in a black pair of panties and shimmying them down.

"Dan?" Big eyes blinked at him. The panties went down. His mind ... going, going, gone. Because oh, yes. A dark tuft of pubic hair and not much else visible in this dark, but he could feel his way just fine.

And hell, he wanted to take his time.

Yeah.

His face belonged between those thighs. He needed to nuzzle the glossy wet lips of her sex. Licking and laving and breathing her in were all that mattered now. Hell, he would imprint himself on her if he could figure out how.

"Why are you waiting?" His girl tilted her head, mystified, reached up and grabbed his hand. "I want you in me."

So when it came to talking he said the only thing he could possibly bring himself to say. "Yes."

He collapsed back down on top of her, taking his weight on a hand at the last.

Ali grinned, planted a kiss on his mouth and pressed his hand to her hot, wet sex. He set about making her hotter and wetter. A finger ran up and down the lips of her sex, making her squirm and pant. Two fingers pressed slowly inside her. She squirmed against his hand, taking more, faster. Forcing the pace.

"Easy, babe." His thumb stroked her clit, working it side to side till her back arched, offering up her breasts to him. He hunched down to suck a sweet, stiff nipple into his mouth and worked it with his tongue. Her noises were perfect; all the moans and gasps building him to a fever pitch. He was already barely hanging on.

"Dan. Please. Hurry."

"Soon, babe. Very soon. Come for me first." The need to be in her was driving him mad, but there was no way in hell he was going to give in and mess this up.

Daniel swirled his long finger about inside her, searching out the sweet spot, right behind her clit. He worked her from inside and out till she was trembling, shuddering and panting his name. "That's my girl."

He slammed his mouth down on hers when she came, muffling the cries as her pussy convulsed around his fingers.

Perfect.

So absolutely damn perfect.

Screw watching football, he had found his new favorite pastime for the next fifty years at least, or however long his dick held out. He rubbed his thumb gently above her clit, dragging out the last of her pleasure till she sagged limp beneath him, every muscle lax, spent. Her thighs stopped trembling, her breathing evened out. Eventually.

Wow. Talk about humbled. The total relaxation on her pretty face and the slow smile when her gray eyes blinked open once again had him hooked.

"That was hot," he said. "Again. Come again for me, babe."

Her brows rose as her mouth opened. The wondrous look she gave him held more than a touch of "are you crazy"? Well, he would have to prove himself to her. No hardship.

She watched as he licked her juices off his fingers, lip smacking involved. This was his girl. He had every intention of spending some very serious time with his mouth between her thighs, but right now, his instincts told him to keep eye contact. If she got skittish then he wanted to be there, talking her back down.

He finished sucking her honey from his fingers, and then he ever so gently, very tenderly, began to stroke her anew. Taking care to go easy while, he knew, she was still reeling from coming, still ultra sensitive to every touch.

"No, Dan. Your turn." She grabbed his cock and did some stroking of her own.

Her lovely hot hand.

The punch of heat to his gut was insane; the tightness in his balls from touching and watching nearly did him in.

He covered her hand with his own, stilled it before he embarrassed himself and came all over her belly like some overeager kid. Oh, man. The mental image of her soft, pale skin splattered in his come. Marked by him.

He had to close his eyes, will it out of existence before it became truth. This woman made a mockery of his control.

"Why not?" She gave him a cranky, confused frown and a squeeze. He swore a blue streak.

"Ali, babe, wait. I want to be inside you."

"I want that too."

Fine. She was onboard. Further foreplay could be post-play. No problem.

Daniel leant across the mattress, grabbed his pack and rummaged for the condom he had stashed away for such a joyous

Flesh

occasion. He used his feet to push off the jeans holding his ankles captive and tying him in knots.

"Hurry, Dan," she urged. Her pussy, fiery hot, rubbed against his thigh as he moved back between her legs. Her hips pushed at him. It was exhilarating, the way she wanted him. Exactly what he needed, craved. "Hurry."

"My greedy girl." He ripped open the wrapper with his teeth, rolled it on without preamble. Fingers kneaded his shoulders like a cat working on a lounge. He rubbed the head of his cock up and down the seam of her sex, teasing them both before positioning himself against her and pushing in, sweet and slow.

Holy shit. The feel of her taking him sent heat licking over his skin. They fit together just right. He had known they would. Some things were facts of the universe. It didn't do to question them.

She was a little tight. He was a little big. Together, perfect.

"Oh." Her mouth formed the letter perfectly.

"Oh?" he asked, rubbing his lips along her jaw. Thoroughly enjoying the long, slow slide of his cock gaining ground inside her, the way her body hugged him tight. His whole world was remade on the journey. His breath was choppy and his toes curled. Everything as it should be. "Ali, baby?"

His girl gasped as he pulled back, pushed in anew, fingernails dug into his skin, clinging onto his shoulders. When she answered him she tried to play it cool and calm. Didn't quite manage to pull it off with her mouth trembling like it was.

Nice to know he wasn't the only one affected.

"Hmm?"

"Oh, good?" He freed up a hand to pluck at a nipple, roll the tight bead between thumb and finger. True cause and effect. She got wetter, and he got hotter.

"Yes," she said.

He knew he was in serious trouble. Legs wrapped around him, holding him to her, urging him on with the upward tilt of her hips. And when she had taken all of him, with every inch of his dick in heaven, he knew this couldn't last long, no matter his good intentions.

"Oh, yeah." Her eyes were huge and dark, her teeth biting into her bottom lip. "That's ... that's so good."

Daniel dropped his head onto her shoulder, grazed his teeth over the line of her collarbone. Loving the way she shivered, wanting as much skin-to-skin contact with her as he could get.

All his. Every last bit of her.

His cock jerked inside of her. She gasped, tightened on him till he had to count backward from ten to hold out. Not good.

He had grand plans. Romance. Fireworks. Everything and anything to make her his.

"I need to fuck you," he admitted in defeat.

Her tone when she answered was bewildered, indulgent. "I thought that's what we were doing."

"No. I was trying to make love to you. I had intentions. But ... I can't."

Her cunt squeezed him again. His last coherent thought fled. As far as non-verbal communication went, it was loud and clear.

He turned his head, hid his face against her neck and gave in to the need to have her. Hard and fast, losing himself in her. Taking everything she gave. The slick sounds of flesh slapping against flesh filled his ears, competing with the roaring in his head and heart.

He fumbled his hand down her, searching the length of her with unsteady fingers, finding the place where her clit poked out, all ready for him.

Didn't take much to send her over.

Her arms wrapped around his head, holding on tight. The muffled cries in his ear as she came and her cunt clenched at him set him off in turn with perfect synchronicity.

He might have bit at her soft, sweet neck, said something along the lines of, "Fuck yes, I love you." But really, who could blame him?

CHAPTER ELEVEN

Ali woke up coming.

The dream of hands and mouth on her were real, the soft brush of hair and the scratch of stubble against her inner thighs not even vaguely imagined.

She lay spread open, horribly exposed. His broad shoulders were wedged between her thighs, and his focus was total. He didn't leave her any room to hide. Daniel was terrifying.

She bit down on her bottom lip, smothering the noise before it could begin as the muscles in her legs and belly danced to his tune. He sucked at her, drawing it out. And out. And on, and on.

When he finally finished, she felt like she had been blown apart and put back together one molecule at a time. The whole mix was wildly unstable. She could fall apart at any moment. It was un-precedented, in a good way. But still, unnerving. This made it past time to face some facts.

Sex with Daniel was ... unpredictable. Intense. There was no control. She had been kidding herself. No, lying. Lying to yourself was well and truly messed up. She couldn't contain the emotions he stirred up inside her. There would be no managing this. Daniel swiped his tongue gently up her center, dragging a needy whimper from her. Her hips twitched as he placed a ticklish kiss above her mound. Then he wiped his mouth with the back of his hand and grinned up at her, obviously well pleased with himself.

"Breakfast of champions."

She tried not to smile. It didn't work out so well. Her defenses were shredded. Part of her wondered how long it would take before she stopped fighting it altogether and let herself get carried along with his romantic craziness. "That was a sneak attack."

"You're welcome."

Her feet rested on his back, his shoulders and arms holding her open. His two big hands spread across her stomach. There was more than a little "this is mine" in the positioning of his hands, and not an ounce of dignity in the pose, but who cared? There was no one but him to see her.

Stuff it. She couldn't raise the energy to mind.

Ali gave in and slumped back against the mattress to catch her breath. One breath, two, and then curiosity got the better of her, and she was up on her elbows, watching him. Fascinated by him.

He nuzzled her thigh. The man looked spectacular spread out across the bottom of the mattress in the small hours of the dawn. Bare ass naked and really ... yeah, a lot of burnished skin on show. Along with one very tight white ass.

He was gorgeous, with the lean angles of his face and his big body. Short dark hair spiking out every which way, care of her fingers the night before, dark stubble on his chin, and his smile ...

A girl could let it all go straight to her head in a very nice way.

Time to admit she was drowning, her lungs working hard but getting nowhere. She was losing the war despite her best efforts. God, she always confused good sex with love. Great big mind blowing sex was certain to break her in two. The way he watched her, he didn't play fair. As if he wanted to know every stupid thought wandering through her head. No one had ever looked at her like that.

The illusion of guarding her heart kept her going. Because, reality-wise, it would be one hell of a loss when this all went to pot.

Screw it. Why worry it to bits? The pounding of her rabbit heart made her queasy, but irritation prodded her to make a decision. She'd grab happiness with both hands while she could. Life had become more precious now than it had ever been. She needed to make the most of it. Decision made.

Ali turned away from him, studying the gorgeous dawn. The beauty removed the scariness, gave her a chance to calm down and quiet the panic attack in the making.

Already sweat dripped between her breasts. It would be an absolutely sweltering summer's day.

"So, given you're a female and all," Daniel began, fingers tapping either side of her belly button as if it were a tribal drum, "I'm guessing you want to talk about last night. More specifically, what I might have said last night in the throes of coital bliss."

"The throes of coital bliss? Do you even listen to yourself? No, I don't actually feel the need to discuss anything right now."

The drumming ceased. "You sound pretty certain about that."

Out by the highway there was a flash of light. A whole lot like the slowly rising sun had reflected off something. It was there and gone. "Dan ..."

"I meant it. If you're wondering, at all."

"No, I ..."

"Don't feel the same way. I know."

"By your own rules, I now get to spank you." She wrestled her legs back, not kicking him in the head when it might have been excusable. She sat up and searched their surroundings. "There's someone out there."

"Infected? It's still early. They might be stumbling on home after a big night chewing on the local wildlife or something."

"No. There was a light. Like sunlight reflecting off something."

"Well, that can happen." Daniel shrugged, rolled over onto his back and stretched out, supremely unconcerned, totally at home in his own skin. Totally turned on, too. Long and hard, the thick head flushed a deep dark red.

Her body lit up in sheer instinct at the sight. She was liquid and alive, ready to go. Came close to forgetting what she saw out there, waiting.

"Babe," he said, winking. The arrogance worked for him, unfortunately. "There's a better topic of conversation for us right there."

She faced him straight on. It was easier said than done. Maybe not the time to have been caught checking out his cock, despite knowing each other in the biblical sense. "Daniel, concentrate. The light wouldn't be there and gone. Wouldn't the metal or whatever have to be moving to do that? Otherwise it would still be happening."

Slowly he nodded, the heat in his eyes dimming. "Alright, alright. How about we pack up, move on. There are some back roads we can use, less cover on them for anyone following. If anyone is, which I doubt. My bet, it's infected."

"Thank you," she replied drily.

He gave a pained sigh and one big hand reached down, wrapped around the meat of his cock. He stroked once, twice. "I call rain check on oral, though."

Her mouth watered. How the hell did he take her from irritation to lust in two-point-oh seconds?

She had never had much of an opinion on the subject of oral. It was the polite thing to do. It was expected. It made a guy happy. With Daniel, she wanted to know if she could reduce him to the same mindless whimpering state as she fell into whenever he put his hands on her. She wanted to know what he tasted like, what he felt like. Would he pant and plead?

She wanted to please him and show him without words what he was starting to mean to her.

She could imagine herself on her knees for him, sucking him off. It was no great stretch of the imagination. Her mind leapt at the idea and her pulse thumped hard down low. The strong, sure way he handled himself held her captivated. A muscle jumped in his jaw and his stomach tensed. With lips parted he watched her watching him. He really was beautiful. Her body heated further every time she met his gaze.

But the light she'd seen, it hadn't been her imagination. She tensed as the old familiar stress slid through her. They weren't alone. This wasn't safe.

"Dan," she whispered harshly, torn in two. She'd love to watch him make himself come. "This isn't safe."

"I love that expression on your face, all hungry and curious. And there it goes." The man gave up stroking his still-hard cock with a truly agonized groan. Surprisingly, she was ... disappointed. Disappointed that he had stopped, disappointed that she had shut down on him, her and her rabbit heart. "Oh, well. We are making progress, babe. I can feel it."

It was on the tip of her tongue to deny or retract. But she held the old standard in. Ali reached for her clothes, liking the ache between her legs. She gave him a long look over her shoulder, a playful look. Impressed that she remembered how to flirt. He gazed back at her in rapture. Maybe her skills weren't so rusty.

"I might be willing to honor that rain check," he said. "Later."

"That so?" Daniel came to his knees behind her, pressed his front to her back and took the weight of her breasts in his big hands. A shiver ran straight down her spine, a baby jolt of lightning.

"You're gonna mess with me all day, aren't you, mean woman?" he said.

"Probably." She didn't stutter too much as he rubbed himself against her ass. The hot length of him was melting her down. "We can discuss it once we've found somewhere safe tonight."

"Oh, I guarantee we'll be discussing it."

He whispered the most terrible things in her ear, half of them unintelligible. Her surprisingly dirty mind filled in the gaps.

Still, the feeling lingered ... they weren't alone, someone was watching. "Daniel. The light. Remember?"

His breath sounded choppy against her ear, his groan loud. "We may need to up the ante from oral. Be warned."

CHAPTER TWELVE

Daniel knew she would be the death of him. But he couldn't keep his eyes off her.

Ali wedged her upper body beneath a line of supermarket shelving as she stretched and strained to reach wayward cans of caramel goo. The words pouring out of her sweet, sweet mouth were gutter talk by any standards. Daniel wouldn't have gone anywhere near her had he been the subject of that particular discourse.

What a lie. He was a total sucker for her, fair weather or foul. Ideally he should help her reach the cans of goo. He really, honest to God, should get down and lend her some assistance, only her butt was wriggling in the most intriguing way. He couldn't move to save himself. The sight held him transfixed. A few hours previous he had lined the length of his painfully hard cock up with the crack of her very sweet ass.

Awfully close to heaven on earth as he knew it.

It made a man wonder what he could talk her into, given a little time and plenty of patience. And he had both. The possibilities were endless.

But back to the present.

"Yes! Eureka!" Said butt wiggled back and several cans rolled forth. He really wanted to cup her ass, take it in hand and call it his. Lick it, bite it, and own it completely. It would so make his day.

"Well done, brave young hunter."

Ali climbed to her feet, with a victorious grin. "Thank you."

"You've got, ahh ..." He gestured to the smattering of dust bunnies that had attached themselves to her front. Who could blame them? He himself loved to be plastered against her, preferably without clothes.

"Hmm." Her hands started brushing off her shirt, beating off the dust and dirt, setting her boobs to moving in a wondrous manner. Hard to say whether watching or doing would have been more fun.

He grew very hard.

"I'd offer to help but you'd take it the wrong way, wouldn't you?" One side of her luscious mouth kicked up, and he recalled with much joy, she still owed him a blow job. Life was sweet.

"Are your intentions pure?"

"No. Not in the least."

Her smile widened. His heart jumped.

"You're honest," she said. "That counts for something."

"I'm glad you think so." Daniel held the shotgun out to her. When her slender fingers wrapped around it he towed her in, not stopping till their chests bumped. The sweet mounds of her breasts pressed up against him. "What say we call it a night. Find some-place safe to hole up and practice our repopulation methods. Do it for our country. What do you think?"

His girl arched her neck to look up at him, the long line of her throat calling to tongue and teeth. "It's only a little past midday. We could go for hours yet. I thought towns made you twitchy."

"I could definitely go for hours. You make me twitchy."

"Daniel. That's the strangest compliment I've ever received."

"But you like it, right?" He leant down and brushed her cheek with his lips, slid his free hand around to cop a feel of her. "Tell me this is calling to your inner patriot, babe."

She smiled and angled her face so their mouths brushed. Lips soon locked with everything hot and wet and good. Kissing Ali was so divine he forgot to breathe. Her kisses made him giddy. The way she opened her mouth to him was exactly what he needed. Her hand moved up his chest hesitantly, turning him rock hard. He oh so welcomed her touch.

Far less welcome was the shrill wolf whistle from the end of the aisle.

Daniel shoved her against the shelving behind him. He kept the shotgun in hand as he faced the strangers. Five of them, all wearing the remnants of military uniform with a dash of "fuck you" thrown in for good measure. Harley t-shirts and shit kickers, mirrored sunglasses and backward ball caps. It was a wonder they could stand, they were so heavily armed.

He had failed her.

"We'll have the woman," one large and ugly specimen informed him. Daniel could smell the scotch and marijuana perfuming the bastard from meters away.

"Bad idea, seriously. She's very mouthy, difficult. I won't even start in on her trust issues."

"And yet ..." The big bastard licked his chops and ran his fingers up the barrel of his machine gun.

Clearly, the gun overcompensated for something.

The bastard resembled an ape. Hairy shoulders displayed by an undershirt that had to come back as something less tortured in its next life, if fairness counted at all.

Knuckles slid against his skin and her hand gripped the pistol tucked into the back of his belt. The gun slid out and his heart hit the bottom of his chest and broke in two. The pain was shattering.

"I'm sorry, baby," he whispered hoarsely.

She was mooshed up against his back, caught between him and the shelving. Her frantic breath made a damp spot on his t-shirt. His sweet girl, what the hell had he done dragging her out into this? He had failed her. So angry he was shaking, Daniel bit down on his tongue, focusing on the pain. He wanted to rage at them, but she couldn't afford for him to lose it. Not now.

"Drop the gun, asshole, and step away from her," snarled the behemoth.

Ali's fingers dug into his hip in response, holding him in place. She had obviously connected the dots as he had. They only wanted her. He was expendable.

"Now!" Bastard screamed, his four mates making menacing motions with the weaponry at hand.

Ali pressed a hot kiss against his back. She had a gun. He knew exactly how she planned for this to go down, and while it broke him inside, he had to agree. Leaving her alive at the mercy of these bastards was out of the question.

Pity he had the shotgun instead of his pistol, but he would ...

A bright blossom of red erupted dead center in Bastard's forehead. Daniel's heart caught. They were in play.

Whoever they were.

Machine-gun fire tore into the roof as Bastard fell, his finger caught on the trigger.

Daniel turned and took Ali to the floor, covering her with his body. Noise and color lit up the supermarket aisle. It had turned into the O.K. Corral. He emptied his shotgun at the bad guys, trying to keep his head low.

The remaining four fell back fast. They sheltered behind the shelves, one full of soup cans. Liquid was flooding the floor, surrounding the dead in a pool of blood and French onion soup.

At the other end of the showdown was one man. One, lone guy. Blonde, twenty-something and serious as shit. He had a pistol in each hand when he ducked out from behind a diaper display, squeezing off rounds at Bastard's mates.

"Move!" their new best friend roared.

Daniel shoved a hand beneath Ali's waist and scooped her up. He dropped the spent shotgun and snagged his pistol from her grip.

The bastards didn't want to kill her, yet bullets filled the air. It was pandemonium. Daniel sheltered her with his body, threw a hand back and emptied his clip helter-skelter. Hauling his girl to her feet, they ran toward their lone ranger.

"Back exit. Go." The blonde guy nodded toward a "Staff Only" hallway, and Daniel dragged Ali toward it, past a row of fridges full of rotting food.

"Gun. Give me a gun." Her words were rough, but she had found her own feet.

"Can't. We've lost the pack. Go." He let her pull free of him and followed her into the dank hallway. The guy wasn't far behind. Daniel heard cursing and gunshots following them.

A body held the exit door propped open, army boots lying in blood, throat ... Oh, shit. Throat gone. Ali hesitated at the gruesome sight. He tugged at her arm. "Don't stop."

"Gun." Without flinching, she scooped up the dead guy's handgun smothered in thick, congealing blood.

Her face blanched and her throat worked, but she kept it together. Of course, she hadn't yet seen the second body, dispatched same as the first.

The blonde guy sprinted through the hallway after them, moving like six feet worth of athlete. He crammed a fresh clip into one of his pistols without slowing. He was pretty fucking impressive.

The hallway led to a loading bay, roller door pushed up. Heavy, gray clouds covered the area. Nothing moved in the parking lot. A delivery truck sat idle, stripped down, and a large gas tank lay nearby.

Daniel faced the stranger, heaving in breaths. "Getaway plan?"

"I'm going to blow the tank," the stranger announced without preamble. "Run."

CHAPTER THIRTEEN

They ran.

Along the back of the supermarket, behind a couple of refrigeration trucks and on to forever; forever these days being not so impressive. They ran down a line of specialty shops, through parking spaces and a row of storage sheds. Debris covered the area.

And damn, she hurt. The side of her face felt fit to explode where it had connected with the supermarket floor. Her head spun and pounded until she couldn't have found the ground. The tang of blood lingered, thick and cloying, but the gun stayed in her hand. She was done with being a dead weight. Done with panic attacks.

The gas tank exploded behind them, splitting the early afternoon in half. The ground buckled beneath her feet and she nearly hit the ground with her wits cracked and scrambled.

Daniel caught her, dragged her on. He pulled her into one of the sheds as the smoke and haze hit the overcast sky. It had looked like rain, now it looked like hell.

The cool brick wall felt good against her back. The shady inside of the shed was a welcome change from the weak sunlight. Fuck her head hurt, every little last part of it. It spun and pounded and throbbed all at once. Her stomach churned and she swallowed hard, trying to keep its contents down. So damn not good.

Ali rubbed the pilfered handgun against her jeans. What a mess. Some bastard's lifeblood smeared down her side.

Shit.

Some bastard had wanted to make her a personal fuck toy. Someone who was willing to kill Daniel to do so. Bloody hell.

She had been in the middle of her very first gun battle. Her ears still rang, though it might have been the head wound.

The stranger slipped into the shed like a shadow. Calm, with his gun still in hand, everything about him at the ready. "Hey," he said with a nice, deep voice, serene despite all the bloodshed and crazy in the supermarket.

Her eyesight blurred, and he was just a shape, crouching down before her. Everything around her was a painful gray haze. She had no recollection of sliding down the wall, but it was probably all for the best.

"H-hey." Ali frowned, concentrating till things swam into focus. It took some time.

The stranger frowned too, which was fair enough. She didn't sound so great to her own ears, probably looked awful. Stupid thing to worry about, but the man watching her, he was pretty. Take a picture pretty. A few years younger than her thirty-two, blonde hair on the longish side, with pale green eyes staring back at her. Still frowning.

Her focus wavered as the pounding in her skull kicked in anew. Curling up into a ball in the corner would be for the best, but she couldn't. If she fell apart now they were fucked. Those people were still out there, ready to murder and God knows what else.

"Put your head between your knees." The stranger used that voice again, smooth and authoritative. He controlled the situation. Exactly what was required. She did as told and hung her head. "That's it."

She nodded. Or tried to.

"Hey you," he said, referring to Daniel. "There's water in my pack there ..." Fingers rubbed at the back of her neck. The stranger's fingers. Nice of him.

"Thank you," she mumbled.

There came the sound of footsteps and ruffling, then more footsteps headed straight for her. Daniel. Daniel was close. Good.

Everything was better already.

"Babe?"

"I'm okay," she whispered. Willing it to be true. Hoping she didn't pass out.

"Course you are. Here, drink some water." Daniel coaxed her head back and held the water to her lips.

God, he was so good to her.

She tightened her grip on the pistol and gave pulling her shit together another shot. They really didn't have time for this. Water trickled into her mouth, and the world slid slowly back into focus.

"You're going to have quite a bump there," the stranger said, pulling at her scattered senses.

He no longer frowned, but still looked pretty.

Her head spun, and she put it back between her knees. Preferable to puking on the pretty man or her shiny brand new boyfriend.

"I'll second the thank you for saving our asses. Who are you by the way?" asked Daniel.

He moved closer to her other side, and she ever so slowly reverted her head to the upright position. Seeing him was a medicine all of its own.

Daniel leant in to brush her bruised cheek with a quick kiss. "God, I'm sorry, baby. You alright? Keeping it together?"

No. Not really. "Yep."

"Atta girl." Daniel winked and sat back on his haunches, dealing the stranger an assessing look. He raised his chin and gazed at the guy frankly. "You saved our asses, all power to you. And yet ..."

"Finn Edwards. I was an officer, a cop, before ..."

"A cop," Ali echoed in surprise.

"Yeah. For what it's worth." The stranger took a hefty gulp of water. She tried not to notice the blood stains on his arm and the sleeve of his blue t-shirt. No uniform, just jeans and a t-shirt. What use would a police uniform be? The blood and gore would have been from those two bastards on the floor with their throats missing. Two people he had dispatched to protect her. It was surreal.

Her hands started shaking. About time the rabbit hopped back onto the scene. "You're really a cop?"

"Hang on. I've got my badge in my pack." Finn hopped up and made for a pack waiting by the half-torn away shed door. He returned with a black leather wallet and flipped it open with practiced ease, displaying the shiny silver shield within and a picture ID. "If it helps any."

His jeans were hitched up on one side; a knife in its sheath jutted out from one of his big brown hiking boots. What a weapon. Probably the one he had used to slit those throats.

"You haven't told me your name." Finn bent down, putting himself back into her line of vision. He cocked his head, smiled briefly.

More choirboy than killer.

"I'm Ali. This is Daniel." She tried to smile back, but the expression wouldn't quite work. "Why were you following us?"

Finn rubbed his chin with the palm of his hand, his forehead furrowed. "I spotted you two on the highway heading west yesterday, heard the gunshot the day before. I figured I'd follow. A man and a woman alone ... perhaps you don't want company. Making new friends is difficult these days; there are a lot of dangers to consider. You weren't likely to just accept whoever came along."

He hesitated, seeming much older for a moment, and very serious. "Humans are social creatures. I didn't realize how much until nearly everyone was gone. Then there's security, safety in numbers ..."

Daniel made a noise. She couldn't tell what the noise meant, but apparently, it made sense to Finn. He nodded solemnly in reply.

"They got the drop on you. No offense intended. They were halfwits, but they were trained halfwits. They came prepared and they outnumbered you." Finn gave the badge in his hand a long look, eyes going blank. "I can help you protect her," he said to Daniel.

Daniel cocked his head. "And what do you want in return for this help?"

"Good question." Ali pulled herself up, let her hand drop down to rest atop the gun beside her. Hopefully, a valiant show of strength.

Finn tracked the movement. "No, Ali. Guys ... I'm not asking for that. Shit." He kept his hands low and out front. "Eventually you two are going to run across more people and not all of them are going to be assholes. Eventually, you're going to want to find someplace safe, settle down, rebuild. That's what I want. I want to know there's something after all this. Us banding together, that's a beginning."

And what was Daniel's take on this?

Her boyfriend shrugged, gave her a small nod. She had to make the final decision. Odd, Dan had pushed at every turn up until now.

Finn's elegant face was all seriousness. Pale green eyes honed in on her. It felt like his hopes were on a tight leash, but his heart was on his sleeve. He had seemed so contained, controlled, but not so much now. She knew what it was to be alone and without hope.

"You want to be friends," she said, feeling her way tentatively. She'd lucked out with trusting Daniel. Twice in one week might be pushing it. But Finn had saved them from certain horrible deaths. There was a familiar edge of desperation in his eyes, a craving. She'd seen it in Daniel and she'd also seen it in the mirror a time or two. Everyone was scared of something these days. Her rabbit heart sped and her skin felt too small. She couldn't leave him on his own without hating herself a little. They'd just have to take the risk.

"I want to be friends," he said.

"I appreciate what you did for us in there. Stepping in when you didn't even know us."

His eyes searched her face. "I'll have your back, Ali. I promise."

"Okay." She stopped, sniffed the air. "I smell fire. It's close."

CHAPTER FOURTEEN

The supermarket was burning but it wasn't alone. Thick plumes of black smoke rose into the air, much too reminiscent of the bombings down south for Finn's peace of mind. He had enough to contend with without lobbing flashbacks into the mix.

Every now and then a car would go, exploding as the spark hit the gas tank and "whoosh". He had to empty his mind, de-escalate the tension and get on with the job. Depend upon his training. Things were getting more dangerous by the second as infected stumbled out of nearby buildings, lured by the noise and drama.

It could work for or against them.

The gunmen were having fun for the moment, setting the whole world on fire, but still making their gradual, inexorable way toward them. The drugs and liquor and whatever they were on were slowing them down, but not stopping them.

As a fear tactic, the extra fires worked a treat.

"They're helping the blaze along." The big guy, the civilian, Daniel, scowled in the direction of the bonfire.

It was far too fucking close for comfort in Finn's professional opinion. "Let's get moving."

Daniel helped Al to her feet, tucked a strand of hair carefully behind her ear. It was a tender moment that spoke volumes. The way the big guy could step into her personal space without her blinking. The way he could touch her.

Finn watched while Daniel melded his hands to the curves of her hips. Al fit the length of her body against him. It hadn't even occurred to Finn that he wanted that, not until right then.

A thorn caught in his throat.

Okay, it had occurred to him. Of course it had. The usual hot, sweaty thoughts passed through his mind. But this was specific, wanting to fit her against him.

Just. Like. That.

"Baby, good to go?" Daniel asked. "We need some distance from these dickheads."

Al didn't look good. She was dazed, the bruise on the side of her face bloomed in dark gray and blue. The gun was still in her hand and at the ready. What were the odds of her shooting straight with a concussion to guide her? Shit.

"What about a car?" she whispered.

Finn cleared his throat, and her eyes darted to him nervously. "Ali, there's still four of them that we know of. Going further into the center of town would be a bad idea. Probably we'd be flanked with more infected around to manage. Plus, they came from that direction; they'll know the area. There's only one road heading back to the highway from here, and it's a mess. We'd be slowed down and exposed. If we made it to the highway there's too much open space. They would run us to ground."

Al's arms tightened around Daniel. She opened her mouth and nodded slowly, her gaze at her feet.

Finn didn't blame her in the least. While he might not like the report, he would give it fully.

"I didn't think of that," she said.

Finn settled his pack over his shoulders. He picked up a pistol, double-checking the clip, from habit more than necessity. It was full. "To sum up, a car or a bike would be bad. Stealth is more important right now."

"What's your plan, then?" Daniel asked. He deferred without antagonism. This time at least. They didn't have time to butt heads and clash antlers.

The man ran a hand down Al's back. Part territorial, part reassuring himself maybe. It had to be killing him what had gone down in the supermarket. Her getting hurt because of him, no matter the circumstances.

Finn knew he'd been right. All round nice guy or not, Daniel could not keep her safe. Not like Finn could.

Not like Finn would if it came down to it, when it came down to it. Daniel could fend for himself.

"There's a river about a kilometer west. I say we make for—" An almighty explosion shook him, the ground trembling beneath his feet. It was soon followed by a second. No time for talk. "They're getting closer. Let's go."

They ran, keeping careful and low. They dashed from shed to shed, then along a line of dumpsters.

Ali did well to keep up, sequestered between them. Daniel led. Finn found it easier on his concentration if he could keep her in sight. She was less of a distraction right in front of him than she would have been behind.

Plus, the assholes were back there.

Flames roared in the distance, but they could still hear the pack of gunmen over the fiery cacophony. They yelled and fired their guns into the air. The assholes were doing their best to round them up and hunt them down.

Suburbia surrounded the shopping precinct, older-style wooden buildings mixed in with newer brick and tile.

They moved as fast as they could. Daniel helped Al scale a chest-high wire fence while Finn stood guard. A few feet from the ground, she lost her footing and tumbled down, landing hard. The big guy hurried down there in a flurry of action. He landed deftly beside her while she stood and rubbed at her fine ass.

"Umm, I'm okay."

Daniel cupped her chin and gave her a good long look. "Hurt anything?"

"My butt, my pride, otherwise, no."

The big man gave a tight nod, walked her back from the fence so there was room for Finn amongst the shrubbery. "Come on over. We'd better keep moving."

Finn got up and over while the big guy watched their back trail, gun in one hand, Ali in the other.

Moaning drifted up from within some of the houses where the infected had been sheltering from the daylight. The situation grew worse.

"This is going to get ugly fast," Finn reported.

The big man grunted, keeping his eyes on his woman. She barely stood her ground, swaying like a wind buffeted her.

Daniel didn't wait for her to throw a leg over the next fence. The man grabbed her about the waist and lifted her over the hip-high wooden palings. Setting her down, he kept a hand on her while following her over.

Doing his best by her. But, had she been in Finn's care from the start, she wouldn't have been hurt. He hoped she didn't have a bad concussion, internal bleeding or bruising.

They moved through a long line of suburban backyards, slowly, steadily gaining ground. The scenery altered little. Children's swing sets, a soccer ball and line after line of washing. Colors had paled from days and days of exposure.

A motorbike tore up the street in front of them. They changed direction, running alongside the river, as opposed to toward it.

Swimming pools were swamps, with the water turned algae green. They clambered over fences and pushed through bushes and gardens running wild.

They had to cross another street.

"Wait." Finn stepped up from behind them, leaving Daniel to watch their backs and her.

Up the street an infected stumbled onto the asphalt in the remains of a suit and tie. Its bald head swayed from side to side, coated in dirt and old blood, and blinded by daylight. Gunfire drew it back toward the shops, away for now. Another infected lurched along beside it, a child in the tattered remains of pajamas, joining the chase.

What he wouldn't give for a silencer. The first time they were forced to shoot would give up their position. "Go."

Ali jerked to life, crossing the street with Daniel hot on her tail. He wasn't more than a step away from her, one hand wrapped tight around her arm.

Another bike drew close. It hummed and growled like a hungry animal. A street over, no more.

"We're being herded," he said.

"Yeah. We gotta head west," Daniel said.

"Agreed." Finn motioned them on, staying at their backs as promised.

They cut through some open-air car parks beneath a block of apartments, climbing the hood of a vehicle when it blocked their way. Another chorus of moaning came from close by, thankfully behind them. The fire and noise was drawing the infected away.

The ground fell between one line of houses and the next, a sharp decline of more than a story from the top of the fence to the grassy yard below.

"Pass her down to me." The big guy made the drop then held his hands up for Al.

She gripped the hip-high fence as if a hurricane was causing her havoc, her knuckles white with pressure.

"Al?" Finn stood beside her at the fence and turned her to face him. He pried her hands from the railing and set them on his shoulders instead.

His reaction to the contact was instantaneous. And damn ill timed. His dick stirred, and his heart rate sharpened.

She clutched at his shoulders. In theory, good, neutral territory. He didn't dare dwell on the scent of her. Getting hard would not earn her trust, and he wanted it. Wanted her to know he would follow through. That she was protected.

"Al? Are you with me?"

She blinked furiously as if she was straining to see him, but her pupils didn't appear too bad. It was a good sign. "I'm okay."

"Headache?"

She nodded; a bad idea with a concussion. Her fingernails pricked at his skin through his t-shirt as she reasserted her grip. "I did have some painkillers. We, umm ... we lost the packs."

"I've got mine. Once we get out of here I'll get it sorted, alright?"

"Thanks, Finn."

One hand remained on his shoulder as she stuffed the handgun down the back of her belt.

"Tell me the safety is on, Al."

"It's on." She licked her lips, visibly straightened her shoulders, pulling herself together. His trail of thought ended at her mouth. Her lips. Christ. He had a job to do.

"Ready?" Finn gripped her hips, steering his mind clear of the fact that several of his fingers wrapped around soft, warm skin. But he could deal with that. The warm, female scent of her got him where it hurt. Burying his nose in her neck was right out of the question. Concentrating was fucking impossible.

His stomach drew tight, his cock swelled in his pants. Not the time to go there.

"Take it slow." He held her steady as she inched one leg over, then the other. She balanced on the narrow strip of concrete by the toes of her shoes, fingers digging into his shoulders for dear life. "Give me both hands, Al. I'll lower you down."

"Okay." She hesitated. He waited, long minutes that they couldn't afford.

"I need you to trust me, Al," he confessed. "Just like you trust him. It's the only way we're gonna get through this."

"Don't ask for much, do you?"

"Only what's necessary."

Her hands slid down from his shoulders, down his arms. It was the trip of a lifetime, charged with meaning despite his best efforts to keep it simple. He wanted her trust for a myriad of reasons, but he needed it to get the job done.

Her fingers, slick with sweat, met his palms. Gripping was a bitch, but he held on tight, easing her down. She hovered above Daniel's grasp.

The noise came from his six. A footfall heard too late.

Finn released Ali's fingers, trusting the man.

The bullet lit bloody fire across his shoulder. He swore, dropped and drew his gun from the holster at his side. A second bullet cut through the air his head had just vacated. Too late. The asshole had had his chance.

No time to worry about noise or positions. Training and instincts took over. Finn aimed for the chest, going for the kill shot.

Once, twice, three times and done. He put the shooter down. One of the assholes he had missed at the supermarket, something he really fucking regretted.

His heart hammered loud. Job done.

The body toppled to the ground in a contortion of limbs. Blood-soaked clothes and gun falling from limp hands. Everything seemed slow, his focus tight.

Getting shot was well overrated. Blood oozed from his shoulder. It fucking hurt. Al wouldn't be the only one investing in some of the painkillers in his pack.

Finn moved over to the body, pocketing the man's weapon. He gave him a quick frisk, took anything of use. An expensive-looking pocket knife and some ammunition. A battered Zippo lighter, mostly full. He didn't have time to search for more.

His pack slumped to one side, the weight of it pulling at him. The strap, torn by the bullet's passing, had given way.

He dropped the pack over the fence, then followed, awkward and slow.

Daniel pulled Al out of the way.

The fall jarred his wound, and he cursed more than once. Steady pain bore a noxious beat, turning him inside out. He peeled back the neck of his bloody t-shirt. Every nerve in his shoulder screamed bloody murder, but he had only been winged.

It should have been more spectacular for the amount of pain.

"Have you got something we can tie that off with?" Daniel kept an arm around Al, propping her up. Chances weren't high she would remain upright much longer.

By the sound of the roar, he knew the bikes were closing in fast. How they could tell a firefight over the bedlam was beyond Finn. Very in keeping with their current shit luck.

"Later." He tipped his chin at Al and Daniel nodded.

Finn doubted the woman even knew what was going on. She pressed her face into the big guy's shirt, hands clutching him to keep upright. Without comment Daniel set his shoulder to her middle and up she went, draped over his back in a fireman's hold.

"Hey." Startled, her feet kicked out, but Daniel slapped a hand down over her ass.

"Hush, woman. Phase two of the plan?" The big man asked, hand settling on her rear with a final, affectionate pat.

"Run."

CHAPTER FIFTEEN

They had found a hovel to hide beneath for the night. Daniel knew it was a hovel. Bone deep. No debate. He lay on his back in the dirt, staring at the shadowy wooden floorboards a bare meter above his head. When he was a kid they'd lived in a similar place. A small two-bedroom cottage with walls so thin they'd shake. His father would stomp about, rattling the panes of glass in the window frames. The old man loved to intimidate with his size. Prime perfect example of everything Daniel never wanted to be. No, he'd only wanted to protect Ali and he'd ballsed that up royally. Guilt smothered him like lead-lining. It was amazing he could breathe.

He saw Finn crawling around in the near darkness, patrolling, watching the street. A machine had nothing on the kid as he went about his duty. Daniel didn't know whether to be jealous or grateful or what. Mostly, he just felt tired. He could feel himself sinking into the ground, wanting to give in to it. A yawn cracked his jaw and he opened his eyes wide, trying to stay with it. They needed to be on the alert. Ramshackle fence palings hung on all sides of the cottage, little protection against anything, should anything manage to find them. The situation was well and truly fucked.

His girl was out cold, a lovely load strewn across his chest because he beat the dirt floor, comfort-wise. And because he needed her close. If he were some cynical, sorry son of a bitch, he might have had a moment. He might have figured playing mattress was the most he was good for. There was no sugar coating it, he had failed her. He had lured her out of her hidey-hole, and then been too high on life and love to protect her. It couldn't happen again. For the last couple of hours he'd been picking their problems apart, trying to come up with a solution.

If Finn hadn't turned up, then he or both of them would be dead. Or worse, because there was worse. Her trust issues began to make sense. What those fuckers wanted her for would be a living nightmare, guaranteed. His stomach roiled at the thought of them hurting his girl. Scrubbing the inside of his head out to purge those pictures would be a mercy. There weren't any limits to how far he'd go to keep her from such a fate. He'd do anything.

The bastards riding up and down the streets intermittently blocked off their lone escape route, a rickety old railway bridge. It didn't seem to bother them that infected roamed the night. Because of their patrols, the only pissy footpath to freedom wasn't an option. No one was getting across the river tonight.

Beautiful.

Smoke remained thick, but the flames hadn't reached them yet. No more fires had been lit close by. Even the bastards had to have deduced they risked being caught between the fires and all the infected.

Finn crawled over on hands and knees, favoring one side. His arm was tucked up against his chest. Daniel added that to his list of worries. But Finn could take care of himself.

"There are less infected on the streets than there were a month back," the kid commented, dropping onto his belly with gritted teeth. "Noticed that while you were out and about?"

Daniel nodded, traced a hand over his girl's back. She slumbered on, on top of him. He slid his hand beneath her shirt, pressed his palm to her back. Feeling her breathe, taking in the warmth of her skin soothed him. "Yeah. They're running low on food."

"Fine. How is she? Woken her up recently?"

"About an hour ago. She threatened me." Dan grinned, heart swelling with love. He was just beginning to understand the things a man would do for love. "She has such a creative mind."

Finn chuckled, casting an eye over his sleeping beauty. His gaze glommed onto the side of her breast where it pressed against Daniel's chest.

After a hell of a long moment, wherein he was certain the guy had stopped breathing and quite possibly swallowed his own tongue, the kid's gaze shot back to Daniel's face. Hungry-looking eyes turned guilty in an instant. "Shit. Sorry, man."

"Don't worry about it. I know what it's like." Yeah, he knew what it was like. He still wanted to hit the pretty asshole, but he did know what it was like.

Therein lay the root of the problem.

Sharing was not in his nature, but nature would have to adapt. Ali needed this kid. Finn was a modern day gunslinger. Deep down he fucking hated it, but his girl needed this one nice and close. Preferably wrapped around her finger and deeply concerned about her health and happiness.

Every goddamn minute of every goddamn day would be best.

Daniel did not want to share her. Not with the kid, not with anyone, not even a little. He knew it would work, this insane idea of going halves, he just didn't want it to. He had only recently found her and she was his. But he couldn't keep her safe on his own, a fact that bit deep and hard and hung on as a pit bull would. How the hell to convince her? What Ali wanted and what would keep her safe and alive would likely be at odds in this case. She'd accused him of being pushy a time or two. His girl had no real idea how far he'd go to protect her.

The kid hung his head, shoulders rising awkwardly with a deep breath. "I'll go do another lap."

"No." Daniel sealed his eyelids tight, then opened them. Belief that he was actually about to take this step was a long, long way off. "You've been at it for hours. It's my turn at guard duty. You be the pillow."

There was a moment of relief followed by a flash of "what the fuck?" on the kid's face. "What? Whoa, aah ... I don't think she would be okay with that. Let's not upset her."

Funnily enough, the thought of his girl upset at Finn didn't bother Dan. Still, it wasn't a step in the required direction. "I think she would be less keen about having the hard ground beneath her when she's feeling tender."

"I can get my towel from my pack, roll it up for her. You know, like a pillow."

Puh-lease.

Even in the low light, he could see the emotion playing out over the kid's face, wary and want going to war. Desperation lit his eyes and he licked his lips before locking them tight. There was a certain satisfaction in making Mister Cool and Calm squirm. He didn't hesitate to lie to the dick. "She has nightmares sometimes, loud ones. You need to be close. We can't afford the noise. Lie down on her other side."

Finn's eyes flared in panic.

Sweet baby Jesus, the man could go all urban guerrilla warfare but was too shy to snuggle up to Ali. And he knew the kid wanted to.

"Dan, it's been a while, and ... Man, I ..."

"Like her?"

The kid nodded. Emphatically. "Yes, I like her. Uninfected female, how could I not? And we've got enough on our plate."

"Yeah, she's very likeable. Especially when she's asleep, all soft and cuddly."

"Sort of my point. I don't want to cause any trouble here."

"I appreciate that, really, I do. But take in the big picture here, buddy. World gone mad, chaos, carnage, we all nearly died today. That we've survived this long is pretty wild when you stop and think."

The kid groaned. "So you're saying you won't shoot me in the back if I'm jonesing for your girlfriend?"

Tempting, but no. Dan shook his head. "Nah. You're more use to her alive than dead."

"Right. Thanks. I think." The kid shot him a wary glance but lay down, setting his gun close by.

Daniel rolled Ali over, shuffled and rearranged her so she splayed out across the kid instead of him. It hurt.

His girl grumbled something beyond comprehension. Actually, it was a direct assault on his familial line, but she'd had a really hard day, so he let it slide. "Easy, baby. Go back to sleep."

"What's going on?" Her eyes drifted open. She blinked up at him, knocking him for six without even trying, bruised and dusty or no. His girl. "Are we making a move?"

"No. I'm swapping guard duty with Finn. Go back to sleep."

"Finn?" She raised her head and peered down at the face in question, rearing back in surprise when she registered his proximity. "Oh, hey."

"Hi, Al. I'm your stand-in pillow," the kid explained, shrugging, then flinched when he remembered his shoulder too late.

"My pillow?" Her voice sounded slurred from sleep. She couldn't be badly hurt. He wouldn't allow it. They'd dosed her up on some super strength aspirin. Knocking her out for hours with something stronger was out of the question in case they needed to move.

"Is that okay?" The kid's voice held a boatload of tension, like this girl could make him or break him. Daniel would have found it cute if it had been about any other girl than his. "Or not? Your call."

"Sure. How's your wound?"

"Fine, thanks."

"Good."

She was fine. Finn was good. Hell, the kid had those lush breasts pressed nice and tight against him. Daniel wanted to gouge the jerk's heart out with his fingernails. Bathe in his blood and howl at the moon. Shit like that.

But no.

He forced himself to crawl away as Ali mumbled something to her brand new very best friend. Some something that made Finn chuckle all low and rough and reeking of sexual interest.

Slutty bastard.

It was like giving candy to a baby.

He didn't hear any noise for a long time. Just as well. A man could only stomach so much in the name of true love and the survival of same. He peeked out front through the guardrail, watching the street for a while. Gunshots fractured the silence farther down the lane, and a couple more infected ambled past, drawn by the noise.

Same old, same old.

When the view from the front got dull he meandered over to the side, followed soon thereafter by the back. He skulked about, not letting himself catch too much of the two bodies entwined.

Yep, he didn't see Finn's hand kneading the muscles of his girl's neck. He also didn't see her sleeping like a baby, curled up and draped over him, out like a light.

And he especially didn't need to see what the kid was packing behind his zipper. No matter how pronounced it might be.

"I hate you, man," Finn bitched, somehow making everything better.

Daniel smiled.

CHAPTER SIXTEEN

"Al? Al. You have to wake up."

Problem was she didn't want to. Really, honest to God, did not want to.

And they couldn't make her.

Screw them.

Her face pounded, and her brain ached like a rusty nail had been embedded deep. The worst of hangovers didn't measure up to this.

"Al?"

Despite it all, he had a really nice voice. Low, smooth, and ... earnest, that was what it was. Earnest was the word for the day, earnest and sleep. Besides, her bed smelt nice. The sort of warm, male scent her hormones cried out to curl up to. No way she'd move.

"Come on, Al. Time to make a move." Earnest turned edgy, not at all in keeping with her mellow, no-moving frame of mind. Best if she ignored it. But a hand gripped her chin, tilting it upward, and the voice went all hard-assed and demanding. "Al, wake up. Now."

She huffed, but did as directed. Pale green eyes set in a breathtaking face watched her determinedly in the pre-dawn light. Holy shit.

"Finn?"

The hows and wheres of her situation took a moment to hit home. When they did, the embarrassment floored her. She stopped breathing for a moment. No morning after walk of shame could measure up to this.

"Hey," he said calmly.

"Hi," she croaked.

"You had me worried, I couldn't rouse you. Come on, we're making a move." He sat up, taking her with him on account of her being wrapped around him like melted plastic. "We think they drank themselves unconscious. There hasn't been any noise for over an hour. The infected have dispersed with dawn coming. Streets are clear."

"Okay." Business. Right. She could talk business and peel herself off him at the same time. Hurrah for multi-tasking.

"Could it be a trap?" she asked, hand fumbling on the ground for her gun. Her gun. Shit. Her shotgun had been lost yesterday. She had loved her gun, stupidly enough. The rabbity heart squirmed in her chest.

"Here." Daniel pressed a pistol into her hand before planting a kiss on her forehead. Reading her right. He was magic. "Good to go?"

"Absolutely." She grabbed onto him, the human rock that he was. Used his greater weight to pull herself onto her knees and off Finn, whom she had no business being plastered over. "What's the plan?"

"We run." Daniel informed her with all due sincerity.

"Iluh. One day soon can the plan involve a touch more complexity? Not that I'm complaining or anything."

"Complain, you? Never. You're a constant delight."

Right before she could tell him how full of it he was Daniel grinned and slid his hand behind her head. He drew her forward and sealed his lips to hers.

Firm lips and a wet warm mouth setting her head to spinning. The best medicine in the world.

He really was magic. And he still wanted her, his hunger right there, open and honest. A part of her had forgotten in all the confusion and fear of yesterday, but he was giving it back to her in spades, right when she needed it most.

God, I needed that.

"Anytime, anyplace," Daniel murmured before letting her go, smirk firm on his face.

"I said that out loud?" she asked.

"Yes," Finn confirmed. "You did."

The man pulled on his pack, carefully setting the mended strap on his shoulder alongside the dressing covering his wound. The ripped neck of his t-shirt hung caked with dried blood.

He was a sublime mess. Sandy hair all untidy and stubble lining his elegant jaw took her breath away. Women attempting to cozy up to him would be no new thing, but she hadn't woken up smeared over a stranger for years.

Or at least a couple of days.

Looking at him, it was easy to forget what he was capable of. The killing he had done had saved their lives. The debt she owed him was massive.

"I can take it for you." She pointed at his backpack, tried for a smile of competence, though it probably fell short. "You should be careful with your shoulder."

"Thanks, no. Pack's pretty heavy. You keep yourself upright and moving. We'll do great." Finn made no eye contact, checked over his gun, tone curt, professional.

That told her. She pushed back her shoulders and drew a deep breath. Embarrassment oozed out of her pores.

"Finn, I'm really sorry I was all over you."

"Relax, Al. I knew I was signing on as third wheel."

Good. Great. So long as he wasn't feeling used and abused because of her treating him like a couch. How had that come about anyway? The events of last night were fuzzy and distant in her battered head.

He glanced up, found her watching. His blank facial expression never changed. There was no chance of reading his thoughts. "How's your headache?"

"It's fine," she replied coolly.

One brow rose. Perfectly.

She gave him a double thumbs-up, full of exuberance. Also jam-packed full of bullshit. "Upright and moving, no problem."

"Really? Because you look like Tokyo after going a few rounds with Godzilla." The lovely jawline tensed, cop eyes staring her down. "No offense intended."

"None taken." Her face throbbed and tingled and was numb all at once. Managing a smile was an exercise in slow and awkward. "Interesting reference though with Godzilla and ... I don't think we can be friends, after all."

A brow rose again in query. It was a neat trick. "You always run from a challenge?"

"Really? You failed to notice that?"

A beatific grin split his face and her belly tumbled, the traitor. He was heavenly. Angels wished they could be so cool. "Why don't we both make use of some of those pain killers?"

Finn eased the pack back off his bad shoulder, rifled around until he found aspirin and a bottle of water. He picked up two tablets with careful fingers. "Open." She did. He popped them on her tongue, then unscrewed the bottle of water and held it out to her. "Drink."

She did. "Thanks."

He gave a terse nod. "You're welcome. Don't worry about last night."

"Then thank you, again."

"Why are we always stopping and chatting when we should be moving our asses?" Daniel hissed from the front of the house.

"Let's go." Finn urged her forward with a hand. "Do your new friend a favor and try not to get shot crossing that bridge out there, okay?"

Her rabbit heart stuttered. "Yeah. Sure."

CHAPTER SEVENTEEN

The quiet when they approached the old wooden railway bridge didn't soothe Finn.

Fog and smoke made their world gray. With dawn, the smell of lingering fires cut the air. Fire evoked all sorts of shit he didn't need to be dwelling on. Memories of the bombings down south cluttered up his head. There'd been so much death and destruction, innocent civilians leveled where they stood. Charred flesh had a particular, pungent smell he'd never forget. He concentrated on his elbows to stop the shaking in his hands, an old trick a detective had taught him. Finn had to clear his thoughts and focus on the job to hand.

It was not going well.

The bridge would be tough, which sucked, seeing as it was their sole option. Heading back into the burnt remains of suburbia would be a death trap. They had to get across the river somehow.

Some enterprising little shit had trashed the stairs leading up to the fenced-in walkway that ran alongside the train track. To cross the bridge they would have to climb the hill and walk along the railway tracks. It would take longer. Time was at a minimum.

No one spoke.

The railway was perched atop a mound, built up a couple of meters above street level. They turned and made their way up the slope. Someone's stomach growled. Finn could empathize. They were running low on supplies; he had had no plans to cater for three.

Loose gravel sprinkled the side of the hill, not the optimal climbing surface. They crawled more than walked, the tumbling stones similar to the roar of an avalanche in the pre-dawn quiet. Dan had one hand wrapped around Al's arm, the other flat against the hill for balance. The gravel slid down the mound like a landslide.

They were so exposed, wide open and awaiting an attack.

"Easy, feel out your foothold. No rush," the big guy instructed Ali in a low voice, which was good advice. The problem was, they needed to haul ass, clear the area as fast as possible.

Finn scrambled to the top of the mound, checking every direction and seeing nothing. That did nothing to appease the itch between his shoulder blades.

Time seemed to slow down to a deliberate, painful crawl while he watched them make their way up the incline. He wanted to grab her and run the minute she hit the top. Get her somewhere safe and never let her out again. Lock her up for her own protection.

The world was too dangerous. He couldn't keep her safe this way.

"Let's go," Finn said.

Dan appeared solid enough with a gun back in his hands, and Ali was managing. Just. What parts of her not bruised or dirty were white as a ghost. She panted from the crawl up the incline.

Up ahead, the coal train looked like a giant hand had picked it up and draped it across the bridge. Two cars, one on each side, sat in the muddy water below, as if they were toes, testing the temperature. The fenced-in walkway beside the tracks would have been a dead end after all.

The other two hadn't seen it yet. There was no excuse, he was plain tired, and telling them versus waiting the minute or two at most that it would take ...

"Oh, no ..." Ali saw it.

Daniel groaned.

"They're going to try to trap us up here." Daniel drew Ali in front of him with a hand to her hip. "No wonder they let us get this far."

"So where are they?" she asked, sneaking around the big guy's side, as far as his grip allowed.

"There's got to be a way around." Finn flashed them a smile, more teeth and determination than goodwill. He was feeling a little feral, all things given. "It'll slow us down, not stop us. How about we not accommodate them by standing around?"

Daniel ushered Ali on, fingers fixed around her arm. "Solid notion."

As the sun rose, long shadows crept out from everywhere – the trees lining the riverbank, the houses up and down the street. Color faded into shadows, providing plenty of cover for both sides.

Their feet shuffled along the tracks, which were cluttered with coal spilled and scattered from the train wreck. The wreck they were heading straight toward. The same one they somehow had to magic their way past. Their only option lay beneath the iron beast.

Maybe they should have tried the river. But with its swift current and so much debris in the water, the bridge had seemed the safer option.

Finn tried to look everywhere at once, but the shadows and smoke prevented him from seeing much at all, which meant stumbling every other step. From the trickle of warm liquid down his back, he knew his shoulder had started bleeding. He could feel the wet bandage against the open wound. It was just another irritation to ignore.

The assholes were out there. He knew it. His head quieted, the whole world shutting up, shutting down as he went to work. His mind took on a clarity he couldn't explain.

Finn caught the flare of light on the edge of his field of vision as the bottle arced through the air. It struck the chain wire fence separating pedestrians from trains and then fell toward the bridge. Two, three meters away at most.

The Molotov dropped, smashed against the wooden boards of the walkway far too near to them. It lit up the old planks like tinder, the flames burning bright, hot and close. The stench of the petrol filled his head and clogged his throat, making him gag.

"Go! Get to the train!" Finn yelled, turning to watch at least two of the bastards struggle up the side of the hill not far from where they had just come.

Daniel hustled Al along, keeping her between them. They were only halfway across the bridge. A solid head start but no cause for celebrations yet. They still needed to slide beneath the wreck and escape into the maze of housing estates on the other side.

Another two of the cocktails made their graceful descent. These ones cleared the fence to smash onto the train track, one of them exploding a bare few steps in front of Ali and Dan. It went up with a loud "whoosh", black smoke rising into the air. They used it for cover even though it slowed them down.

Ali pulled her arm out of the big guy's grasp and ducked down, gun in hand, searching behind them. Finn ground his teeth. Two of the bastards were trying to follow in their footsteps by climbing up onto the tracks, but someone was also back on the riverbank.

"Don't stop!" Finn fired a few shots at the top of the mound, forcing the two bastards to keep their heads down. "Al!"

She either ignored him or didn't hear, pausing to fire off a few rounds at the trees. Her bruised face the picture of concentration, but her shots going wild because her aim was shit.

They might have ideally wanted her alive, but even these dick-heads had their limits. Someone shot at her from the bank.

"Fuck's sake." Finn sprinted for her, heart jammed in his throat. He jumped boxes and rubbish and the thick steel train lines. He didn't turn at the smash of glass behind him, nor the rush of warmth from the resulting fireball, hot on his tail, warming his back.

The smoke started to dissipate around her. She fired again and a bellow of outrage could be heard from the riverbank below. Al had managed to hit someone.

Her face broke into a self-satisfied grin as Daniel's arm scooped her up and dragged her off.

The two bastards had made good on the threat of clearing the top. Bullets flew wild, care of the smokescreen, but a breeze stirred, their cover dispersing.

The big guy charged straight ahead with Ali tight against him, struggling to keep up. Her feet barely touched the ground.

Whatever had derailed the train lay up ahead. Here, the cars had buckled and tumbled, spilling their cargo of coal. The crash had wedged two big trucks together. Going over would leave them open and exposed. Going under was the only way.

The others had apparently reached the same conclusion.

Ali dropped to the ground and proceeded to burrow, pushing lumps of coal aside to make a tunnel between the wheels.

"You're next." Finn ducked down on one knee beside Daniel, making for a smaller target. He took another shot at the two who had climbed the mound, kept them tucked behind a beam.

"Nope, I win most likely to get jammed, so I go last," Dan answered. Ali's feet disappeared beneath the wagon and the big guy reloaded and fired. "Keep her close, Finn. You hear me?"

Finn nodded, then pushed his pack through the gap ahead of him.

The clearance was abysmal, and the going slow. He got a grip on the far railway line, dragging himself through the tight space. His fingers fought to keep their hold on the metal bar, and his shoulder throbbed in time with his heart. Coal dust choked him, making him cough. He tried to spit it out but it did no good. Everything in front of him was a dirty haze. The chances of Dan making it through were minimal to nil.

"This side's clear." Al grabbed his pack and pushed it aside, took a step back as he squirmed low on his belly between the bridge and the wagon. Something hanging low scraped painfully along his spine.

"Keep watch." His foot caught on a beam, and he pushed off hard with the other, sending himself surging forward. His bad shoulder rammed into the edge of a metal wheel. Fireworks exploded through him. The world flashed white for a long, tense moment. He was not passing out. "Oh, you motherfucker."

"Come on." Her hands wrapped around his good arm and tugged, prying him out. Finally, his torso cleared the truck and his knees came into play. "Finn, you're bleeding again. Take the shirt off. We'll tie it around your shoulder."

"Yup. Just a sec." He really wanted to refrain from crying in front of her. Easier said than done. He covered the wound with his hand and applied pressure. It didn't feel beneficial but had to be better than bleeding out beside the train wreck. "Okay."

"You two get moving," the big guy yelled from the other side. "Right now."

Ali dropped onto hands and knees, gun clenched tight in her hand. "Come on, Daniel."

"The kid barely fit. I'll need to go another way. Get moving, I'll catch up."

"No! NO!" Al screamed, skittered forward, then stopped as guns fired up on the other side. There was the sound of someone hitting the water, an almighty splash followed by shouting from the bastards left behind.

"He jumped in the river," a helpful soul called out.

They heard the bastards shooting at the water, calling out to someone to come join them on the bridge.

Then nothing.

Ali didn't breathe. Her shoulders hunched over like she was drawing inward, protecting herself from harm. The woman grew smaller before Finn's eyes and there wasn't shit he could do.

"You heard the man. Let's move." He grabbed her shirt, dragging her back. There was the sound of an engine revving up on the other side. His heart beat harder, faster, rattling his rib cage. "He'll catch up. Move, Al. They're going to be searching for a way around."

She stared at him with eyes blank as the dead. The material in his fist stretched and strained, ready to rip. The woman didn't move an inch.

"Al. I need you to keep it together."

Nothing.

"Al!"

Her gaze slid back to the wreck. A fine tremor worked through her, taking her over till she shook like she held a live wire in her hand.

Finn grabbed her chin. Beneath the dirt her cheekbones stood out starkly, as if the life was being sucked out of her. She bucked against him, trying to turn away. He got up in her face and prayed she understood. They didn't have time for this. Not now. No time for pain in his shoulder making him dizzy. No time for her to mourn. "Listen to me. We have to go. Now. Do you understand?"

"He—"

"No. Now!" he snapped.

"Yes. Alright." Her movements were sluggish, deliberate. She lugged his backpack up onto her shoulders, her back bowing beneath the weight, but her feet moving forward.

He kept her in motion. People had survived worse, she would too.

They stumbled along beside the tracks until a break in the fence gave them their exit. Smoke drifted overhead, the smell of burning wood and worse filling his head. He just needed to get them clear of the scene. Then they'd be fine. Clear of the scene and clear of this fucking city.

No sound of engines getting closer. Nothing stirred. The sun had barely risen any further than when they had started out.

"God, Finn."

"Hmm?"

She was looking back. Not the wisest thing to do. Didn't she know how that had worked out for Lot's wife?

The sun rose over a black wasteland, the remains of the city smoldering still. In the distance the fire raged on, consuming everything. Eerily similar to after the bombings, complete and utter devastation.

"If the wind had turned ..." Ali took it all in with a mix of numb wonder on her dusty face. "They're going to have trouble getting back to the highway. It should give us some time."

Finn nodded, couldn't speak. Yes, they were going to have a shit of a time. She spoke the truth.

Finn bent double and dry heaved.

CHAPTER EIGHTEEN

Finn was asleep. Ali had watched him for hours, less a few minutes spent running an errand. She had split her attention between him and the laundry door, and was guarding him, if the gun in her hand counted. At least it wasn't shaking anymore.

Finn hadn't moved, not since she'd re-bandaged his shoulder and he had popped a magical pain pill. They spoke very little.

He slept upright, his bare back propped against a concrete pillar, head canted back. The stark white bandage was bright against his tanned skin and the dark smudges of dried blood.

The garage stank of old oil stains and laundry detergent. The back door had been open, barrel bolt intact, the roller door undamaged and locked down. It made for a perfect hidey-hole.

Except for that one infected upstairs. Every now and then it would move. The sound of a dragging footstep or two would break the silence. Creepy. Happily, there was no internal staircase for it to come visiting.

Between the infected and the biker assholes, they could easily get trapped here, sitting and waiting. They should be on the move. Despite their various injuries they could be hot-footing it across the countryside, getting to a safer place out of reach of those assholes, right now. Finn hadn't needed to say it. She knew it.

But she waited for Daniel. Apparently it hadn't needed saying either. Finn had opened his mouth, looked at her face and shut it again without a word uttered. End of conversation. And so, they waited.

Her mind wouldn't still. The adrenalin surge from this morning had crashed, leaving far too much of everything bubbling around inside her brain, none of it good.

Daniel would find them. He would. Deep down inside it almost felt like a test of faith or some such. She just had to believe and be patient, find something to occupy her mind.

Not fixating on the door would be a positive start.

Kylie Scott

There was a rainwater tank outside. A big modern number; the type everyone had scrambled to install during the drought. She pondered the basin beside the washing machine, the pipe jutting out from the brickwork above it. They both needed a bath after lying in the dirt last night and crawling beneath the train this morning.

"You should try to sleep." Finn's eyes were open, half-lidded, but he hadn't moved otherwise. He watched her with a preternatural stillness and a calm most probably fake. Guilt slid through her.

"Hey," she said.

"It'll be okay, Al."

"He'll be okay," she corrected.

Finn gave no response.

For a long, tense moment silence reigned supreme, almost as if they were giving the dead a minute's tribute. Only Daniel wasn't dead. Not even a little.

She wrestled the panic back down, subduing it one more time.

"We should go upstairs, see if there's food," Finn said.

She shook her head. "No."

His high forehead creased, and his nostrils flared as he drew in a deep breath. "If we're quiet, keep our heads down, we'll be okay. It's a risk we need to take."

"No, Finn."

Like magic the thing upstairs chose then to bump and grind, as if it knew it were the topic of conversation.

"Shit." Finn straightened himself and stretched, rolling his good shoulder in slow motion. "Give me a sec. We'll try the neighbor's house."

"Finn, there's no need. This lot was getting ready to run. The car has a box of groceries, not all of them have gone off. There's not much else, a couple of blankets, some bottled water and beer. A stack of photo albums ..." She cast her eyes toward the second story, wondering. Not a good place to go. "Anyway, we're good for the immediate future."

"Alright." This one word finished on a weary sigh. It seemed to say this man's reserves were running low, and the blame lay with her. Dark shadows sat beneath his eyes and lines bracketed his mouth. They were still in danger because she refused to move on without Daniel, and he might not be coming.

Except he was. Nothing else was acceptable.

"He'll come, Finn. You don't know him. Dan is very resourceful."

Finn did the raising of one brow thing, giving her a long look. The type that said nothing and everything. The type bound to piss her off.

"I know you think he's—"

"We should put a sign out, something only he'd recognize. What do you think would work best?" He cut her off neatly, face expressionless. Nothing to see here, move along.

"Oh. Well, I already took care of it," she admitted.

His green eyes hardened, lips flat lined. "Al ..."

"I think we have a decent water supply. The tank seems to run in to the laundry." She waved a hand in its direction, a blatant bit of distraction. Who had the energy for subtlety? There was no softening of his glare. "Don't go there, Finn. I was careful. It needed to be done. You needed to rest."

The man raised a knee, draped an arm over it. It had the feel of another cop thing, the silence and watchfulness as he waited for her to stumble into his trap. He observed her, elegant face cool and composed despite the dirt and stubble.

Two months ago, his level of scrutiny would have shaken her down to her shoes.

Now, not so much.

Things took on a different perspective when you knew what real fear was. A good cop face wouldn't send her running for cover anytime soon.

"Do you have a spare shirt I could borrow? I want to give my clothes a wash while we have the chance." Ali stood, brushed off her hands and butt. Like a few specks of dirt would make an imprint on top of everything else they'd been subjected to. "Anything you want done?"

"Laundry wise?"

"Yes, laundry wise." She needed to keep busy, keep her hands occupied.

Ali wandered over to the basin, said a silent prayer and pushed in a plug. Slowly, she turned the tap. There came a trickle of rust-colored water. A dirty dribble could be accounted to water sitting in the system, nothing to get excited about yet.

She turned the knob farther. Oh, yes. Out it came. Stupidly, her eyes welled. Daniel was missing, and she was crying over running water. How messed up. Everything inside her had been rewired wrong.

Her entire life, running water had worked just fine, her love life, not so much. Where was the balance? It served her right for letting Daniel be her crutch. Now her weak knees were quaking.

Running water didn't begin to fix the wrongs. But, it did give her hands something to do. A bar of old yellow soap, cracked with age, sat on the sink just waiting for her. She set to it with a vengeance.

Ali scrubbed her arms and hands, built up a lather to attack her face. The need to get the grime was all consuming. When he walked in, she would be waiting, in one piece, not looking as if she had been rolling in mud.

Fuck no, she would pretty herself up for her man. Hope was a sly bitch.

Strands of hair stuck to her wet face and Finn's hands were there, pulling them back. He resurrected her ponytail. She could feel the warmth of him at her back, not quite touching, but near enough to soothe and scare.

She wanted Daniel, and she wanted to feel safe. These days, she wanted all sorts of shit she couldn't have.

Finn took a step back and she breathed easier.

"I get that you needed to do it. Just wake me next time. You can't go out on your own, Al."

"Shit. I've got soap in my eyes." Ali fumbled around for the threadbare hand towel that had been hanging from a hook beside the trough. "Damn it."

"Hang on."

Something soft and dry dabbed at her face. She dared blinking. That was one thing that hadn't changed – getting soap in your eyes still sucked. "Thank you."

Finn's face was solemn, mouth set and eyes decades older than they should have been. His gaze made her feel juvenile, foolish. Like she had hurt him somehow, disappointed him.

Making the mad dash outside had seemed perfectly reasonable at the time. Why did she feel yet more guilt creeping up on her?

"What sign did you put out there?"

"Oh, it's subtle. Don't worry." Her eyes were hot, stinging from more than suds. Ali scrubbed the soap off her face, searched for a distraction to stop the tears. Every damn subject felt razor-edged. "Thanks."

Finn tipped his chin, accepting the meager show of gratitude. "You're welcome."

It was wildly insufficient on her part, and she admitted it. "For everything, I mean. In case I haven't mentioned it before. You've been ... amazing, Finn. Really."

Finn nodded again, set the requested t-shirt aside. His face was calm but somber, lips slightly parted and eyes full of concern. She blinked back tears like crazy, refusing to let them show. As if he was fooled.

Not even a little.

He was no more fooled than embarrassed. "You need to be more careful, Al."

"I know. I understand."

"Good. Because you need to give me the opportunity to watch your back. You need to trust me." And then he turned his back, gave her a chance to shut down the waterworks. What a gentleman. After a moment or so he cleared his throat, giving her warning. "How about you wash my back and I'll do yours. Deal?"

"How about I clean yours up, and help put on a new bandage. Deal?"

He gave a gruff nod and showed her his back.

The intimacy of it unnerved her. So, she talked. "When I ran into Daniel I had been hiding in a neighbor's roof for months. No baths."

"So I'm getting off easy?"

"I was ... fragrant, let's leave it at that. Once upon a time, I never bathed with veritable strangers at all." The smile felt awkward, strained.

"Small-minded of you. There's nothing wrong with sharing a shower with new friends." He flashed her a grin as he glanced back over his shoulder. There and gone in a moment.

"You know, the Japanese have public bath houses, have done for centuries," he continued on when she failed to pick up the thread of the conversation.

"I don't believe the men and women actually mix in those." Ali rubbed her hand against the slab of soap, working up a lather for round two. "I'll get the dried blood off your back while you tell me sordid tales of your youth."

"I have two older sisters. My adventures couldn't even begin to compete."

"I'm sure you underestimate yourself."

He flashed his teeth again.

"So you were the baby of the family." She ran her fingers over his back, aiming for impersonal. She rubbed at the build-up of blood and dirt. Reddish-brown soap bubbles trailed down his spine, soaked into the top of his low-slung jeans. Her throat closed at the sight of the bloody gash in his shoulder. A hand-span lower and the bullet would have killed him. No Finn. The thought of it had her tearing up once more. "You've lost a lot of blood."

"I'm fine."

"Got some hard evidence to the contrary back here." Her voice wavered. Damn it.

The look he gave her over his shoulder made no sense but it froze her in place. Finn held her gaze for a long moment. And then turned away. Said nothing.

She had no idea what it meant. Her hands hovered, hesitating, waiting for enlightenment. He kept his face averted. "Finn?"

"We should eat soon."

"Okay," she agreed, letting it drop.

He nodded. Mission accomplished apparently, whatever the mission had been.

She couldn't read him for shit. Then again, she'd always been clueless when it came to the other sex. Men were complic-ated. Straightforward one minute and riddles the next. It irked the crap out of her. In the face of her new upfront and open frame of mind, she wasn't letting it go after all. "Finn, what was that?"

"What?"

"The look."

"Nothing." His tone of voice firm and flat.

Okey dokey. Apparently she hadn't grown enough to chase it down. Awkward feelings flooded her.

"It's a good thing you had antibiotics," she said. An innocuous enough topic, surely.

"Got the bag of wonders."

"Yes." She offered him a smile. He looked over his shoulder and almost returned it. The corner of his mouth hesitated at the last. "Your bag of wonders rocks, I must say."

"Personal preparedness. I was a Scout." He braced his arms on the edge of the basin and dropped his head forward. She scrubbed at his back and neck, gently pushing her fingers into solid muscle. "Can you do it harder?" he asked.

"Sure." She dug in, keeping a safe distance from his shoulder, wanting to soothe, not harm. From her, it was the least he deserved.

"Where was your family?"

"Down south. We grew up on one of the Northern Beaches, running wild half the time. I don't know how Mum put up with us." The strong column of his neck tensed beneath her fingers. The warmth in his voice when he talked about his family made her heart ache. They had obviously been close, something she had never quite managed.

"How long have you been with him?" he enquired. "If you don't mind me asking."

"No, I don't mind. Only a couple of days, though it feels longer. Things work differently now, don't they?"

"Times of war, the rules change."

"War ... I guess that's one way to put it." Her eyes bored into the back door. If she stared long and hard enough then magic might happen. Bullshit. Daniel would make it. He would.

And what the hell would he see when he walked in? Her fingers flinched back from Finn, covered in suds. "Wet the towel for me so I can clean you off, please."

He did as asked.

"So, do I want to know what you saw when you were watching us?"

"I don't know, Al. Do you?" He watched her over his shoulder, something akin to amusement lighting the pale green of his eyes. The corner of his mouth twitched.

The tease.

"No. No, I don't. Forget I asked." Heat swept her face. He handed her a wet cloth, and she washed off his back as carefully as possible, sopping up all of the gray suds. "Can I get to the water, please?"

"Let's see ... You two fight. A lot." He turned to face her, blocking her way with his arms crossed over his chest. "Opposites attract, I guess."

"That would be it."

"Sucked when I dropped the night-vision goggles. Smashed the lenses. I had to go by guesswork after that ..."

Her jaw fell. "You did not have night-vision goggles. Pervert."

The elegant face gave away nothing. He was fibbing. Had to be.

Suddenly a dimple flashed, he shrugged his shoulders. "Be fair. Without TV what was I supposed to do for entertainment?"

"Aren't you funny?" She bumped her hip against his. "I know you're lying."

"Do you?"

"Yep."

"Alright then. I would hate to make you feel uncomfortable about any lewd, unnatural acts I might have witnessed."

"I think I liked you better without a sense of humor." The clean, if threadbare, hand towel would do fine for washing them off. "Turn around, please."

He did so without further comment. Thank God.

And he couldn't have seen anything. Jerk.

With gentle strokes, she washed off his back, wary of touching his wound. "You're good to go. Got more bandages?"

"Yeah, I'm fine. What about your back?"

"I haven't been shot lately."

"I'm not trying anything, Al. Let me wash your back. Consider it a stress remedy."

"Wow, that offer isn't dubious in the least. I'm fine."

A sly sort of mirth lit his eyes. "Are you? Or are you ... a chicken?"

She laughed, delighted at the unexpected silliness. Amazed to be feeling anything at all. "Bawk, bawk, bawk."

Childish sniggering ensued until a loud crash from upstairs stopped them cold.

CHAPTER NINETEEN

Finn watched her in silence.

They sat in the parked car inside the garage passing a can of chicken soup back and forth, along with bottles of lukewarm beer. It was the car seats or the concrete. Most of their clothes were scattered over a wire rack, drying.

She didn't speak, so neither did he.

He watched her watching the door. She barely even blinked.

He could almost feel her hope waning. There was no point cracking bad jokes now to try and make her smile. He had done his fair share of delivering bad news. Between confirmed death and missing persons, the latter was the cruelest.

"Al." He nudged her elbow with the beer bottle and she started. Enough to let him know her thoughts had been a million miles away from the dodgy Datsun with the mission brown interior.

A billion miles away from him.

"Thanks." With an ever-present hand at the bottom of her t-shirt, the only item of clothing on her, Al accepted the bottle and took a swig.

There was a lot of skin on display next to him. Who'd have known that beneath those jeans her legs were so long? She had the nicest curves. He tried not to enjoy them, given what she was going through, but it wasn't easy to keep his mind off track. Those legs, and the way her knees kept rubbing together, came close to causing him pain, especially knowing she wore nothing underneath the shirt.

Not a damn thing. He knew it for a fact. Just like there had been nothing under her dirty jeans, hence the hand on the hem.

Her confidence in him keeping his back turned while she bathed was sweet but misplaced. Each tug on the shirt's hem seemed to ramp up the heat in the airless garage a bit more, for him at least. She remained oblivious. It frustrated the shit out of him but then, that was the situation, wasn't it? Shit.

There was only one spare pair of boxer briefs in the bag and he wore them. All other assorted items of clothing had been washed and hung up to dry. Not that he hadn't offered her the boxers. He was comfortable with nudity. Guess she wasn't. Guess maybe it was insensitive on his part to let his thoughts dwell in that direction. Again.

He never had been good at going without sex. Previously, there had never been a need to. Nearly nine weeks into the celibate lifestyle, and he found it as overrated as getting shot had been.

"It'll be dark soon," she said. Her voice sounded smaller each time she spoke, making him wonder how long till it disappeared entirely.

"Yeah."

"Daniel will find somewhere safe to hole up for the night."

He didn't answer. She'd said it more for her benefit than his.

She passed back the bottle of beer and he drained it, put it aside and twisted the cap off number five of the rapidly diminishing six-pack.

The owners might have had dubious taste in vehicles, but he could only applaud their priorities in packing the brew. It had been a shit of a day, well worth throwing back a couple.

The edge of gold around the door was fading, the shadows growing. He could do nothing for her but be there and wait this out. He couldn't leave her alone. He would never leave her alone.

But the days of being able to fix something were gone. There wasn't a chance he could salvage this. It was one more loss amongst so many.

At least she was alive, safe beside him. Protected.

Upstairs, the infected moaned, growing agitated as night set in.

The rat-a-tat-tat on the door seemed part of it at first. Just more of the dragging footsteps from overhead and a "ker-thunk" as something hit the floor. It all blended for him. But Al was up and running, the length of the t-shirt forgotten in her dash to get at the door.

"Daniel."

"Al, wait!" He freed his gun as she did likewise the locks, throwing open the door to all comers. Adrenalin surged through him with fury hot behind it. She'd get them killed for sure this time.

110

Al launched herself at the tall figure waiting on the other side.

Disappointment had a taste, and it sat on the back of his tongue, hot and sour as acid, making him sick. He truly fucking hated himself for feeling it. No one had canceled Christmas. A man had survived. Bad had been trampled. Al's heart remained unbroken.

This was a good thing. A good thing. Yeah.

He just needed a minute to catch his breath and find his happy face.

Dan appeared none the worse for wear. He shuffle-stepped her backward, sparing a hand to close and lock the door while she clung to him.

With the shirt riding up he got a great view of Dan's hands clapped over the curves of her bare ass cheeks. The man murmured to her, soft and low, over and over, "I know. I know. I know ..."

"You made it," Finn said. Lame as it was, it was the best he could do without actually lying.

For some reason, he didn't want to lie.

Dan nodded. Nothing needed to be said. And Finn didn't need to see the understanding in the man's face. Anger would have been easier to take.

Simpler.

He flicked the safety on his gun, pointed it elsewhere.

"Lose something, baby?" A piece of black fabric hung from one of Daniel's fingers, dangling against the back of Al's thigh. Dan raised the black fabric high above her head, and she set her chin on his chest, peered skyward. "Finders keepers."

Finn had to squint and take a step closer to make them out in the fading light. But yes, they had a winner. Daniel had found Al's panties.

Finn's sense of humor, however, had long gone. "You risked your life to hang underwear off the mailbox? This is what you couldn't wait till I was awake to do? Fucksake, Al."

"Actually, it was the shrub beside the mailbox, discreetly positioned unless you knew what you were after," Dan explained, dangling the item higher when Al took the bait and made a grab for them. "I knew what I was after."

"This was the agreed upon sign?" Finn asked in a brutally tight voice. No point hiding his ire now. These two were all loved up and he was on the outer, the audience, not required. No one was interested in his mood or his issues.

"Not exactly, needing a sign hadn't occurred to us. We weren't planning on getting separated. I guess that was short-sighted." Daniel planted a kiss on her forehead, ignoring her grasping arm. "Mmm, you smell of soap, all shiny and fresh. Me, on the other hand ..."

The big guy slowly eased his shirt up. "Shit. That hurts."

"There's water for washing," she said. "What's wrong with you?"

"Bumped into something. Gonna have some beautiful bruises tomorrow."

"How bad, Dan?" Ali gave up on the attempt at grabbing and held out her hand with all due decorum. "My underwear, please. I'm done with flashing for the day."

"That's a damn shame." Daniel brushed his nose against hers, Eskimo style, and handed over the plain cotton panties. "Not too bad. I'll get cleaned up."

Al was glowing with good feeling, panties in hand and fingers fidgeting. "Finn, thank you for putting up with me. For everything. Again."

She was so happy. Alight with love. And he wished, just for a second, that he was the one on the receiving end. He gave himself a moment to wonder what it would be like to not sleep alone. Because if he had been just a couple of days earlier, then he could have been the one she threw herself at.

A few fucking hours earlier was all it would have taken and it would have been him. There it was. He was dismissed. Job done.

Time to take it on the cheek and roll with the punches. "We're friends, Al. It's all good."

CHAPTER TWENTY

She was scarily happy.

Blissfully happy and scared shitless all at once. Of course, the rabbit had issues with making such a gargantuan leap of faith. Bad luck. It was too late for any rabbit-type retreat.

"Talk to me," Daniel demanded from beside her. They lay on a nest she had concocted for their comfort out of old blankets and towels.

Finn had bedded down on the far side of the room, behind the car and out of view.

While Daniel washed up, Finn had made a small production out of plugging into a tiny MP3 player, affording them as much privacy as possible.

"What about? You've only been gone a few hours." She stared back at him, bewildered, full of joy, amazed he had returned to her. She hadn't lost him. Maybe there was a God of some description on high.

"Talk," he demanded again. "I want to hear your voice."

"Okay, okay." He was wonderful. Her stomach wouldn't quit somersaulting. The light from one lone candle flickered and fluttered over the planes and angles of his face. Those blue eyes fixed on her. Waiting. "Ah, well ..."

"Come here, babe." Daniel's impatient hands grabbed her. No. He grabbed at her one lone item of clothing. Soon enough he'd ridded her of the t-shirt and she lay bare, body and soul. He had total access without even trying.

She had no idea how it had happened. Before she could worry about exposure, he was there, covering her, distracting her. He was a master at distraction. Her breasts filled his hands, thumbs stroking the tight peaks of her nipples, sending warmth flooding through her. The way he touched her lit her up from inside. "I love these. So, you got away okay? Everything was alright?"

"Y-yes." His hands coaxed and teased, there was no chance of coherency. He was crazy to expect it and it was well past time to return the favor.

The hard muscles of his stomach jumped beneath her touch as she slid her hand down the front of his pants, loving the liberty to touch him how she pleased. Wheresoever she pleased.

His cock was at the ready, hard and hot, perfect. Her fingers wrapped around him, stroked and caressed. All for her. What a gift he was. And she had nearly lost him.

"Good. That's good. Knew I could count on Finn." His lids dropped to half-mast, eyes glittering with a lust that thrilled her.

"I can take care of myself." There was no impact. The words came out more breathy than bold. Hopeless.

No chance to get angry when her heart and mind were melting.

"Course you can. You're my uber girl." He moved, winced, abruptly stopped. With a pale face he muttered something deeply profane.

"Right, that's it. On your back, buddy." Ali eased him over with careful hands, abandoning the hardness and heat of his cock for now. She hustled up his white t-shirt, revealing a spectacular black bruise the size of her hand. Her throat shut tight. The mark covered the entire right side of his ribcage.

"You said you were fine. Holy shit, Daniel. This is not fine. This is a really long way from fine."

And whoa, there went her voice. She screeched at him by the end of it.

"Shh. Don't go ballistic. I can explain ..." He lifted up, flinching all the while. Hands gripped her hips and rearranged her till she sat atop him, aligned with his groin. She stared down at him, careful to keep her knees back from the damage. Where was it even safe to touch him?

Daniel sighed. "Actually, you know, it's not worth explaining. But, okay, don't get mad. There was all sorts of crap in the water. I hit something when I went in. I lived to tell the tale. End of explaining. Feel free to rub yourself against me in a show of sympathy. Hang on. Up."

His hands urged her to rise up sufficient to drag down his boxers. Going skin to skin with Daniel sent her out of her mind. The contact hot, hard, and soft, and wet. He hissed as she let out a sharp, shock of a breath.

"Babe, you are so wet. Fuck, that's good." Daniel's hips pressed up, his hands on her pressed down. "Oh, yeah."

"Dan. Shit. Stop."

The grip on her shifted, moved up till her breasts were back in his hands. Her own hovered, uncertain where to land. Oh whoa, that bruise. And who knew how to tell if he had cracked or broken something. Then again, surely a man with cracked or broken ribs didn't go around lifting women and positioning them where he wished. Surely.

For the four-hundredth time in twenty-four hours, she thought she might burst into tears.

"I'm not hurt. Touch me," he implored. Fingers lightly pinched her nipples, and he toyed with her while his hard cock slid against her pussy. She became dizzy. The combination set her senses to reeling, so much sweet sensation. Her body rocked against his of its own volition, out of control.

It was so good, so right. She wanted to cling to him, rub herself against him till they both got off in a spectacular fashion, spectacular but without hurting him. The thought of him in pain undid her. Poured cold water on the rocking and rolling and grinding herself against him.

"Wait. How bad are your ribs? Are you hurt anywhere else?" Ali covered his hands with her own, stopped the action going on with her boobs. Necessary for straight thought, hard as it was. "We need to talk. I thought you wanted to talk."

Daniel scoffed, drew her fingers down to his mouth and kissed them. He rubbed his lips over her knuckles, the palms of her hands, making her feel treasured.

"Please," he said. "With you sitting on top of me bare ass naked? Are you kidding? Nah. No way. Come here. Let me get my mouth on you."

Hands slid back down to her hips, tried to lift her, move her up his body. She swatted at his arms, which were unblemished, therefore a fair target. "Stop. Dan, I'm serious. Are you hurt anywhere else?"

He groaned and rolled his hips against her, sliding his cock against the seam of her pussy, nudging her sensitive bits and getting her even slicker. Her insides squeezed tight. The cheat. "Oh, I'm hurting, babe. But it has nothing to do with any bumps or bruises. That much I can promise you."

"Dan." Ali scowled, wrestled back her hands and set them by his head. She bent over him, careful not to let her knees nudge his sides. "Why can't you give me a straight answer?"

"Why can't you ride me like a pony?" He scowled straight back at her, unrepentant. "Don't pretty girls like ponies? I thought they did."

"Daniel Cross. Tell me if you're hurt anywhere else. Please."

Dan licked his lips, studied the ceiling above her head. Talk about avoidance. He blatantly hated any hint of weakness. Bad luck. She cared about him a lot. Possibly more.

"No. I'm not hurt anywhere else. The ribs are bruised but I'm pretty sure they're not broken. Okay?"

"Thank you."

A huff was all she got in reply. Then, eventually, a pout from the man between her thighs. The bastard. It was hard not to smile at the disgruntled moue. "Whatever."

"I'm sorry if I killed the mood. I am, however, positive I can revive it."

"Like to see you try," he grumbled, keeping a firm hold on her hands beside his head.

"Okay." Ali took him at his word, pressing her lips to his, soft, firm and perfect. And closed.

They did not open to her again until she nipped at his bottom lip, sunk her teeth in sufficient to get his attention. When his mouth opened, it was to bite back, teeth snapping. "Careful, baby, two can play at that."

"Decided to get back in the game, have you? Let me have my hands."

"Why should I?"

"Because, with my hands trapped I'm not sure I can reach your cock with my mouth."

Daniel stopped and stared at her with open fascination, blue eyes darkening. "That might just be the best reason I've ever heard."

"I'm very glad you think so. I choose however not to ask how many women you've caught in this position."

"My girl." The big man grinned, brought her hands to his mouth and kissed them elaborately. "I love you."

Her insides quivered alarmingly. "Shuddup."

He winked, freed her hands with a flourish. "I'm yours to command."

Biting her tongue against further comment, she crawled down his body, everything in her feeling hyper sensitive, totally in tune with him. Even the brush of his leg hairs against her nipples was a sensual thing. The whole of him worked her up to a fever pitch.

Already half erect, he lay thick and proud against his belly, beautiful as sin.

She lightly drew her lips down the length of his cock, turned her face and pressed her cheek against him. He smelt good, warm and male. And she had to be crazy about him to be thinking such things. Ali closed her eyes tight, breathed him in deep. Tenderness for him filled her. Such a beautiful man, she couldn't get enough of him.

Hot and smooth as silk, the pronounced veins wending up his length calling to the tip of her tongue to trace and tease. So she did. No matter how he urged her on she did not hurry up about it either. She'd set out to savor him and that's just what she did. From the touch and taste and scent of him through to the feel of him in her mouth. The sounds he made were the finishing touch.

"You win," he murmured, watching her with a singular dedication. As if he were committing this to memory, the view of her huddled over his cock, savoring him. The picture she must make.

And she had almost lost him today, could lose him for good next time from one thing or another. The world was a dangerous place.

Ali took him in hand and rubbed the flat of her tongue against the underside of the head. Dedicated to pleasing him, she would stop worrying about shit that didn't matter, future things she couldn't effect. They were together now. That was all that mattered.

She studied him with her mouth, lips, tongue and teeth, gave herself over to his pleasure with enthusiasm.

He mumbled her name as she took him deep. Not as far as she would have wished, but then they always said the head of a man's cock was the most sensitive part. Duly, she lavished it with attention. He groaned when she gently dragged her teeth up the underside of his cock and pride and heat filled her in equal measures. Maybe she wasn't so bad at this. Maybe she could drive him as wild as he did her with a little practice. God, but she wanted to give to him. She clenched her thighs together, redoubled her efforts. Not stopping till he threaded his fingers through her hair, tugged her gently off him.

"Babe. Stop."

She blinked at him, dazed and confused and more than a little caught up in the moment. Her lips felt swollen, mouth tingling from all her efforts. She had been waiting for the pay off, waiting to taste him on the back of her tongue. Further proof of just how far he had managed to sink beneath her skin. "But ..."

The man shoved a condom at her and oh man, he could only have gotten it from Finn. She and Dan had lost their packs with all required supplies. Mortification swept through her.

But now was not the time to dwell. Really and truly not.

"Babe, I love you," he said, and her rabbit heart twisted and turned. "Trust me. You can suck my dick whenever you want. You're a goddess at it. I'll actively encourage it to happen often. But right now, I want to be inside you."

When she hesitated, he took back the condom. Daniel ripped it open and set about rolling it down his cock, still wet from her mouth. "Let me rephrase. I need to be inside you now. Right now. Up."

"I thought I was in charge."

"And you did great." His big, strong hands gripped her arms, taking her weight and drawing her up his body. She knew was safe with him. He wouldn't drop her. Drive her insane with his alpha bullshit, yes, that he would do. Hurt her though? Never.

Once in position, her slick pussy hovering above his sheathed cock, he set a hand to her hip to still her. A finger trailed down her torso, through the valley between her breasts, down over her belly, stopping to circle her belly button, round and round until she ground her teeth in frustration. "I can't begin to say how proud I am of you. You did brilliantly."

"Well, thank you," she panted. "But no teasing."

Ali gripped his hand and pushed it down toward her center. A part of her in dire need of attention, as the noise she made when his finger drifted, feather light, up and down the seam of her pussy attested to. No one had ever affected her the way he did.

"No teasing," he promised, while his fingers did exactly that.

Long before his fingers ceased to thrill, he changed tactics. He took his cock in hand, teasing her with the thick, blunt head. Her eyes nearly rolled back into her skull. Heat coiled low in her belly till she ached with it. She was so turned on it hurt. Daniel stared up at her, studying her, gauging each and every reaction. His absorption in her was disarming, distracting.

She couldn't come with him watching her. He saw too much.

"No." He grabbed the hand she moved to cover his eyes with. "Let me see. You like this, don't you."

"Yes, but ... Dan. Enough. Let me ..."

He obligingly fell still beneath her. She let her body be her guide, his and hers both. Gave up on the worry and gave in to the feel of him. It was all so simple, concentrating on the prod of his cockhead against her opening. The slow, steady push of him into her stole her breath. But the lust and love in his eyes stole her heart. It washed away the bitterness and fear of a lifetime's making. The raw feel of so much emotion stunned her. She didn't know whether to laugh or cry. Somewhere in between fit best.

"Okay?" he whispered hoarsely.

"Yes."

His hand stroked her cheek. "So pretty. Ready to come for me, babe?"

She nodded, beyond words. The fit and the fullness of him had her there, teetering on the edge. That and his teasing.

And this position, it was the perfect angle for grinding her clit against him. Her body wasn't interested in slow and sweet. And her body was definitely in control. Or more accurately, her pussy. Her brain had been shelved, though her heart was wide open.

It had been a hell of a day. The rush of it, the sensation building as she took his cock inside her again and again thrilled her. She was burning up. All of the emotions, the love and fear and all the rest, were pressure packed inside her. She had to have release. Every cell screamed out for it. Her body was mindless in its pursuit of it.

It shocked her when it hit. Like freefalling. Her heart faltered. All the air left her body on a cry, dragged out from somewhere deep inside. Somewhere she hadn't even realized existed.

Dan's fingers dug into her waist, pushing her down onto his cock as he pressed up and came with a gasp.

They both lay still, slicked with sweat and silent, for a long time.

Her bones felt hollow, the whole world light and floaty. The noise had emptied her out. She pressed her forehead into his shoulder, letting the aftershocks have their way with her. Daniel's ribs moved in and out between her knees, bringing her back to reality.

"Did I hurt your ribs?" she murmured.

Sweat slipped from his forehead, and he gave a small smile. "Forget my ribs. I can't feel anything outside of good. My girl, I think you needed that."

She could only nod her agreement. What she needed was him, but she wasn't sure she could admit to it yet.

"I know *I* did," he said. "And you were loud."

She tensed. "I was?"

"Oh, yeah," he laughed. She considered giving the strong column of his neck a nip but settled for a kiss instead. Partly to hide her face as it heated.

Dan trailed his fingers over the line of her spine, exerting pressure to hold her in place when she tried to rise. He brushed his lips against her ear, lulling her into a false sense of security as he mumbled, "Spectacularly loud. You're a security risk. Finn had to have heard you."

"I'll have to be more careful. Finn's listening to music."

"Bullshit. He's listening to you."

"No. He's not." She frowned, carefully rolled off him and settled in against his side as he dealt with the condom. "You're just trying to mess with me."

Daniel smirked.

No way. Impossible. "Aren't you?"

"Whatever you say." He wriggled an arm beneath her neck and drew her in closer against the heat of his body. Summer nights be damned. "No teasing. That's what I agreed to," he said.

"Hmm." A world of doubt filled the sound. He turned his head toward her, stared her down. "Dan. I don't want him. I want you. You know that, right?"

"He's a pretty boy. Smart. Lethal as hell. And most importantly, in my humble opinion, very keen on keeping you safe." His hand stroked over her, trailing down to the curve of her hip and back up again. "Important things, especially these days. Well ... pretty is overrated."

Guilt bit her ample ass. Had she been flirting? Not with intent, most definitely, but still. His voice had not been accusing. It would be closer to say amused. Talk about confusing.

Ali wriggled out from her safe place against him, rose up on an elbow to better gauge the expression on his face. "Where is this coming from? Are you tired of me or something?"

"What? No. Of course not, babe."

"Alright, so you don't want to pass me on." She paused, listening for movement behind the parked car. No sign of life. "That's nice, and yet ... God, Daniel. Do you think I'd cheat on you?"

"No. Ali, look at me," he insisted, waiting her out till she did. No accusation, no judgment. So why was unease slicking over her skin? This was dangerous territory, but his face was calm and close. "I trust you. I'm yours, babe. No matter what, okay?"

"Okay."

"You don't need to worry about that." His hand cupped an ass cheek, thumb stroking the curve of her hip. Not lighting her up, but placating. "I'm just saying that the world has changed. The rules have changed. It might pay to have an open mind where this situation with the three of us is involved."

"What are you trying to push me into now?"

He cocked his head. "My love, I would never try to push you into anything. You wound me. Relax."

"Right." Ali nestled back down next to him. Hiding. Maybe. A little. She was just pulling it all together in her head, what to say and how to say it, when he pre-empted her again.

"He's attracted to you. I don't think you see how much."

"I get that things have changed, but ..."

"But?"

She said nothing – for all of a minute. "But I'm probably the first female he's seen in a while and his alternatives aren't great, Dan.

Sex-wise it's down to you, me or his fists. His being attracted to me doesn't necessarily mean a whole lot."

"Hmm."

What the hell did he mean? Hold up. What if it wasn't about her? "Are you attracted to him?"

"I'm very attracted to you. I'm not letting you go." He brushed his lips over hers, reassuring, teasing. "But what, hypothetically speaking, would you think if I was attracted to him?"

The picture hit her full frontal. Finn and Daniel naked and sweaty, hands and mouths all over each other. Her heart raced. Her mind was a far filthier place than she ever suspected. "Ah, really?"

"No, hypothetical, remember. I love your inner kink. You always have this vaguely stunned expression when it rears its head and bites you on the ass. A dead giveaway," Daniel chuckled, then groaned when the movement jarred his ribs. "Damn. But the fact is, you wouldn't mind if I did want him."

"I might get jealous. I don't know. I've never been in that situation. Am I in that situation?"

"Again, no. But ..."

"But ..." Would she deal with it? Yeah, probably she would. There were no doubts in her mind that Daniel was committed to her, and yet, this conversation had a dangerous feel to it. Like the ground was shifting beneath her feet. The topic they were covering was all highly unstable. "It's a risk, Dan."

"Babe, you over-think everything. Our life is one God-awful risk these days."

"True," she sighed. "Is there a point to this bewildering conversation about who you have no interest in sleeping with? I'm a straightforward kind of girl. Just spit it out."

"Straightforward? Yeah right," he said, again with the laugh. "The point, my girl, is this. If you wouldn't mind me doing it, what makes you think I would mind in the reverse-case scenario?

"Because if you wanted Finn it would possibly mean you're after something I can't give you, namely a real-live working penis. Maybe that's small-minded, I don't know. This is complicated. I wasn't expecting ..."

She cleared her throat, tried to form a straight line in her head. Maybe that was the problem – straight lines didn't always apply.

"I won't risk losing you for a frolic. You're too important to me. Not to mention Finn deserves better. I won't treat him like a cheap thrill when we're talking of building a future somehow somewhere. Sex complicates things."

Dan nodded. "Alright, though I never said short-term. See how it goes. Be open-minded. Two men devoted to pleasing your very sweet self? Have you ever thought about that?"

Her filthy mind filled with images.

"Holy shit. We're gonna need more Eves in this garden." She moaned and hid her face against his side, taking comfort in the warm and familiar scent of him. Admitting to any sex fantasies did not feel smart. Nothing about this was safe. She might be in love for the first time in a long time and he was talking about adding someone else. Historically, one-on-one proved enough of a challenge to her. How could she possibly keep two men happy? The idea was ludicrous.

"Daniel ... You're so cool about this and, and I'm so not. At all. What happens if we find another woman? We turn it into a circus act and take it on the road? Sounds like you're using the end of the world as a flimsy excuse to have an orgy every other night of the week."

He grunted in disapproval. "I disagree, and you're getting jealous. There's no need. This is about you and me and possibly him. That's all."

"The three of us?"

"The three of us."

"Wow" Right. Sure. It sounded so simple. No chance for broken hearts at all. "No, Daniel. No."

"Okay."

Ali raised her head, mouth tense. "That easy?"

"Yep. It's your choice. I just wanted to make sure you knew you had one."

"Right. Well, my choice is no. Meanwhile, this is doing my head in."

"Enough of that talk then." Daniel nodded, satisfied. "Instead, let's discuss why you tried to cover my eyes earlier. Because baby, if it had been a kinky sex game I would have been on board, but I'm thinking it was something else."

"It was nothing," she said. "You need to rest. Sleepy time."

Daniel rubbed his jaw against the top of her head, ruffling her hair. "Nah, I'm fine and so, very much, are you. Time for round two, cowgirl. And this time, we're going to take it nice and slow with our eyes wide open."

CHAPTER TWENTY-ONE

The criminals were back at it.

Smoke lingered in the air at first light, making Finn's pulse spike and his brain snap to attention. Adrenalin had it over caffeine any day of the week, even after a shit night's sleep. He jumped to his feet, circumnavigated the Datsun to find the lovebirds tangled up and sleeping. "We have a situation on our hands."

"Finn?" Al asked in a husky voice. She blinked big gray eyes at him from where she lay wrapped up in Daniel. Her hair was all tussled, and there was a general well-fucked appeal to her.

He was nowhere near as immune to it as he would have liked. Which pissed him off.

And she wore his t-shirt, having gasped words along the lines of "God", "yes", and "Daniel" before slipping into it.

"What's wrong, Finn?"

His. Shirt.

"We've, aah ..." He took a nice deep breath, focused on the essentials. Things besides what was going on beneath his shirt and inside his head. "We've got trouble."

"Again."

"Again," Finn agreed.

She shook the big guy's arm. "Smoke. Wake up, Daniel. They're lighting more fires."

"Ah, man." Daniel rolled onto his back and stretched. He really was big. Civilian or no, taking him on hand-to-hand for her was not the best idea. Tempting as it was. Better to woo her away. "We were out of beer anyway. It's time to move along, kids."

Finn turned his back on the love nest to get his shit together. It also gave him a chance to get his temper back under control. Not that those two were messing around, not taking the threat seriously. The man donned his pants while Al made a dash to the spindly clothesline.

"Finn, your stuff's dry too," she announced.

He turned in time to catch the flash of ass as she stepped into black cotton panties. Oh yeah, the swift revelation of the long line of her back as she tugged his shirt off over her head. Breathing didn't matter and blinking was right out. Anger slipped from his immediate reach in the face of this.

Strangely enough, once removed, he wanted the shirt straight back on her.

Ali fished about for her bra, found it and slipped the straps up her arms. Dark blonde hair fell over her shoulders, sliding across bare skin. Porn had nothing on this.

He needed to get laid.

Pity about the chances.

"Great." He joined her by the laundry, started dragging on his own clothes before she noticed anything was up. Not that she ever did seem to notice. Living in close quarters with strangers brought politeness to an art form.

The roar of a motorbike gunning up the street had them both jumping. He simply hid it better.

"Fuckers," the big guy muttered, bending over the sink to drink from the tap.

"Yep," said Finn.

"So." Dan clapped his hands together, rubbed. "Who's up for playing another round of hide and seek?"

Hours later, summer showers had messed with the bonfire tactics. Unfortunately, the vigilant bastards patrolled the streets, making it hard to move far or fast.

The noise of the motorbikes kept the infected stirred up. They'd shamble out looking for action, and the bastards provided it. Whittling down the zombie population of the surrounding area kept the bastards distracted at least. Important to note, petrol was plentiful, but their ammo had to be running low the way they went for maximum effect.

Al, Dan and Finn managed to waste the morning skulking four blocks through the ongoing drizzle. A patrol had them seeking cover inside a rusted garden shed. They rested amongst the garden tools and towers of empty plastic pots. The place smelt of damp earth and fertilizer.

Dan shut his eyes, legs spread out in front of him, and his back to one rickety wall. There was nothing from him for a long time, care of the painkillers Al had all but stuffed down his throat. The man obviously needed the sleep after his busy night and war wounds.

Yes indeed. A very fucking busy night.

Behind them lay the river and before them suburbia soon petered out. Acres of sparse bushland and the occasional farm or homestead ahead. Acres of next to no cover with few roads, even if they could bypass the bastards. Options dwindled.

It didn't help his pissy mood. Close to being cornered. Dan injured. Still no sign of winning the woman. And the woman had been suspiciously quiet all day. Al rarely met his eyes. He had no idea what was going on, nor did they have time for it, given the situation.

"Al?" He turned his head sufficiently to put her in his line of vision. The pistol Dan had put in her hands the day before sat close by. A higher caliber than he would have preferred, but then again, a .22 wasn't going to get the job done. "Come over here and bring your gun."

She blinked. "Why?"

"Because you aren't as proficient with it as you should be. You need to practice." He crooked a finger and beckoned. "Come on."

There followed a wary glance, but she did as directed. Al shuffled over on her knees, weapon in hand. No mind at all to where it pointed. Finn caught her wrist in one hand. Her smooth skin and fine bones felt perfect in his grip. Images of her restrained for their mutual pleasure flooded his mind. It took him a moment to remember the gun. "The safety had better be on. Turn around. I need to be behind you."

"Sorry."

Once she faced the wall, he knelt behind her, put his arms around her and covered her hands with his own. Knowing it was bound to unnerve her. Knowing part of this was just a good excuse to rub up against her.

Pitiful, but true.

The whites of her eyes flashed as she glanced at him over her shoulder. Her ponytail brushed against his face. It could have been his imagination, but she seemed to smell of laundry soap and sex, the most bizarre combination ever. It shouldn't have worked but, of course, it did. She had his dick's total and immediate attention, proving he could wear his hand out all he wanted. Wouldn't help.

"Relax." He lifted one of her hands off the butt of the pistol, checked the safety was on, then released the clip and set it aside. Tasks he could do in his sleep, perfect for keeping his mind occupied no matter how good she smelt. He couldn't stop breathing her in. It was all about sex, or the lack thereof, not her in particular. An important fact to remember.

"Okay, keep both hands on the gun. Grip it like you're holding a bird. Firmly enough that it's not going to get away from you, loose enough that you're not going to hurt it."

"Alright." The frown line above her nose deepened. Her slender fingers realigned beneath his. "Like this?"

"That's good." Finn held his hands up, made the peace sign then stuck a finger in the middle. "This is what you're after, line up your front sight center between the two at the back. Raise the muzzle. You're pointing low."

Al adjusted her aim.

Finn brushed aside a piece of her hair tickling his nose, tucked it behind her ear. He resisted the urge to rub it between his fingers, to feel it and sniff it. Yet his hand lingered. He breathed in deep. Again. Finding words got hard. "Good, good. Don't forget to breathe."

She nodded, her face the picture of concentration.

"Pull the trigger nice and slow. Squeeze it. The gun," he said, more for his benefit than hers.

Sex and soap.

Daniel slept on in the corner. Or appeared to. His eyes were shut, shoulders rising and dropping with deep, even breaths.

Finn felt no guilt. Refused to.

"Go on, Al. Do it," he urged and she nodded hesitantly.

Her finger tightened. So did her shoulders, her arms, her everything. By the time the gun clicked, her aim was, once more, shot to shit. She had held her breath throughout the entire process. "Okay?"

"No. You're too tense. That's why you jerk the gun up when you fire and your shot gets wasted."

"I hit someone yesterday."

"You got lucky. Not something we can depend on. Go again. Relax. Breathe this time." He leant in close to the rim of her ear. She shivered, frowned, but whether over his proximity or the gun, he couldn't tell. Didn't want to know. It was nice to let his mind run wild. "Let your breath out slowly as you squeeze the trigger, okay? Don't get all wound up over it going off. You know it's going to happen, so let it. Relax, Al. Let it surprise you."

She nodded, lined herself up and dry fired. Little changed the second time round.

"Again."

The third time she marginally improved.

"A little better. Keep going," Finn said.

"Maybe ... if you weren't hovering."

"Al, this is the least stressful situation you're going to find yourself in when it comes to firing a weapon. Concentrate on what you're doing. I need to be behind you. Deal with it." Finn placed his hands on her shoulders. She flinched. "Easy. They're there to remind you not to tense up. Go again."

She scowled and fired.

He didn't move his hands an inch. "You rushed it. Again."

One pained expression later, she did so. Being told what to do clearly wasn't her forte. Maybe she just needed to learn about the benefits it could bring. He'd certainly love to teach her.

"Much better. You're focusing now. Maybe you don't mind me hovering after all," he said, and she snorted, lined her sights up on her imaginary target once more. "That's it."

She nodded and the side of her mouth lifted. Then she relaxed the hair's breadth left between her ass and his dick, shoving against the front of his jeans. She stilled instantly. "Finn?"

"It's a predictable reaction, Al. Ignore it."

"But ..."

"Go again." He squeezed her shoulder, returning her focus to the task at hand. "Concentrate on what you're doing."

Her chin jerked, and she breathed nice and slow in a deliberate, steady motion. And fired.

He would have felt proud if he could feel anything beyond the light press of her ass against his crotch. Direct contact couldn't have been better. "Good. You're getting the hang of it. Keep going."

"I held steady that time." The edge of her mouth tensed, muscles moving, and she glanced back over her shoulder. "Are you sure we don't need to talk about this?"

He turned her further with gentle pressure on her shoulders and waited. Watched her watch him until she had some iota, some notion as to his thoughts.

The way her face heated up satisfied him as nothing else could. "Are you offering to help me with this, Al?"

Her lashes fluttered – a nervous reaction. "You know I'm with him."

"Then we're not discussing it. We're doing necessary target practice so you have the required skills to help you stay alive. Understood?" In the end, he was the one who moved away. It was simpler.

For now.

"I'm sorry. I don't want to hurt you," she said. Because she didn't understand a single thing. She turned on her knees to face him, and her gaze shifted to where Daniel lay in the corner, apparently oblivious.

It took everything in him not to grab her, make her look at him. He shoved his hands in his pockets for safety's sake.

"I'm not hurt. I'm horny," he explained. Maybe the tone edged toward patronizing, but bad luck. "Two different things."

"I'm aware of that." She gave a frustrated growl. He did his best to ignore it. Him and his dick both. "Why are you trying to piss me off? Why can't we just have this conversation and clear the air?"

"Because, Al. We. Are. Not. Fucking. Understand?" He resisted the urge to shove a hand through his hair. Or hers. "Nothing is going on between us. Therefore, we don't need to have these kinds of discussions."

She stared at him, her brow channeled and lips tight.

"Okay? Can we just let it go for now, please?" He waited.

"Alright." Her gaze dropped to his groin, danced off him and plummeted to the ground. There it steadfastly remained. "Thanks for the practice."

"It needs to be a regular thing."

"Sure." Al turned away, concentrated on a huntsman spider making steady progress up the wall. She shook her head like she was shaking off an errant thought. "There are going to be other females out there, Finn."

"Al ..."

Other females weren't his problem. She was. He stared and her face blossomed into color. He almost felt bad for making her so uncomfortable. Then again, she did have a charming tendency to blush at next to nothing.

Ridiculously, he welcomed any reaction from the woman. He couldn't take his eyes off her and those twin spots of red sitting high on her cheeks. They'd be warm to the touch. Fiery hot and flushed with blood. He knew the feeling.

Daniel cleared his throat and drew up his foot in the corner, watched them both through a slit of an eye. "Give him the 'I'm not the only untainted vagina in the country' speech. That'll put him in his place."

Al glared back. "If you're finished napping, we need to move on."

"Yes ma'am."

"Wait. I've been thinking," Finn announced, amused to see Al's head whip up at the declaration. Startled eyes searched his face, proving she was still thinking about sex. Which made him curious, but they didn't have the time. "We keep running and sooner or later we're going to start making mistakes. We're going to get cornered."

Dan's gaze had been light, sleepy, but now he snapped to attention, face serious. "How many of them do you think there are?"

"Group was ten strong when they came in. After the losses they took in the supermarket, I'm guessing they're down to six," Finn said. "Enough to keep us pinned down for the foreseeable future."

The man nodded. "Alright. How do you want to do this?"

"One at a time and very, very quietly." Finn rested back on his heels, pleased there wasn't a pissing contest looming. At least not today. "We need to corner them, draw them in."

"Sounds dangerous." Al gestured with the pistol again and, loaded or not, he snatched it off her on principle.

"If you need to talk with your hands then do it without a gun in them," Finn said.

Al opened her mouth, paused and rethought whatever words she had been going to lob his way. "Sorry. You know, I could play bait. That would work. Get them off the motorbike ..."

"No," said Daniel.

"It would work," Finn confirmed, much to Dan's displeasure. The man's fingers flexed like he was warming them up, readying for a fight. "We do have to get them off the bikes, you're right about that. But they'd never believe you would be on your own."

The big guy's frown morphed into a grin. "You suggesting I play bait, kid? Keep this up and I'm going to start thinking you're trying to get rid of me or something."

"Neither of us want her hurt," Finn answered without hesitation.

"True."

"But we need to get the upper hand in this situation."

"True again."

"Dan, I won't let anyone touch her. That's not going to happen."

"Serve and protect, hmm?"

"What are you two on about?" Al barked, voice strained. "You're not bulletproof, Daniel. You're not doing it on your own."

"Neither are you, Al." Finn rubbed the pad of his thumb against the side of her gun. "Neither am I for that matter. However, I think we can safely assume they still want you alive so they're going to hesitate to shoot ... at least at first. Dan's covered you bodily before so they'll be comfortable with that scenario. They'll be expecting me to put in an appearance but it can't be helped. If we don't give them time to think, it won't be a problem. You show your face then dart for cover, that's all," said Finn. "Lure them in one at a time. I'll deal with them. It's a viable plan. Probably the best we've got."

"We should take turns at jumping them," Daniel said.

Finn shook his head. "No offense, but it's better if I take care of it."

The man gave a reluctant nod.

"They'll figure out what we're doing. There's ..." Al's hands fluttered about. "No. They don't know Dan survived yesterday. If we do this then I'll be the bait on my own. The less people at risk the better. It's bad enough Finn could get hurt."

"It's too dangerous, and worrying about you would split my focus," said Finn. "I want to know someone's watching out for you. We only need to take out a few to even the odds. To my mind it's worth the risk."

"I agree," said Daniel.

"I don't." Her eyes cut to the doorway. "Finn—"

"Enough." The big man cleared his throat and sat up like an Indian Chief, cross legged with his palms on his knees. "No God damn way you're doing it on your own, sweetie pie. It's against my better judgment to even have you involved. So, you're going to be a good girl and stay behind me or I'll get Commando Kid here to bind and gag you while I play lure. You know, I've got this funny feeling he'd jump at the chance. I think he enjoys being in control."

Finn did his best to confirm nothing with a smile.

"Babe?" Dan reached out a hand to her, but she made no move to take it. After a long moment, the big guy let his hand drop back to his knee. "You won't even chip a nail, pretty girl. I promise."

She stared at his hand. "Not funny, Dan."

"Not meant to be, honey. You gonna play nice for us?"

"I don't have much choice."

"That's true, Al," Finn said. "You really don't."

An expression promising all sorts of pain turned Finn's way. He was past being concerned that he liked it. Her attention was its own reward.

"You know, you're growing on me, kid." The big man beamed. "So, now that we're all in agreement, where do you want to set it up?"

CHAPTER TWENTY-TWO

Outside, no one commented on the lack of rain. Daniel had never been so irritated to see blue sky. Fires would be raging in no time.

This particular house and garage sat side by side, a clear view to the street. The garage door was pulled up and Finn waited within, tucked away out of sight. Daniel and Ali lurked in the slim corridor between the two buildings, waiting on their prey to come find them.

The tension wasn't only getting to him. His girl stood beside, and ever so slightly behind him, tapping the barrel of her gun against her leg. Tap, tap, tap. In time to some beat playing out in her head. Finn had dealt her and the weapon one sharp glance then let it go. It was probably for the best.

He had a feeling they might have used up their cooperation points for the day. Dan did, however, find it interesting the way her gaze kept returning to the other man. Very interesting.

There was a body or two close by. The smell of rotting flesh permeated the air. Nothing quite compared to it, especially when you knew the remains used to be people.

Finn turned, glanced back at them as the sound of a motorbike drew closer and closer. Checking they were still with him. Dan gave him a nod.

A big shiny Harley idled along, slowly moving up the block toward them. The bastard rode one-handed, fussing with something, not watching where he was going.

The kid was about to signal when glass shattered down the street. There was the "whoosh" of a Molotov being thrown, the crackle and pop of the fire gaining momentum. Next came the scent of petrol and the sight of smoke billowing into the air. Damn but the smell had reached them fast. It made Dan's stomach lurch. Things were moving in their direction.

Finn motioned them forward while he himself moved back, blending into the shadows of the garage, out of sight.

It flowed fast then.

His girl took three fast steps forward, planting herself out in plain sight. The biker was so surprised to spot his quarry standing out on the front lawn, he came close to stacking his big ride.

Daniel grabbed Ali from behind, lugged her back into the gap between the buildings. The chopper lurched up onto the grass to follow. Had the dickhead gone for less chrome he might have succeeded but, having chosen to be a showy fuck, there would be no joy. He couldn't follow them on those wheels into the tight space.

Finn slunk out of the shadows with a knife in hand.

The motorbike stalled, and the dickhead yelled something nasty. Dan hustled his girl down the corridor, getting her away from the action.

The dickhead's greetings died as Finn pounced. That should have been the end of the story.

"Come on." He grabbed Ali, tried to move her along as per the plan. They were meant to get behind the house and keep their heads down. Meant to keep out of the way. But no, she pulled at his grip and dug her heels into the stony ground, sunk her fingers into his arm. "You don't need to see this, babe."

"Wait. We're not leaving him on his own."

"Babe. Don't." There was a grunt and a groan and some blood-curdling gurgling going on behind them. Her breath caught, and her body jerked against him. He held her tight, swearing all the while. "Finn can look after himself. Will you not watch, please?"

"Dan ..." She shook her head and actually fought his hold when he tried to walk her back. Which hurt. He kept his arms around her waist as the whole grisly scene played out on the front lawn.

It was probably swift. The kid was good at what he did. Still, it seemed to take forever.

Eventually her nails released him. "It's done. He's finished."

The gravel lining the walkway crunched as Finn came their way. Dan didn't bother to turn. He had seen enough blood splatter, and Ali was doing enough watching for the two of them.

"What are you doing here?" Finn asked, as well he might.

Ali tensed, pressed herself into Daniel as if she needed shelter. Who knew what looks were being passed behind his back. Doubtless, not good.

"Waiting for you," she said.

"We had a plan," the kid said.

His girl said nothing.

"Is there a problem, Al?" the kid asked in a quiet voice.

There was a definite delay to her answer. "No."

A low moaning started up nearby, the kind of noise only an infected made. She pulled back and Dan let her go.

And no, Finn was not happy, features so strained his jaw looked disjointed. His girl's expression was of a similar ilk but her eyes were two times wider. Spooked. Big time.

Across the street a zombie crawled out from beneath a parked car, one leg mangled. Its fingers were no better than bloody stumps. It began to make its way across the street toward the fresh kill.

Unlike his girl, he didn't mean to see the dickhead's remains.

His throat gone, the surrounding grass glossy with blood. The kid was lethal. And there wasn't a drop of gore on the blonde-haired bastard outside of his hands, but they dripped with it.

Ali took a step back from both Finn and the zombie. It was a move hard to miss.

"We better go," she said.

***

"I love you like the sun loves the soil," said Daniel.

His girl turned her head toward him, eyes somber in the darkness. Which worked. It was a somber kind of night.

They had hidden in a house. Finn, crouched in the front room, kept watch through the remains of a front door. Someone had decided to rip the door off its hinges, and the gaping hole could be seen from the street. No one would settle down for the night in a place with no door. In turn, no foe, infected or otherwise, would come close without them knowing.

Another canny idea from the kid.

The second feature of the night's shelter was the body decomposing in the tub. Not infected, the kid had reported. The person had chosen to slit their wrists and bleed out. Morbid, but Daniel could almost understand. The place reeked of death. Infected wouldn't to be able to easily detect their live, uninfected flesh.

There'd be no bedding down for good times tonight. The dickheads were well and truly stirred up. Gunshots regularly scattered the quiet as they revved their big bikes up and down the streets. Finn had only managed to dispatch one of the gang, but it was sufficient to get their attention. Nearby, fires raged, filling the air with smoke. The idiots might yet end up toasting themselves along with their quarry.

Outside, the wind was blowing like crazy and there was an electric buzz in the air. Hopefully the storm would hit soon and douse the flames. God, Daniel hoped it would. Something had to go their way, for once.

"I love you like the moon loves the stars," he said.

She cuddled in closer.

"I love you like the fishes love the sea," he said.

"Hmm." His girl gave a tired little smile, leant her head on his shoulder. "Do the fishes love the sea?"

"They would be screwed if they didn't, my love."

She sighed. "True. Where are you going with this, Daniel?"

He smooched the top of her head, rubbed his cheek against it. The softest silk had nothing on his girl. "Well, because I have this great love for you, I feel compelled to confide in you when you are behaving like an ass."

Her head fell back, and a hurt look flashed, then faded. If anything, she looked a little defeated. Lovely lips turned down at the corners and sadness filled her eyes. "You mean Finn." She didn't move away and didn't proceed to rip him a new one. It told Daniel much. "Yes, Finn. You're not being fair, baby."

"I know." Ali huddled against him. "The way he just ... I mean .. He didn't even blink. Just killed that guy."

And as much as he would have wished to protect her from all sorts of stuff, protecting her from this would not be to her benefit. Not in the least. The brave new world required skills just like the kid's. His girl needed Finn more than she needed her pride or her delicate sensibilities. Jealousy niggled at Daniel but he pushed it aside.

"Shit, Daniel," she said.

"So, you're worried someone you know and possibly have feelings for could kill like that?" he offered, finishing the sentence.

"I guess. I don't know. Shit. Shit. Shit." There followed further heartfelt sighs. And he couldn't have fixed this one for her even if he wanted to. Which he didn't.

"You should never have started up about the three of us," she grumbled. "I am not equipped to handle this crap."

"I disagree."

Her dark eyes honed in on him. "Why are you pushing for this? Really?"

"I want you to be happy. Also, I want you to be safe."

"You want him to protect me. That's using him, Daniel."

He made a noise of disapproval despite her being spot the fuck on. Sometimes survival came first. Actually, always survival came first. "He's already protecting you. He chose to protect you."

"Be honest."

"Babe, I'm open to the idea of sharing you. Okay? And the fact is, there's something between you and Finn. Now there's a damn good chance the three of us are going to be sticking together for the long haul, so ignoring it is plain dumb. This is my reasoning." He patted her on the head and gave her a smile, one that he hoped conveyed more love than sales tactics. "But yes, his ability to protect you has been noted. With the world the way it is these days, how could it not be?"

Al's mouth widened in a pained expression, her lips thinning. "I get why you might think this is a good idea, Dan. I do. Did it ever occur to you that pushing me in this direction might screw things up spectacularly between all of us?"

Yes, it had occurred to him, and fuck he hoped not. Sincerely to the bottom of his soul.

Dan set his chin on her crown, caught one of the hands fiddling with the seam of her jeans and held on tight. "Okay. Let's focus here. Finn acted today to protect you. He risked his life and what he did was for you. He does not deserve to reap your shit for his efforts, babe. No matter where you are on the you and him getting together front, okay?"

She said nothing.

"Leave it for now. Why don't you sleep on it?"

She snorted. "Right. Sleep." There followed a long pause. He could almost hear the cogs turning in her overactive mind. "I know he killed for me, and I know I'm not being fair. I just ... I don't know how to do this."

"Do what?"

"Feel this way ... Twisted. Confused."

He deposited another kiss on the crown of her head. "Let it go for now. Give yourself a chance to get your head around it. You know, I have every faith in your good judgment."

"Right," his girl murmured. "You think fishes love the sea."

Thus began one of the longest nights of his life.

The fires crept closer until a reluctant drizzle arrived. The air filled with smoke and steam and the scent of damp ashes. The rain made listening to the night much harder.

No one slept.

Dawn was a curiously quiet thing. No birds. No bike engines. Nothing. After all the chaos and commotion of the last few days, it was downright creepy.

Finn wandered over and hunched down in front of them, staring straight at his girl, who was studying the doorway over the kid's right shoulder.

"We should move," Ali murmured. The shadows beneath her eyes were as bad as the bruise on her face. They were all well on their way toward wretched. "Maybe they passed out."

"Maybe. Or it could be a trap," Finn said. "We need to be careful."

"Everything could be a trap," Dan said. That they might not survive the next fuck up was best left unsaid. "Yesterday's plan is still on."

The kid continued to watch his girl with a steady gaze. "Alright, the vote is in. Let's find another place to stage it."

Progress was slow. Daniel had a bad feeling the end was approaching, for better or for worse. More skulking between flat, squat, square brick housing, doing their best to avoid high fences and dead ends as Finn turned down site after site to set the trap.

Delaying.

Who could blame him? Who knew how his girl would react the next time Finn had to kill?

The sudden wailing cut the air. It came from close by. They all dropped low, grasping their guns. They heard another long, pain-filled howl. It sounded solely of loss and anger. There had been a lot of it in the weeks after the sickness first hit, when people were dropping like stones.

He locked his hand around his girl's wrist. Finn led them forward, over a buckled wire fence and into another overgrown backyard.

"Wait here," the kid ordered.

Ali's chin jumped up, and she shook her head. "No. We stay together."

Finn took a step toward her.

"We stay together," his girl reiterated.

The kid turned to him for backup. He just shook his head, wondering what came next.

The sound, shit, it had rattled him. Had rattled all of them, but Finn was still waiting. Problem was, he understood. He couldn't let either of them out of sight. Fuck knew what would happen next. "What she said."

Finn bared his teeth but they went forward.

A lone man was crouched over a massacre. Or the remains of one.

Trickles of blood stained brown ran across the twin lines of concrete leading out to the road, and it was black where it had soaked into the earth. Shreds of bloody clothing lay scattered here and there. People had been torn apart every which way. There was the odd shard of white bone sticking out of drying chunks of flesh. Half a rib cage lay tossed aside. God knew how many people had been butchered. Breakfast tossed about in his belly, wanting out, but his throat had shut up shop. He could barely fucking breathe. A lot of blood and unidentifiable chunks of who knew what? There was a sick fascination to it. Even Finn seemed stunned, hovering on the edges. One of the dickheads was making the racket, identifiable by the leather biker vest he sported. A couple of choppers lay tipped over nearby, chrome shining bright in the morning sun.

The man cried so loud he hadn't heard them coming, didn't notice them there. Yet.

Too late, Daniel tried to grab her, hold her back. Her mouth opened. "Oh ... God."

The biker raised his head, face red from all the caterwauling.

"Dead. They're all ..." With a rumble of a noise he raised the gun and pointed it at Ali. "You did this."

Finn's bullets hit him at the same time as Daniel's. They minced the man's chest, leather and blood and meat. The bastard toppled backward, his bullets flying wild over their heads. Daniel felt one trim his hair. He hadn't even thought to duck. He had, however, made his girl do so by pushing her down.

Ali knelt on the grass beside him. His hand had wrapped around the back of her neck, her skin bleached next to where his fingers gripped. She had nearly been killed. His pulse pounded through his ears. Nothing seemed real.

"Dan." Finn stepped closer, face calm. "Let her go. It's okay. He's dead."

Daniel blinked at the kid, waited for the words to hit him from a long way away. His hand remained wrapped around her neck, fingers set. He had given her more bruises. Shit.

Dan looked up and the kid nodded.

Slowly, he pried his fingers loose. "Sorry."

"S'okay." His girl put a hand to her neck, rubbing tentatively. The kid pulled her to her feet, dusted her off. "It's fine. Really. That was close." Her gaze found the dead body, the man's chest laid open.

"Babe ..."

Ali held a hand up, tottered a couple of steps sideways. She turned, bent at the waist and lost the half a muesli bar from breakfast.

Dan's stomach pitched in empathy. The hand remained up, and she remained over.

Impossible to tell how many bodies had been involved out of the few remains left. Finn hunkered down, inspected what had to be a part of someone's leg, going by the thickness of the bone. "An animal did this. Or a pack of them."

Daniel swallowed back bile, stared into the sky till the shit in his head calmed down to a dull roar. "Sure it wasn't infected?"

The kid cocked his head, inspecting the scene, doing his job. And he was so cool about it. So matter of fact. Dan could almost sympathize with his girl's freak-out over Finn.

"No. Not with teeth marks like this," Finn said. Then his gaze moved to the figure behind Dan. He stood, reached for the bottle of water in his pack. "She'll want this. We need to find a car, move on. What the hell could have done this?"

CHAPTER TWENTY-THREE

Al and Daniel needed time alone. Finn knew this, understood it. Didn't mean he had to like it. Even with things the way they were between him and Al, he didn't want her out of his sight. It fucked with his head just a little.

They had driven for hours, putting a good distance between them and that scene. Found a small country town to hole up in for the night. As exhausted as they were, they needed to shore up and stock up. Finn could have slept for a month. Yawning and rubbing his eyes became second nature.

Which went nowhere toward explaining why he was out doing the shopping while they played.

Screwed around. Fucked. Frolicked. Whatever.

Poor him, left out in the cold on a hot summer's day. Or afternoon, as it was. Jealousy made a poor companion.

The sun was sliding into the horizon, the light in the small general store growing dim. He should pay attention.

Finn had left them to fortify the chosen abode, amongst other activities. He tried not to ponder those other activities.

Sadly, he sucked at it.

The place they had chosen was a detached concrete granny flat with one bedroom, one bathroom and an attempt at a kitchen. Someone had hated granny. But, small windows and one door made it simple to lock down.

Maybe they'd spend a few days, take the time to lick their wounds.

Lick was a bad word, a word to steer clear of.

Same went for suck, which rhymed with fuck and led nowhere good at all.

He scrubbed his face with a hand, took a deep breath.

Finn grabbed a spare shirt and a few other goodies. He set off for the flat as the sun sank low and the violet of evening set in. His heavy pack aggravated his shoulder, but it was full of the required supplies.

Moaning started in the west. Something close answered the call. He picked up the pace, put his gun in hand. The first star twinkled overhead. Shit. Where the hell was his head at?

He had taken too long. Been careless.

He was sprinting by the time he turned onto the rutted gravel lane leading toward home. The pack bounced about on his back, which the gunshot wound did not appreciate. He hadn't secured the pack properly, not for this. So careless.

There were noises behind him, back at the corner.

He kicked up dust as he pounded down the dirt driveway, along the side of the house and through a hastily thrown-open doorway.

Someone had been watching for him. What a feeling. Home. Safety.

The door slammed shut and the lock was thrown behind him.

Finn dropped to his knees, eased the pack off slowly. His shoulder throbbed in time with his heart.

"What the fuck were you doing?" He glanced up to find Al towering, hands on hips. Her was a flat, unhappy line. Fury radiated from her. "It's nearly full dark. What were you thinking?"

Finn just blinked at her, stunned.

Dan gave him a careless shrug. The big man lounged on the couch, feet crossed at the ankles. And not that Finn wouldn't do similar should their roles be reversed, but good God, what an asshole.

Actually, what bullshit. Finn would have tried to talk her down and assured her everything was fine, when time and again it clearly wasn't. That was about when he realized this situation wasn't working. Not for him.

And it if wasn't working then it was time to fix it.

"I was worried about you. You were gone for hours. It's dark outside, Finn. You could have been hurt. Or killed. Did you even think of that?" She stood taller than a tower, righteous indignation blazing in her eyes. "What the fuck were you doing that was so important it was worth risking your life for? Well?"

Normally, he would never have stuck around for shit like this, but from her ... a large part of him loved it. Her going toe-to-toe with him, taking him on. She did the same with Daniel, and Finn wanted in. The fishwife tone was even worryingly endearing. All of this, however, did not mean she was getting away with it.

"I was getting supplies, Al, just like I said I would," he said lightly. "What's the problem here?"

The woman slammed her lips shut and crossed her arms over her heaving breasts. The same ones he was developing a serious fixation on. He had found her a t-shirt a size too small, solely for the chance to magnify those babies. He'd feed her some bullshit about the lack of appropriate sizing, not much caring if she believed him. The shirt would be worn because the current one was trashed.

Some things in life were simple. But this was not.

"I thought you'd appreciate some private time with Dan. Did I get that wrong?" he continued, nice and calm, keeping everything off his face. Unlike her. Frustration poured off her in waves. There were red spots high on her cheeks. She was flammable. "What do you want?"

Her gaze fled to Daniel, her safety blanket. Of course. Finn almost groaned in frustration.

But the odds were, the man wasn't going to interfere, not with this. After a long moment, she reached the same conclusion. Her shoulders sloped and the gray of her eyes brightened as if in disbelief.

"What do you want from me, Al?"

She watched her boot toe at the carpet, rubbing at the gnarled pile. A large part of her bravado appeared to have fled. "Finn ..."

"No excuses. What do you want?"

Her gaze lifted at his harsh tone. She looked stricken. "Finn ..."

He didn't know where she was going with pleading his name, but it didn't matter. He was done with it. "No."

He took the irrevocable step forward till they really were toe-to-toe, cradled her face in his hands. Ignoring the flinch, the way her mouth snapped shut. "No, Al. We're not doing this anymore."

Finn brushed his mouth over hers, the barest whisper of contact. Not sure if she was even breathing, her body so tense. He slid his fingers down her arms, gripped her hands and placed them right where he needed them. She shut her eyes tight, and her fingers fisted in his shirt, dragging at the bandage on his shoulder.

He didn't mind.

Their mouths were so close he could feel the warmth of her breath on his lips. He wanted to kiss her like he might die sometime soon.

Which was the truth. He might. She might. Some random act could wipe them out any day now.

Finn wasn't going out without having had her first. Not even if he had to do some pleading himself. "Say it."

She said nothing. Not a single thing.

Nothing, and then everything.

CHAPTER TWENTY-FOUR

Finn was like a giant magnet, the pull of him irresistible. Or beyond her control.

Ali clung onto his shirt and her body swayed into his.

Such a small space to cross. Miniscule, unimportant and momentous all rolled up into one.

His lips covered hers, and she opened her mouth to him. The only thing she could do.

She wanted him.

Finn kissed her till her head spun. He plundered her mouth and his hands slid through her hair, pulling lightly. He pressed his mouth against her jaw, down into the crook of her neck, breathing deep before dragging his tongue over sensitive skin, raising goose pimples.

Everything he did turned her into a weak-willed mess of a woman. A woman who had no compunction about being involved with two men at once.

"Open your eyes," he murmured in her ear, teeth sinking into the lobe in a sweet sting of a bite. He made it all so good. Her body was buzzing, heat taking her over. This was actually going to happen. The knowledge made her giddy. "Say it. Tell me what you want."

With complete honesty, she told him. "I want you."

"You want him too," said Finn. He looked at Dan. The hands threaded into her hair, cupping her head, prevented her from following suit. "No. Answer me."

She wasn't going to lie to him now, but her response took a while. Some things were hard to own up to, suburban middle-class background notwithstanding. "Yes."

"He's right. You are greedy." Finn tucked her in against his neck, the scent of him perfect. Warm and heady and all male, her fingers pawed at him, wanting in. And yet, there was something going on behind her back, some communication passing between Dan and Finn. The hands fisted in her hair weren't permitting her to see.

"Finn." She pushed against the wall of his chest, and the fingers in her hair tightened as he rubbed his cheek against hers like a big cat. The tenderness in direct contrast to the hold he had on her hair. The whole thing working far too well. "Finn, what's going on?"

"I think our boy has a point to prove," Daniel provided when it became obvious Finn wasn't going to. "He shouldn't worry so much. There will be times when I'm not in the mood for sharing either."

Finn's sighed. "Tell me this isn't just a one off, Al."

"No." Hard to tell if it was a question or statement but Ali shook her head, as far as his grip allowed. Her body wanted him, but so did her heart. "It's not."

Finn's grip on her eased at those words and his fingers rubbed at her scalp, soothing instead of inciting. He winced as his shoulders rose on some great intake of air, like he had been deep underwater and had surfaced. He eased back. She could only stare at him, the light green of his eyes much darker now than normal. There was an edge of desperation, a sense of being lost. Two emotions she knew intimately. Her heart ached for him.

"Good," he said.

But then Finn returned his attention to Dan. The pissing contest going on behind her back needed to stop. The air was getting thin. She was nervous enough already.

Daniel had made his decision. Finn had made his. Last, if not least, she had made hers. No going back now.

Ali reached up to press her lips to Finn's, snagging his attention. She opened her lips, sliding her tongue into his mouth, slipping past teeth, taking it slow. Seducing him.

Finn coaxed her mouth open wider and took over. He didn't ease into it. Daniel had warned her. Finn enjoyed being in control.

His hands held her, keeping her where he wanted her. Giving and taking. Where Daniel played, Finn took. Both ways apparently worked for her.

The low ache in her belly escalated, flooding her pussy and curling her toes. She could feel him hard and ready against her, making her all the more excited. She wanted to climb him like a tree, wrap her body around him and not let go. Her legs trembled and every nerve in her seemed set alight.

He kissed her long and deep, teasing her mouth with his own. He drugged her more effectively than any chemical. It was a little scary to react to him this strong and fast, the same way she did to Daniel.

It proved all the worst things she had imagined about herself. Someone needed to run her out of town, pin a nice big red "A" on her chest. Pity the only two people around to see it seemed to be encouraging the behavior.

Ali couldn't get close enough, fast enough. Her hands roamed far and wide over smooth hot skin. It was hard to remember to be wary of his shoulder. His mouth slid over her jaw line, nipped at her ear. The pinch of his teeth sent a shudder down her spine and a gasp from her mouth. Her cunt ached.

There hadn't been any conscious thought about climbing him bodily, but she obviously had been. And he came to her aid.

"Come here." His hands cupped her ass and lifted, and her legs wrapped around his hips. Finn pushed off from the door, staggering toward the small bedroom with her wrapped around him, strangler-vine style. She looked over his shoulder, holding on tight.

On the couch, Daniel watched with his hands behind his head. Her boyfriend. Her man. Holy shit. He gave a small self-satisfied smile right before Finn kicked the bedroom door closed behind them.

What did that smile mean? Guilt slid over her like a second skin. Lust kicked hard in her belly, and it slipped straight off.

Finn laid her out on the bed, loomed tall above her. A lantern she had found beneath the kitchen sink sat glowing on the bedside table. It was good not to be in the dark, very good to be able to see him. The shadows on his beautiful face made him appear all the more menacing as he scowled down at her.

"No going back," Finn warned in a voice she hadn't heard before. It sounded low, rough and thrilling. He took hold of one of her boots, dealt with it swiftly before starting in on the other. "Undo your jeans."

Her fingers fumbled on the button and zipper. "What about you?"

"Soon." Finn put a knee on the mattress, leant over and sped up the process, peeling her jeans off her legs. He hooked his thumbs into the sides of her panties and pulled. The feral grin he gave as he stripped her underwear down had her heart tripping in her chest. "These are wet."

"You have that effect."

"Good to know."

Ali leant back on her elbows. Finn folded her underwear and tucked them in his back jeans pocket.

"Those are the only pair I have, Finn."

"I'll get you more." He sunk down onto his knees on the carpet at the foot of the bed, pried her legs open with gentle hands. The reverence of his gaze as he stared at her sex caused her mouth to go dry. If he hadn't been holding her legs open she'd have snapped them shut in a fit of nerves.

"Closer," he urged, wrapping his hands around her hips to drag her toward him. "A bit more."

Firm hands slid down, the rough tips of his fingers smoothed over her inner thighs, tracing lightly over her skin, getting goose pimples raging. His warm breath fevered her skin. She just about jumped when a fingertip traveled the seam between her pussy and thigh. Her shoulders shook and there was a noise in her throat, fighting for release.

It all grew out of control the longer he studied her. The more he touched her.

This was going to kill her.

When Finn's mouth touched her sex, she sagged with relief. Her back hit the mattress and her whole body shook. She would have liked to watch him, but maybe next time. There had to be a next time, because the tongue swiping through her was heaven-sent and blessed from on high. It felt of sweet deliverance making everything right.

His firm lips rubbed and his tongue tickled and teased. Swift swipes followed by a long, lazy wander from the flat of his tongue through slick flesh. She didn't know what she was going to get. What he would give. He drove her steadily toward the edge. He suckled her lips, fingers pressing hard into her thighs, keeping her legs spread wide.

Her back arched and her body hummed.

"God. Finn." Nothing else existed outside of the way he was making her feel. The pleasure he inflicted.

When he restricted his oral worship to her clit she was done for.

"Oh ... GoddammitFinnyes." White lightning struck behind her eyelids and her back bowed. The muscles in her legs pulled taught and her heart punched at her rib cage. Bones were surely broken. She pushed her pussy into his face, all sense of shame long gone.

Ali came and came, body shaking and shivering as he eased her down. His mouth stayed on her till the last, hands holding her tight. She drifted till the strong hands gripped her hips and thumbs stroked over her skin.

His low, rough voice called her back.

"Roll over, Al. I want you on all fours. I want to fuck you from behind," he said. She was well and truly back in her happy place with the erotic image planted in her mind. "Can you do that for me?"

"Yes." She nodded and rolled her lax body, pulled herself up onto hands and knees. Muscles turned to liquid trembled, but determination won through. She felt exposed, putting herself in his hands. Anxiety spread through her at not being able to see him. But wasn't it always this way with sex? The trust involved. The desire to please. To be pleased in turn.

Considering he had so recently been up close and personal with her privates, it was foolish to worry, but it lingered nonetheless. A tiny mirror above the bed provided few clues as he stared at her with intent.

His hands positioned her just so, toes hanging off the end of the bed. The clink of his belt buckle. The small sounds of him undressing. A condom wrapper ripped open. Then his hands were back on her, fingers kneading her ass just hard enough to leave a mark. Which was exactly what she wanted.

"I think you can get louder." His cockhead brushed against the swollen lips of her pussy and a shiver shot through her.

This was it. He parted her and pushed, entering her slow but sure, not stopping till he was seated fully inside. Until she was full of him.

Finn groaned, long and low. She could have sworn it carried straight through him and on into her. "Al?"

Took her a while to recall a question had been asked. And how was she supposed to converse, with his cock buried deep inside?

Her mind was mud, every thought focused on the feel of him. "Ahh, maybe."

"Hmm." His hands soothed down her sides as he ground himself against her. The light scratch of his pubic hair and the heat of him against her thighs and ass, so primal. "Al. Are you with me?"

"Yes." She tensed around him, testing the feel of his cock inside her. Deliciously good. Her whole body felt alive with him. "Please, Finn. Fuck me."

"Yesss." His voice was victorious as he pulled out slowly, his cock dragging over places inside, bringing her back to life. Then he pushed in. Then he pulled out.

Over and over, fucking her slow and sure. Working her. The pace coldly calculated. Every move controlled. Something was wrong.

"Finn, wait ..."

Beads of sweat struck her back and he continued his game.

The tension built but it was wrong. Wasn't what she wanted. Mindless passion, losing themselves in each other ... yes. Which would have been honest. But no, he had shut her out.

And it felt a lot like he was proving a point in here with her much like he had out there with Dan.

If it wasn't so good she would have throttled him.

There was nothing wrong with his sexual technique. Over and over he fucked himself into her, saccharine sweet and mechanically slow. His thrusts timed like a metronome kept pace. He had closed himself off completely.

She could hear his belabored breathing. Feel the tension in his hands, shaking and gripping her hips. This was taking its toll. "Finn. Please. Stop."

"You don't like this?" he asked. A hand settled onto the mattress beside her. He leant over, reached beneath to slip his fingers over her mound, in pursuit of her clit, of course. "I think you like this. You're going to come again for me. Then we'll get to work on number three."

The strength left her arms as he found the tight bundle of nerves and stroked. Her body shook as the orgasm stole over her. Stars. Sunbursts. The whole setting sun. "Oh God. Finn."

The bed cushioned her cheek, as her lungs fought for air. Her eyes were full to brimming with scalding hot tears. Seizures still racked her when she gave in and asked, "Are you finished?"

The man behind her stilled, his cock still buried in her.

"What?"

"You heard me," she said.

He pulled out of her and the loss was devastating. Everything was cold and empty.

"What the fuck is your problem?" Finn's voice was quiet and cold with anger.

Ali turned over, legs locked. Finn's cock was hard, his hair disheveled. He was so beautiful it hurt, and she hadn't even gotten to touch him.

She sat up straight, tucked her feet beneath her. Faked the dignity sorely lacking. What was even happening here?

"Good question," she muttered.

"I just made you come. Twice." He waved two fingers in her face in case she needed the visual aid. "Twice, Al."

"Because it's a competition. Right? We really need a scoreboard in here, don't we?"

Finn shoved a hand through his blonde hair, his mouth a strict line. "Al ..."

"Are you finished proving whatever you felt you needed to?" The first tear spilled onto her cheek, and she hated herself for it. She wanted to yell with frustration, batter at him with her fists like he was a locked door. "That's what I meant, Finn."

He stood at the foot of the bed, his eyes stunned, horrified. He looked at her like they were strangers. Of course they were, really, weren't they?

She had been stupid. Breathtakingly dumb to have thought this meant something. It was almost funny, to be making this mistake. She was too old for this shit. Crying was for pussies. Making a mess of herself served no purpose at all. Now was the time to toughen up.

"Remove the condom. I'll finish you off," she said, just wanting it done.

He flinched like she had hit him, green eyes locked on the latest dumbass tear trailing down her cheek.

"Sorry 'bout that." Ali flicked off the offending tear with her fingers, forced herself to face him. Still beautiful. The whole situation still wrong. "Well, are you —"

He grabbed her without warning, hauling her up onto her knees. Shock held her rigid. His mouth slammed down on hers, and his tongue forced its way inside. Forced a reaction from her.

She thought briefly about biting the bastard. There was no doubt he deserved it. But she couldn't. Because she was stupid. Clearly. Instead she found herself kissing him back, holding onto him as hard and tight as he did to her.

Both of them desperate.

"I'm sorry, Al." Her name was an agonized groan as he dragged his mouth over her cheek. His arms around her so tight her ribs creaked. "So sorry."

"Okay. It's okay, Finn."

"No." He wrapped an arm beneath her butt, one around her back, and lifted, taking her back down into the middle of the mattress with him above her. The weight of him pressed her down, and her legs wrapped around him, her hips cradling him. "No, it's not. I want you so much."

"You have me." She slicked her fingers over his back, comforting him. "I'm right here."

"With conditions." Face against her neck, his teeth sank into her. The sting of it had her body bucking beneath him, her pelvis pushing. He was still hard, amazingly enough.

"Yes." And she wanted him worse than ever. She still wasn't going to lie. "With conditions."

Finn drew back, up onto his elbows, and studied her hungrily. Her neck stung, her body ached and she still couldn't read him for shit. Whatever was going on in his head, she remained out. It nearly started the tears again.

"Don't," he said.

"Don't what?" she asked.

"Don't cry. Shit. Don't." His hand slid between their bodies as his mouth slid over hers. Sweet and hungry and perfect.

The press of his cock against her pussy seemed natural and right. She canted her hips, tightened the pull of her legs around his waist. The head of his cock nudged her entrance and his hand guided it back into her. They both panted.

Finn stared at her. She followed suit, watching the pleasure take him. The tongue swiping out over his lips and the clench of his teeth. He started slow but it didn't last. Long, satisfying slides of his cock inside her made everything right. His strokes grew harder and faster. He held nothing back this time.

Not performing.

Blonde hair clung to his forehead and the pale green of his eyes seemed swallowed by black. He was beautiful. So fucking beautiful she didn't know what to do.

He took possession of her hands, first one and then the other, pinned both of her wrists to the mattress above her head. Her rib cage tilted, her back arched. Her nipples scraped against his chest as he moved, sending sparks of pleasure through her.

The feel of him all over her was deliriously good. Him moving inside her, building the hot and brilliant sensation. The tension running through him, making him shake, took hold of her too. But nothing compared to the surge she got from watching him. He was exquisite.

Finn dropped his head and his teeth found the place on her neck he had made his own. He came, body shuddering above and inside her.

She didn't feel the least bit alone.

CHAPTER TWENTY-FIVE

A line of smoke rose into the blue sky, cutting the horizon neatly in half.

Finn sat on the front step and watched the world wake, enjoying the birds singing and the sun rising. He felt happy, relaxed. But then the smoke snapped him to attention.

What signal was it sending, good or bad? Distances could be deceiving, but he didn't think it was more than an hour away. Perhaps less.

"Hey." Dan stomped out onto the concrete and tipped his chin at him. "Ready to move on?" And for a second, just a second, Finn thought he was being given his marching orders.

"Is that smoke?" Dan asked.

Finn cleared his throat, shook himself free of the flash of panic. Neurotic idiot. "Yeah. I thought we should check it out."

Al wandered out with two cups of coffee in hand, and passed one down to him. He overreached on purpose, letting his fingers slide over hers as he took the cup. He wanted to touch her. Resisting those impulses hadn't gotten him anywhere, so why fight it?

"Thanks," he said.

"You're welcome." She smiled at him, and the tight knot of tension in his chest eased, unwound. Because the smile was pushing at the edges of her lovely mouth, threatening to morph into a grin, and it was just for him.

"Babe, we got smoke signals."

She raised her face to the morning sun and squinted into the distance. The bite on her neck was prominent against her pale skin. His handiwork. He couldn't help but be satisfied in some way. What a lie. His face hurt from smiling. They'd woken wrapped around each other and taken their time leaving the bed. Then she'd gone to talk to Dan and Finn had given them space. Making the only decision he could in the circumstances, the one that would bring her back to him.

"Huh," she said, staring at the smoke.

"Huh?" the big guy enquired, slipping an arm around her waist. Finn wanted the ease of familiarity. To be able to tuck her in against him whenever the mood hit him as Dan did. Finn would have it. "Care to elaborate on that, my love?" the big guy asked.

She shrugged. "Last time we did a meet and greet it didn't work out so well."

"We'll be careful. Scout things out," said Finn, watching her carefully. "I think we need to."

Dan nodded approval. "I agree."

"Okay." The frown on her face did not lessen. Her reluctance made sense after the past few days, but they needed to know if these people were legit. If they stayed on the road they'd eventually run into trouble beyond their ability to handle. Their chances of survival were lower alone in the open.

"But you're not happy about it." Dan kissed her forehead, rested his chin atop her head. Finn had seen the man do similar a dozen times, still didn't stop a twinge of jealousy running through him. He didn't normally get territorial. Nothing about this situation was normal behavior, however.

She shrugged.

"We will be careful," said Dan.

Al forced a smile, nodded. "Yep. I know."

"Baby ..."

"No, really, it's okay. I know we need to do this, check out other people and such," she said. Al squared her shoulders, ready to fight. The way she picked herself up time and again got to him. Taking her back to bed right then was out of the question, but he wanted to, badly.

Finn watched her, sipping at his coffee. Not hot coffee, room temperature, but he would take what he could get. "Time to hit the road then."

In the end it took them forty-eight minutes to reach the fortified settlement to the north. It wasn't the Great Wall of China, but an impressive barrier stood before them all the same.

The wall consisted of everything from a string of semitrailers to a toppled freight train. Bulldozed buildings filled in gaps here and there. The barrier stood as tall as a house and surrounded the bulk of the center of Blackstone. A sign told them the town had been founded in 1875 with a population of 1150.

Finn revised the figure to approximately a hundred. Stunning, given the severity of the plague and how quickly most places had succumbed to the accompanying chaos.

They had paused at a rest stop just outside of town. He gave a low whistle and swung down from the tree limb he had perched on while Al watched on nervously. Whether she was nervous over his jump or the township, he didn't know.

"Seems they've managed to save whole families," he said. "There's a creek running along the front so they've got water. A cleared area over the other side of town, maybe a sports ground, for livestock. A few guards at the front gate, some along the wall. It's impressive, reasonably well organized."

Dan dug at his front teeth with the tip of his tongue. "Wonder what their welcome wagon's like?"

"Good question." Finn shoved the binoculars back into his pack.

"Finn, have you still got your badge?" Al enquired. The first words she had spoken since they set out.

He nodded. "I'll test the waters."

"No," she grabbed at his arm, held him in place. Her gray eyes were emphatic, deadly serious. "We go together or not at all."

Dan shot him a look, and he met it with one of his own. "Al ..."

"No. Again," she growled, "to the both of you."

"Yeah, ah ..." The big guy started, sighed and stopped. "But it is two against one, sweet. We do kind of have the majority here."

Al let Finn loose but appeared the antithesis of cooperation. Her hands rested on her hips and her mouth tightened as she looked between the two of them.

"Don't make the mistake of believing you make decisions for me, either of you." Her fingernails tapped against the butt of the gun tucked into her belt.

He knew the safety was on. He had checked it himself. Still, he wondered if the threat of her finger was real or imagined.

"I wouldn't appreciate it," she said quietly. The tapping of her nail grew louder.

Finn stepped forward. "Al, we just want you safe."

"If we misrepresent ourselves to these people they're going to mistrust us from the start. There are families in there. You said so, Finn. They're going to be cautious, not crazy," she said. It made sense but he hated the thought of taking her into the unknown. He checked out the trail behind them to hide the grimace on his face. Weighing the odds gave no comfort at all. There wouldn't be anything controlled about this situation. She could get hurt. Or, this could be their ticket back into civilization. What remained of it at least.

"Think about it," she said. "They might be less likely to send us packing if they see we're together."

The big guy nodded slowly, eyes glued to Al. "Like a family. Alright. I happen to agree with you this time. Sending the kid in on his own doesn't feel right. Shall we walk it? Might seem less aggressive, more open. Show them we come in peace."

"I hate it. Though I think it would be best." Finn nodded. "Al, if I tell you to get down at any time, you do it. No hesitation. Understand?"

She gave a tight, brief smile. "Okay."

"Okay." Finn wanted to reach out to touch her, but didn't. In all likelihood she was right. A group with a woman would seem less of a risk than a lone male. It had already been proven that women were a prized commodity. If anyone was in danger of being shot on sight, it wasn't her. "I'll lead. Stay close to Dan."

Time to go to work.

Al dragged her heels along the dusty road, kicking rocks and looking straight ahead. A recalcitrant school kid would have shown more enthusiasm. Even she, however, couldn't put off the inevitable. They were going to meet other people.

A big surly guy who most closely resembled Santa with a sniper rifle met them at the gate. The gate being a garbage truck with a few extra sheets of metal welded on. Crude, but effective.

"Weapons on the ground, nice and easy."

"That leaves us at your mercy," Finn pointed out, but laid his two pistols on the street just the same.

"You came to me, not the other way round. Therefore, we play by my rules," Santa grumped, nodding to a couple of others who emerged from the slim gap between dump truck and wall. How Santa squeezed through, Finn didn't know.

They lay down their assorted guns and knives, leaving Finn

feeling naked and vulnerable in the hot morning sun. His body hummed with adrenalin as he gave them an easy smile. One wrong move in Al's direction and he would end them. Her safety meant everything.

"Keep your hands out in front of you. Don't move. Where have you lot come from?" Santa motioned and his juniors came into play. Two young white males crept out and gathered up the weapons, placing them in a plastic laundry basket. They kept sneaking looks at Al, but it was more curiosity than covet, for now.

"The coast," Finn said.

Santa grunted. "We had some people come through last week from the east, sent them on their way. They didn't give me the warm fuzzies. Know what I'm saying?"

"These are dangerous days," Finn agreed. "I was a cop. I have my badge and ID in my back pocket if you want to check it out."

A black-haired junior, the one not holding the laundry basket, stepped forward and slipped the leather wallet from the back of Finn's jeans. Inspected it with care. "Could be legit, Sam."

Santa canted his head, grimaced. "Maybe. When did you three arrive in our beautiful area?"

"Just now," said Finn. "We saw smoke earlier, came to investigate."

"Sure about that? My scouts have seen some movement just outside of town the last few days. The truth would be best, son."

Finn shook his head. "Not us. We were almost an hour south this morning. First time we've been out here."

Another grunt from Santa. "Pretty girl you've got there."

"Our girl." Daniel stared the fat, round, not so jolly fellow dead in the eye.

"Known each other long?" Santa enquired.

"Long enough," said Finn.

"That so, sweetheart?" Santa's beady blues narrowed on Al. "You with them by choice or should I send these two assholes on their way? Don't be afraid. You can answer me honestly. Those bruises on your face are a concern. No one here will hurt you."

Al's chin rose as she gave Santa a faint smile. "I go where they go, by choice. But thank you for asking."

The old man nodded, as if he had expected the answer. "Which one is your man?"

There was a beat before she answered, a long, slow one, stopping his heart. Finn waited for her to deny him. Fully expected it and braced himself for the rejection. They'd slept together once. One night didn't make a relationship by anyone's standards. God knows, he'd walked away often enough without looking back.

"Both." Her tone was firm though her face pinked.

Finn couldn't hide the look of relief.

"Busy girl. That should raise a few eyebrows." Santa barked out a laugh, the sort only lifetime smokers were capable of. His belly shook beneath the stretch of his shirt. "Good. Women are scarce, local boys wouldn't like the competition."

The man pursed his lips and lowered his gun. "Let's talk inside. I wanna get the hell outta the sun. I'm Sam Cotter, that's Andy. The one with the basket's Owen."

Al made introductions as Santa waddled away, acknowledging one and all with a wave of the back of his chubby hand.

The skeleton-thin kid decked out in all black, Andy, handed the badge back to Finn. Owen gave a wary nod and gave back nothing.

"So, what use are you people to us?" Santa enquired. He proceeded to push himself through the gap between dump truck and wall, testing the laws of physics and muttering all the way.

"Ali worked in an office, and as Finn said, he was a cop. I was a mechanic," Dan said.

Finn concentrated on details. The weapons being carried, the vehicles being used and the good organization of these people. Pretty much everything he saw impressed.

"I'm liking you more already. Of course, I would have outright loved you if you'd been a doctor, but a mechanic I can use," Sam said.

"You're in charge?" asked Finn.

"There's a board, a council of sorts. I'm mayor for the time being."

Dan smiled, rubbed at his chin. "And how are things going, Mr. Mayor?"

"We're getting there," Sam hedged. "It's not going to be easy, lot of work to go around."

Inside the wall was a graceful old country town in the grip of fierce change. Half of Main Street was being ripped up by a bulldozer. A flock of children watched the machinery in awe from beneath the shade of one of the grand old jacarandas occupying the median strip. Many of the trees stretched up to two stories high, their boughs covered in clumps of small purple flowers. The sweet scent filled the air.

"We'll use the space cleared for planting wheat and corn. People are growing the basics in their yards but some things we need to make certain of." Santa waved to a couple chatting out in front of a petrol station. They eyed their group curiously. "We're making daily supply runs to the outlying areas, gathering up anything useful. You three'll be expected to pull your weight one way or another, same as everyone else."

The fat guy never slowed, hustling them down Main Street as people emerged from every nook and cranny to gawk at the newcomers. On the whole they looked clean and well-fed. "All the domestic residences are at capacity, the motel's pretty much full as well. If you lot are staying, then we'll put you up above the real estate agent's old office. There's a small kitchen and bathroom, plenty of room to move in a bed and whatever you need."

"Sounds fine," Dan answered.

Finn tagged along behind with Al beside him, her arm brushing against his. Blackstone was perfect. She could be safe here. He smiled and nodded to one and all as they passed. These were ordinary people inside the walls, ordinary people in extraordinary circumstances. It was everything he had been hoping for. A way to start over with his woman beside him.

On the other side of the street, beyond the noise and commotion of the bulldozer, was an old motel. There was an antique shop beside it, then a big hardware store stretching back the width of the block. The interior of the building was packed to the rafters.

"You're stockpiling like you're preparing for a siege," Finn said.

Santa rounded on him, face grim. "You never know, Finn. You never do know. There's been infected gathering along the fence line at nighttime. Pays to be prepared for anything. Now, why don't we discuss the checking you over physically requirement? Wouldn't do for anyone to be hiding a bite, would it?"

CHAPTER TWENTY-SIX

Santa had a daughter named Erin. She showed them to their designated lodgings above the real estate office. Ali tagged along behind as Erin and Finn did the getting to know you thing. Already Blackstone gave her a bad feeling. Though that might have just been due to the company she was keeping.

Erin was a pretty, sporty sort, around Finn's age, with shoulder-length brown hair. Womanly wise, Erin was on the smallish side and didn't require a bra. This fact was made glaringly obvious by the thin tank top she wore.

And if Erin didn't get her tea-cup tits out of Finn's face, then Ali was going to start scratching shit up.

The lust on the girl's face when Finn had stripped off his shirt for the physical had made Ali want to pull hair. She had never gotten into a catfight in her life, but apparently, there really was a first time for everything.

There was only one small problem. Finn was flirting back.

She had never seen him so happy. He was lapping up Erin's tales of daring deeds done on supply runs. How she must pale in comparison, sleeping with a gun under her pillow and fear in her heart.

Bleh.

Ali turned her back on their shenanigans and kept busy checking the place out. The kitchen was a small corner unit consisting of a sink and a two-ring gas stove, the bathroom every bit as elaborate and dating back to the 1960s. Otherwise, the large expanse of what had once been storage space was perfectly vacant, completed by two rickety sets of French doors leading to a veranda overlooking Main Street. It would do them fine. Whoever "them" wound up being.

Santa had taken Dan off to organize a king-sized mattress sufficient for the three of them, which had prompted much guffawing from the old man. Sam was getting great mileage out of the ménage thing.

"Al, Erin's leaving now," Finn announced.

What a shame.

"Bye," she called back over her shoulder, saving her "fuck you very much" for a quieter moment.

"What do you think? This'll be okay, won't it?" Finn wandered up behind her and leant an arm on her shoulder like she was part of the non-existent furniture.

Her skin felt paper thin and ready to rip, doubtless already worn at the edges. The scene brought her ex-fiancé to mind, horribly enough. The uncomfortable but haughty glances as he packed his shit and took off with her sister sat front and center in her head. There'd been enough hurt and betrayal to last a lifetime. She couldn't do this again. The need to tear Finn a new one boiled beneath the surface. But he didn't belong to her. There was no commitment made. She had slept with him, end of story. It was just sex.

With Daniel she knew where she stood, that ground was rock solid. But with Finn ...

She heard voices drift up the stairwell.

"Finn, get your ass down here and help," Dan hollered from below. Even his raised voice calmed her down some. Her shoulders sunk back to a more normal level and left her earlobes alone.

"Duty calls." Finn brushed her cheek with a finger and headed for the stairs, leaving her to wonder if he filed her under the same heading. Duty.

The weight of her pity party would grind her down to rubble at this rate.

Bed installed and guests gotten rid of, they spread out on the end of the mattress for dinner. Each awkward second passed slowly with her tummy pitching like she was at sea. The need to do something with the mess of emotions inside her drove her nuts. What had ever made her think she could deal with two men? The blame sat squarely at Dan's pushy feet, except it didn't. She'd stumbled straight on into the mess with eyes wide open.

"We need to talk," she announced. Her voice sounded way more confident than her quivering rabbit was making her feel. Two sets of eyes rose from their canned dinners and focused on her. The desire to scurry off into a corner reigned supreme.

"About?" asked Daniel.

"This place."

"You don't like it?" Dan gave the room the once over and shrugged. "Babe, I know it's not much, but—"

"No, not this room. This town. About being here." She turned her attention to Finn. His blonde hair fell into his eyes, brushed the tops of his shoulders. Maybe he would cut it now they were back amongst society. Maybe he would put on his uniform, become someone else entirely. "Finn, I know Sam said they weren't keen on single guys coming in, but I'm sure they wouldn't evict you if that was what you wanted."

Finn gave her cop eyes. "What exactly does that mean, Al?"

"You really hit it off with Erin."

"I'm with you."

"You don't have to be. You're free to choose, I won't ..." She paused, flustered. "It's up to you."

Finn set aside his food, moving like his shoulder pained him. "What won't you do?"

"There are going to be other women here too, not only her," Ali said. "You're free to make your own choices. I won't get in your way. That's all I wanted to say."

Finn blinked furiously. He sucked in his cheeks and his lips pressed tight together like it was taking a lot out of him not to lose it. "Fuck!"

"Easy," Dan cautioned.

"Easy? She's trying to set me up with someone else. How the fuck do I take that, Dan? Tell me."

"Finn—" she started.

"Don't." Finn stood, brushed off his hands against his jeans legs. "Thank you for your permission, Al. Can't say what it means to me. I'm gonna go check out their cop shop."

She heard the thump, thump, thump of him jogging down the stairs, followed by the God almighty slam of the door at the back of the shop.

"Finn has left the building," Dan said mildly, watching her over the top of his can of Irish stew. "Wanna tell me what that was about, babe?"

She shook her head. The rabbit was well riled up. Even meeting his eyes again was right out of the question.

"Why doesn't that surprise me?"

She had no answer.

"Come here." Daniel set aside his dinner and she all but scurried into his lap, taking refuge. His big hands cupped the back of her head as he fed her a steady stream of kisses, long and deep and lovely. They almost took away the pain. "Talk to me."

Ali slipped her hands beneath his shirt, held her palm over his heart and huddled in against him. The scent of him was so warm and familiar, a balm to her jagged edges. "I need you."

"I'm yours. But I don't think sex is going to solve this one. God help me. Why don't you talk to me for a minute instead?"

"Dan ..."

He made a sharp, exasperated noise and pushed his nose into hers.

"Please, Daniel." Her hands slid up to his shoulders, over his hard, hot skin. Ali climbed up and straddled his lap, covered his mouth in kisses. "I need to know you still want me."

"Of course I want you."

"Show me. Please."

"Babe," he groaned. His hands shredded her clothing while she worked at his. She needed him now, had to have that connection. The heat and strength of him could comfort her no end. They'd be okay. Nobody's heart was broken.

Daniel got her naked faster than she'd imagined humanly possible. Her fingers clawed at him as she rubbed herself against him. Close enough wasn't good enough. She needed him inside of her. Desperation rode her hard and he seemed to understand. Arms wrapped around her, squeezing her bones breakingly tight. He held her together and kept her in one piece. Then took her down to the mattress. His hands and mouth were all over her. They lay skin to skin with his cock nudging at her opening.

"Yes. In me. Hurry," she moaned. He swore as the hard length of his cock surged into her, healing every ill.

He drove her hard and fast toward climax. Her legs clenched tight around his hips. Her arms locked around his neck. She moaned and mumbled words of love as she came. Ali didn't even realize she was crying until he kissed her face, brushed away her tears.

"I love you," he said, his panting breaths hot against her ear. "I'm not going anywhere. Ever."

She balled her hands and held onto him tighter, ignoring the stupid tears. The muscles in her legs and arms burned from gripping him so tight. But no way was she letting go.

"Everything will be okay," he said, smoothing back her hair. "Just wait and see."

CHAPTER TWENTY-SEVEN

Daniel had seen some pathetic sights in his life. At two o'clock in the morning, Finn was right up there. He lay sprawled out on the bunk in the Blackstone police station's sole holding cell, wide awake and humming sad old songs by the Man in Black.

"I brought supplies." Dan held up the bottle of scotch Santa had handed over earlier in lieu of a welcome mat and dumped the kid's pack by the cell door.

Finn arched a brow at the luggage. "Throwing me out?"

"No. You idiot." He twisted the cap on the scotch and took a mouthful of the fifteen-year-old malt, letting it sit on his tongue before swallowing it down. "Man, that's good. We should have cut crystal for this but we're gonna make do with the bottle. I figured you'd want some of your things seeing as you're obviously not planning on returning tonight. I have every faith you two morons will sort this out, eventually."

"Then you have more faith than me." The kid swung his legs over the side of the bed and sat up, holding a hand out for the liquor.

"What happened with Erin?"

Finn's brows shot up high while he downed a healthy amount of the superb single malt, thus proving it was wasted on his immature twenty-six year old taste buds. Both the scotch and quite possibly Al, but what exactly could Dan do? He'd kickstarted the situation between them. It was his own damn fault if his girl had feelings for the fool. Finn hadn't gone to find Erin, however, and he sure as hell wasn't happy. Which answered the most pressing questions regarding whether the situation was salvageable.

"Nothing happened with Erin," said Finn.

Daniel settled himself down the other end of the bunk with his back to the wall. Happily, his first time inside a jail cell. "Try again."

"It was harmless."

"So harmless that you're crashing here and Ali's asleep curled up in a ball like she's waiting for someone to come along and kick her," Dan scowled. "Harmless enough that she was crying. Not over something I did. Over something you did."

The kid scowled back at him, sampled further from the bottle before shoving it back in his face. "It was harmless. She overreacted."

"You kids, I swear."

"Don't expect me to call you daddy."

Daniel choked down the scotch, laughing and drinking at the same time. "You really are an idiot."

The kid just grunted.

"You know, I don't have to be here trying to smooth things over between you two. This would be the perfect time for me to phase you out."

"That so." Finn tensed his shoulders, ready for a fight.

"This is my chance to have her all to myself again. I think we'll be safe enough here, even if she isn't thrilled with the idea of rejoining society just yet. You'll find someone else. Maybe you already have ..." Dan passed the bottle back, feeling the warmth of the alcohol spreading through his veins, despite the kid's icy stare. "So, that's about where I'm at."

"Sounds like you've got it all worked out. Why are you here, then?"

"Because I love her, and I want her to be happy. But her idea of happy now includes you too. Therefore ..."

Finn winced, rubbed at his chin with the palm of his hand. "And why are you okay with sharing her, anyway?"

"Because, she comes first with me. And ... because I'm partly responsible for getting you two together." Daniel took his turn at the bottle, unable to raise any remorse for the way they were burning up the liquor between them. "A long time ago, I had one messy-ass marriage and made some mistakes I won't ever be repeating. Hopefully. You want it to work then you have to work at it. Whoever said this sort of thing is easy?"

"Nice bumper sticker. Pity no one's buying." Finn snatched back the bottle, downing it fast and hard enough to make even Dan wince. "Maybe it should be easy if it's meant to be."

"Give me strength. What are you, twelve? You fucking show pony. She's not a present your Mummy left for you under the Christmas tree. Not everything in life is given to you, Finn. Sometimes you're actually required to put in a little effort." Feeling more than a touch pissy, he grabbed the bottle before the kid could throw some more down his undeserving gullet. "Dickhead."

"This thing with Erin ... Al could have talked to me about it like a rational adult. Did you lecture her like this, you prick?"

Dan shook his head and the world spun some. "No, I don't need to. She knows she messed up. But you intimidate her so it's going to take a little time for her to work out how to deal with it. Then maybe a little more time to work up the courage to actually do it. Who knows, she's awful fond of you. I'd be surprised if you're left to rot here too long."

"I intimidate her?" Finn scoffed, held his hand out and clicked his fingers for the bottle. "Stop hogging it. Why would I intimidate her? I'm not the oversized old man always on her ass trying to push her into things."

Dan shrugged. "She has a very nice ass."

"Trust me, I'm aware of that. Gimme the bottle."

"I don't push her into things. I make helpful suggestions regarding her future wellbeing is all." Daniel gave up the liquor, feeling the effects of their speed drinking hitting him hard. "Shit. She's gonna be so pissed we're pissed."

The kid shrugged and drank. "It's all on you. I'm not going home."

"Rebel, suit yourself. I'll have her all to myself, half-asleep and cuddly as a kitten. My very own pretty pussy, I can't wait. We had sex after you stormed out. She felt needy after that scene. I feel so ... used. Dirty, almost." He grinned wide and the kid gave him a face made of lemons, all puckered lips and squinty eyes. What a situation, mediating between his girlfriend and her other boyfriend.

Ridiculous.

"Go fuck yourself."

"Finn, she didn't want you to leave. She was giving you the choice. Come back with me." Dan held up the last quarter of scotch and swirled it around in the bottle. "Come on, we're running out anyway and that bed does not appear comfortable."

The kid shrugged.

"Come on."

"What did you learn from this messy-ass marriage?"

Dan sighed again, loud and proud, and rested his head back against the cool of the concrete wall. It felt nice. "Well, it's important to say you're sorry, even if you don't mean it. Sometimes, especially if you don't mean it."

Finn choked on a laugh. "That's terrible."

"Terrible but true. Sometimes you need to make the peace and work it all out later. Being together is what's important."

"This is your version of wisdom? I think I'll pass." The kid leant back on his elbows, laughed again and shook his head.

"I better head back. Certain you're not coming?"

"No."

CHAPTER TWENTY-EIGHT

Finn woke up alone just before dawn with a brain-splintering headache. A shave and wash in the police station bathroom did nothing to alleviate it.

People started dropping in shortly thereafter, small-town gossip having made the rounds. He greeted all comers, sunglasses firmly in place. The dark lenses were small protection against the glare of daylight bursting through the front windows, threatening to boil his eyeballs in their sockets.

It seemed like everyone in town had come calling. Everyone except for the person he wanted to see.

He ignored the pounding in his head, smiled and nodded and said nothing. Committee members stopped by, Sam included. He waddled in with his big belly leading the way. Plenty of people dropped by, smiling and making the right noises about his promotion to town cop.

Time would tell. Finn had wanted to wear the badge since about the age of five, but what it meant now, he didn't know.

Two bored teen girls were practicing their wiles on him when Al wandered in midmorning. The sight of her did things to him that made life less simple. She was a punch to the chest. He could feel his heart flop over and offer up its belly.

The girls stopped and stared at him and Al. And then stared some more. Then they scurried out with much excited whispering.

"Hi," she said.

"Hey," he said back.

She wore a denim skirt and a t-shirt with her hair down. Morning light did beautiful things to her, while it had tried to annihilate him. How fucking unfair he'd only had her the one time. His fingers itched to touch her, to grab her and run.

Not being able to touch her would kill him. He would leave. Al would be safe here with Dan. Finn was unnecessary now. He couldn't spend the next however many years watching her and wanting. Being kept at a polite distance would kill him, because this need he had for her wasn't going anywhere.

"How's your head?" Her fingers twitched at her side, her arms knife straight.

"It's been better. Mind locking the door behind you? I'm done with visitors for a while." Pain flashed across her face. He back-pedaled fast. "No. Al, I meant with you on this side. Please."

"Oh." She turned her back and fiddled with the lock for a moment. Finn opened the internal door beside the counter, ushered her through to the back of the station. Out of sight of any spectators while they tied up loose ends seemed a good idea. Probably best not to have witnesses just in case he actually gave in to the temptation to beg and plead on his knees. Shit.

"Dan's still sleeping it off," she said. "I don't know what time he got back."

"He didn't wake you?"

"No."

Finn shook his head, surprised over being surprised. "Manipulative son of a bitch."

Al smiled, the love she felt for the big man obvious in her face. His overly familiar answering pang of jealousy made him silently snarl. But she was here. She had come to him, and it had to mean something even if this was the big kiss off. That she cared enough to do it face to face was nice, though of course a phone call or an email was out of the question these days.

She wandered amongst the office desks out back, touching things here and there, looking awkward.

Smelling great. Soap and sex again. He never stood a chance.

"I have something to say," she announced at last.

Finn sat on the nearest surface, a desk across from her. He nudged ancient piles of paperwork aside. "I'm listening."

Her shoulders rose on a deep inhalation of breath that made the skin above her nose bunch up. "If I'm still what you want, then I need you to not grin at girls who stick their tits in your face."

She paused for effect. He could only blink.

"I realize you're an attractive guy, you're going to get attention, that's a given. I mean, you're beautiful, I know this. But if you're sleeping with me, then flirting like that is disrespectful. I'm a long way from being okay with it," she said. "It hurts. I need you to understand that."

He made to shrug and stopped. This was too important. "Alright."

"There's more," Al warned, wearing her game face. Her serious eyes studied him, making him thankful the sunglasses still sat on his nose.

"Keep going."

"If I'm not what you want then I still want to be your friend. I care about you a lot, Finn. That doesn't change ... whatever you decide."

Rendered dumbstruck by her honesty, he took off his sunglasses and dumped them on the desk, giving himself a minute. It took guts to put herself on the line. Shit, he'd had no business flirting with any girl. He knew it. Had known it at the time.

Maybe he had been jealous. Spending the night with a woman and then handing her back to her boyfriend ... Not knowing where he fit in with her did not sit well. In truth, he'd never not come first with a woman. If only he had found her before Dan. But he hadn't. This thing between them would always be more complicated than normal. Still, he'd gotten involved with her knowing that.

Ali shuffled about on her feet for a minute then ceased that too, her frown increasing. He realized she fully expected him to tell her they were done. Expected it and hated it. It left them both in the same fucked up place neither wished to be. What a revelation. His heart thundered and he stared at her, mute.

"That's all," she eventually prodded. Her gaze darted around the room, diligently avoiding him. "It's what I should have said yesterday, as opposed to what came out. I'm sorry for that."

He gave one cautious nod.

"Say something."

Finn pushed off the desk and walked toward her, taking up her hands when they were toe-to-toe. Her fingers, warm and a little damp, slid through his own. Sweaty from the burgeoning heat of the day or nerves, he didn't know. It didn't matter. Everything was going to be okay. He'd promise her whatever the hell she needed him to so long as he could stay close to her. It was that simple. "I missed you last night."

Air left her lungs on a sigh. "I missed you too. I guess I'm selfish. I want both of you with me, or I'm not happy."

He brushed the pad of his thumb over her bottom lip, loving how her eyes dilated. Loving her saying these things to him.

But he wasn't interested in hashing out their issues right there and then. Maybe Dan was right, sometimes the being together was more important.

"I want you," he told her. "Right now, Al."

"Here?" She looked around, perplexed. "In a cop station?"

"Right here. Right now."

Her answer was the hitch in her breathing and the hunger on her face. It was enough.

He held her hands a little tighter, taking them behind her back. Just far enough to arch her spine and press the soft mounds of her breasts against him. "You know how I held your hands down last time?"

Al's throat worked. "I remember."

"Yeah. I remember too." Finn took her mouth, kissing her with all the pent-up frustration lingering from the night before. Kissing her till he couldn't remember what had caused all the fuss in the first place. His jeans strangled his dick as his balls became hot and heavy. Getting her off and getting into her were the only things that mattered. But he had this mental image of exactly how it had to happen. God help him, it had to come true. "Trust me?"

"Yes."

"Turn around, hands on the table."

Gray eyes blinked open, dazed and confused. Her lips were swollen and wet. She watched his mouth move but he couldn't be sure she got the message. And the message was all important.

"Turn around, Al." He helped her turn, then helped himself to two handfuls of her curvy ass. "Put your hands on the table."

"The table?"

"That's right." She took far too long to bend forward and place her palms flat, but finally they were there. "Good." Finn pushed his boot between her sandals and pushed her left foot to the side, widening her stance. It was a simple enough matter to pull her denim skirt up to her waist and push her panties down to her knees. "Al, I wish you wouldn't wear underwear."

"That why you're arresting me, officer?"

The spicy scent of her arousal filled the air, and he groaned aloud. He hadn't actually thought he could get any harder. "I'll cuff you later when I can find some. Damn, you smell good."

Finn dropped to his knees behind her and swiped his tongue through the folds of her wet cunt. She tasted exactly as she should, familiar, hot and female. Never would he get enough of her. Al squirmed and he took the opportunity to use the flat of his hand on the curve of her ass. The slap of his palm on her soft, warm flesh was shockingly loud in the quiet of the station house.

Yes, just like that.

Al jumped beneath his hands and pale skin turned a nice shade of pink. "Finn! Shit. Warn me next time."

"No." The next smack hit her other cheek, and there was a nice sense of balance to it. Pink handprints all in proportion. She made to move, trying to cover her rear with her hands. Protecting her rosy ass. Not. Happening. "Put them back on the table, Al."

She growled and stomped a foot. He couldn't keep the smile off his face, not that she could have seen it. Finn indulged it.

Her muscles tensing, she slowly returned her hands to the table. "Damn it, Finn."

Actions speaking louder than words, he put his mouth on her, tonguing her sweet flesh. Her pussy was hot and wet and right there. It was perfect. A dying man's last meal. He hadn't been certain they would be like this again. The future had been bleak, empty. Gratitude swamped him.

And ... and the moment she started moaning and her legs trembled he pulled back. Al was less than impressed. "You bastard, don't you dare—"

The crack of his hand on her ass drew her litany to an abrupt halt. "You going to throw me out again?"

"I didn't throw you out," Al snapped, giving as good as she got. He fucking loved that about her. "You left, remember? Are you going to fall down the front of other women's shirts again? Huh?"

"No," he promised, and placed tender, sucking kisses on her labia, one on either side. "No, it won't happen again. I'm sorry about that." Took him a minute to realize the shudders racking her body weren't tears or excitement but laughter. He didn't even bother spanking her, it was so out of place. "What is your problem?"

"You're apologizing to me with your face in my pussy."

"It seemed prudent." He bit the curve of her ass, pressing in with his teeth just enough to mark her. Because he needed to. Visual evidence was required. She was still with him. She was his. The noise she made brought forth all sorts of needs in him. All kinds of demands. "Do you accept my apology?"

"Yes."

"Good." He scattered kisses over her hot ass cheeks, held those perfect curves in the palm of his hands. There came another sound from the back of her throat when his thumb stroked over her asshole. Soft and gentle, teasing and testing. "I'm going to want this."

She looked back over her shoulder at him, eyes dark with passion and something else. A little wary maybe. Cautious. "Are you now?"

Finn rubbed his mouth over the fading pink marks on her flesh. "Talk to me, Al."

"I tried it." She shrugged with one shoulder, bit her lips. "It didn't really work for me. But if you want ..."

"You'll give me that?"

She nodded.

"Thank you." Finn took a minute, savoring her trust. A warm flush of feeling rose in his chest when she surrendered to him. He brushed his thumb over the tight, puckered hole again, and she shivered.

Probably not from pleasure.

Some idiot hadn't respected this gift. He wouldn't be making the same mistake. "Easy. We'll just experiment a little. Okay?"

She nodded, but didn't visibly relax until he got back to kissing and licking her gorgeous pussy. Hot, open-mouthed kisses that got them both steamed up. The taste of her infused him, filled his every sense and pore. He didn't leave a cell unclaimed.

The need he had for her was bigger than he had imagined. He had known giving her up wouldn't be easy. But it wasn't until now he could truly admit that it wasn't something he could see himself ever doing. Not a chance. He'd fight for her till his dying breath.

When he slipped his other hand between her legs, his fingers finding the hard nub of her clit she moaned. A loud, wake-the-neighbors sort of noise. His balls curled up against his body.

With her suitably distracted, he moved his attention back to her ass. She didn't seem to notice what he was up to with his tongue, she was too busy pushing her pussy into his hand. The noise of her panting breath and another one of those moans filled his ears. He lavished her with attention, front and back.

"Come for me, Al."

"Yeah ..."

And she did. Spectacularly. Her spine seized up and her whole body shook in his grip. The way she said his name licked over him like heat. His need to be inside her was paramount.

Finn gave her sex a parting kiss and lick. He rose to his feet and undid his belt buckle, got his jeans open and freed the hard length of his cock. Donning the condom tucked in his back pocket, he told her with all due sincerity, "You're lucky I'm an optimist."

"Maybe I'm just easy." He could hear the smile in her voice, slow and sweet as honey as she struggled back to reality. "Oh, Finn ..." Her back arched and her hair slid forward, covering her face, as his cock pushed into her pussy. "That's so good."

He could only agree.

"Be easy for me, Al. That's all I want." The air went out of him as he pushed home, filling her with his cock. The play of her muscles over him, her heat and humidity. He had to take a moment, get his bearings. Get his head in gear before he blew.

"That's all?" she moaned as he pulled out, thrust back in. Nothing had ever felt this good. Nothing.

He grunted and she didn't speak again as he got busy fucking her in earnest. Talk could happen later.

Finn bent over her, one hand beside hers on the desk, his other arm wrapping around her, holding her tight against him as she came on his cock with a surprised shout.

Saying his name.

No way could he hold out.

CHAPTER TWENTY-NINE

There were two people waiting for her back at the apartment. Daniel appeared pained and Erin looked perky. Perky but subdued.

Her boyfriend sat at a battered table opposite their visitor. He slouched down in a camping chair, a cup of coffee in hand. The slow smile he gave her lured her in, held her tight. Letting her know without words everything was alright. "Erin just arrived. She wants to talk to you, baby."

There were dark circles beneath his blue eyes, still bloodshot from the previous night. His hair was damp from the shower and dark strands clung to his gorgeous thick neck. Everything about him called to her.

He pushed himself out of the chair and came to her, as big and beautiful as ever. Without thought, she slipped her arms around his waist, cuddled in close enough to catch the scent of him.

"Everything okay?"

"Yeah." She looked up at him and smiled, pulled him down for a kiss because she wanted to and she could. If there was some territorial display attached then so be it. Erin could go screw herself, and Daniel didn't seem to mind. He kissed a path down her neck, stopping at a fresh bite from Finn. "I'm glad you got things sorted out with him. I'm gonna go find Sam and investigate these plans of his for keeping us busy. Stay close to home, okay? I shouldn't be long."

"Hmm." She watched as Daniel clomped down the stairs, her heart beating double time from love and lust. Everything about him called to her, from the breadth of his shoulders to the strong lines of his chest. The movement of his ass in particular was enthralling. He looked up and caught her hanging over the railing, ogling him. The side of his mouth kicked up, and he gave her a wink before he slipped from view.

Which meant it was time for the unpleasant part of the day.

"Why are you here, Erin?"

The girl winced and got to her feet, abandoning her cup of coffee. "I owe you an apology."

"Alright."

"I didn't realize when Dad introduced them as being with you that he meant they were *with you*. The both of them." Erin tucked her dark hair behind her ears, studied her shoes for a moment. "I'm sorry. I know I caused trouble between you guys."

"Yes, you did." Ali leant back against the wall. "And Finn was giving off conflicting signals, which didn't help. But that's between me and him."

"Look, you don't know me, but I would never come on to someone else's boyfriend. I don't do that," Erin said. "I really didn't realize that's what was going on here."

"The situation's unconventional, but it's our choice and no one else's business really."

"Don't get me wrong." Erin put out her hands. "The three of you, it's great. Two men, you're my hero."

"Why don't we let this go?"

Erin's smile was megawatt. "I would appreciate it."

"Please sit, finish your coffee."

"Oh, thanks, but I'm due next door at Riley's to help with sorting." Erin paused, considered. "Why don't you come? Good chance to start meeting some people. I could show you around town a bit later if you like."

When Ali hovered, undecided, Erin took a step toward her with a tentative smile. "Come on, let me be useful here. I feel terrible about the way we got off on the wrong foot. Plus, if you don't go out, they'll start popping in, and trust me, that's bad."

"Oh?"

The girl shook her head emphatically. "No. You do not want that. Civilizations may crumble and fall, but small-town gossips never change. Give them an in and you'll never get rid of them. They'll be in here, searching for the satin sheets and mirrored ceiling, the candelabra you swing naked on, that sort of thing."

Ali smiled despite herself. "Going out it is."

A few minutes later, Ali stood on the sidewalk outside Riley's department store, proudly established in 1903. There were towers of boxes piled high. "You guys are serious about stockpiling," she said.

The place was a hive of activity as people unloaded even more off the back of a pick-up truck. These people were dropping off weapons, faces somber, obviously fresh back from a trip outside the town walls.

"As Dad says, you never know." Erin greeted the two men and one woman busy handing down boxes from the back of the truck. "This is Ali. She came in with the party yesterday."

The two men nodded hello and got on with their work, faces tense. Made her wonder what they had seen out there.

"Let me take that." She held her hands up for a box and the woman smiled and passed it down. More helpers ambled out of the shop and got in line behind her.

"Thanks." The woman was in her forties, handsome rather than beautiful, with ash-blonde hair in a braid. Add the rifle slung on her back and she looked eminently capable and all business. "Welcome to town."

"Ali, this is Lindsay. My other personal hero." Erin put her hand over her heart and the woman smiled, snorted a laugh. "When the men tried to protect us poor weak women by taking us off watch-and-supply rotation, she led the charge to defend our rights."

"They were being asses," the woman announced, loud enough to snag the attention of the two males nearby. Neither smiled in reply. "And now they're not. End of story."

"They saw the error of their ways," sang Erin. "Hallelujah!"

"Erin, go do something useful for once," one of the men chided, earning himself a hastily flipped finger. It was Owen, the one who had been with the wire-thin goth at the front gate.

"You shouldn't take the Lord's name in vain," a young, dark-haired woman hissed. Her hands clutched a well-worn Bible. Behind her, a gaggle of people held similar books and flocked close, as if they fully expected the young woman to protect them from the big bad world.

"I didn't, Rachel. I said 'hallelujah', somewhat out of context. Get a grip." Erin charged past the woman, who took a hasty step back to avoid colliding with the side of a box. "Move on."

"It's disrespectful."

Lindsay jumped down from the back of the fast-emptying flat tray. "I believe you were told to restrict your God bothering to the hours after dusk, Rachel. It takes work to keep everyone fed, to keep the town running. Work needs to be shared equally. It's time you did your share instead of leaving it to others."

"We're doing God's work."

"Then I hope God will feed and protect you when they throw your lazy, self-righteous selves out of town." Lindsay gave the girl a long look, tiredness seeping into her eyes. "Go away, Rachel. Your father would have been appalled."

Rachel's cheek twitched, her mouth dwindling into a tight little orifice. "Don't you talk about him."

Lindsay walked off without further comment.

A crowd had gathered to witness the confrontation, making it impossible to follow Erin into the shop as the doorway was now clustered with curious folk. Ali balanced the box in her arms. It wasn't heavy, but it was sizeable, long and awkward.

The wicked witch with the Bible spotted her balancing act and took a step closer, beady eyes narrowing in on her. "You must be the one who came in yesterday, the one with the two men. Whore."

She had been worried about people's reactions but, funnily enough, this didn't hurt at all. "I prefer the term 'high-maintenance'."

Several of those squished into the doorway tittered, and the woman sneered at one and all with a pantomime face. Her finger pointed skyward like she could summon thunder. "God is not finished judging ..."

"Oh, for fuck's sake, Rachel. Take it elsewhere," Erin snapped, elbowing her way through the crowd. "People, show's over."

Andy, the goth from the gate, appeared beside Rachel. They argued in hushed tones. The young man looked genuinely pained as she shook her head furiously and stomped off down the street, her devotees rushing to keep up.

Erin sidled up to her. "Ignore Rachel. Her father was a minister, one of the first to die. He was eaten by one his parishioners right in front of her. Safe to say it doesn't make for a healthy mental outlook. Just the same, someone really does need to stick her head down a toilet."

Ali could only nod her agreement. "I wonder if that would make the water holy."

Erin snickered and watched the group disappear around a corner. She wasn't the only one watching them, but Andy's face held no anger. The young man looked like his heart was breaking.

"Dad put the snatch and grab expeditions on rotation; everyone over eighteen and able to fire a gun takes their turn. Unless someone's willing to cover for you." Erin tipped her chin at Andy as he resumed work, a worried frown fixed to his face. "He and Owen have been covering for her while she harasses everyone in town. It's bullshit."

"Everyone goes out?" Ali asked, a familiar chill sliding beneath her skin. The box in her arms suddenly held the weight of the world.

"Yeah. Actually, can one of you ride out with us tomorrow? We'd really appreciate it," Erin said. "Ben shot himself in the foot this morning, showing off for some kids. The idiot. We're lucky he didn't kill someone. Serves him right that a dental nurse is the closest we have to a doctor. Anyway, talk it over with your men."

And there wasn't a single chance of it happening. She already knew how the conversation would go. It wouldn't be her skin at risk. The thought of one of them out there ...

Ali nodded, clutched at the box before it slipped straight from her numb hands. "They've already been given jobs, but I'll be here. No problem."

The woman smiled. "Good. We take a decent-sized group, post lookouts. It's not as dangerous as you'd think."

CHAPTER THIRTY

Daniel woke up not long past dawn with the sheets twisted around him, half a leg hanging off the side of the mattress. Three in the bed made for cozy conditions, but right now, there was just one. Him. Which was curious.

Finn had been raring to get back to the cop shop, which accounted for his absence. But where was his girl? Because all being right in his world, she should have been in bed beside him, all sleepy and warm and ready to be ruffled. But she wasn't.

"Babe? Ali?" No answer.

The silent apartment felt empty. A bad feeling set in. She might have gone with Finn. Or she might have been next door, sorting supplies, despite their discussion regarding her not wandering off on her own. They barely knew these people; security still mattered.

Daniel vaulted out of bed, pulled on some cargos and a t-shirt, stuffed his feet into joggers and pounded down the stairs. An overreaction probably, but he'd gotten used to knowing her whereabouts. Her absence jangled his nerves. The world felt wrong, more off-kilter than usual.

Outside, there were people out and about on the street, going about their day. A child shrieked and giggled, chased by an older sibling around one of the huge jacarandas filling the median strip. A tractor started up somewhere close, the engine coughing and spluttering to life.

"Morning," someone called. Dan nodded back.

He stuck his head into the department store, where a couple of people were gathered around a middle-aged man with a clipboard. "Hey. Anyone seen Ali this morning?"

They looked at him with blank faces. The guy with the clipboard answered. "No. Sorry. We only just got here."

"Thanks," he nodded, backed up.

She had probably gone with Finn. That's where she was. An ache akin to fear poured through his chest.

He broke into a jog. Down to the end of Main Street, hang a left, feet pounding against the pavement. He covered the half a block and stormed down the station's front path. His hand hit the heavy glass door, shoved it open.

Finn was bent over the reception desk, looking at papers. Immediately he straightened, hand shifting to the gun at his hip. "What's wrong?"

"Is she here?"

"No," Finn frowned, shook his head. "You two were asleep when I left."

"I woke up alone."

The pain in his chest accelerated and the front door was thrown open once more. A boy stumbled through the opening, face ashen, dyed black hair sticking out every which way. One of the guards from the gate, if his memory served. Andy.

The young man's red eyes fixed on Finn, and his thin shoulders caved. "You need to come. It's Lindsay. She killed herself. They found her hanging ... just ..."

Finn shot Dan a questioning look he could only return. The capable woman who went on raiding parties seemed the least likely person to check out in such a fashion. But these days, who the hell knew anymore?

"Maybe Al's there with Erin or something," said Dan.

"Maybe. Let's go." Finn headed for the door and the sniffling young man scampered alongside.

A crowd of people milled about outside a tiny weatherboard cottage two streets over. Despite the bright summer day the mood was distinctly dour. People lined the concrete pavement and overflowed into the garden, crushing the lettuce and tomatoes growing there. Lots of weeping ladies and pale-faced men were present but some kids played a game of footy out in the street, apparently unaffected. Death happened so often these days that it could be regarded as mundane.

Al didn't seem to be amongst the gathering, but she couldn't be far. Stupid of him to worry – grown women could come and go as they pleased. Of course they could, without question and all that. Still, if she didn't turn up soon he might take a jog around town.

Finn strode up the path and straight into the shadowy house. Daniel followed.

"What's going on?" Finn asked Santa.

"She was found 'bout half an hour ago." The fat man huffed out a breath and frowned, his sunburnt face heavily lined.

More people loitered inside but Al wasn't among them. The place was packed, and stank of death and decay. Piss and shit and all the things the body secreted at the end of its use. The combination turned his stomach.

Lindsay's body was laid out on the dining room table with the length of rope beside her. The rope gleamed vibrant orange against the dark wood, the sole bright spot in the room. They'd drawn every curtain but let in half the town. It defied logic. Certainly Finn looked pissed, despite the professional face. His eyes were narrowed, taking everything in.

"You shouldn't have moved the body." Finn motioned people back from the table and inspected the dead woman's bloated, blackened neck.

"We couldn't leave her hanging out there," said Santa in an outraged tone.

"Out where?" asked Finn

A chubby hand waved toward the back door, visible through a poky little kitchen. "There's a little back pergola. She used one of the beams and a kitchen chair."

"Who found her?" Finn surveyed the crowd.

"I did." Andy stepped forward with his eyes downturned. No wonder the poor boy was so shaken up. Even after everything he had to have seen to survive this long, suicide would come as a shock.

"Everyone but Sam and Andy can leave," said Finn in a no-nonsense tone. "Now."

People muttered and murmured about uppity newcomers taking over, but they did as told. Finn's cop face brooked no nonsense.

Dan stepped out of the doorway to make room for the exodus. "You want me to head off?"

"Gimme a minute here." Finn pulled out a notebook and opened it to a fresh page. "Andy, was there a note? Anything?"

Andy shook his head so hard his teeth clattered. "No. I didn't see nothing."

"We already searched," reported Santa with another gusty breath. "Andy, you're fine, son. Run on."

The boy lit out the door.

Finn wet his lips and studied the ground for a moment. "Sam—"

"Hold up. I know what you're gonna say, but this is a clear-cut case." Sam shook his head over the corpse, bushy brows pulled tight. "Spirits around the place aren't good as it is, Finn. We need to deal with this as fast as we can. This isn't the first case of someone taking their own life, and it probably won't be the last. We don't need to encourage anybody, alright?"

Finn said nothing.

"You saw them out there," said Sam. "Some of them are barely holding up as it is. We cannot afford to make a big thing out of this."

"A woman's dead, Sam," growled Dan, letting his temper slip through. "That's kind of a big thing."

Finn turned back to the body without comment.

Lindsay wore a pale pink summer nightgown and her long hair hung loose off the end of the table. Daniel might have believed her asleep if not for the state of her neck. Shit, what a mess. The kid didn't seem fazed. He retained the supernatural cool as he did his job. Other bruises littered the woman's arms and legs. Of course, she'd gone out daily on supply runs. People got knocked around moving supplies and climbing in and out of pick-up trucks, for certain.

Dan took a long hard look out the door, needing a minute. With the windows closed, the scent of death hung heavy in the warm air. When had death become so commonplace? He fucking hated it. And he should be busy looking for his girl because he sure could do with one of her smiles right about now.

"She lost her husband a few months back," Santa sighed. "This isn't a complete surprise. Everyone's doing it tough. Hell, I had a fifteen-year-old OD on painkillers three weeks back."

Finn stared at the older man for a long time before answering. "Alright. We, ah, we have to find Ali at any rate."

"Your girlfriend? She went out on a supply run with Erin," Santa said with a sigh. "They headed out just after dawn. Can't even keep my own daughter safe."

Finn's professional face gave way to horror. Ali was out there? The ground beneath Daniel's feet seemed to give way. The pain in his chest almost brought him to his knees. How he kept to his feet he had no idea. "Oh, fuck."

***

Daniel stood beside Finn, staring at the mammoth garbage truck serving as Blackstone's front gate. The sun was setting, lighting the horizon in shades of gold. It had been the longest day of his life. Fear and fatigue should have long since left him numb. It would have been kinder. Thoughts of Ali lying dead somewhere kept repeating in his head. He couldn't escape them.

But she'd be okay. She would be.

The raiding party had been headed for a town forty minutes due west. They should have been back by now. They would be back any moment. Damn but he wanted his girl back – like, yesterday.

Daniel knew she was independent, knew she wanted to take care of herself. But there had to be a happy middle ground that allowed everyone to sleep at night. Something to stop the heart attack, or whatever it was, threatening to throw open his chest.

He wasn't the only one in pain. Finn stood beside him, buzzing with tension.

"She's fine." Daniel leant against the side of a pick-up.

"Fine like Lindsay?" Neither man spoke for a minute. Then Finn turned on him, face set. "She doesn't do this again. Run off out of our sight."

"You gonna put her in a cage?"

"Fuck's sake," the kid bared his teeth. "You cannot be okay with this."

An older man approached, hand in hand with a young woman. The fair-haired prince might have been strung out, but no one else knew. Finn was in pillar of the community mode, answering questions and offering reassurances. Yes, it was very sad, a great loss to the community. No, plans had not yet been made regarding the funeral. On and on it went. Death might be familiar, but Lindsay's supposed suicide had rocked the town.

When the couple wandered away, Finn turned back to him. "You're going to let her pull this shit? Are you serious?"

187

"I didn't say that."

"Then what are you saying?"

"Same thing I've been saying all day. Calm down, wait and see what she comes out with."

The kid grunted. "You could not be more fucking wrong. I thought you wanted to keep her safe."

"How do you think you got an invitation into our bed in the first place?" Dan snapped.

Finn scowled at him, eyes furious. Yeah, well. It was going around.

"Her safety comes first with me. Always. Bossing her around will only drive her away. Trust me, I already tried it."

An approaching rumble of engines brought the argument to an abrupt halt, as did the cry of the lookout sitting atop the cab of the garbage truck. The truck powered up and slowly reversed, clearing the entrance. A minute later, the first of the vehicles, piled high with supplies, cruised in.

The raiding party was in good spirits. Didn't last long.

The flow of greetings cut off sharply as the pall engulfed the returning crews. And there she stood, all intact. Oh, thank fuck for that. Seemed sensation returned where he'd been deaf, dumb and blind before. His girl lived on and all was okay.

Finn marched up to the pick-up truck Ali rode in. She stood in the cage on the back of the bed, hair windblown and nose pink from the sun. She stilled at Finn's approach, reading his body language just fine.

"What's wrong?" she asked.

"Lindsay's dead, amongst other things," Finn said, shoving a hand at her. "Come on."

"What?" The color dropped from Erin's face. Her father beckoned her down while Finn cursed in a low voice. Apt, since he had well and truly messed up breaking the news.

"How?" asked Erin.

"I'm sorry, honey. She killed herself." Santa scowled, helping his daughter down. "I don't know what to say."

"She wouldn't. It doesn't make sense." Erin stepped into her father's waiting arms. "She ... No. Why would she do that, Dad?"

"I don't know. I don't know." He wrapped a beefy arm around his child and led her away, holding up an arm to keep others back.

"Come on." Finn ushered Ali through the crowd as Daniel fell into step by her side, taking the hand she offered. Needing the connection.

Everyone spoke in hushed voices. Like the pro he was, Finn avoided getting them held up by the gathering. They were hustling her up the staircase toward home in no time, the sliding glass door downstairs firmly locked behind them.

The kid gripped Ali's elbow like she was a criminal about to make a run for it. Nothing Dan could do. This spat was going to happen. Probably needed to. He had his own concerns with how she had taken off without a word, but going medieval was not going to work. He stayed close, ready to intervene if required.

"Finn." She wrenched her arm free and turned about, facing them down. Something in the kid's face had her flinching, mouth pinched and pained. "Relax, would you?"

"You think this is a joke?" Finn roared. Very young male lion. It would have been funny, except it wasn't.

Dan opened his mouth to intercede, but his girl held up a hand, flicked him an unhappy but entirely capable look.

"No, I don't think this is a joke," she said. "But you do need to calm down. One of us needed to go. I went. End of story."

"Like fuck. We're trying to protect you here, Al," Finn bit out. "You just go ahead and make the decision to put yourself in danger? Without discussing it with us first?"

"I want to protect you both too. Can you get that?"

"Protect us?"

"Yes." Al threw herself into the nearest camp chair and started removing a boot with angry tugs at the shoelace. "If I'd mentioned the supply run to either of you, you wouldn't have let me out of your sight."

"Babe ..." Dan took a big step forward, making to touch her, only to receive the stop-sign hand again.

"No." Ali wrestled off a boot, dropped it with an almighty thud. "Did you think it would work differently for me? I care about both of you. The thought of either of you going out there ... I couldn't do it. Just couldn't. It was easier to go myself. I'm not going to apologize. I'm not going to promise not to do it again."

"Like hell you're going out there again," Finn said. "Ever. Over my dead body, Al."

"Don't you get it?" Daniel cleared his throat. "That's what she's afraid of."

His girl glared at Finn, ready to re-launch the war. Shit, enough already. "There are going to have to be rules, for all of us," Dan said.

"She'll get herself killed!" Finn hissed. "How could you agree with this?"

"'This' being our girlfriend? The woman we're supposed to be in a mature, adult relationship with?" Daniel enquired, tipping his chin at the foxy if furious Exhibit A. "Because we're meant to be on her side. Within reason. I didn't talk her down from the roof just to lock her up somewhere else. I do not want to lose her."

The kid growled, and paced like a caged animal. Up and down, up and down, while Ali watched, nonplussed. "Fine, we'll ease up. But you do not go out again."

His girl rose to her feet, radiating fury. Dan was singed just being in the same room. "Not good enough. I won't be wrapped in cotton wool while you two take all the risks. Do you really believe they'll let us stay in your precious town if we're not seen to be contributing? Seriously?"

"Al ..."

"I'm not budging on this."

"Then we have a problem," said Finn.

"No, Finn. You have a problem," his girl said. "There are some things I can't do. Standing back while you're in danger is one of those things."

Finn's nostrils flared. "I'm trained to handle dangerous situations. You are not."

"I don't care."

"Al ..."

"No, Finn. I love you, but no."

The kid gave a good impression of a man who'd had the fight sucker punched right out of him. He stopped and stared. "You love me?"

"Yes. I love you," she said.

Finn stared at her, face rigid and hands balled tight. "Shit."

"Is that really so bad?" she asked.

The kid grabbed her and held on tight. And his girl fitted herself against Finn, her face in his neck, arms wrapped around him like she couldn't let go.

Inside Dan's ribcage something hurt, just like it had earlier today when he thought he'd lost her. No amount of rubbing the heel of his hand at it helped.

CHAPTER THIRTY-ONE

Ali stood belowground in a hardware store basement a half-hour north of Blackstone. Her itchy scalp and damp hair lay beneath her helmet-and-flashlight combo. The confining, dark, hot and dusty space reminded her of old times, only this time she was under a building instead of above a house.

She and her supply buddy, Andy the goth, sorted stock. Others did the same above, clearing the shop floor. Boxes of rope and nails, flashlights and batteries sat in nice piles. All of the useable items were moved beside the stairs, where Andy then hauled them up to the trucks.

Dan was somewhere aboveground helping load, it being his day to babysit from afar. Keeping her men at home was no more feasible than their hopes to ground her were. No one was completely happy. The last few days had been full of terse words and tense silences. Eventually, something was going to have to give. Sweat covered her, sticking her t-shirt to her back. Hours must have passed because her muscles ached and her throat was bone dry. She squeezed by the stacks of boxes, searching for her water bottle.

"Andy?" He had mentioned getting a drink and disappeared a while back. She wore no watch. Had no clue what time it was or how long they had worked. "Andy, you there?"

And it was quiet, too quiet.

No reply came to her call, the echo of her own voice and her breathing the only sounds. Labored and loud. Shit.

She couldn't say when the dozen sets of feet thudding overhead had petered out, but she knew she was alone. The building sat silent.

They had left her behind. How? No way in hell would Dan leave her, and yet the quiet was complete.

Her water bottle sat on a box containing snail bait, right beside where her gun should have been. Without a weapon, she'd be dead.

Panic bent her double and her lungs flattened like a hand held her down.

"Stop it," she snarled, wincing when it echoed back. Quiet. She should be quiet. The sun couldn't have set yet, impossible. Where was a fucking watch when she needed one? "Calm down," she whispered. "Think."

All comfort bled out of the space and the dark pressed in claustrophobically. She needed to get upstairs. She forced slow steps, made her way over and around the boxes. Tiptoed up the stairs and through the door with its broken lock. She flicked off her light, set her helmet aside, delaying.

What was the point? Either way, she needed to know.

Ali stepped out onto the shop floor. It was empty. Nothing moved. Things were scattered here and there, articles deemed unimportant. The afternoon sun shone through dusty plate-glass windows with splendid shades of copper and red. It lit up the dust motes floating about.

Her heart fisted as a meltdown commenced, which helped nothing.

Something nudging the side of her boot snagged her attention. It was the weight of the holster shifting on her leg. Finn had buckled the ankle holster onto her himself this morning before heading for the station, making her love him that much more.

She was so fucking scared it was hard to think straight. Trembling fingers fumbled for the catch, pulled the weapon free and flicked the safety off.

The hardware was wide open, front doors busted, the back the same. Things were stirring out on the street. Shadows moving. The moaning might have been her muddled mind, but it was doubtful.

The sun ducked behind the line of buildings across the way. Above her was a foam ceiling. It wouldn't hold her.

Out on the street there came a low, drawn-out groan. Her muscles trembled.

Move.

She bolted for the back door, keeping low, trying not to make a target of herself. The building behind this one was three-stories high, blocking out the afternoon sun and casting her in shadow. Still a better bet than the open space of the street front.

There was an overgrown patch of grass running alongside a fence, a docking bay with a van parked in it. The windows had been blown out and a long-dead body sat in the driver's seat, rotted arm hanging down, skin like leather.

A forklift was parked alongside the back of the building, a pallet stacked with bags of potting mix weighing down the front. In lieu of a ladder, it looked good. It was also the only option.

More moaning.

"Go. Go. Go. Go." Ali chanted under her breath, navigating the climb from inside the forklift's cab onto its front load. The gun in her hand slowed her down.

Something grabbed her. She almost screamed. The noise stuck in her throat, wanting out.

A grasping hand clutched at her boot. She kicked out, dislodging it for a moment. Where the hell had it come from so fast? Over her shoulder she saw decaying features smeared with dirt and dried blood, eyes empty of color, as though the irises had bled to white. The remains of his torn greasy shirt named him "Mike". In less than a minute she could put a bullet smack bam through Mike's forehead. Be done with him, no matter the noise. But noise would draw more of them.

Fuck. The rabbit went wild in her chest.

She scrambled onto the forklift roof. Mike tugged at the hem of her jeans, scratching and clawing at her pants, trying to pull her back, skewing her balance and sending her onto one knee.

Nothing could save her sweaty grip on the gun.

The pistol slipped from her hand, clattered to the ground. Going, going, gone.

She gave a helpless groan, shaking with fear and adrenalin. "Oh, fuck you, Mike."

She kicked out, boot connecting with the hard bone of his skull. Mike reeled back onto his ass.

Ali scrambled to her feet, perched atop the forklift. There was a narrow window off to the side of the building, about the right height to give her the leg-up required. It would be difficult. She stretched out. Her fingers could just reach the edges of the gutter. The muscles in her legs screamed in protest, thighs and feet and everything in between. Ali pulled herself forward, increasing her hold on the gutter inch by inch. Metal dug into her fingers, but she had it. It held and she wasn't letting go. She stuck her left leg out to kick in the window, the crack in the glass painfully loud.

Ali wedged her foot into the space and reached for the moon. She was stuck stretched between the window and the forklift. Mike, the tenacious bastard, yanked on her boot, still sitting atop the machine.

Mike moaned, a noise that wound down to a death rattle. It sounded like someone had squeezed the air out of him, accordion-style. The poor guy was probably frustrated over watching his meal get away. Another infected stumbled around the corner, drawn by fuck knew what instinct.

God help her. Panic reduced her to an implausible leap of faith.

Ali pushed off with her toes, dislodging Mike's claw, and put her weight on the leg stuck akimbo in the window. She clutched at the gutter and dragged her sorry self up. Her arms felt like fire, no, like lead. It took forever. Her ribs scraped on the gutter and her fingers tingled, thick and numb.

She didn't fall a story to the street below and become a broken-boned meal for the horde. Fucking up wasn't an option because she was getting home. Yes, she was.

The aluminum roof blistered her hands and cheek. It was a piss poor welcome to safety.

Ali rolled onto her back, folding her arms over her body, trying to keep her exposed limbs off the scorching metal. The hot pain through her t-shirt was the final insult.

She lay there and cried from relief and horror both as the sunset faded and the infected gathered below.

CHAPTER THIRTY-TWO

"What do you mean she's missing?"

Santa blanched, held up his chubby mitts in a placating gesture. "Now then, son, calm down. She's a smart girl."

"I. Want. Facts." Finn clamped his teeth shut, his stomach ready to spill. People milled about amongst the pick-ups piled high with the day's takings. He ignored the audience and the pounding of footsteps behind him. "Explain to me how she was the only one who got left behind."

"What's going on?" Dan demanded, landing a heavy hand on Finn's shoulder. "Finn?"

"They lost her. They fucking lost her."

The big man's mouth opened then closed. "What? Andy said she took the first truck back."

"No. Where is she, Dan?"

"Finn, I swear, I thought she was already home. I was going to give her a serve for leaving without me."

Erin stepped forward. "Andy came back in one of the other trucks. We don't know where he is now. He told me the same thing."

"You left her there." Finn grabbed Dan's arm, ignoring the tremble in his fingers. "How the fuck could you leave her there, Dan?"

"I ... I thought ..."

"You were supposed to watch her!" Finn raised his fist. Dan didn't even flinch. Just stood there, patiently waiting to take what was coming. He didn't even say anything. Just looked completely gutted. Soul destroyed. His gaze vacant and the color gone from his face.

Finn knew how he felt.

"We need to go get her," Finn said, letting his fist drop. He couldn't do it.

"I'm in," Erin said. No hesitation.

"Calm down, people." Santa's bushy brows clumped. "It's nearly dark. You cannot—"

"Like hell I can't," Finn snarled. Dan's fingers dug into his shoulders, holding him back. "She is not staying out there alone. Move that truck now!"

"Son ..." Santa started up again.

Finn literally felt himself snap, heard the noise like a crack in his skull. He lunged at the prick.

"Finn! Shit." Dan's arm grabbed around Finn's waist, dragged him back. "Calm down. This is not helping. You wanna hit someone, hit me."

Finn snarled, pissed off beyond belief. But he let Dan pull him back.

"It's nearly dark," Dan said. "We can't do a damn thing by going back out there now but get her into more trouble."

"Explain," Finn demanded, his heart racing.

"Ali knows how to hide. She's really good at it," said Daniel. "We go out there now, we'll put her in danger. She'll try to come to us."

"I want her back."

"I know." Dan's arms wrapped around him. The man was the only thing stopping him from hitting the ground. "I know. And I'm so fucking sorry, but we've gotta be smart about it."

His mind raced, and his heart sank, so far down it was through the ground. The thought of leaving her out there was abhorrent. "Fucking hell," muttered Finn.

Dan nodded in perfect understanding, eyes glassy. "Yeah."

CHAPTER THIRTY-THREE

It was oddly peaceful on the roof. There was nothing to be done until dawn and infected didn't climb. They lacked the coordination, the muscle strength, who knew. She was safe for now and resolved to take it easy.

It was hard to block out all the moaning going on downstairs. At least she was out in the open air, not caught in a dust-ridden attic. And she was safe enough for the night. There were two positives.

She counted stars to pass the time and keep her mind off her bladder, tested her memory for song lyrics. Hoping she didn't hear any vehicles, hoping they wouldn't try to come out at night, hoping they were safe.

The lights of Blackstone shone like a beacon in the darkness. No wonder they were attracting zombies to the walls. It seemed a long way away. Then, another light came to life near the settlement. That was odd. She squinted, peering out into the dark.

One lone light outside of town. It was there, then gone. Poof! Like she had imagined it. No one went beyond the town walls at night. Better not be Finn or Dan out there, trying to get to her. God, she hoped it wasn't them. Please.

There'd been a lot of angry words lately between all three of them. When she got back she'd fix that. Whatever was brewing between Dan and Finn would be dealt with. She loved them both too much to lose them. The pissy silences between her and Finn needed addressing, too.

She swallowed, trying to conjure up some moisture in her mouth. No water bottle; it was downstairs somewhere. What a mess.

But she was still alive and breathing, still uninfected and still getting home. She watched the light and ran the opening lines to Gloria Gaynor's "I Will Survive" through her head. Over and over. Her memory for lyrics was shit.

A menacing growl shut down the disco. Snapping and snarling rose up out of the dark. Scratching and scraping. Her skin prickled. She wanted to huddle against the cooling tin roof.

The moaning escalated to counteract the competition. The zombies sounded agitated, afraid.

She lay like the dead, staring into the heavens, her focus entirely on what played out below. The noises reached new heights and the battle began. The sound of breaking bones and tearing flesh came to her, noises unique and horrible, indelible.

Something was enjoying the infected she had drawn. Safe to say Mike was done. Poor Mike. Poor everyone.

There were several somethings sniffing the air, followed by whining and howling. Dogs. What would the infection do to dogs? More importantly, dogs couldn't climb buildings, no matter what their diet entailed. She was safe for now.

Ever so quietly, she rolled onto her belly, crawled to the side of the building and peered over the edge, not daring to breathe.

Several sets of gleaming red eyes stared back at her from below.

CHAPTER THIRTY-FOUR

Finn squinted into the rising sun, bracing himself against the side of the tray as they drove out of Blackstone.

For a moment he had a funny sensation, racing past the remains of the town. The hairs on the back of his neck vaulted. It felt a lot like someone had him in their crosshairs.

He scanned the lines of dull weatherboard houses and over-grown gardens, but there were no signs of life. Nothing.

He shook it off, got back to the gnawing anxiety over Al.

Dan sat beside him, face lined with guilt. That wasn't right. They both loved her, and both did their best. There'd been a lot of tension lately, but that was the truth of it. No one had been expecting an attack from within. Blackstone had seemed a haven up until now. The big guy's face showed the strain of the past twelve hours, dark stubble lining his jaw and heavy shadows beneath his eyes. Finn knew the feeling.

Patience was non-existent, and frustration rode him hard.

Dan caught him looking and gave a tight nod. "Not far now."

He nodded back, hoped it was reassuring.

Two of the other men sat further down the bed of the truck with guns in their laps, gazing at anything but him and Dan. No doubt skeptical they would find her in one piece. Idiots. She would be fine.

Dan sighed, staring off into the red dust clouds trailing behind them. "Andy's a dead man."

They'd spent the night searching for the little prick. He had been the one who told Dan that Ali had left in the first truck. He had also been the one who came across Lindsay's body. What would have happened if they found him? He didn't know. And there was the line in the sand. The moral quandary Finn could see himself stepping over. But he gave the same answer he had all night. "No. We can't go there."

"Sure we can." Muscles jumped in the big guy's jaw. "I have no problem with having his blood on my hands."

All too believable.

Andy's disappearance left a lot of unanswered questions. Unfortunately, he could hide, even in a small space like Blackstone. Especially since they were newcomers, and Andy was the hometown boy. If he had crossed the wall then the chances of locating him were none. The last thing Al needed was Dan going out into the wilderness, guns blazing. They needed to stick together, all three of them. That would be the new rule, if he had to cuff himself to her to make it happen.

"She's alive." Finn had to be over the century mark on churning out the statement. Those words were as hollow as they had been each and every time.

Another nod from the man.

In between searching for Andy and worrying about Al, Finn had done a lot of thinking. Not just about the jealousy between them all lately, but also about Lindsay's death. Turning over everything he had seen since arriving in town. Second guessing everything because nothing made sense, at least not to him.

"There were extra marks on Lindsay's neck. Might have been fingerprints. But I'm no expert. I have no proof." Finn rubbed his hand over the stubble on his jaw. "Why would someone want to kill her?"

Dan stared back at him. "Why would someone want to set up our girl?"

"I don't know. But quit saying it was your fault."

Dan said nothing.

Miles and miles of bushland passed them by.

Eventually, a neat line of houses surrounded by hip-high grass and weeds announced the beginning of another town. Erin dropped the speed to negotiate the typical assortment of cars and debris.

Everything was still. The town permanently asleep, already neglected. It wouldn't be long till it verged on ruin.

She did not end here. She could not be dead.

Houses gave way to a line of shops. Lots of busted glass and dark patches on cement walkways. It was the same story everywhere, death and destruction.

And suddenly he was tired and cold. He realized if she was dead, then he wasn't certain he wanted to live. He wouldn't leave Dan on his own, but still. Fear of commitment had nothing on this. She had ruined him for anyone else. Her prickles and quirks were as potent as her soft touches and tender ways.

She could get all fired up, but he could talk her down, get her under him, get inside her.

"Pony up," murmured the big man.

There were no signs of a fresh kill nearby; the street was clear. The pick-up pulled up outside a typical country hardware store. The building had probably stood for eighty-odd years. They jumped down off the truck to the clicks of weapons being loaded. The others milled about, waiting on him and Dan to make the first move. And Dan did move.

Straight up the sidewalk, long legs striding into the cavern of the store. Finn followed, his blood thick with fear. The place looked well-raided, rubbish strewn about.

"We'll head downstairs." One of the other two guys produced a flashlight and off they went.

Where was she?

"Yelling isn't smart," Santa rumbled. Far too close.

He gave the guy the evil eye but it was true, he wanted to let loose, bring the hick town down around their ears, shouting her name.

Erin headed toward the back door and the street. Santa fell in behind her without further comment.

"I'm going to check out back," said Finn.

"Yep." Dan turned on his heel, stalked out the front door.

A noise on the roof had Finn's eyes and ears up. It was a scraping sound, followed by the creak of wooden beams. It wasn't just the normal stretch and strain of an old building. Something was up there.

"Dan!"

Finn bolted for the side exit, throwing the door open so hard it slammed back against the interior wall. Who cared about noise now?

"Al?" He searched the skyline and the gutter framing the building. "Al, you there?"

The door slammed open once more and Dan joined him on the strip of weeds. "Where? Where is she?"

"Heard something on the roof."

"The roof?" The big man grinned like someone had flicked all his best switches at once. "She loves roofs and attics. How do we get up there?"

Dan hoofed it down the side of the building with Finn following tight. He nearly ran into the man's back when he suddenly halted. "No, no, no."

Blood and gore splattered the rear parking lot. It was far too familiar a scene. Flies lay thick on the ground. The place stank.

Finn's words petered out as they both stood and stared. Something nastier replaced the fear and worry that had dogged him through the night. "What do we do if she's been bitten?"

Daniel gave him a glacial look, his face like a stranger's. "Then we're too late. She would have already ... she'd have ... you know, if she could."

Finn nodded, the warmth of the morning sun leaching straight out of him. Because yes, she would have killed herself rather than turn.

The building beside him made the same creaking, groaning noise. There she was, climbing down in slow motion. One foot was wedged into a broken window while the other gamely searched out the platform provided by the forklift below.

His lungs swelled in his chest like his ribs couldn't hold them. She was alive.

Her fingers were clutching the edge of the roof. If they made a noise, she might startle and fall, but she was not being left to deal on her own.

Finn moved before he was even aware of it. He scaled the piece of machinery, climbing onto its roof, hands reaching for her. She squeaked and kicked back, nearly nailing him in the balls with the heel of her boot. One grimy hand slipped and she flailed in midair, twisting and turning, trying to fight him off.

"Al. Stop." Finn fisted his hand in the waist of her jeans, throwing the other arm around her thighs to steady her. She hung suspended by one arm, her feet still a foot or two off the roof of the forklift. "Al, it's me! Calm down."

Her other hand gave way and she fell the remaining distance. One foot missed the forklift's roof, slipped into the abyss between machine and building, and sent them both off balance. His arm had ridden up to her chest, but his hand was still tight in the back of her jeans, caught nice and snug between them. Al slapped her palms against the side of the building, which stopped them from falling. No way he was letting go now. Not now and not ever.

"I've got you, Al. Everything's fine." Finn put his mouth close to her ear and tried to talk her down, because she shook like a leaf and still wouldn't acknowledge him. "Pull up your foot for me. I'm right here, Al."

She made no move. The back of her dirty t-shirt rose and fell chaotically.

"Al, please. Listen to me."

After a God-awful time she turned, showing him the shiny red mark taking up half her cheek. It sat on the same side of her face as the fading brown and green bruise from her concussion. Her eyes were wide and glassy. Their poor girl. Anger and fear filled him all over again.

He waited.

"Finn?" she asked, voice a scratchy whisper.

He smiled. "Hey. Everything okay?"

She blinked twice before lowering her chin. "Yeah."

"Alright, that's good. Lift your foot up onto the roof for me."

"My foot?" Ali gazed down, mystified, but her foot duly lifted. "Dan?"

"Here, babe," the man said from behind them.

Finn carefully turned her.

Dan's face showed nothing at the damage done, from her scalded hands to the burn on her face. His voice was calm and measured. "Hey, hon."

She tried clearing her throat, coughed. "I'm not bitten or anything. Can we go now?"

"Sure." Dan held his arms out and Finn guided her down, not letting go until she was firmly in Dan's grip.

She was okay. She was fine. Finn put his hands on his knees, bent double and breathed deep. He kept his eyes on her. Handcuffing himself to her held appeal. Man. The feeling of relief almost dropped him to the ground.

Santa clapped his hands lightly, applauding Al's reappearance. Erin beamed. Whatever. Apart from Daniel, he didn't want anyone near her until they sorted this shit out. The big man obviously felt the same way, keeping an arm tight around Al while he held a water bottle to her lips.

Al gave the two a brief nod, gazes stuck on the sticky mess on the street. "It was dogs."

"Dogs?" Dan pulled her in closer.

"A pack. They had red eyes. It was … it was crazy."

"I bet," the big man rubbed at her arms, like she needed the heat put back into her despite the morning sun that was now beating down.

Santa squinted. "Dogs? Honey, are you sure?"

"It was. I saw them, well, I heard them."

Santa's mouth contorted into a grimace, vaguely sympathetic, but mostly skeptical. "Ali. You've had a dreadful experience. We are going to get to the bottom of what the hell went on here yesterday. But don't you think …"

"Stop. Right there." Finn slid down off the forklift, stood beside her. "She says it was dogs, it was dogs."

"Look at this. Look at what they did. You really think it could be anything other than an animal?" Dan gestured to the mess of blood and gore with the water bottle. He turned Al away from the scene, herding her toward Finn.

Finn put his arms out eagerly, unashamedly. He tried not to let it bother him when she frowned and turned back to face off with Santa.

"I wasn't imagining anything. I wasn't hallucinating. They were dogs, a pack of them, and they had red eyes." Their girl stared down the old bastard, daring him to argue. "I've never seen anything like it. A bunch of infected had gathered down here, I think they heard when I kicked in the window. It was over so fast … There was another light, too, near town."

"Ali …" Santa started.

"We believe you," Erin said, when her father didn't make the right noises.

And Santa might have appeared chastened, but he didn't seem convinced. "Right. Well, let's take this discussion somewhere safer, hmm?"

CHAPTER THIRTY-FIVE

Standing in the shower, Daniel's girl was a kaleidoscope of colors.

Finn washed her down with the utmost of care. There were bruises ranging from black and blue to murky greens and yellows. There were fresh red scratches and the softer pink of older wounds. They needed to take better care of her. But any attempt at discussing it was met with her silence.

The kid was down to her knees, rubbing at some imaginary patch of dirt. Their girl was squeaky clean. Finn probably just wanted to keep his hands on her, keep touching her. Who could blame him?

Dan watched the slow, delicate process with his arms crossed and his back to the wall. He was barely holding himself together, just waiting for her to snap out of it and come back to life. She remained as silent as a living doll.

Her gaze, however, kept sliding back to the pistol in his belt. They were back to that, God help them. He really hoped she wasn't going to try to sleep with firearms under the pillow.

He still buzzed with adrenalin, wound up with no one on hand to beat the living shit out of. Yet. Thank God she was safe.

The kid kept on and on with the bathing.

Finally, when she wavered on her feet, ripe with gooseflesh, Finn reached for a towel. Much patting and dabbing of shiny pink skin ensued. Then the kid slathered her in antiseptic cream. He treated her like spun glass, a fairytale princess receiving her due.

Sweet, but enough. His girl was ready to collapse from exhaustion.

"My turn," he said. "Up and out, babe. Time for bed."

"Wait." She gripped his shoulder, most likely to push him away, but he already had it sorted. Ali was up in his arms and halfway to the bed piled high with pillows before any coherent argument could be found. "Dan, I can walk."

"No. Finn?" Dan lay her down on the mattress. Finn was already pulling off his soaked shirt, toeing off shoes and socks. "Everyone's getting some sleep. See?"

"Definitely." Finn, naked in a nanosecond, climbed in beside her and lay on his side. He shuffled over till his nose nearly brushed the side of her face. When she made to rise, the kid threw an arm over her waist. Carefully. "Stay put. What do you need? Dan can get it."

He didn't even need those rosebud lips to impart it.

"She wants a gun. She's not getting it. You are not reverting to sleeping curled around a firearm, babe. Not. Happening." Dan yanked his shirt off over his head, not bothering with buttons, then got to work on the lower half. "Don't even try it with me."

The sudden mutinous glare she shot back bumped up his heart rate. Their girl had come back to life. It did him good to see it. He knew then she'd be okay.

"Shh, it's fine." The kid touched his lips to her cheek, stroked her arm with his fingertips. Trying to instil some peace and calm, for all the good it would do him. His girl was overtired and wired, ripe for a fight. "There are two handguns and a rifle behind the bed. All within easy reach, Al. You can get to them in no time if you need to. Okay?"

Their bristly babe frowned, thought it over a moment, then nodded. "Okay."

"Good." Finn's eyes drifted closed.

"Suck up." Dan muttered at the kid, then finished getting undressed and crawled onto the bed. He settled in flush against her, threading her fingers through his. Ignoring his ever hopeful dick.

Ali squeezed his fingers lightly, letting him know she wasn't set to castrate him over the gun issue right here and now. Later, when she had her energy back, he might be wise to worry. But for now they were good.

Her skin was cool like the sheets and the smell of the antiseptic cream lingered. Beneath the soap and the shampoo came the scent of her. Warm and lovely and his.

His and theirs. Whatever.

They had pulled the curtains, locked the doors. Wellwishers and the curious alike could take a flying fuck. They were not home to visitors.

"Close your eyes," Finn ordered her without opening his own.

She did not.

"I don't think I've ever been so awake in my life." Al stared at the ceiling, placed a hand on the arm the kid had thrown across her chest.

"You're safe, babe. Everything's fine," Dan told her, wanting to believe it. Needing to believe it. Because he was more than willing to throw himself off cliffs for her, but that wasn't stopping the bullshit from happening. It wasn't keeping her safe. That had to change. Ali appeared to have gone ten rounds with the champ and not emerged the winner. "No more adventures for you. Either Finn or I will keep you company for the foreseeable future. You need to stick close to home for a while."

She said nothing.

In days of yore, circa late last week, her silence might have been cause for concern. He knew her better now, knew she was mulling things over, choosing her words with care.

Finn broke first, rising up on one elbow and dealing Daniel the death glare. "You could give her some space to recoup."

"You disagree with me?"

The kid's pretty face drew tight, and he shook his head. "No. I just wasn't going to lay it all out on the line at this particular point in time."

His honey snorted. "You were going to attempt to manage me, you mean."

"I was going to attempt to protect you. Not that you make it easy." Finn put his hand to her face, and her focus shifted off the ceiling and onto him. Neither smiled. "You're not stupid, Al. The situation isn't right. You're at risk. We need to know why."

"Oh please, I'm at risk over my sleeping arrangements. Kind of obvious since it's the only standout thing about me right now, given the state of the world. Also, I don't want to be a job for you." Her bottom lip trembled, gray eyes shone.

Daniel stared, spellbound. He loved it when her mouth did that. The stern set of her jaw, however, didn't alter in the least.

"Can't you understand?" she asked. "Or are you too far gone on your serve and protect bullshit to figure it out?"

The kid frowned, surprised. "My serve and protect bullshit?"

"Yes," she said.

And then in one smooth move Finn rose up over her. He nudged her legs apart with a knee and settled between them, an arm set beside her head to take his weight. Daniel scooted over to make room, curious about the kid's plans.

"Finn." Her brow furrowed as she pushed at him. "Get off me."

"No," Finn said. "We're talking."

"We can talk without you lying on top of me."

"No, we can't."

"Finn—"

"See, I've got all sorts of warning bells going off in my head, Al. That statement you made sounds far too similar to the last time we had one of these talks. After that talk, I ended up sleeping somewhere else. Remember?" Finn's voice was all reason as his hand burrowed down between their bodies.

It was the first time the kid had touched her in an overtly sexual way in front of Dan. They were covering new ground here and it felt right, hell, it felt good. His blood raced. Voyeurism just might be a field sport he could get right into after all because it certainly wasn't jealousy rising to the fore. Ali's mouth opened on an "oh", her hips kicking upward. The bed shook as the kid found his target. Dan's cock stirred against her thigh.

"I hated that," said Finn. "Hated fighting with you. Hated being away from you. Then, I was partly at fault. But this time, I'm not. So I'm staying put."

His girl growled and squirmed and got nowhere.

"Your logic escapes me. Get your fucking fingers out of me." Her hands shoved at the kid's thick shoulders, not moving him at all. "Finn!"

"My fucking fingers aren't in you. Yet. Be patient."

"Daniel ..."

"He does have a point," Daniel said, relishing the whole scene more than a little. "You do seem to be starting a fight for no reason."

Her mouth twisted and those familiar twin spots of red lit her cheeks. So pretty.

He sighed, dramatically. "Hon, it's not really fair to expect me to get involved in a fight between you and your other boyfriend."

"Get him off me," his girl gritted out.

Finn looked at him, eyes fierce, daring him to do it.

"Easy, tiger. This is between you two." Dan held up a hand in surrender, grinning broadly. "So long as you're not hurting her, I'm not interfering."

The tirade this set loose from his babe was mighty. They both ignored it.

"I would never hurt her," Finn snapped, fingers still busy between her legs.

"I know," Dan said, shifting his hard-on to a more comfortable position. "That's why I'm not interfering. So ... what happens next?"

CHAPTER THIRTY-SIX

Frustration had her fit to fight.

She wanted to stay mad. Mad felt safe. Instead she was moving against his hand, ostensibly to get away, but it wasn't working. Her sex was slick and far too willing. A moan escaped her, and she almost sobbed at the betrayal.

Being wet didn't play into her mood. But she was panting, out of breath and overexcited.

And the real problem was that she was going to cry, fuck it.

Her eyes were gritty. Her heart going rabbit crazy in her chest. The fluffy white menace was going to break a rib in its bid to run away this time.

"Don't. Finn, please." Her voice caught, which she hated even more. "Stop! Just stop."

"Stop what? This?" His hand stilled against her pussy, cupping her sex. Oh man, the ache it left behind. The bastard. "You don't want this?"

"I don't want you touching me when you're angry at me."

Finn smiled. It wasn't comforting. "I'm not angry at you, Al. You're angry at me. Doesn't matter though. I'm not going to play this game with you anymore."

"What game?"

His beautiful face dipped, firm lips aiming for hers.

She turned her head aside. There Daniel lay, twirling a strand of her damp hair around his finger. His face was impassive, concentrating on her damn hair without meeting her eyes.

She was on her own as promised. The wanker.

Finn rested his forehead against her cheek, his breath warm on her skin. The heat of his body pressed her into the mattress and everything became good and right. He made breathing an effort.

"Look at me." He rubbed the tip of his nose against her cheek, waited. Sighed and kept on when she didn't comply. "The game I'm referring to is the one where you start a fight when you're scared.

The same game where you don't say what you mean. Those kinds of games, Al. Do you love me?"

"What?" Ali tried to turn her face back to him. She needed to gauge his feelings, figure out where he was going with this. But now he didn't let her move. His face pressed against hers, lips sliding along her skin, stopping near her ear.

"You heard me," he prodded. The feel of his mouth moving against her skin sent shudders through her. Resisting him was doomed to failure, she should have learned that by now.

"Finn."

"Answer the question. Truthfully."

Her mind reeled. The rabbit fought harder than ever, rattling the bars of its cage like a lion. "You know I do."

Finn said nothing, lifted his head. His face eased and he nodded. Nothing more.

She swallowed hard. Stared back up at him. "I mean it."

His angel's lips curved into a smile. "I believe you. Now tell me what the real problem is."

She turned her face to the other side, eyeballing the bulge of his bicep. He was so strong, willing and able. His strength set the perfect example. They both were perfect, and they were far more than she deserved. Not that she would give them back.

The rabbit kicked hard, frantic. Letting them down terrified her. It was a nasty little knot inside herself. Being petrified of everything all the damn time made her sick to her stomach. Up on the roof she'd sworn to sort all this out and she would. Right about now.

Ali shut her eyes tight and opened her mouth. "What if this crap against me involves you two? What if they go after you, if they hurt one of you? I couldn't ... I can't be the reason for one of you getting hurt. It was all I could think of last night. What if you tried to come get me while it was dark? You would have died." She couldn't look at them without her eyes going hot with tears. It felt like there was a stone in her throat, but she had to tell them everything. There was no turning back now. "And this place. I'm not sure I like it, but you two love it. You're like local gods here. You fit right in. What if I never do? Some asshole here already wants me dead or infected. And what if I get pregnant? How do

213

we protect a child? Let alone the lack of modern medicine. I'm not sure I could do that without drugs. Dan and I forgot to use a condom the other day. What if one of you decides you don't feel like sharing anymore and opts out? What if ..."

She pressed a hand against his chest, turned her face away again. Finn's heart beat reassuringly against her palm.

"Actually, that's it," she said after a minute. "I'm all whined out."

Silence. More silence. It was really quiet out there.

She dared a peek. Finn lifted a brow at her in response.

"I think I'll wait for both eyes." He took his hand from her crotch, set an arm on either side of her head. The tangy scent of her lingered on his fingers. "Still waiting."

Ali opened her eyes, stared back at him. He was so beautiful. Her defenses were shredded, lying in tatters around them, but she put on a brave face. "What?"

Finn frowned. "Where to start ..."

Dan cleared his throat like a pretentious bastard. "I find chronological order works best. Clear, concise, that kind of thing."

She snorted. They ignored her.

"Right." Finn shifted against her, getting comfortable. The heat of his cock rested against her inner thigh, hard and heavy. He made it near impossible to lie still. Fear and lust made for odd bedfellows, but lust was winning.

"Point one, Dan or I getting hurt? We're both capable. We're both on the alert. Point two, this town?" He turned to Dan, questioning. "Was it this place? Is that next?"

Daniel gave one judicious nod and got back to playing with her hair.

"Right, this town ..."

"Hold it. You can't just discount one of you getting hurt," she said, her voice strained. "Not that simple."

"Ali, I can't promise you Dan or I won't get hurt. I can promise you we'll try our best not to," Finn said. His throat worked and his pale green eyes searched her face. "We'll be careful."

"Absolutely. I hate getting hurt," Dan interjected, all sincere. "Pain does nothing for me."

The hint of a smirk on Finn's lips became a full-blown smile, as beautiful as the rising sun. Heaven sent. A dimple flashed and he licked his lips, the gesture doing things to her nether regions, even if it did nothing to soothe her nerves. "See? All due diligence."

"Great. I'm so glad my concerns amuse you both," she bit out, sounding the bitch. And not particularly repentant. Egotistical wankers, the pair of them. "Thank God we're done with that."

Dan rolled onto his back, finger still entwined with her hair, tugging just enough to keep her attention. "Ouch. Babe, we just spent the night wondering if you were alive, unable to do a damn thing to help you. A little levity won't hurt things. You haven't told her you love her yet, either, moron."

"Fuck's sake," Finn said. "I was getting there."

Dan clucked his tongue. "You were taking too long."

"Thought I was handling this."

"Again, you were taking too long." Dan rose up on one elbow, taking a strand of her hair with him. He stopped when she yelped and gently untangled it from his finger. "Oops. Sorry. Anyway, Finn loves you, babe. So do I. You already knew that, right?"

She held out a hand to him, and he took it, holding on tight. Yes, she knew it. Hell, she counted on it.

"Give me strength." The voice against her neck was muffled. The tone, however, was perfectly clear. "I don't suppose he's a passing fancy?"

"Sorry." Ali wrapped an arm around Finn, holding him close against her heart. Something she hadn't been sure would happen again when she'd been stuck on the roof. It had been so dark, so lonely.

She clutched at him till the muscles in her arm ached, ignored the pain and hung on some more. A low rumble sounded his approval. She was so wet, pinned to the bed beneath him, her sex throbbing.

Finn rubbed his lips over the sensitive skin below her ear.

"You know you'd miss him if he wasn't here," she said.

It earned her a sharp nip to the neck. The sort of sweet sting she associated solely with Finn. "If you say so."

Daniel squeezed her hand. The three of them together thrilled her all over, inside and out. Already the scent of sex seemed to linger in the room. Her head swam with it.

Finn's cock rubbed against her. He swore fervently. "The only thing I can think about is being inside you bare. But you're hurt."

"Not that hurt." Al pressed her short nails into his back in warning. "Don't even think of stopping now, or I will definitely go for the guns."

Daniel chuckled, sighed and rolled onto his back beside her. "So, children, are we making babies or sleeping? Just wondering."

"Oh, we're making babies alright." Finn's hand trailed down the side of her body with a happy hum. Fingers stroked the length of her thigh, then lowered to her knee where he dallied, delivering feather-light touches. She rolled her hips, rubbing herself against him. It felt so good, her heart racing for all the right reasons. "Put your legs around me and tell me again."

"That you'd miss Dan if he was gone?" she said, smiling as Finn began to press into her. The slow stretch was perfect, the heat and hardness of him just right. A ragged groan slipped from her lips.

Utterly shameless.

"That you love me, and I can be inside you without a condom," he corrected in a voice gravelly low beside her ear.

His hand glided up from her knee and cupped a butt cheek, bringing them closer together. "Never done that before with anyone. God, I love how wet you get. Love how ..." Finn groaned against her ear, the sound vibrating through her as his cock did a long, slow slide into her body. "Fuck. There, right there, as deep inside you as I can get."

"Finn."

Ali didn't know what to say while he gave her the full body tingles. It felt too good. He was all the way inside her, buried to the root, his pelvis flush against her and angled to rub just right.

She was still overexcited from his earlier touches and toeing the edge already. "I love you, Finn."

"She's blushing." Dan chuckled, still holding her hand like they were on a date while Finn fucked her. The whole set-up made her dizzy with want.

"She's being seen to," Finn replied.

A bark of laughter escaped the big man beside her. "She certainly is."

Ali ignored the both of them. It happened to be a simple enough task, given the sensations engulfing her.

Finn rose up above her, pale green eyes hazy and half-lidded, beautiful beyond words.

He pulled out of her, pushed back in, owning her heart with the force of his gaze. Being loved like this deserved sonnets, ballads – the most she could manage was a stuttered "oh, w-wow, Finn."

"Yeah," he rumbled. "You see? We fit perfectly."

Having long since been converted to a true believer, she could only nod.

His cock stroked all sorts of magic places inside of her, places going crazy for the attention. Sweat pooled between her breasts, trickled over her belly. The heat made her insane. Her fingers slipped against the smooth, slick plains of his back. He was just as hot and overexcited as she was.

The connection was everything.

"Hold on," he murmured, moving his hand from her butt, slipping it between their bodies and touching her. "Listen to me, Al. Are you listening?"

"Yes. Please, Finn, I need to come."

"You will." He circled her clit with the tip of his finger. Round and round till she couldn't think straight, could only feel. The pressure nearly hurt, building to a pinnacle inside of her she couldn't possibly contain. Overwhelmed, she clung to him. He played her so soft and subtle, but not quite enough. Then his words were there, making everything just right. "I would never leave you by choice. I will always want to be whereever you are. I love you. Do you understand that?"

"Finn ..." Her climax hit her hard, stealing the breath from her, making her body shudder and shake beneath him. The whole world went away. She wasn't the least bit scared, bound to him like this.

"There we go," Dan murmured.

Finn swore profusely and held on tight, hips pressed hard against her. He was still there when her vision cleared. The tendons in his neck strained, pulse visible. Still hard and buried deep inside her. "That's what I wanted, the full body blush. I can make her cheeks pink by talking dirty any time, old man."

"Old," Dan snorted, shook his head. "And it doesn't make it any less fun."

"True." Finn's hand moved back beneath her butt and hoisted her upward, angled her pelvis higher so he was rubbing her still-sensitive clit. She didn't know whether to push him away or pull him closer. But she clamped her thighs around him tight on the off-chance he had any intention of trying to escape. "But nowhere near as much fun as this."

Dan shifted closer, got within whispering range. "That's my girl. Does it feel good, having his cock inside you?"

She nodded, beyond words.

It was dirty, decadent, to have Dan whispering in her ear with Finn above her and inside her. They had never all been in the bed at the same time for anything other than sleep. By some unspoken agreement, one of them had always made himself scarce during intimate moments. They had shared her fairly, equally, and apparently by common consensus.

Having the both of them present was a whole new thing. Everywhere it counted, she loved it. Her head, her heart and every inch of her body craved it.

Her pussy contracted around Finn's cock, making him groan and grin at Dan. "Man, keep going. Keep talking to her. She loves it."

She might have suffered some embarrassment if she hadn't been otherwise occupied.

Dan, of course, took up the invitation with a squeeze of her hand. "You do love it, don't you? Having both of us here in bed with you?"

Her mouth fell open but nothing that made any sense came out.

"We weren't sure it was what you wanted," Dan informed her. "But then, you can be a very dirty girl sometimes."

Another shaky nod.

He lifted her hand to his mouth, kissed her fingers, stopped and sucked at the tip of one. "I can't wait to be inside you." He moved up the bed, placed her open hand over the hard length of his cock. Curved her fingers around him. The feel of his hot bare skin was enough to make her lick her lips in want. Wanting to pleasure him. To please him. "That's it," Dan said.

Suddenly Finn pulled out of her, sat back on his haunches. She wanted to kill something at the loss but wasn't given a chance.

His hands reached beneath her arms, turning her before her sex-addled mind could work out quite what he was up to. "Finn?"

"Ass up, Al." Hands pulled her hips into place, and she set her elbows beneath her. "You want him in your mouth, don't you?"

"Yes."

"What a wonderful idea." Dan moved into position in front of her. Those muscular thighs, dusted in dark hair, the flat planes of his stomach. Not to forget his penis. Thick and full, the tip weeping salty pre-cum. "Babe?"

"Please," was all she could say.

Dan's fingers rubbed at her scalp. "Best idea ever."

"I hate to see a grown man cry." Finn slid back into her, his body bumping against her ass with each thrust, hands tracing over her spine.

Dan's chuckle ended on a groan as she curled her tongue around his cockhead, drawing him into her mouth. He fed his cock to her slowly, one hand threaded in her still-damp hair. Eagerly she took him in. The taste and feel of him against her tongue like a drug.

She wanted to reduce him to the same mindless mess they made her.

There were the dual sensations of Daniel in her mouth and Finn in her pussy. Splitting her focus. It made her giddy, so much at once. Her body and brain couldn't keep up. Fuck drunk was exactly the word for it. So she let go, let it happen.

Finn thrust into her steadily but slowly, as if wary of the cock filling her mouth. All she could do was feel, caught between the two of them and loving every minute of it.

This was her reward for surviving. For not giving in somewhere along the way when it would have been so easy.

She gasped around Dan's cock as Finn picked up the pace, filling her harder, faster. The scent of sex and the salt of their sweat filled the air. A heady concoction.

She didn't want it to end. Never wanted to let either of them go. Never would.

They were hers. She was theirs. Screw the rest, it could see to itself.

Daniel pulled out of her mouth as Finn finished.

"Al." Her name was an agonized plea on his lips as he came.

The nicest thing she had ever heard. Apart from when they said they loved her.

Finn's fingers pressed into her waist and he ground himself against her. With nothing between them it was hot and sticky and perfect completion. She never wanted anything between them ever again. Everything was just right, from the heat of him at her back to the fumbling hands stroking her sides as he caught his breath. Sweat dripped off him and onto her, sliding over her skin and soaking into the sheets in the warm room.

She didn't want to forget a single detail. Wanted it all seared in her memory like the precious gift that it was.

Finn's cock eased out of her and the mattress sunk as he shifted to kneel behind her. Not leaving the bed like she had first thought, but staying with them, as the palm smoothing over her rear attested to. Another hand snaked between her legs, fingers stroking, teasing her wet cunt. Working her up again till she didn't know her own name.

Before her Dan held still, waiting out the moment, fisting his cock in one hand. The musky scent of him was tantalizingly close. "Remember me?"

"Very well."

Daniel's cockhead bumped against her lips, and she opened to him, taking him in just far enough to work the sensitive underside with the flat of her tongue. His size didn't allow for much more.

One hand cradled her jaw, the other wrapped around the base of his cock. It was a powerful thing, the giving of pleasure. If it hadn't been for the clever fingers choosing to deliver a soft pinch to her clit, she would have been quite smug over it. Her insides clenched.

One of Finn's fingers tickled over her ass, his teeth ... His finger. The tip pushed, gently, slowly gaining admission. The slight pressure felt strange, but not uncomfortable. Little-used nerve endings came alive.

"Is he playing with your ass?" asked Daniel, hand stroking her jaw.

She couldn't have answered with his cock in her mouth had she anything to say.

"The shame of him."

Finn's teeth grazed the curve of an ass cheek, the low chuckle teasing across her skin. His finger slid into her, eased back while his other hand strummed her clit. It lit up her spine, the insane heat coiling in her belly. She might not last much longer, but Dan was going first.

Harsh, guttural sounds praised the greedy pulls of her mouth. He didn't even try to hold back from her.

His cock jerked against her tongue, hot liquid filling her mouth as she swallowed as fast as she could.

The fingers playing over her swollen cunt intensified. The finger in her rear stroked still. Everything inside her tightened, coalesced, and expanded in a sudden burst of heat.

Daniel withdrew from her mouth and dropped to his knees in front of her, watching her. His blue eyes never left hers, holding her gaze. Good God. Her elbows trembled. Everything quaked. It went on and on.

Finn gave her back a parting kiss, climbed off the mattress, headed for the bathroom. Dan's arms wrapped around her, drew her down onto the mattress.

An almighty yawn took her as she settled against him. Body blissed out and mind blessedly quiet.

"We boring you?" Finn lay down beside her on the mussed sheets.

She shook her head. Would have expounded on that answer, but sleep had already taken her.

CHAPTER THIRTY-SEVEN

Finn sat at the table, watching Ali sleep. It was evening, he had been up and dressed for hours, but she slept on. The book in his hand kept him occupied. It was ... interesting, to say the least. It gave him a greater appreciation for her concerns.

"Hey," she murmured. Al blinked sleepy eyes at him and then the room, taking in the dark, the lantern beside him on the table. "What time is it?"

"Nearly eight. You slept all day."

The red stain on her cheek had paled. The dark circles beneath her eyes had lessened. Sleep had done her good, despite the odd disturbance.

Several times she had stirred from nightmares, lulled back to sleep by him or Dan or both. One of them kept his eyes on her every second, taking turns watching. Eventually their agreement to haunt her every step would earn a negative reaction, but not yet.

He found he liked being needed by her. He liked it a lot.

"What are you reading?"

Finn held the book cover high for her inspection. "Are you aware contractions are like warm waves caressing you?"

She screwed her nose up at him. "Sounds like some fantastic bullshit, Finn."

"Attitude's important, Al. The book said so," Finn chided, dropping the baby manual on the table. They'd avoided those concerns of hers because, truth be told, he hadn't known what to say. Information had been required.

He rose from the chair and slunk over to the bed as she watched, all wary eyed. The frown eased some as he sat beside her on the mattress, leant in to press his lips against hers. "Wonder what a baby of ours would look like?"

"Beautiful, I guess ... You're both beautiful." Her eyes dropped, hesitating, but then she kissed him back, sweet, soft kisses easing him. Al was safe, secure. He needed the physical proof. They were both worriers in their own way. "Would it bother you if this imaginary baby looked like Daniel?"

It wasn't like it hadn't occurred to him. He kissed her some more before answering.

"No. You're mine, and I want a part of any baby that's yours." He opened his mouth wider, incited her to do likewise. Her tongue stroked over his in welcome, the touch light, thrilling. Behind his zipper his cock stirred, the electric hum of arousal spreading through him. "We're family, Al, the three of us." Finn hooked a finger over the sheet she was holding against her breasts, lowered it. "They said some interesting things about the sensitivity of nipples during pregnancy."

"Did they?"

"Hmm." Finn traced over the line of her collarbone, tried to ignore the twitching in his pants. Touching her didn't help, but the low rumble of her stomach did. "You need to eat before anything else."

"Is that a euphemism for something?"

He smiled. "No. It's closer to, 'I have some fresh fruit and half-stale cereal for you.' You have such a lewd mind."

"You like it," she said.

"I love it." Finn breathed in deep: sex and soap and antiseptic lotion. Plus the special something, solely her.

"Where's Dan?"

"Helping Sam fix a generator. Shouldn't be long." He climbed off the bed. One of them needed to before things got out of hand. She really should eat.

Al wandered off to the bathroom as he set the table, poured juice into a glass, cereal into a bowl. Everything was ready and waiting when she emerged a few minutes later dressed in the usual jeans and t-shirt, her hair tied back and face damp from washing. He welcomed the normalcy of routine. They could live like this no problem. Mostly petty jealous bullshit had fueled the recent fighting. A near-death experience tended to clear up communication issues pretty damn fast. Or maybe it reshuffled priorities back into their pertinent order.

Finn smiled at her, and she smiled back.

The guy from the supply runs appeared at the top of the stairs. The one who had collected their weapons the day they arrived.

Finn hesitated, surprised, certain Dan would have locked the door. Owen. That was his name. And the first thing that came to mind was that something had happened to Dan. This guy was bringing the news.

"What ..." Finn stepped forward, and the guy raised his hand. There was a gun in it. Owen's eyes were empty and his mouth set. Owen, not Andy, and the gun had a silencer attached. Owen was working with Andy. They wanted to hurt her. His heart beat frantically.

Fuck.

"Al!" A muffled crack, followed by the impact of the bullet. It sent Finn stumbling back and a world of pain ensued. A universe of it.

Then everything went black.

CHAPTER THIRTY-EIGHT

Ali watched Finn stumble, fall. Her head spun sickeningly. There was so much blood.

She scrambled forward as Owen barked something, waved the gun at her. It was all peripheral, unreal. She couldn't make out the words. Her brain wouldn't accommodate them.

She had to reach Finn. Had to.

His closed eyes and ashen face tore at her. He looked like he'd been tossed aside by an uncaring hand, lying slumped against the brick wall, blood seeping from his chest. The front of his t-shirt slowly soaked it up. He might have only been asleep if it weren't for all the blood.

She moved jerkily forward and Owen's hand closed around her wrist. He gripped tight enough to grind her bones together, to drag her to a halt. He twisted her arm up behind her back. It should have hurt, but she had gone numb.

Finn.

He pushed the barrel of the gun beneath her ribs. She saw it, but she didn't feel it. It made her wonder if the punch of a bullet would hurt, wake her up.

"Let's go," Owen said. "Cooperate or I go find your other boy-friend and shoot him too. Move."

Her jaw flapped but no sound came out.

Owen strong-armed her toward the stairs, down them, the gun shoved beneath her ribs the entire time. He was strong and handled her easily.

She had to get back to Finn. Had. To. Had to stop this before Dan came strolling in and the prick shot him too. Owen needed to die before this nightmare worsened. He would die whatever it took.

Owen pulled her along, keeping her close, keeping up the grip on the gun and her wrist. If he had been behind her on the stairs, it wouldn't have worked. Halfway down the stairs, she threw her half-formed plan into action. With a strangled scream, Ali smashed herself into Owen. She threw all of her weight against him.

Surprised and caught off balance, he toppled to his knees. Gravity took over.

She had hoped he would let go. He did, but only of the gun. It bumped its way down the steps ahead of them.

Next came the tearing and the pop of her arm being wrenched from its socket. A blaze of white pain shattered her like a bolt of lightning, shearing her in two. She knew her shoulder was dislocated. No more numb. Oh fuck did she feel it.

They both fell, tumbling down the stairs to land one on top of the other. Owen grunted and shoved her aside, setting off all the pain receptors in her body once more. Black pinpricks danced and the world swam, murky and bright. Her breathing came in agonizing puffs. Every bit between her top and toes felt broken. When her vision cleared she stared down the barrel of the gun, her arm limp at her side.

Owen kicked out, caught her in the leg. He even sneered for good measure. Or he tried to. There was a bruise blossoming on his jaw, bloody drool on his chin. He was a mess. She wasn't much better. Her shoulder drowned out all other sensation.

"Fucking thtupid bitch."

She blinked, again and again. Poor Owen had apparently bitten his tongue.

She lost it. A manic giggle frothed up. It came out as a gasping groan of a noise.

The prick's face turned pink.

"Up. Move." Blood bubbled on his lips. He grabbed the front of her shirt, wrestled her back up onto her feet. Whatever damage she'd done him, he still had her in strength. "Move!"

Owen dragged her, limping and swaying, to a vehicle parked out front of the building. It was one of the pick-ups used for supply runs, nothing anyone would notice. The night was deadly quiet, the street empty. Dinnertime, everyone was busy. There was no one nearby to hear them.

"Don't make me thoot any more people," Owen hissed in her ear, hustling her into the passenger side of the pick up. He flicked on the child lock and slammed the door closed in her face.

She had to get back to Finn.

Ali nursed her injured arm, breathing through gritted teeth as the pain ebbed and flowed. In and out, in and out, in time with her heartbeat.

Oh, God. Finn. He had to be alright. He couldn't die. She had to escape. Get back to him. Stop the bleeding.

The truck's interior stank of old cigarette smoke. She peered out through the dirty windscreen, hoping for rescue so she could get someone to save Finn. Not many lights out there. A few of the empty steel storage drums dotted up the sidewalk, the tips of flames dancing over the steel rim, smoke winding up into the night air.

No one knew to help Finn. He was still up there, bleeding and alone. There had been a silencer on the gun but still, someone had to have heard something. She didn't want to think of him dying, but there it sat, front and center. No chance she was going to give in and cry in front of the prick, though her eyes watered. Her trembling sent pain lancing through her. Fuck but it hurt. Her breath stuttered and she held in a groan.

Owen climbed into the driver's seat, a gruesome trail of slobber dripping down his chin. It hung, suspended, catching the light from the nearest fire before falling to his lap.

The drive was short. Blackstone wasn't big. Neither spoke. Owen drove with the gun still in hand, braced against the steering wheel. He darted looks at her every other second, waiting on her next great escape attempt, no doubt.

What the hell could she do?

They made slow, steady progress through the streets. No point in making a grab for the wheel, he could easily overpower her. Besides, she only had one hand at her disposal and it wasn't her right, which was a bitch. Another opportunity would present itself and she'd grab it when it did. Rage and pain roiled through her.

They passed a group of people standing on a street corner. Several raised their hands and Owen nodded back, lowering the gun from view.

"Don't move," he muttered as they rolled past the scene.

The church spire came into view, the solid old brick building set with panels of colored glass. It was too dark to make out what stories they told. A trio of massive pine trees circled the place, standing guard. They made it even darker.

Owen pulled into the churchyard. Her teeth clattered as they covered the uneven ground. She clung onto her wounded wing, doing her best not to pass out. She needed to be coherent to kill the fucker and get back to Finn.

Andy stuck his head out the church's side door. There was a flashlight in one hand pointing down, casting a circle of light around his shoes. He held a gun in his other hand.

"What is this about, Owen?" she asked, trying to think her way clear of the pain, trying to find a way out.

The prick turned off the engine and wiped his chin with the back of his hand. "Come on, we'll thow you."

Fresh air rushed in as Andy opened the passenger side door. Owen had kept the windows up. She hadn't realized how cloying the temperature and the stink of old cigarettes had been until relief was granted. Maybe she should just try to make a run for it. Her rabbit heart beat faster at the thought. But getting shot here wasn't going to help Finn.

Andy stood there grim faced, looking far too young. "Told you to be careful with her."

"Thwew herself down the stairs. She's a fucking nut job." Owen flung open his door and spat onto the grass. "Shit."

"Come on. She's really agitated tonight," Andy said.

"Who is?" Ali levered herself carefully out of the car. The barrel of Andy's gun hovered by the side of her head.

"Inside," the boy waved the gun in the desired direction.

They marched her into the cool, quiet of the church building. It smelt nice at first, wood polish and the lingering scent of flowers. It was peaceful, still. Her shoulder beat in time with her steps. The farther they got down the dark red strip of carpet toward an open internal door, the more a pungent odor rose to greet them.

She knew the stench. Once she had caught it, it was all she could smell. The rank and putrid stink of rotting flesh. A low moan echoed up from below. Everything in her slowed in horror.

Al shook her head, trying to step back. "No! No."

"I can thoot you in the leg now and we'll drag you down there," Owen pressed the butt of his gun to her thigh. "Your choice."

The lack of options beat her about the head. Her ears filled with gray noise. Her steps toward the dark, open door were small, measured, and each and every one took a year off her rapidly dwindling life.

"Down the thteps. Don't try anything thith time." Owen tapped her head once more with the pistol in warning.

Andy led the way with his gun and flashlight.

Below, the cellar was lit with candles, big and small. Altar candles. The room glowed with light. Rachel was chained to an overhead beam, a dog collar around her swollen, gray neck. She had been fighting her imprisonment. One hand tugged at the collar while the other reached out to the three of them, bloody lips spread wide. The chain jangled as she tested her reach. It almost sounded merry.

Ali searched for an escape route. There was a line of three small windows halfway between them and Rachel. Pity about the guns pointed at her. The room wasn't very neat, not up to church standards. Old candelabras and brass vases were scattered about on the tabletop closest. A line of shelves filled with junk covered the far wall.

"Rachel went to see her dad," Andy said, his voice breaking. "He was hanging around the section of the wall up by the railway yard, trying to get in. She didn't understand ... infected don't ..."

"You think she would want to live like this?" Ali clung onto her wounded arm.

"We can look after her. There's no reason she can't still have a good life." Andy threw back his shoulders, stood tall. "We can do that for her."

"We will do that for her," Owen corrected. He spat a wad of bloody saliva onto the ground and Rachel snarled, yanking on the chain.

"People will find out," said Ali.

"People need to change their minds about infected. You'll help with that." Andy flicked off his flashlight and set it on a nearby table. His gun trembled in his hand.

"How?"

"We'll turn you. Your men won't let them hurt you. They'll have to let Rachel thtay too," Owen supplied, a wary eye on the homicidal maniac leashed up in the corner. "It'll work."

"No, it won't. My men will put a bullet in my head and give me a decent burial." The two idiots dealt her dubious looks.

"Bullthit," Owen growled and spat some more blood on the floor. "They would never kill you."

"You're wrong," she said. "They would never let me suffer, like you're letting Rachel. I guarantee it."

"We can't let you go. I guess that makes you dinner." Andy swallowed hard, his Adam's apple leaping in his scrawny neck, despite the tough words.

"You really think you can kill someone?" Ali asked. "It's not like you imagine it would be, Andy. It's not fast, no matter how quick they die. It stays with you. Plays over and over in your head till you think you're gonna lose it."

The boy's eyelids went into overdrive, fluttering like a fan. His gun dipped, trembling.

She almost felt sorry for the idiot when he teared up.

"We love her," the boy sobbed.

"Enough!" Owen jabbed the barrel of his gun into her head and pushed her backward, toward Rachel. "Think you're tho fucking thmart."

"How's your tongue?" she enquired, her own voice cracking. Back they went. Her hold on her arm slipped and slid, her palms damp with sweat. "Cause you're still sounding pretty shitty, Owen."

Rachel growled and Owen repeated it.

Closer and closer.

"Can I just say, you are one sick fuck of an individual. How did it feel, killing Lindsay?"

The young man's eyes fired with rage and his bloody teeth clenched.

"It was you, wasn't it? Just because she called poor little Rachel names."

"Sthe detherved it!"

"Right, course she did. You're one sick puppy, Owen. Honest to goodness, deep down where it counts, you really are. You are all fucked up, my friend."

She could almost feel Rachel's stale, fetid breath on the back of her neck, hear her snapping and snarling next to her ear. Fear stiffened every hair on her body. Pain brought tears to her eyes. Fucked if she was dying here.

Being marched backward to her doom had only one positive. Ali kicked the prick in the balls with her bad leg. Gave it her all.

She didn't want to die. But taking a bullet to the brain from Owen versus getting munched on by Rachel was a no brainer.

She'd take the bullet.

Owen howled and clutched at his junk, gun forgotten in his agony. Ali skipped aside and shoved the prick with all her might while he was still doubled over. Balance gone, Owen stumbled into the waiting clutches of his infected girlfriend.

Rachel fell upon him with malevolent glee. The infected woman had a good grip on her prey, fingers gouging into his flesh as she tore at the side of Owen's neck with her teeth. Owen's gun slid behind Rachel, out of Ali's reach. The man screamed, and Andy ran toward the couple, caught in their morbid embrace.

The still sobbing boy started yelling something, but Ali didn't stop to listen. Hell no. She made straight for the stairs. Her shoulder throbbed and her bruised leg dragged behind her in her haste.

Shards of wood hit her bare feet and the noise of Andy's gun firing echoed through the concrete room, bouncing off the wall at top volume. The sound made her ears sing.

No stopping. Again and again, he fired wildly.

Owen screamed.

The top of the stairs was so close, if she could only reach the door. There were no footsteps behind her, only Rachel's snarls and Owen's wailing.

Andy didn't follow her.

Ali hauled herself up onto the small landing, threw herself through the door and slammed it shut. There was no lock, and the heavy christening font would need two good arms to shift it. She had to keep going.

Down the red carpet and through the shadowy church. She bumped off the ends of pews like a pinball. Her choppy breathing and the muffled yells from below were the only noise.

The side door was unlocked and she threw herself through it, emerging out into the open air.

Thank fuck.

Her body ached but she couldn't stop yet. Ali hustled her ass into the pick-up, the key still helpfully sitting in the ignition. It wasn't like people stole cars anymore. She pushed in the clutch and shoved the gear stick into neutral, turned the key. Every movement was awkward and slow with her one good hand all over the place. The engine didn't care, it roared to life.

Lift-off.

Ali threw it into reverse and the pick-up truck shot backward like a rocket, taking out a panel of the wire fencing. A bullet cracked the front windscreen and her foot slipped.

The engine stalled.

Andy started walking toward her, tear tracks lining his face.

She swore, threw it into first and turned the key, wincing at the stabbing pain and keeping her head down, lest Andy's aim improved.

The truck took flight again and she was off. Bullets slammed into the side door as she careened past the little prick, almost clipping him along with another section of fencing. Her foot nearly slipped again when she jumped the curb but no, no way.

Ali roared down the quiet street.

Things were happening in her rearview mirror. People wandered out onto the footpaths, weapons in hand, alerted by the shooting. Finally.

Andy took off at a run, disappearing into the darkness behind her. She wasn't alone. The little prick was not going to get to kill her. Not today. A noise came from low in her throat, relief and anxiety and fear.

"Fuck, fuck, fuck." Ali eased up on the pedal, turned the corner one-handed in a great arc of a circle and headed back toward Main Street.

The group on the corner had grown. There was help. The pick-up slowed to a crawl, seemingly of its own volition. Strength seemed to be seeping straight out of her as the adrenalin eased.

It was Santa who threw the truck door open, surprise and concern dragging at his face. His mouth hung open. "Ali? What the ..."

"Finn's shot. Back at the apartment."

"What?" His bushy brows met. "Who?"

"Owen," she said. The big man scrunched his face up at her and she lost it, yelling at him. "Owen shot him and took me to the church. He and Andy have got Rachel there, she's infected. Do something for once, would you?"

"I'll check on Finn." Erin said from behind him and took off at a run.

"Good." Ali rubbed gingerly at her shoulder, tried to catch her breath. "That's good."

Santa gave her a dubious sidelong glance and pulled a walkie-talkie from his belt, pushed the button. "Tom, anything happening at the front gate?"

"Nuh —" was all the man got out before the sound of more shots came from exactly that direction.

One. Two. Three shots. Then an almighty tempest of gunfire. Andy had lost it, too.

"Give me a gun." She crawled out of the pick-up and shoved her good hand at Santa.

"You're hurt. Stay out of the way."

At the sound of shots, the people he had been standing with had started back down Main Street, running toward the gate. Santa followed at his heftier pace.

Ali followed the path Erin had taken and hobbled toward home, her arm nursed against her chest. Finn was propped against their downstairs front door, a gun in each hand. His skin was pasty and covered in streaks of blood.

Erin slipped out of the doorway beside him and sprinted toward the front gate.

Ali burst into violent tears, startling herself. They ran down her face unchecked while she crossed the distance between them. "You're alive."

"Course I'm alive. He only got me in the shoulder." Finn gave her a lingering kiss, eyes squeezed tight. When they opened, he had his game face on. "Where's Owen?"

"Dead, I think. And Andy's at the front gate."

"That's where Dan headed to get help looking for you. What's wrong with your arm?"

"Dislocated, maybe?"

"Al," Finn sighed. "Upstairs and stay there. Lock the door. Lock every damn door."

"You just got shot!"

"I field-dressed it. Go on." Finn turned and broke into a steady if slow jog.

A chorus of moaning rose in volume down the street. But it wasn't enough to drown out the noise of the garbage truck serving as the settlement's front gate chugging to life.

Andy was going to let in the infected. The whole settlement was dead.

CHAPTER THIRTY-NINE

Daniel had an aneurysm. He could feel it. Without a doubt it was going to pop if he didn't find his girl right fucking now.

He jogged down Main Street, his small semblance of calm thinning with Finn's blood on his hands. He rubbed his palm on his jeans, spread his fingers out and wiped off the blood in between them. His gun was slippery.

The kid was alright. He was on his feet, swearing like a trooper and finishing padding the bullet wound in his shoulder.

Daniel headed up the search party. The group gathered at the Blackstone gate would do fine for his search and rescue squad. Someone here had to know where Owen would have taken her.

He dodged the tractor they had been tearing up the tarmac with, less than 50 meters out when he saw Andy. Then, Daniel's feet faltered.

The young man came streaking out from beneath the shadows of a line of shop awnings to the east. He held a small sub-machine gun in his hands. The weapon pointed straight at the four men standing clueless by the garbage truck.

Andy's mouth opened in a silent scream. A war cry.

"No!" Daniel raised his pistol, fired off three shots in the boy's direction.

Andy started firing. His victims were clustered so close they didn't stand a chance. The four men toppled, torn apart by the volley of bullets. Blood sprayed the road, the truck. It went everywhere, bright and beautiful in the light of the rising moon.

Andy's head turned and the weapon followed. Bullets sprayed up stone at Daniel's feet. He threw himself behind the tractor, hitting the ground hard while bullets punched into metal. His teeth clinked and his shoulder sang, jarred by the impact.

Then the bullets stopped. The sudden silence chilled him to his bones. His ears still echoed with the inferno of noise from a moment ago.

Shit.

Daniel pushed to his feet, feeling every day of his forty-odd years. He snuck a look around the side of the tractor and his gut plunged. Andy was climbing into the cab of the garbage truck, slamming the door shut. "Oh, no."

He aimed at the door, firing at the little prick as the truck came to life like some monster of old. Or maybe more akin to the monsters of new. The infected were well revved up – moaning and snarling on the other side of the big machine.

"What happened?" A hand clapped down on his shoulder and one of Santa's buddies puffed to a stop beside him.

Others didn't stop to ask questions, opening fire on the garbage truck's front windscreen. Glass shattered. Inside the cab Andy jerked and fell, spread across the steering wheel. His head was a ruined, red mush.

It didn't matter. Mission accomplished.

Andy had managed to reverse back two, maybe three meters. He had almost cleared one lane of traffic and it was more than enough.

The infected spilled into town.

Gunfire filled his ears. Daniel ejected his empty clip, reached for the spare in his back pocket. A weird kind of calm took him over. His hands held perfectly steady. They were fighting for their lives now. No question about it.

More of the townsfolk arrived, standing alongside him, taking aim. Before them, bodies staggered and flopped and fell, soon replaced by more. The horde gathered on the bridge and along the fence lines poured through the gap in their defenses. Some fell upon the four men Andy had killed until a hive of moving limbs surrounded the bodies.

Several tried unsuccessfully to climb the front of the garbage truck to get at Andy.

There were too many of them pouring through to get close enough to reach the truck and close the gap.

Close by, something howled, loud, long and mournful. More joined in and the noise eclipsed all the weapons with ease. Yipping and snapping sounds came from the other side of the truck.

"What the fuck was that?" Santa looked as good as Daniel felt, cheeks puffed up and purple.

"At a guess?" he yelled back at the man. "The dogs Ali saw, or something like them."

Santa blanched, turned and hollered, "More guns in the hardware."

Daniel grabbed his thick wrist. "Where's Owen?"

Santa squinted, shook his head. "Your woman's fine. Sent her home."

It was all he needed to know. The relief was exquisite. Breathtaking. He stupidly grinned, ignoring the look from one of the townsfolk near him. The apocalypse could wait. Or not.

The assembled were slowly being pressed back by the onslaught of infected. Some were slipping through the gap to collapse mere meters before them, but others were spreading out into the town.

This was not a fight they were likely to win.

"She's safe." Finn elbowed in beside him, a rifle slung over one shoulder and a pistol in each hand. The front of his shirt was stained dark with blood and there was a tangle of bandages spanning from around his neck to beneath his left arm. An almighty wad beneath his left collarbone, where the bullet had hit.

"You're a walking happy meal looking like that." Daniel jutted his chin at the kid's chest.

"They won't get close enough." Finn took aim, popped off a few rounds. "We need to get her somewhere safe. This is going to go south."

Screams echoed from one street over as infected found prey.

Back down the street more people hurried, loaded down with weapons. More still would be locking down in hopes of surviving by staying put, others loading up to run. He doubted any had planned for this.

The first dog came through, red eyes ablaze and bloody foam dripping from its jaws. Fucking hell. Daniel had never seen anything like it. The hot stench of urine hit his nose as someone pissed themselves nearby. More than one on the front line turned tail and ran.

Finn shoved his pistols into his jeans pockets and drew the rifle from his back, the both of them walking backward. "I want you to get her out."

"If we're leaving, we all go together."

Finn fired and the first dog fell, its body flung aside by the force of the bullet and its own momentum. Two more jumped atop the growing mound of dead bodies to take its place. "Stop talking. Start moving."

"She won't go without you."

"Make her."

"Finn, neither will I."

The horde had them on the run. People appeared in upstairs windows, seeking shelter and a decent firing position off the street. There was more screaming in the back streets of Blackstone as the infected spread.

Finn swore, lined up another shot and pulled the trigger, dropping a second of the hellhounds.

"We're just going to leave these people to die?" asked Daniel.

And they were dying. The front line was a jagged, hole-ridden thing, doing little to stop the barrage of infected, let alone the dogs.

A truck pulled up behind them, headlights on full, casting shadows across the crowd of infected. It lit things up nicely for the shooting gallery. If anyone but his girl had been behind the driver's seat, he would have thanked them.

"How we doing?" Ali yelled from the driver's-side window.

He and Finn both swore.

An infected fell upon someone to their far left who was caught out reloading. A high-pitched squeal filled the air. Finn quickly shifted, lining up his target. The top of the thing's head turned a red mass as its brains exploded.

But it was too late.

The man fell to his knees, clutching at the remains of his throat, helpless to staunch the flow of blood pumping out through his fingers.

"I need to get to the garbage truck," Finn said. "We have to close the gap."

"There are too many," said Dan.

"We have to push through." Al revved the engine. "Get in the back."

Finn turned to Daniel with teeth clenched tight. "I'm begging you, get her out of here."

"If we need to make a run then she's right where we want her," Daniel said. Panic ripped through him like broken glass in his gut.

The thought of letting either one of them out of his sight squeezed those shards tight. "Here's the cavalry."

Another pick-up truck pulled up alongside them, Santa behind the wheel. Erin and three men were in the open-top cage up back. They were armed to the teeth, with an assortment of guns and ammunition lying loose around their feet. Erin handed Dan a couple of pistols, popping off shots at the gate all the while. The woman stayed strong despite the pallor of her face.

"Thanks," he said.

"We're going for the garbage truck. Cover our backs." Finn seemed to avoid Ali's worried gaze when he passed her by and climbed onto her pick-up's tray in one smooth jump. "Wind the window up, Al. Whatever happens, you stay put."

Daniel followed the gunslinger, standing up high, hanging on to the metal frame sitting behind the cab. If possible, things looked worse from up there. He blocked out the cries of panic and pain from nearby, muted the moaning and concentrated on doing his part, gunning down the infected shambling toward them. They were taking her straight into it.

His shoulders tightened and he prayed the gun wouldn't start shaking.

If they could just all live through this, all three of them get through it in one piece – it was all he asked. And it was a shitload to ask at such a time.

Finn knocked once on the cab roof and they were off. A hot, putrid wind rushed toward them as they drove into the oncoming sea of infected.

CHAPTER FORTY

Finn stood behind the cab on the back of the pick-up, concentrating solely on one lone target at a time. He took it nice and easy, though he could feel the sweat dampening his back, and the trickle of blood running down his front. Not letting the fact that his girlfriend was driving straight into danger mess with his focus.

Shit.

He wanted Al away from this, but Dan was right. Keeping her close was best.

Shit. Shit. Shit.

More dogs appeared, slinking in, cautious now. They growled and bit at thin air. They fell upon the scene like it was a feast. Infected or no, it didn't seem to matter.

Finn laid the rifle at his feet and Daniel slapped a semiautomatic Browning into his hand. The two trucks moved forward, side-by-side, toward the garbage truck, lowering the risk of friendly fire. It was a bumpy ride, since many of the infected had fallen. There was no clean path.

It was less than a hundred meters, but it felt like miles.

Al kept going till the vehicle's front grill bumped against the side of the garbage truck. She had made the vehicle into a walkway, delivering him straight to the driver's-side door.

A zombie banged against her window and Daniel dealt it one to the head.

Finn slipped his pistol into his belt, climbed up and over the cab, and stepped onto the pick-up's hood. The engine vibrated beneath his feet.

None of the garbage truck windows survived. Andy lay where he fell, slumped against the steering wheel.

Finn pulled open the driver's-side door.

The world lit up from the wrong direction. Lights appeared, dazzling him, shining in from out of the darkness beyond Blackstone. From the outside. Finn shielded his eyes with his hand.

An army Hummer rolled toward them, heading for the gap in the wall. Men walked alongside, picking off the infected as they came close. Some carried pistols, not unlike his own, but not all. The staccato bursts of an Uzi or something similar cut the night apart. About nine men, max, dressed in haphazard uniform. Ex-military, perhaps.

What the fuck is this?

Five, six of the dogs stood snarling, caught between guns firing inside Blackstone and this new line of attack. Trapped. They were going to lose civilians to friendly fire if these new people weren't careful. The moaning of the infected picked up. Many were milling about, likewise caught between Erin's truckload of gunners and this new development.

"We're here to help," someone yelled before one of the men up front struck up a flame thrower. "Stand clear!"

The blue and gold of the flame flared and shot out, painting the scene in vibrant light. The dogs scattered and ran. The clothing of the infected lit up like dry grass. Burning flesh scented the air along with smoke and gunpowder.

But who were these people?

Finn pushed Andy's body across the seat then climbed into the truck, turned the key and ...

Nothing. Absolutely nothing.

Finn shoved the gear stick into neutral, motioned to Daniel. "Need a push!"

The man grimaced, nodded, shot another infected wandering close to the vehicle. Two of the men from the back of Santa's pickup had jumped down and were working through those closest, thinning out the infected. No more came through the gate.

If the hole in their defenses could be plugged then Blackstone might survive after all.

There was a strangled cry from one of the men. An infected had managed to come up behind him. It dug its mouth into the male's thigh, tearing through cloth. Blood gushed from the jagged wound.

Erin stood on the tray of the second pick-up, her face drawn back in horror. She raised her gun and shot twice.

The infected fell.

Without hesitation the man who had been bitten put his gun in his mouth and pulled the trigger. Finn forced himself to look away. Nothing he could do. Besides, the job wasn't done. Not yet. On the bridge, the Hummer drew closer and the strangers rigged out in military gear started wandering in, picking off any stragglers lumbering nearby. Erin and her friends focused on the newcomers for a moment but hesitated, shifting back to targeting the infected, the most immediate and pressing threat. Gradually the infected were being thinned out.

"Truck's dead. Help us push it up." Finn called out to the nearest newcomer, a big, boxy looking man with a take-no-shit face.

The guy nodded, signaled to his squad. There was a lot of yelling and movement while the two forces combined, the strangers and the townsfolk. People rushed to the back of the truck while others straddled the gap, keeping any remaining infected from entering the town.

Slowly, the garbage truck rolled forward.

The men standing before it eased back, making certain they were on the right side when the gap closed. Finn tugged on the handbrake. They had done it. Amazing.

He pulled out a pistol and swung down from the truck too fast. His vision grayed. He gripped the side of the truck, gun clattering against the metal. Weakness from blood loss crept steadily through him, draining him. The desire to sink down onto the bitumen and sit a while wasn't easy to resist. But they weren't finished yet.

Santa wandered forward, a messy, bloody wound on his forearm. His face was taut and white from pain. He had been bitten. "Who are you boys?"

"I'm Emmet, the leader. You been bit?" He nodded at Santa's arm.

"It'll be dealt with," Santa said.

Everyone stood silent for a moment as realization sunk in.

"Dad?" Erin grabbed at the man's shoulder, eyes red and wild. "No!"

"Hush." Her father patted her hand. Then he pushed it aside. "Who are you?"

"We're the people that just saved your asses." The big, boxy man who had identified himself as Emmet strode forward. A malicious smile bent the man's face and Finn readied his gun. "I believe some sort of suitable payment can be worked out. We ..."

Whatever the man had been going to say was lost in a sea of red. His body slumped to the ground.

Finn looked around, his finger on the trigger. He was unsure who to aim at. The place sunk into pandemonium.

Everyone's guns were in their hands, pointing every which way. It was about to be a fucking disaster. But most people targeted the eight remaining strangers in their midst.

Another man opened his mouth, eyes bulging at the sight of his fallen commander. There was a pop from somewhere and then he too dropped.

"Don't shoot. Please," one of the strangers said, open palms rising above his head.

"Explain your intentions," Finn yelled.

The man's eyes settled on him. He nodded and set down his gun.

"What the fuck is going on here?" Santa bellowed. Erin stood beside him, the gun in her hand trembling.

"We are all going to put down our weapons now," the unarmed stranger said loudly.

The rest of the newcomers slowly put down their guns. Several wild-eyed men took longer than the rest.

"I'm Captain Sean Manning," the stranger said. "The two men we just executed were planning on kidnapping some of your females. That was the payment Emmet was seeking."

Santa swayed on his feet but his face seemed set in stone. "Is that so?"

"Three more of these men were not openly opposed to this plan of taking your women. But we can't speak to their intentions. We would request you send them on their way. Unharmed." Captain Manning pursed his lips, his gaze wandering over his companions. "Enough people have died. Emmett killed anyone who defied him. He executed men earlier this week for speaking out against him. These three didn't necessarily have a choice."

"But you didn't trust them enough to include them in your coup?" Daniel asked, keeping a hand on the truck door so Al couldn't climb out.

"No," Captain Manning replied. "The fewer who knew, the safer it was."

Santa nodded, lips pressed tight. Blood seeped steadily from his wound. The man had strength and then some. "I take it the other four of you wish to remain with us."

"Yes. Please."

"They have nice manners," Daniel said.

"Right now we need to clean up the rest of the town. Make yourselves useful and we'll see." Santa ran his eyes over the men, weighing their worth. "Send your three friends off."

The soldier nodded, clearly pointed out three of the men. "If any of you show your faces here again you'll be shot on sight."

Two started arguing, denying. Their movements were sharp, aggressive. But there were a lot of guns pointed at them. The third dropped his gaze, frowned hard at the ground, his mouth working noiselessly. Finally he looked up, nodded. "Can I have a gun?"

"There's more in the Hummer outside, Nick," Captain Manning answered, not unsympathetically.

Nick nodded just the once. The man was tall, well built. Lethal. Out of the three, he was easily the most dangerous. Finn kept close.

The man's eyes never stopped moving, hands clenching and releasing, but when he spoke, his tone was resigned. "Alright."

The other two men said enough for everyone standing. Insults mixed with denials. Their hot and greedy eyes slid over Erin and Al. It was all Finn could do not to end them there and then.

"They can stay the night in the lock-up at the police station. We'll release them during the day," Finn said. He turned to the men. "And if I ever see any of you three near town again after tomorrow, I will kill you."

CHAPTER FORTY-ONE

Ali wound down the window, curious and frustrated and just a little afraid. Her heart would calm down eventually. Probably. "Will you move your hand, already?"

"What's wrong with your arm?" Daniel snapped back, throwing the door open himself. He leant down and ducked his head into the cab and kissed her soundly. His hand burrowed through her hair to clasp the back of her head and hold her to him. Like she would try to escape. Idiot.

They had survived. Her men were alive.

Daniel rubbed his lips over hers, nuzzling her face. "Babe, what have you done to yourself now?"

"I'm fine." Her shoulder throbbed, the joint swollen and hot. "I love you."

"I love you too. That being said, you can't lie for shit. I honestly don't know why you bother." Daniel's hand stroked her bad shoulder and she whined, the pain excruciating. Gray dots hovered at the edge of her field of vision. "Damn."

"I think it's dislocated," she panted.

"You're going to have to pop it back in for her," Finn said from behind Daniel. "She shouldn't have been running around in the truck. She should have stayed locked in at the apartment."

"*She* can make her own decisions. And you. You have a bullet in you!" Ali shifted around in the driver's seat, a slow and agonizing process.

"Children ..." Daniel chided. "Come on, sweet."

His big hands gripped her waist as he ever so carefully helped her from the vehicle.

"Thanks."

"I'm gonna help them run the rest down," said Finn. One-handed, he checked the remains of his clip. "You get her help."

And out came her fretful tone of voice. High-pitched and panicky, she didn't even bother to try and rein it in. "No, you're not,

Finn. You're bleeding, aren't you? And we need to figure out how to get the bullet out."

"Later." Finn turned his back on her and reached for his rifle in the back of the pick-up. Dismissing her, apparently, which didn't work. She knew better now.

"Hey." Ali slipped her good arm around his waist, pressed herself against his back. "Stop. Turn around."

With an exaggerated sigh Finn did so, careful of bumping either of their shoulders. The lines around his beautiful pale green eyes were embedded deeply. "Al ..."

"I love you."

He canted his head. "I know, but you need to stay put when I tell you to."

"Love means sticking together. Thick and thin. Good and bad." She leant against him, rose up on her toes and kissed him. "I needed that."

Finn put his pistol on the pick-up's bed, stroked her neck with the tips of his fingers. The scent of blood and gunpowder was thick in the air. "I need you. I nearly lost you again today."

She shrugged, put on a stoic face. "Things are bound to calm down eventually."

Finn sighed, pressed his forehead against hers. "I'm gonna lock you up."

"You'll try. We'll fight. There'll be make-up sex. Life goes on."

"Sam said there was a dental nurse," said Daniel. "She can dig out the bullet. I'm probably going to have to pop your shoulder back, babe. Sorry."

"It'll feel a lot better once it's done," Finn said.

"Okay." She nodded, lips compressed. Her eyes stayed on Santa, huddled aside with a crying Erin. Things could have been much worse. Daniel and Finn stood beside her, close and comforting. So many dead lay about them. "We got off light, considering."

CHAPTER FORTY-TWO

Dan stopped to catch his breath. He leant against one of the big old jacarandas. A couple of members of the militia stumbled past, dragging bodies toward the mammoth bonfire burning bright at the top of Main Street. Several of Blackstone's remaining citizens stood close to the funeral pyre, saying prayers. Mourning. There was no time for burials and no space in the little town cemetery. And fresh blood attracted infected.

Long as he lived, he didn't think he'd ever forget the smell of the bodies burning. Twenty-one of the townsfolk were dead. A hell of a toll. Lindsay's body had also been consigned to the fire. So too had the remains of the slain infected, including Rachel and Owen.

Death made all things equal.

Ali and Finn lay tucked up in bed, safe and sound. Finn had wanted to be down here, overseeing things, but Ali wouldn't rest without him. She'd won this round with the use of big, sad eyes and a healthy dose of common sense. The dental nurse, a lovely lady by the name of Lila, had dug the bullet out of Finn without too much hassle. Fortunately, it hadn't been deep, but the kid had still lost a good amount of blood. Dan had popped his girl's shoulder back in. Her pretty face had blanked, and she'd passed out for a couple of minutes, her skin whiter than he'd ever seen. It felt like his heart had stopped. Causing her pain, no matter the reason, was not on his list of things to ever repeat. It had all left his nerves a little raw.

Maybe Finn was right. Maybe they should lock her up. Something to consider. He sighed, hung his head. She'd just figure out how to pick locks.

They were all okay. They were good. Everyone would recover. Unlike Sam.

Dawn neared, the sky a hazy mix of violet and pink in the east. The renewed build-up of infected on the other side of the wall slowly dispersed, the moaning and groaning gradually calming.

They'd attracted more than their fair share of attention tonight with all the noise and commotion.

Time was running out for Santa. In the eight to ten hour incubation period a fever took hold, causing the person to sweat profusely. Skin turned from tan or pink to an eerie gray. With the light of dawn, Dan could all too easily see the toll the sickness took in Santa's sunken eyes. It was hard to look at him, but even harder to look away. Any minute now, Santa could turn from man to mindless predator. Erin remained at her father's side, posture rigid and face set. She wasn't crying. Her hand lingered on the butt of the pistol holstered at her side. Waiting.

Her father was filling his last hours with organizing the small community before the virus took him. Talking to everyone. Solidifying the council. He had already asked Finn to step up and take a seat. Erin would lead them for now. The locals weren't ready for so much new blood so fast. Finn had agreed.

"She shouldn't have to do that," said Sean, the militia captain, tipping his chin at Erin and her pistol.

He and his men had helped hunt down the last of the infected inside the walls. Then they'd moved on to the grisly job of dealing with the dead in a respectful but efficient manner.

Everyone watched the newcomers, waiting for a misstep. Acceptance wouldn't come easily. Considering how trigger-happy folks were feeling after the carnage tonight, it wouldn't take much for all hell to break loose once more. The militia seemed to appreciate that fact, moving slowly, wary of spooking anyone. There were lots of sincere nods and wary greetings. As to their true intentions, time would tell. The fact remained that the town needed them. The wall wasn't without its weaknesses.

And who knew what the hell else was out there, ready and waiting to come at them?

"I agree. Erin shouldn't have to deal with her own flesh and blood." Dan stretched, cracked his neck and winced. Another death on his hands. Better his than Erin's.

They walked toward the small group. A couple of remaining Council members with grave faces stood beside Erin and her father. It wouldn't be long now. Dan had seen the signs often enough to know.

"Wait," Sean said, watching the scene with tired eyes. "It's already being taken care of."

Two militia men were waiting close by, behind Erin, out of her line of sight.

Santa turned to his daughter and his whole body started shaking, twitching. He clutched his arms to his chest. "I, ahh ... I may have left it too late."

Erin's face fell but she nodded.

One of the strangers stepped up to Erin, put a hand to her elbow. He leant in close, mouth moving fast. Whatever he said was too soft to hear.

"Let him." Santa fell to his knees, lips curling back in a pained snarl. "Do it!"

"No!" Erin leapt forward, toward her father, as a low growl escaped him. His fingers curled into claws and his eyes rolled back into his head, tremors racking his body. The stranger grabbed her, hauling her back.

"Dad!"

The second militia man drew and fired, the blast of his revolver echoing through the quiet town, reverberating off the neat lines of old buildings.

Santa's body tumbled to the ground. Dead.

Erin gasped, mouth slack and eyes wide. The man who held her released her, drawing back. But a hand remained stretched out to her, in case she stumbled.

Daniel swore fervently beneath his breath. Aah, man. What a thing for her to have to see.

Her fingers flexed and closed, flexed and closed as she stared down at her father, lying in an expanding pool of blood. Somewhere in the distance kookaburras started laughing, greeting the dawn. The wood in the funeral pyre popped and crackled, the scent of charred flesh heavy on the breeze. Daniel swallowed back the nausea. Death wasn't something you ever got used to. Not really.

Erin spun and stepped up to the man who had killed her father. His gun was still in his hand. Her fist caught him fair in the face, slamming into his cheekbone, leaving a smear of blood in her wake. She drew her hand back again, her intent clear.

The man grimaced, straightened and holstered his gun. He stood tall, not moving an inch, with his eyes wide open, waiting to take anything she had to give him. Not saying a word.

Her fist trembled in the air between them, wavering.

Erin's shoulders crumpled first, caving in. Her hand fell next, spine bowing and knees folding. She made no noise at all as she knelt beside her father's body.

Captain Manning nodded at the two men standing guard behind the woman. "They'll look after her."

Daniel raised a brow.

"You'd have her live with killing her father on her conscience?" the captain asked.

"No. Just curious about exactly how they're going to 'look after her.'"

Sean's tired gaze stayed on him a long time. "We realize we're going to have to prove ourselves." He narrowed his eyes at Erin. She remained huddled beside Santa's corpse. "It'll be easier for her to hate them than herself, or anyone else here for having to kill him. They'll look after her by dealing with his body, if she wants, when she's ready. They'll make sure no one bothers her if she wants to be left alone. That's all."

Daniel rolled out his lips. "Yeah. That's what I thought you meant."

"You think you're funny, don't you?" asked the captain in a low tone.

"No, not particularly. Sure as hell, not right now." Dan smothered a yawn, widened his stance. "You'll get your chance to prove yourselves. Be careful though. People are going to be edgy for a while. It'd be sad if there were any accidents and one of you got shot by mistake."

The captain's eyes lit with a wolfish grin. "Wouldn't it be?"

"Now then, I'm just saying."

Sean grunted, frowned off into the distance. "How did the world get so fucked up?"

"Dunno. Why don't we all just concentrate on helping each other stay alive, hmm?"

"Believe me, that's the plan."

CHAPTER FORTY-THREE

Un-fucking-believable, they were arguing again.

Finn climbed the steps silently. Loath to interrupt, because not all arguments were bad. Especially not if the room reeked of sex.

"Dan ..." Al's voice was low and urgent.

Finn knew that tone of voice. Finn loved that tone of voice.

"You have to wait," Dan said.

"You're not being fair."

"Of course I am."

"No, you're not," she moaned. "You're really fucking not."

"I would remind you, babe. This was all your idea."

Their girl took a sharp breath. "Damn it."

"You're doing so well. The secret, my love, is lube – lots and lots of lube."

Finn's imagination had presented many varied scenarios. The one that met him topped them all.

Al was naked and on her hands and knees, a personal favorite of his. Watching her tits sway was awesome. Dan knelt behind her, two fingers buried in her gorgeous ass. His pants were still on, despite the definite bulge at the front.

And there were balloons, strangely enough, balloons in every color imaginable. A whole room full of them.

"You're in trouble," Dan said to Finn. His fingers never ceased their slow, careful thrust and retreat.

"Why is that?" Finn asked, his gaze glued to Dan's hand.

"It's your birthday, and you didn't tell me." Al's face was flushed pink, her mouth open, and jaw tight. Her gray eyes were glazed with passion. "You were supposed to be home quarter of an hour ago."

"I forgot about my birthday." Finn dropped to his knees beside the mattress and leant over, kissing the life out of her. He couldn't get enough of her. "I'm sorry I'm late."

"He wouldn't let me come," she tipped her chin at Dan.

"It was polite to wait for the birthday boy," said Dan with a wink.

Finn grinned so hard his face hurt, hand stroking her healed shoulder. "Can I guess what my present is?"

"Get your dick out. I'm tired of waiting. You need to catch up fast." Al's gray eyes glanced up at him, mouth open and waiting, her beautiful lips moist. "Hurry."

He loved her so much it hurt, along with being so damned turned on it hurt. And she had been more careful the last six weeks, conceding to some, if not all, of his demands. Things really had calmed down.

"Catching up is not going to be a problem." He was already hard, the surge of blood to his groin dizzying.

Finn unbuckled his belt, tore at the button and zipper of his jeans. The minimum required to free his cock and feed it into her waiting mouth. Sweet heat and tension. Ali's lips closed around him, sucking at the engorged flesh.

Perfect.

The muscles in his stomach jumped and clenched as she drew on him. Her tongue got busy, and his head fell back, hands cradling her skull. "God, Al. That's so good."

She moaned around Finn's cock. Daniel gave a short, pained laugh, scissoring his fingers more obviously in her rear entrance. "She likes this more than she has let on."

Al hadn't been the only one waiting.

The man licked his lips, watching his fingers gliding into the nicely stretched little hole. Finn's cock pulsed in her mouth. Waiting really wasn't an option. That she gave to him like this drove him wild. That she had planned this for him.

Best. Birthday. Ever.

"I think we're about ready," Finn said.

"Alrighty." Dan slid his fingers free of her and wiped them on a waiting towel. He gave her ass a final squeeze, shuffled back on his knees.

Finn reluctantly withdrew from the heat of her mouth. Her tongue swiped over the head of his cock, taking a drop of pre-cum before he could draw away completely. Her fervor for him was the only gift he needed. Not that he would turn down her ass.

"Happy birthday," she said.

"You have no idea." He kissed her deeply, giving her everything he had. Thanking her without words. "You want Dan beneath you?"

"Both of you?"

"If you want."

Her teeth worried her lip and her eyes wandered away briefly. She was nervous, but that had never stopped their girl before.

"Okay," she whispered.

"We'll go slow." Finn whipped off his shirt, nodded to the man. "You're on the bottom."

"Excellent." Dan dealt with his jeans in a hurry, hand to his cock as he crawled back onto the bed. "Come here, babe. It's been killing me thinking I'd have to wait."

"You like to watch," Al purred, camping it up with a grin.

"I do. But I like to participate even more," Daniel assured her, lying on his back so Al could climb atop him. She kissed him over and over, covering his mouth with her swollen lips. Her hands pressed down on his shoulders, holding him in place. Playing with him. Their wrestling escalated till Daniel took her hip in hand, his other guiding his cock into her. "Give me that pretty pussy."

She inhaled and sank down on him, her hands wrapped around his shoulders and her ass squirming as she worked herself onto Daniel. Finn was almost jealous. He knew how her body welcomed him, the pull of succulent cunt. His balls were in agony.

"Hell," Dan mumbled.

"Lie down, Al." Finn's hands guided her onto Dan's chest and the man's hands slipped up her arms, held her. "That's it. We'll take it nice and easy."

"My brave girl," said Daniel. "I'm so proud of you right now. I just can't say."

"Shuddup," Al choked out a laugh that morphed into a moan when Finn rubbed the head of his cock over her asshole and pressed inward. Christ. The way that tight hole parted for him, softening and giving just enough to swallow the crown of cock. He had to take his time, had to make it good for her. Damn but it hurt to wait. "Aah."

"Push back, Al."

"Stings," she panted.

Daniel stroked her sides, soothing her, pressed kisses to the side of her face. "Relax, babe. You're tensing up."

"I shouldn't have encouraged the oral," she groaned. "You were big enough without it."

Her hold on Finn eased incrementally as he pressed forward. Sweat and heat flooded his spine, building up and up. Slowly, he pushed into her until his pelvis lay flush against her body. He was seated inside her fully now. The presence of Dan inside her made the fit even tighter.

Finn hung his head and sucked in a breath, his lips drawn back. Every time he touched her he doubted it could get any better. Every time, he was proven wrong.

"Good?" Daniel enquired, face strained and damp.

"Fuck." Finn shook his head, unable to elaborate. He rubbed a hand over her trembling back. "Okay, Al?"

She gave a hesitant nod. "Yeah." Which meant not really, but she was committed to persevering for his sake.

Insufficient.

Finn lifted her slightly, burrowed his hands beneath her and cupped her breasts. He played with the pointed tips of her nipples, rolling and pinching until she made one of her happy noises. Her shoulder blades flexed as she pressed herself into his hands. "Show her some love, Dan."

"With pleasure." The man cupped her face and took her mouth, angled head and eyes shut tight.

Finn moved his hands back to her hips and Daniel took over thumbing her nipples. A soul kiss if he had ever seen one. How they breathed through it Finn wasn't sure, but Al began moving restlessly beneath him.

It was time.

Finn drew back. She shivered. He pushed into her. She broke off the kiss and moaned, fingers clutching at the bedding on either side of Daniel's head. He did it again, pulling out and thrusting back into her, Daniel moving in counterpart to him this time. The feel of the other man's dick stroking inside her was a strange, tantalizing sensation. His skin tingled and his balls drew tight. His dick throbbed in the tight embrace of her body.

"I can't last," Finn said.

"Make yourself come, baby." Daniel instructed, and Al complied, fingers sliding down her body. Her hips kicked back against them and the tight ring of muscle clenched at his cock. Finn lost it, fucking himself into her, Daniel following suit.

Their woman groaned, pitching forward against Dan's chest, body shaking and shuddering as she came. Her internal muscles crimped down on him, squeezed him tight. Finn thrust deep and held there, emptying himself into her.

Finn shut his eyes against the flickering lights, gave in to the swell of heat and emotion rising through him.

When he came to, his face was pressed to her back, wet with their combined sweat. His half-soft cock was still buried in her ass. Al's only proof of life was the shallow rise and fall of her rib cage. Going again so soon wasn't an option, birthday or not. He needed to get off her.

"I love you," he said. Gently, he pulled free of her body and rose to his feet.

Dan gave him a lazy wink, one finger wrapping itself in a strand of her hair.

Finn headed to the bathroom, cleaned himself up and took a wet facecloth back for Al. She had crawled off the man and lay on her side, one arm thrown across Dan's chest. Finn eased her knee up onto Dan's hip and ran the cloth over the swollen bud of her rear entrance.

"I like the balloons," he said. and received a tired smile.

"You do?"

"Yep." Finn put the washcloth aside and lay down behind her. "And I really liked your present."

She gave a low chuckle, "That's good."

"Are you sore?" He scattered kisses over her shoulder, the one that had been hurt.

"A little. You know, I'm pretty certain that's not how you make babies, Finn."

"I had that part covered," Dan rumbled.

"Mmm. Yes, you did," Ali said. There was a pause, her shoulders rising and falling on a deeper breath. "I think I'm a couple of days late. I can't be sure, things haven't been regular the last few months."

"Babe." Dan leant over, kissed the side of her face. "I guess we'll see."

Finn curved his arm around her, seaming himself to her back.

Home.

"Best. Birthday. Ever."

Room With a View

Thirty-eight days post-apocalypse

Waves crashed and rolled onto Kings Beach across the road, the white expanse of sand a beautiful thing. The ocean had long since washed away the bulk of the dead bodies and debris. Only the tank remained and each tide buried it deeper.

Angus had abandoned her. Which was probably for the best.

She couldn't stand to watch him die too.

The summer sun was blindingly bright, the weather hot and humid, typical for January. Or was it February? She'd lost track of the days.

Natalie breathed in the salty sea air as she huddled behind the curtains. She watched the world from four floors up. The penthouse apartment, because Sean had to have the best. No matter her terrible fear of heights.

Another sucky relationship indicator she'd chosen to ignore.

Sean wasn't looking so good anymore.

His body was black and bloated, floating facedown on the surface of the large and lavish lagoon-style pool below. The stench of decay didn't tend to reach her unless it happened to be a particularly still day. Sean hadn't believed the reports on the TV and internet. He'd mocked her when she'd filled the bathtub and every other available container with water, shut up the unit and flat-out refused to leave. Sean had wanted to swim some laps, do a little sunbaking. Plus the beautiful blonde from the unit next door had been down there, artfully arranged on a sun-lounge in her teeny, tiny yellow bikini.

It hadn't ended well for either of them.

Hmm.

What was Angus doing?

Had he gotten away?

She bet he had. He was brave. Smart. Resourceful.

And damn fine-looking. Not that a thirty-two-year-old woman should be checking out a twenty-three-year-old boy, but hey ... she might as well get her kicks where she could. Happy thoughts these days were few and far between.

He'd be okay. He'd be fine. She'd know it if something had happened to him. She'd feel it somehow.

Natalie scrubbed away a tear with the back of her hand.

Stupid. Pointless. The resort had become a death trap and she was caught. It was for the best that he'd gone.

The walkie-talkie sat beside her though, just in case.

So did the bottle of sleeping pills.

One of the infected out in the hallway rattled the door handle. Her breath stuck in her throat and her fingers clutched at the curtain. A pounding started deep inside her skull. They couldn't get in. Not a chance. She'd barricaded the door with the chunky Asian-style coffee table. Backed it up with a couple of the heavy dining chairs for good luck and prosperity. She was safe.

Safe, but stuck.

Darkness owned the hallway. There was no night or day for the ones trapped in there. For them, every hour was party hour. She'd long since gotten used to getting by on little sleep. The three caught in the pool area below were huddled beneath the sun-lounges, cowering. Infected didn't like bright light. And they couldn't climb. She'd watched them try to clamber over the shoulder-high pool fence again and again, snarling and growling in frustration.

Like her, they were stuck.

They too would slowly starve.

She had enough food for a few more days, but after that ...

The size of her ass had once been an issue for Sean. He'd helpfully stocked the kitchen cupboard with a variety of diet bars and drinks lest she be tempted to enjoy herself over the Christmas break. She'd been furious. Beyond words.

But without those supplies she wouldn't have lasted a week.

Angus had been a miracle, magically appearing in the garden on the other side of the pool. He'd spotted her somehow, stuck in the apartment. He'd stood below the cluster of palm trees, arms waving madly and a gorgeous, crazy-ass grin on his face. She'd thought she was alone.

Angus played AFL. He also had a decent throwing arm. He'd demonstrated it by chucking care packages up onto her balcony. Protein bars, bottles of water. The walkie-talkie, wrapped tight in a towel so it didn't shatter on impact. Lots of batteries, because they ended up talking for hours about everything and anything. His aim wasn't perfect. One time, he accidentally smashed the glass door of the apartment next to her. Infected had shambled out, emerging from all their various hiding places, alerted by the noise to the possibility of a free meal. Angus could run like a demon, not that he had to. Infected didn't move fast.

Natalie snuffled, blinked furiously. Crying didn't help. So why had it become her favourite pastime?

He was gone. A good thing.

Right.

She sucked in a breath.

Except he wasn't gone.

Suddenly, Angus was right there, below her. Striding into view and marching across the courtyard. Heading straight for the pool gate like he was contemplating a dip in the fetid green waters. There was a pack on his back and a sawn-off shotgun in his hands.

Her heart punched hard.

No, no, no. The noise. They'd swarm him.

Natalie scrambled to her feet and shot out onto the balcony. Too damn scared for the young man below to worry about the vertigo assailing her. Too busy to freeze up in fear. He couldn't be here. It was too dangerous. "Angus!"

The metal lock on the gate clattered as he pulled it up. Rusty hinges squealed as he kicked the gate open. He stomped into the pool area like some warrior of old and the infected stirred beneath their sun-lounges. A blonde head tangled with dried blood appeared from beneath the green and white striped cushions. The gate clanged shut behind Angus, locking him in.

"Angus! No! Get out of here!"

He didn't look up, didn't acknowledge her. His focus stayed total.

The blonde in the dirty yellow bikini struggled to her feet, a low growl emanating from her throat. A middle-aged man with a sunken belly and mangy red boardies followed her.

Angus didn't pause.

He aimed the gun, pulled the trigger.

Boom!

The deafening blast took out the blonde's head and splattered the middle-aged man with blood and grey matter. Blinded, the infected male stumbled back, moaning, his hands waving urgently in front of his face. Angus fired again and the man flew backward, landing sprawled across the lounges. Eviscerated.

Oh, hell. God. There was … there was a sickening amount of blood.

Angus looked up at her, victorious. His blue eyes squinted into the midday sun. "Gimme a minute. I'll climb up."

She blinked stupidly. He'd done it! He'd actually done it.

"You're insane."

His gorgeous face broke into a broad grin and her stomach swan-dived. He was really there. He'd come back for her. She wasn't alone.

But neither was Angus.

A third infected stumbled out from beneath a nearby picnic table, its bloody mouth snarling. Angus hadn't seen the thing yet. Its arms were outstretched, reaching for him.

"Behind you!"

Angus spun and the infected fell upon him, taking them both down. His shotgun clattered to the side, out of reach. The two bodies struggled on the ground directly beneath her, four stories down. Angus gripped the thing's shoulders, wrestling with it, trying to push it off. The infected's head twisted and jerked, yellow teeth snapping.

"Angus!" She strangled the railing, panic rattling her bones. She was going to wet herself. It was so far down. It was. But she had to help him, had to do something.

But what?

The only weapons she had were a set of steak knives and they weren't going to cut it.

What to use? There were pot plants. Two of them. Heavy, ugly, ornamental things, cluttering up the balcony.

If she could just lift one.

Her sweaty hands slipped on the glaze, baked hot from the sun. She could do this. Natalie scrubbed her hands on her shorts, drying them. Tried again. Her back strained, shoulders protesting. It was bloody heavy. Slowly, she lifted it. Not dropping it. Not yet.

"Throw him off, Angus! Get him off you!"

There was a flash of blue eyes from below. Angus kept moving, struggling, but she couldn't see ... oh, shit. Angus was strong. He was fast. He could do this. He could. She'd never been big on faith. But she had faith in him.

Angus gave a grunt and a heave and the infected flew backwards. Angus rolled to the side, scrunched up into a ball.

Now.

Natalie pushed the pot off the railing. Gravity took over and it plummeted straight down. The infected was rising slowly from the ground, ready to attack Angus again. The pot smashed into its shoulder and the thing tumbled back onto the pavement, arm dangling crookedly and a low moan coming from its mouth.

Angus wasted no time. He leapt to his feet, grabbed the shotgun and reversed it. Rammed the stock into the thing's face. Bone splintered and cracked. It didn't move again.

Thank God.

Other infected had gathered below. They stood rattling the fence, wanting in. The chorus of moaning grew louder by the minute. Angus had a hell of an audience assembling, straining against the barrier, bloody hands reaching out to grab him. The glare of the sun obviously forgotten in their hunger.

"Hurry," she hissed. Loudly. "Get up here."

Angus nodded and shoved the shotgun into his pack. Pulled up a deck chair and stepped onto it, stretching, reaching up for the first-floor balcony. He started to climb. He was moving. He was safe. It would all be okay.

But the ground loomed below and blood surged hot inside Natalie's head, drowning out everything like a bass drum beating loud behind her ears. She staggered back from the railing, legs like water. Throat shut tight and her shoulders up to her ears.

It was so high. The balcony was bad.

Really. Just. Bad.

She stumbled inside, sat her butt back on the thick carpeting before she fell down. Breathing deep. Waiting.

It didn't take him long to reach her.

Angus's big hands gripped the bars of the railing and he pulled himself up slowly. The muscles in his arms bunched and strained in ways that took her mind off the height thing. His eyes shone and his teeth were gritted but he gave her a wide, relieved smile when he cleared the top. She grinned back, helpless to resist. If she hadn't already been sitting she would have hit the floor.

He was actually there. He hadn't left her after all, this beautiful boy.

"Hey," he said.

"Hey, yourself." Her eyes welled anew. "Are you hurt anywhere?"

"No." He looked taller than she'd realised. He seemed ... well, it was harder to dismiss him as a boy when he was this close. When he had just risked his life for her. Angus knelt down in front of her, dark brows drawn together. "Are you alright?"

She nodded, hoped it was convincing. Seemed she'd used up her daily allotment of courage. Her trembling hands itched to grab hold of him. To hold on tight and never let him go, keep him safe somehow. Huh. She'd probably scare the crap out of the poor guy.

"You sure?" he asked, eyes not unkind. "You're looking kind of freaked out."

"Oh, I'm fine." She gave a rough laugh. "Another day in paradise."

Angus didn't laugh.

He had short, dark blonde hair and a strong jaw covered in stubble. His nose was a little wide, his mouth a little generous. Pale blue eyes as clear as the summer sky stared back at her. "You went out onto the balcony, Nat. That was really brave."

"No, what *you* did was brave. I threw a pot."

"I'd be dead if you hadn't been there."

"Oh. I was worried about you." Natalie tucked her brown hair behind her ears, studied her toes. Over-aware of everything all of a sudden. The way he watched her was ... intense. Sitting around in her shorts and a tank top had seemed wise back when she hadn't been expecting any visitors. Angus wore sneakers and cargo shorts, a T-shirt of some band she didn't know. The Soviet X-Ray Record Club, whoever they were. He looked good, while she showed a lot of skin – including dimpled thighs definitely not belonging to a girl in her twenties.

Such a stupid thing to worry about, given the situation.

Natalie wrapped her arms around her knees, rocked back. Gave the poor guy some room from the desperate thirty-something eyeing him off like a meat tray at a raffle.

He gave a cautious smile and edged closer. "I can't believe we're finally in the same room together."

"I know! What were you thinking?"

One thick shoulder rose and fell, and he sat back on his heels, nonplussed.

"I'm serious, Angus. You could have been bitten. I thought you'd left town."

"No."

"Why didn't you leave? It was the smart thing to do."

His features tightened and he leant in, getting in her face. "I wasn't leaving without you."

"I wouldn't have blamed you—"

"I would have blamed me."

"There were three of them in there." Her voice rose in pitch. "You can't risk yourself like that. What if you'd been infected?"

"I didn't get any blood on me, Natalie." His lips were a grim line, face deadly serious as he stared her down. He reached out and touched her, curled his fingers round the back of her neck. Stroking. "Listen to me."

Natalie stopped, stunned. It felt so good. He felt so good, his mouth hovering over hers. His body was close, filling her head with the scent of clean male sweat, of the sun and sand. Everything else fell away. It was just a simple touch, but it had been so long. Even before the world went to hell Sean had been disinterested, at best. The press of Angus's hand against her skin, the warmth of his palm. It all served to remind her that she was still alive and so was he.

"I wouldn't leave you," he said. Pale blue eyes so serious and intense and lovely. And young. Best not to forget that amid the haze of dirty thoughts. "I won't do that. Do you understand?"

She nodded, more than a little mesmerised.

"Good. You and me against the world."

"Okay," she said, arching her neck ever so subtly.

"Shit." Angus gave her a startled look and retracted his hand in a rush. "Sorry. I didn't mean to grab at you like that."

"Oh, it's alright. I don't mind."

He frowned, the skin between his dark brows ridging. "You don't?"

"No." He had risked his life for her. He could have been killed, this beautiful boy dead and gone. The thought bled her dry. Her hands shook and her spine bowed. She hunched over her knees and held on tight. "But you have to be more careful from now on."

"Do you mean that?" he asked.

"Yes, emphatically."

"No. I mean about my hand."

"Oh." Her eyelids started batting like crazy, beyond her control. "Yes. It's fine."

Angus stared at her, said nothing.

"So ... any ideas about what comes next?"

"Yeah." He leant forward and kissed her.

***

Natalie's mouth was amazing. But then, he'd known it would be.

Angus slanted his head, kissed her again. Slower. Without butting her in the nose this time. He brushed his lips against hers, stroked her neck. Her skin felt silken warm, her soft hair tickling the back of his hand.

If only she'd kiss him in return.

He set a good example, hoping. Hoping and waiting as ever-fucking-patiently as he could manage. Only, he'd been waiting weeks to get this close. Maybe weeks wasn't long in the old scheme of things, but right now it seemed like a lifetime.

He'd come to the coast with some uni friends for a couple of weeks' holiday. A chance to do some surfing and see out the New Year. The virus hit Christmas Eve and by Boxing Day his friends were dead. Everyone was dead or gone. It spread like a bushfire, the streets soon empty of all except for the infected. There had been the whine of jet engines, followed by ground-shaking explosions as bombs were dropped inland at the hospital, killing infected and innocent alike. Gunfire. Screaming. The power went out two days after Christmas. He'd holed up in the hotel basement for a fortnight, living off cans of spaghetti and dry Weet-Bix. Everything had been cemetery-still when he emerged. So quiet. He'd wandered around, hiding at night, hoping to find someone still alive. Someone uninfected. Then he'd found her.

Natalie.

She'd been pacing past her balcony doors. Stalking back and forth, back and forth, darting the outside world nervous glances. Her long dark hair had been tied back in a ponytail, swinging every time she did her abrupt about-face. She'd been wearing the same denim shorts and green singlet top she had on now. Natalie had the best rack. He knew he shouldn't think shit like that about her, but it was amazing. He'd been lugging around binoculars and finally, that day, he knew why.

"Natalie?" He opened his eyes. Hers were huge. Shocked. Oh, no. Had he read her wrong? His dick was killing him, fucking with his head. Maybe she hadn't meant what he'd thought she'd meant. He swallowed hard and cursed. "Is this okay?"

"You want ..." Her lips grazed his as she spoke because he wasn't moving back. Not until she said to. She looked so much prettier up close. The sweet curves of her face, the dent in her chin. Everything about her worked for him.

"Yeah. I, ah ... I ..." He rubbed his thumb against the back of her neck and her skin goosepimpled beneath his touch. Good or bad? Shit. He had no idea. So what if she said no. He'd survive it, somehow. What he couldn't do was not try. And why this felt harder than storming into that fucking enclosure, he didn't know. "I want you."

There. It was said.

Her eyes went impossibly wider and her breath hitched.

Except he wanted to make sure there were no mistakes this time.

Angus sucked in a breath, let it out. "I mean, I want to have sex with you. Now."

Natalie's eyes darkened and her mouth opened. But she said

nothing for the longest time. Her dark brows drawn tight and lips perfectly still.

He could have choked on the silence.

There was a softly mumbled "fuck it". Then her soft hands cupped his face, drawing him in. And God, he wanted in. More than he could remember ever wanting anything, he wanted inside of her.

"Okay, Angus," she said. "Yes. I want that too. I want us to forget about everything for a while."

Coherent thought sailed straight out the window. He smashed his lips to hers. Shoved his tongue into her mouth. There was nothing smooth or controlled about it.

Natalie made a noise beneath him and it might have been laughter but he was too busy to care. Too taken up with kissing her, deep and wet. The taste of her filled him and he was full to bursting already. His balls aching and his dick so hard it hurt. Her fingers slipped into his hair, holding him to her as she stroked her tongue against his. Nipped at him. Kissed him.

Gave him all the encouragement he needed.

Pure instinct drove him. He slid a hand behind her back, taking his weight on the other, easing her back onto the carpet. Getting her underneath him. Getting between her thighs so he could rub his hard-on against her like some horny kid.

He had to be as close to her as he could be.

His hand fumbled over her shirt, shaking like shit embarrassingly enough, seeking out a breast. He felt sixteen all over again, unsure and overexcited. The hard point of a nipple scraped against the palm of his hand through her layers of material and he closed his fingers around her. God. She was more than a handful, all over. Her body felt so right, soft and curvy. Fucking perfect. But there were too many clothes between them. Far too many.

He was in a mad rush, verging on panic, and he couldn't seem to slow down. Need hammered at his head. "Natalie ..."

"Easy," she soothed, kissing the side of his mouth, his jaw. Her lips swollen and the skin on her chin pink from his stubble.

"You really want this?"

"Very much so."

Relief flooded him. He curved his arms up around her head,

pressed his face into her neck and squeezed his eyes tight. "Thank fuck."

"I really thought you'd left." Her voice cracked and he reared back. Her eyes were liquid-bright.

"No. No, I couldn't do that." How could she even doubt it? He'd told her things on that stupid damn walkie-talkie he'd never told another living soul. "You don't need to worry about that. Ever."

Her chin wrinkled up and he kissed it too. Again and again.

"Tell me you believe me," he prompted.

Her mouth opened and her bottom lip trembled. "I'm sorry. I'm ruining it."

"Tell me you believe me."

She nodded jerkily. "I believe you."

"Good. You're so beautiful."

"You're brilliant for my self-esteem," Natalie sighed and then chuckled. Low, throaty sounds that fulfilled two of the top three items on his list of things to hear before he died. Her hands slid down his body, moulding to his damp back. Clinging to him enough to let him know this was getting to her too. "Let's get this T-shirt off. Hmm?"

"Yeah." Angus pushed back onto his knees, ditched the shirt, started tearing open his shorts while he toed off his sneakers. Naked was excellent. Naked was clearly where they needed to go. His heart pounded inside his chest. Sweat slicked his body and his hands were still shaking. Hopefully she wouldn't notice. "Ah, Nat. Get your clothes off. Now. Please."

"You've got combat adrenaline." Natalie rose up onto her elbows and eyed the bulge in his boxer briefs with interest. "I read about it once."

He frowned at her, confused at the change in subject. "Maybe. Does it matter?"

"No."

"You've still got your clothes on." He pushed down his cargos and boxers, needing to get naked. Needing her to get naked, but Natalie was busy, watching. The expression on her face when she saw his cock for the first time was immensely satisfying. The dart of her pink tongue across her lips like she was contemplating all manner of stuff. Her eyes roamed over him, breasts heaving like there wasn't enough air in the apartment, even with the balcony doors wide open.

She really did have the best tits. The best everything. Her voice alone had kept him hanging on for days. To think she'd imagined him gone. The things she'd said to him, how she'd kept him hoping, yearning. She'd given him a reason to live when every last thing was lost. Now he'd gotten to her there wasn't a chance in hell he was going anywhere without her.

"You're gorgeous," she said.

Angus grunted. Not that her lust for him wasn't nice but he was concentrating on other things. Things like not losing his load right here and now. The need to claim her in some primal way thumped around inside him, burning through his blood.

The effect she had on him.

Getting her top off would take longer so he went straight for the shorts, hooking the elastic of her panties into the deal. Two articles of clothing for the price of one. Eureka! Without hesitation he stripped them both straight down her long, shapely legs, eyeing up her pussy. Every bit as interested in her sex as she'd been in his. No game of 'you show me yours and I'll show you mine' could have measured up. There was a dark strip of hair on her mound and plump, pink lips. So damn nice. Here, too, she was prettier up close than he'd imagined. And he had spent some solid time imagining.

Angus traced her moist slit with the pads of his fingers. Up and down, over and over. Just feeling her. Learning her. Her breathing grew choppy. He eased in a finger, experimenting, sliding it in deep. Pumping first one, and then two, slowly into her. She was warm and wet inside and out, her pussy making soft sucking noises as he finger-fucked her.

"Angus," she moaned.

He could listen to her say his name all soft and husky for a good long time.

Her whole body tensed and she whimpered when he searched out the top of her seam, locating her sensitive clit. Rubbing either side. Her folds were flushed the darkest pink and his dick screamed bloody murder but he couldn't pull himself away from playing with her.

Not just yet.

Dark eyes were on him, huge and hungry.

"I want to lick you." He didn't recognise his own voice. "But later, okay?"

"Okay," she murmured, hips bumping against his hand. Demanding more. The air was laced with the scent of her. It was intoxicating. He twisted his fingers, watching to catch her every reaction. It made him hot, making her squirm. "Angus, enough, come here."

She smiled and arched her neck, pressed her mouth to his. Kissing him slow and sweet. Opening her mouth to him when he licked at her bottom lip. Making his head spin.

His Natalie.

She pushed lightly against his shoulders. "Let me up so I can put my mouth on you."

"No, ah, that's a bad idea." He eased back, started working her top up and off her. Easy enough, but the bra lacked a front closure. Unacceptable. "Time to change positions."

Angus rolled them, taking her onto his chest, her dark hair falling over his face. Natalie's hands gripped his shoulders and she sat up, astride him. What a view. Her breasts jiggled, snaring his immediate attention, but the sudden press of her hot, wet cunt against his tortured cock felt insane. Terrible. Perfect. His jaw locked.

They needed to move forward with this sex thing before he disgraced himself. He hadn't been this worked up in years.

"Why is it a bad idea?" she asked. "You'd like it. I promise."

"I believe you," he croaked. "Take off the bra. Please."

She did so with a pleased smirk, her earlier shakes and tears long since forgotten. Given half a chance he'd have a smile permanently on her face. She threw the black satin aside. Her luscious tits tumbled into his waiting hands. Hard, brown nipples made his mouth water and his blood surge anew. He shook his head, closing his eyes against a wave of light-headedness. Too much to do. Several lifetimes' worth and then some.

He rolled her pretty nipples between his thumb and forefinger, plucked them and played with them, making her breath hitch and her mouth fall open. That was nice, but honestly, he was too caught up in pleasing himself to notice much. Maybe next time. No, definitely next time. He'd be all about pleasing her. She'd never doubt him again. Not in any way, shape or form.

Her fingers kneaded at his forearms, short nails scratching. He hoped she left marks.

"I feel like a dirty old woman when you look at me that way."

"I like you dirty. The old is bullshit. I don't want to hear that. Ever."

"Harder, you sweet talker," she panted, grinding her pussy against him. "Just like that."

"Shit. Stop." He gripped her hips, holding her still. Slamming his eyes shut against the real-life wet dream sitting on top of his cock. He'd played this moment over and over in his head but nothing came close to actually touching her. Need almost made a mess of him. "Nat, I'm a little on edge here."

"Sorry, sorry." She petted him apologetically but the unholy gleam in her eye remained. "So when you thought about our first time, how did you imagine it?"

"Honestly? There was less talking, more action. And you were wearing this red thing..."

She grinned, leant down to kiss him again, good and hard. Teeth chinked. She was obviously as hungry for him as he was for her. So fucking good. Her hips rolled against him and white light edged his vision. The sweet heat of her was killing him. He groaned loudly and his balls drew up tight.

This had gone on long enough. He needed inside of her. Now. "Nat."

"Sorry. Sorry. I got carried away."

He didn't answer. Instead, he rummaged for his pack, pushing aside the shotgun and fossicking for ... "Got it."

Natalie leaned over, inspecting his pack with interest. "Exactly how many condoms did you bring with you?"

"Some." Three boxes, total. They'd been sitting on the shelf of an abandoned pharmacy. He'd grabbed them ... just in case. Which was bullshit. He'd had every intention of using every single one with her and then searching for more. The need she put in him wasn't going away any time soon. He ripped into the nearest then did the same with one of the foil packages within, handed the contents over to her waiting hand. "Please. Hurry."

She shuffled down his body, took his cock in hand. Delicate fingers wrapped around the width of him. His hips kicked and Natalie gave him a look with a hint of mischief. Oh, man. She even licked her lips for good measure. A living dream. "I like this."

Angus moaned and fought the need to thrust into her fingers, breathing out hard through his nose. He was running out of time. She had no fucking idea what she did to him. Her grip tightened and he felt about ready to beg. Propose. God, just do something. Sweat sheeted off him.

Shit, she was going to kill him.

But she didn't. Thank God, because the condom cooled things down, dulled the sensations just enough. Natalie rolled it down with smooth precision, kissed and licked her way up his stomach, his chest, crawling back up his body. Taking her time and driving him mad. He grabbed her beneath her arms and brought her mouth back to his. Kissed her soundly, impatiently, several times. Soul deep. Trying to tell her everything he couldn't begin to know how to say.

Her nipples brushed his chest and she guided his sheathed cock into her waiting cunt. Slowly impaling herself on him, never breaking eye contact.

The feel of her enveloping him. Taking him deep into her body. There was nothing like it.

Nothing.

The very first time of what he hoped to be many, many more. *Mine.* He counted backwards from fifty, locked down his stomach muscles. All that shit so as not to lose it. His ragged breathing was the only noise. But every breath brought her scent to him anew. She marked him inside and out without even trying.

"You okay?" she asked.

Hell, how could he not be? He was in paradise. He was in love.

He managed a nod and she started to move with a dreamy smile.

"You have no idea how often I dreamt of this."

"Natalie," he groaned. Helpless beneath her and loving it.

"But I wanted you safe ..."

"We will be."

She rose and fell on him, hands sliding over his shoulders, his chest. Fingers brushing across his nipples. Teasing him. Her greedy hands were all over him and he loved it. Loved the growing look of intense concentration as she rode him, her dark eyes never leaving his face.

She was his now and he'd tell her as much. Later.

Sensation spread through him, stealing his mind. His spine felt electric with the tension building. There were no words to describe how good it felt when she fucked him, the scent of sex on the air and the slap of skin on skin. Dark hair sliding across her shoulders, the sway of her tits in the sunlight. His dream girl. His miracle. No one before had ever mattered this much. He couldn't even remember a before. But this ... this he wanted to remember every second of. He wanted it to last forever but that wasn't going to happen.

Not even remotely. Not this time.

"Make yourself come," he said, voice harsh and his throat tight.

Natalie held two fingers to his lips and he sucked them into his mouth. Wetting them for her.

And then, bloody hell.

The sight of her touching herself, strumming her clit for him. Not an ounce of shame in her. It was more than he could take. He clutched at her hips, taking what he needed. Her sweet, slick cunt taking him. The hand against her groin picked up speed and her internal muscles fluttered around him, clenched at him.

"Angus," she moaned, working herself onto him harder, faster.

Her sex squeezing him. Fingernails digging into him. It was a whole-body effect she had going on and he was lost to it, heart and soul. He held her hips tight as he thrust up into her tight body, once, twice, three times. He swore and some strangled noise escaped him. Nothing he'd ever heard before. He came, grinding himself against her. Vaguely pissed the condom was between him. Emptying himself totally. Giving her everything. His mind was gone. Floating free. Every care and fear a distant memory. Everything had gone away but her.

Natalie sank down onto his chest, her weight welcome. The mounds of her breasts squished between them, perfect. Angus ran his hands over her damp back. Let reality drift back slowly.

"I think I like having sex with you," he said. "Very, very much."

She smiled against the side of his face, huffed out a laugh. He was crazy for her laugh. "Mm?"

"But I might need to try it a few more times to be sure."

"The three boxes of condoms in your bag kind of clued me into that plan."

He laughed. "If you saw how many were in there, why did you ask?"

"I was testing your honesty."

"Hell of a time to test it."

"Relax," she said. "You passed with flying colours."

"Hmm."

She smacked a kiss on his cheek. Grinning, pleased with herself. "Sullying you further would be a pleasure."

"Time to switch places," he warned. Rolling her onto her back, taking the top.

"Whoa."

"Alright?" He pushed her dark hair out of her lovely face, rubbed his lips over the dent in her chin. Gave it a leisurely lick. "I gave you beard rash."

"I'll survive. Why so serious a face?"

"Do you trust me?"

"Yes," she said. No hesitation. His heart jumped about in his chest.

"Natalie. I've got another plan," he said, all seriousness. "About getting out of here and surviving. You and me. If that's what you want."

He felt the breath leave her, her body tensing beneath him. She went very still. "It's going to involve me scaling the side of the building, isn't it?"

"It's going to involve you trusting me to help get you out of here. Can you do that?"

Her gaze slid off him. "Huh. Climbing the side of a tall building. Well, we're going to need to wait until they calm down. You attracted a lot of infected with the shotgun."

"A couple of days. I brought supplies, we'll be fine. You didn't answer the question."

"I've seen your supplies."

"Answer the question, Natalie." He nudged her nose with his. "This is important."

With a humph, she pushed her breasts against him. Trying her hardest to derail him, apparently. "You were trying to soften me up with an orgasm, weren't you?"

He just stared at her. Waiting.

"You're meant to be young and impressionable. Easily side-tracked by boobs and the mention of sex." She rolled her head to the side, looking out the dreaded balcony window. Her dark brows drew tight. He'd never faced this kind of thing. Walking into the fenced pool area below had been obvious, necessary. There wasn't a damn thing he wouldn't do for her. But he hadn't lived with the fear of it for all of his life, following his every step. Not like she had with her fear of heights.

"I'm not leaving you," he said. "However long it takes. I'm very serious about the you and me part."

Dark eyes turned to him, the column of her throat moving as she swallowed hard. "Okay. For you."

"For me?"

"Yes."

"Natalie," he chuckled, taken aback. Probably blushing again. Bloody hell. "I'm honoured. That's the nicest thing anyone's ever said to me."

Her sudden smile was brilliant. Breathtaking. God help anything that tried to separate him from her now. Not happening.

"I'm not sure I brought enough condoms."

***

Today was the day. Everything was quiet below.

Eerily so.

Natalie peered over the edge of the balcony, her grip on Angus's hand tightening. She was strangling his fingers, throttling them. Close to snapping them in half. But he didn't complain. She really didn't know what she'd done to deserve him.

"Ready?" he asked.

"You're sure about this?"

He just looked at her. Yes, they had to leave the apartment sooner or later. Turned out she could distract him with sex. She'd done so for a solid five days. Thank God for Angus's endless supply of condoms. There wasn't an inch of him she hadn't climbed all over.

And there wasn't a chance she was going to disappoint him now. They were a pair. A duo. Inseparable. He'd said so, time and again, and she'd long since stopped doubting.

Mine.

"Tell me again," she prodded.

He tugged on her hand, drawing her back to his side. She went gladly. "I met a guy who said there was a town out west. They managed to get a wall up. He heard them on a CB radio, talking about it. He was heading there straight away but I had to come back for you."

"Right."

"We climb down. Slowly." His thumb brushed over her knuckles and he brought her hand to his mouth and kissed it. Holding it against his lips. "We head south-west. That's where they are."

"South-west. Okay."

"We have somewhere safe to go, Nat."

The ocean breeze was ruffling his hair. He was the picture of beachside magnificence. Tall and burnished. Hot. *Mine.*

"I can do this," she said.

"Yes. Of course you can. You can do anything. And I'll be beside you every step of the way."

She grinned. "Let's go."

Also Available from Momentum

Skin

Kylie Scott

The hotly anticipated sequel to *Flesh*.

Six months since the zombie plague struck, former librarian Roslyn Stewart has been holed up in a school with eight other survivors. But now the shelves in the school canteen are bare. The stranger at the gate has supplies that will ensure the group's ongoing survival, but at a cost. He wants a woman.

Nick is a man with a plan. He'll treat Roslyn like a Queen, devoting the rest of his life to protecting and providing for her. In exchange, of course, for sexual favours. It's the deal of the century given the state of the world. But Roslyn doesn't see it that way. The first chance she gets she attacks the ex-army man and attempts to escape, forcing Nick to contain her. And so begins his awkward courtship of the woman, with her chained to the bed for security reasons.

Chained like a dog and forced to spend her every waking moment with a creep, albeit a good looking one, Ros is determined to escape. When circumstances force them to band together against a common enemy their very survival depends on their ability to learn to trust each other. An uneasy partnership develops, but can a relationship with such a difficult beginning ever have a future?

Find out more and purchase online at
http://www.momentumbooks.com. au/books/skin/

CPSIA information can be obtained
at www.ICGtesting.com
Printed in the USA
LVOW03s0605170917

548995LV00001B/4/P